EDEN'S FALL

A STILETTOS, STOLI & SCRIBBLES NOVEL

KR BRORMAN

***

CC CEDRAS

***

SA YOUNG

PROLOGUE

Kenna clutched her manila folder of proof. All she cared about was getting inside and showing it to Frankie and Candace.

She ignored blaring horns as she ducked between cars, then elbowed her way through the crowd waiting to be seated. Her friends, at their usual table, stared at her open-mouthed. Kenna didn't notice her haggard appearance anymore. Her looks didn't matter. Nothing mattered but the folder she placed on the table.

"He's not dead, and we're going to find him. Or a body if I'm wrong," Kenna said in a rush. "But I'm right."

"He who?" Candace asked.

"What we?" Frankie said.

"Lucius!" she barked. *Who the hell else could I be talking about?*

Kenna inhaled a ragged breath. She'd avoided these two for so long and knew she should have approached this theory, this belief, with more discretion, but now that she'd made a decision, she couldn't wait for them to catch up. They had to get on board. Right now.

Frankie's large blue eyes filled with unshed tears as she took Kenna's cold hand into hers. "Honey. It's been weeks."

Candace had taken her other hand between her own and was stroking the back of it as if she could transfer her warmth into Kenna.

Kenna jerked free and glared at them. "He's. Not. Dead."

"What makes you so certain?" Candace, always so calm. Frankly, Kenna would be annoyed right now if she didn't recognize her friend's distress in the rising flush on her neck.

As usual, when someone started to show her sympathy, the tears start to well. She'd cried herself dry, but obviously, she wasn't as dehydrated as she'd thought. Before the emotions could get the better of her, Kenna took a shaky breath and shook her head.

"He's out there. I have to find him. You have to help me find him." Her voice cracked. *What if they don't believe me or refuse to help me find Luc? What if they think I'm nuts?* There'd been times over the past few weeks, as denial over his death and the mad search for evidence he'd survived the blast escalated, she doubted her own sanity.

Her friends exchanged a speaking look, one that said they realized how deep her feelings went. They shrugged, nodded and turned to face her.

"Where do we start?" Frankie asked.

"If I knew *that,* he wouldn't need finding." Kenna laughed, her hands and jaws unclenching.

Candace chuckled and raised her glass. "Well, then, we'd better make a plan."

Frankie picked up her Bloody Mary, Kenna lifted a water goblet, and the three clinked their glasses. "'To a plan.'"

CHAPTER ONE

A year earlier, Kenna had been in full battle armor, or her version of it, prepared for a last skirmish in a year-long recovery.

"Power shoes." Will MacKenzie nudged the toe of Kenna's favorite leopard pumps with his own polished Gucci loafers while shrugging into his suit coat and finger combing a thick mass of dark waves away from his face. "Nice touch for your last day." His Scottish burr rolled over his r's and turned "touch" into "tooch."

"Fuck off," she said, elbowing around him to do her own mirror check before leaving Will's Chelsea third floor walk-up. Her curse sounded as forced and unnatural as it was. "Last day should have been months ago. I feel fine."

Will stepped back without comment. At six-two, he could straighten his collar in the mirror over her head, and he knew her tricks too well. The look on her face was sullen and belligerent. Kenna was trying to pick a fight, delay their departure, and avoid another physical therapy session.

Physical therapists and a psychologist had warned him about her defense tactics. "It's all a test for us, you, herself, the memories. She's daring the world to fall apart. Every time it doesn't, Kenna's trust foundation will strengthen. Don't reward unproductive behavior."

So, against his natural and learned instinct to push back when shoved aside and never to let a "fuck off" go unacknowledged, he tolerated her baiting and bitching when it came to the issue of medical care. "Fine" bothered him way more than "fuck" when it came from Kenna.

Will had learned not to argue or try and persuade. He simply proceeded with the plan – holding her coat or bag when it was time to leave, opening the car door, waiting for her to sit, or handing her the pen on a chain at the sign-in window.

In the beginning, Kenna had protested, cursed and hurled coffee cups at the walls, but finally she complied. Her survival had depended on it.

"Ye want me to come with you?" Will asked when he'd stopped his car at the entrance to the Physical & Occupational Therapy Center. He reached over the console and poked a finger through the distressed hole on the knee of her consignment store designer jeans, smiling when her battle-ready, clenched jaw relaxed involuntarily to laugh at being tickled.

Kenna slapped his hand away. "Don't make me laugh. This is war you know." She opened the car door and paused with one foot dangling toward the asphalt. "Do you mind?" She chewed her lip and looked at a string poking out from a button on her "power shirt," a bright orange chiffon blouse that made her green eyes pop and her boobs look fabulous.

"Sign in. I'll park in the visitors' car park." He hated hospitals. Though this was a sleek and supposedly comforting therapy center, it had the same vibe, the same smells and sounds, but he'd go. No matter how many times they walked unharmed through a set of automatic doors into a medical facility, the swoosh took him back to the morning he had carried her through a set of doors, not knowing if she would come out of them alive.

———————

TWO HOURS LATER, Will pulled into the underground parking garage of their next stop at the Federal Building, turned to Kenna, and said, "This isnae gonna take long. You want to wait for me at Starbucks on the corner?"

Emotionally and physically exhausted after the final PT session where she had to prove she not only had full function of her hand, but also was willing and able to continue the routine to maintain the progress, she leaned against the headrest. "Sure. What's this guy after, you think?" What she really wanted to ask was, *"What did you do, and am I going to be alone again?"*

"Och, just jerking my chain." Will half smirked, half snarled. Despite his irritation at the summons, a part of him relished the cat and mouse game. And, if he were honest, he enjoyed having someone care if he went to prison again.

"Well, try not to give him a reason, okay?" Kenna reached for the door handle. "What's his name again?"

Will made a face like he'd gotten a nose full of sewer emissions. "Ross. Palmer Ross. Here it's FBI, home it's MI5," Will shrugged. "They all come out of the same factory. It's no bother."

They parted at the first floor. Will planted a chaste kiss on her forehead, tenderly caressed the recently exercised hand and promised to meet her at the coffee shop.

Seated outside at one of the café tables, Kenna leaned back and closed her eyes. The warm rays kissed her face and she let the weight of PT and Will's FBI summons slip away for the moment.

CHAPTER TWO

E mirates Airline flight 726 out of JFK made its final descent into Muscat, Oman. The setting sun turned the white buildings into terraces of turquoise jewels. Lt. Colonel Lucius Chaerea, Ret., closed his laptop and turned to the window to admire the stunning beauty created by the sun's kiss. He looked over his shoulder to the sleeping passenger across the aisle, a comment about the pleasure of landing at sunset perched unspoken on his lips. Lucius turned back to his solitary enjoyment of the view.

"Colonel Chaerea, may I get you anything else before we land?" asked the exotic and beautiful flight attendant, Nahla. Her full, lush pout curved into an inviting smile. Dark hair draped over her shoulders and curled over full breasts. She bent toward him, a touch lower than necessary.

"No, thank you." Lucius stood and slid his arms into his suit coat without making eye contact or accepting her assistance.

She was always solicitous beyond the demands of her profession, and he was always politely cool to the undercurrent of her attraction that seemed to grow with every trip he made into Oman.

Nahla smiled up at him. "Dare we hope your trip is not limited to business this time?"

"I will have to disappoint once again," he said as he regained his seat.

"I could recommend some wonderful entertainment. Or dining. It's a shame you never see what Muscat has to offer." Lucius simply gave her a small nod and secured his lap belt.

Nahla gently touched the sleeping passenger on the shoulder to alert him of the descent and moved to take her seat. Lucius' gaze didn't follow the gentle sway of her hips as she moved along the aisle. It had been years since he'd allowed himself such simple pleasures or succumbed to the affections that often accompanied physical attraction. Not since his beloved Sophia had been so brutalized and murdered in Sudan. His features, always inscrutable, hardened as he promised his wife's spirit for the millionth time that he'd put a coda on Davit Lazarashvilli's human slavery trade and make him pay for his butchery.

Moments later, as Lucius descended the jet bridge to a waiting car on the tarmac, Nahla leaned against the open door. Along with the standard, "Thank you for flying with us," she placed a small card with her phone number in his hand and renewed an invitation for dinner.

"Are you having dinner later?" Another flight attendant asked peering past her co-worker's shoulder as Lucius debarked.

"We never do, but I'll keep trying," she said with a smile. "I've never seen a man who needs dinner more than that one." Her colleague snorted at the euphemism, "dinner."

Lucius slowed his pace as he observed the rangy form lounging against the rear passenger door of the waiting limo. Absent were the usual baseball cap, faded jeans and well-broken in trainers. Instead, Mike Chapman was wearing pressed slacks, polished loafers, a light blue, starched button-down shirt and navy sport coat. His often unruly ash blond hair was neatly trimmed and combed. The dark aviators were the same though.

"Chapman. Must be important," Lucius said, shaking hands with the smiling man.

Chapman took note of the flight attendants walking past and watching the Colonel. "You alone?"

Lucius quirked his chiseled lips in a small smile and stepped around Chapman to slide into the car. Mike affected a lazy smile and pretended to give the pretty air hostesses a once over as he scanned the area. A red sniper dot bounced in a figure eight across his chest and then disappeared. "Guess I'm lucky I didn't get shot," he said, folding his six-foot-two frame into the limo.

Lucius smirked. Belatedly, he acknowledged the presence of a young woman, sable brown hair falling in a sleek wave from a pronounced widow's peak to above her shoulders. Chapman settled into the seat next to Lucius and nodded at the woman across from them.

"Colonel. This is Layla Gazale, my Egyptian counterpart."

The young woman made bold eye contact with Lucius and extended a slim hand. "Colonel."

Lucius clasped her fingertips and bowed his head. "Ms. Gazale." He turned to Chapman. "I thought we were meeting at the hotel." He tapped the glass partition signaling the driver to get moving.

Chapman shrugged and shifted his legs to accommodate Ms. Gazale's long and shapely calves that had inched into his personal space. "Too crowded. The Sultan's hosting a conference of oil company execs this week, which means the hotel is infested with extra eyes and ears. Besides, I have something on that Cairo thing you asked about." Chapman took the folder Layla Gazale handed him and passed it to Lucius.

"Good work. As usual." Lucius nodded to the young woman, then Chapman, and opened the folder to begin reading. "Have you considered closing shop and bringing your crew on with me full time?"

Chapman leaned back, crossed his arms and grinned. "Have you considered letting that flight attendant take you to dinner?" He laughed and kept talking before Chaerea could voice an objection or offer an excuse. Chapman knew the answer. "I know. I know. Thanks, anyway, but working for you means a chance of getting shot at. And you know I hate getting shot at." As Lucius turned over a page in the dossier, Chapman poked the one beneath with an index finger. "I'll cut to the chase. The Cairo intel is bullshit."

CHAPTER THREE

A s Will watched Kenna exit the elevator on the main floor of the Federal Building, he exhaled a breath that he imagined he'd been holding for close to a year. He knew, better than anyone, what a toll her recovery and rehab had taken on her. It hadn't been easy for him, either, but he'd do it all again in a heartbeat.

Now that she'd been released from physical therapy for the hand, he'd be better able to see how her emotional healing was progressing. He commandeered a corner of the elevator, and his mind drifted to the meeting that was destined to waste the rest of the afternoon.

EYEING the coffee kiosk across the lobby, Frankie Winslow, torn between the desire for a venti iced caffeine boost and holding her place at the front of the horde of civil servants, shifted from one foot to the other. Her dilemma was solved when the doors opened, and the crowd enveloping her packed in. Frankie squeezed her shoulders together and pressed tightly against the back wall, toes curled inside her pumps in case the heavy guy in front of her moved back an inch and crushed her tender tootsies or, more importantly, her new shoes.

The man to her right was taking up enough space for three. Taller than most, expensively dressed, he stood out starkly from the office drones heading back to their offices from lunch. *No wonder everyone else in the elevator was crowded together*, she thought. Frankie didn't take a full breath of the precious oxygen reeking of Indian food and pastrami until enough stops opened up the confined space. When she did, she caught the subtle scent of his cologne.

When the doors opened on the twenty-second floor, the man pushed away from his corner and strolled out, looking left then right and giving Frankie a good view of his imposing profile before the doors closed again.

On twenty-three, Frankie approached an administrative assistant in the FBI offices. The woman remembered her from Frankie's other visits, smiled and announced her arrival.

A moment later, Palmer Ross, Special Agent In Charge, opened his office door. Young for the position, he made it a point to look like he'd been hard at work for hours, shirt sleeves rolled up, wavy hair in studied disarray.

"Miss Winslow! There you are." He moved to kiss her cheek, but stopped short and merely stood close. "Damn, I was hoping you'd stop for coffee on your way up."

Before Frankie could respond, he ushered her into his office with a hand that hovered near the small of her back. Over his shoulder, he spoke to the woman he called his "secretary." "Hold my calls." The administrative assistant rolled her eyes.

"Have a seat, Kitten. I want to give you some more background on this guy. Did you do your homework?"

Frankie sank onto the chrome and vinyl chair. "Palmer, how many times do I have to ask you to please stop calling me 'Kitten'?" She looked around his office with its government-issue furniture. It wasn't much, but he owed her article about his feat of daring, that he had it at all. "Especially not here. It's demeaning and makes me feel cheaper than that desk."

"Huh?" Palmer looked up from his monitor as if he'd just realized she was talking.

"Never mind." She reached into her bag for a notepad. "Okay, what did you want to tell me?"

Palmer came around to sit on the corner of his desk. "What say we grab a drink and some dinner when this is over? Maybe at the Yale Club?"

Frankie's stomach did a barrel roll. "Are you serious? I could have sworn – no scratch that – I know I made it clear this ..." she waved her hand back and forth between them, "was strictly professional. Wait a minute." She stood up quickly. "Did The Senator put you up to this?"

Palmer reached for her hand, but she jerked it out of reach. "Calm down, Kitten." He coaxed in his East Texas twang. "I may have mentioned our meeting, but I promise this was all my idea."

Frankie would never understand why her father would encourage Palmer or consider him a suitable match for her. She picked up the notebook she'd dropped. "Can we do this interview, please?"

Thirty minutes later, Ross escorted Frankie to the twenty-second floor. He stopped at a room with a large window and an agent posted at the door. The men nodded to each other and Ross adjusted a rheostat that cleared the electrochromic glass from dark and opaque to transparent. The subject of today's interview was already seated inside the room, impatiently checking his watch.

"Doesn't look like much, does he?"

"Holy crap," Frankie gasped then covered her surprise with a cough. It was the man from the elevator.

———

OBLIVIOUS TO HER REACTION, Ross reset the smart glass to dark again and held the door to usher her in. When the man at the table looked up, Frankie's face grew hot in time with his slowly spreading grin that eventually reached his smoky grey eyes.

Ross pulled the chair out for her as he greeted the interviewee. "Thanks for coming in, Mr. MacKenzie."

MacKenzie slowly shifted his gaze from Frankie to Ross. A smirk curled his lips. "My pleasure."

Ross narrowed his eyes at him, but said, "Two things before we get started. This is Francesca Winslow. She's a forensic psychologist doing some research." Frankie's head snapped around, her blue eyes wide at the wild exaggeration of her credentials. Her Masters *was* in psychology, but before she dropped out of her PhD program, she was specializing in *child*, not forensic, psychology.

"She will be observing."

MacKenzie spread his hands in a magnanimous gesture, but said nothing.

Ross gestured to an electronics array in the center of the conference room table. "We'll be recording this interview as well."

Again, MacKenzie only shrugged, not looking at Ross.

Frankie hadn't said a word. Between Palmer's elaborate fiction and MacKenzie's intense gaze, she wasn't sure she could.

Ross made a show of aiming a small microphone on a tripod in MacKenzie's direction, another in his, and pressed a button on a digital recorder. He recited the date and time and the names of the individuals in the meeting room. Finally, he read from the pages inside a manila folder. "John William Faraday MacKenzie, aka Wee Mac or Wee Bill, born Glasgow Scotland August 24 —"

MacKenzie half rose from his seat to stick his hand out to Frankie, as if this situation were all perfectly normal. "Call me Will. Francesca, was it?"

"Frankie," she blurted and, without thinking, took his hand. "No one calls me Francesca." She felt her face grow hot again. Now, when she needed them most, her deportment lessons abandoned her.

His Scottish burr drew out her name when he repeated, "Frankie." Frankie glanced at Palmer, wondering if he'd noticed, and then decided she didn't care.

Ross' jaw tightened and his tone sharpened. He'd noticed. He focused on his notes, and talked over their conversation. "Possession of stolen property, possession of firearms, numerous counts of assault with intent, assault with a deadly weapon —"

"All dropped."

"— numerous drug charges – all in the UK – one conviction for several counts of breaking and entering with a plea agreement resulting in a year in Low Moss Prison."

Will sat back in his chair, stretched his long legs beneath the table and laced his fingers together on his stomach. "Yeah, that's me. Ye called me down here so you could read me my biography?"

"How'd you manage to get a green card, Mr. MacKenzie?"

"You tell me. It's in your wee file. What can I say? I have friends –"

It was Ross' turn to interrupt. "Yes, let's talk about your friends. Are you still in the employ of Salvatore 'Big Sally' Tomasi?"

Will shook his head. "Ah, no. Never have been." *Not techni-*

cally at any rate. "I work for Sal Jr. He owns a couple of clubs. I manage one of them for him. You knew that, but it does give me my days free, so I can come down here for a peedy craic. You should return the favor and come in to Spoiled for a bevvy. I'll hook you up." He poured on Scot's slang to irritate Ross.

Ross looked up from his file. "Yeah, something we can both look forward to. Mr. MacKenzie, what is your association with Lorenzo Barzini?"

Frankie thought she saw MacKenzie's jaw tighten. *Interesting.*

"I don't have one."

Ross slid a photograph of what appeared to be a child's birthday party across the table and started pointing at the people in it. "That's Lorenzo Barzini, and there you are, not five feet away from him."

"He's one of Sal Jr.'s cousins. Big deal. There're lots of them. I don't call that a 'association.'"

So it went for the next hour. Frankie'd been told that today's little exercise had to do with a transaction involving the sale of guns to a Colombian drug cartel in exchange for two tons of cocaine. From what she could tell, Palmer hadn't learned anything he didn't already know. He was starting to get irritated. Will MacKenzie looked bored.

CHAPTER FOUR

W hen Will hadn't made an appearance after almost two hours, Kenna, up to her ears in skinny lattes, decided to go look for him. She cleared the security checkpoint and asked a guard where she might find FBI agent Palmer Ross. Having been told the FBI was on the twenty-third floor, she headed to the bank of elevators.

More than a little anxious that this non-event he'd described was taking all afternoon, she was checking her phone for a message from Will when the elevator dinged, and she followed the other occupants off. When she looked up, she was in an elevator lobby that clearly was not the twenty-third floor or the location of the FBI offices.

"Well, hell." She went to the directory mounted next to the elevator to see where exactly she was. Department of Justice, all right, but these included offices for the US Attorney. She was turning back to the elevator when a name caught her eye.

"I'll be damned. Candace Fisher," she mused. "What do you know – I know a guy here. Can't hurt to try for reinforcements." She turned and headed down the corridor to the office number next to the lawyer's name.

She recognized Candace as soon as she saw her leaning on the high counter around an administrative assistant's desk. The long, burnished red hair was a dead giveaway. She was smartly dressed in a black pencil skirt, camel cashmere sweater and heels high enough to cause a stab of envy.

Kenna paused while Candace finished her comments to the administrative assistant and cleared her throat. "Candace?"

The other woman turned with a quizzical look in her whisky-colored eyes that slowly cleared to one of pleased recognition. "Kenna? Kenna Campbell? What on earth?"

Kenna chuckled a little nervously. "I got off on the wrong floor, if you can believe it."

Candace grinned at the curvy blonde, the pale unruly waves just as she remembered. "Oh, yeah. I can believe it. Who are you here to see?"

Kenna thought, *Go for it*, and said, "A friend of mine is here talking to an FBI agent. Palmer Ross, he said. I was expecting him to meet me way before this, but I haven't heard anything, so I thought I'd come see."

"Palmer Ross?" Candace said the name with a grim set to her mouth. "What's your friend's name?"

"Will ... William ... MacKenzie."

Candace expelled an exasperated breath. "It figures, in a strange and highly aggravating way." She turned to her administrative assistant and asked her to find out where Ross was meeting with William MacKenzie. Learning that they were in an interview room on the twenty-second floor, she suggested Kenna wait in her office.

"It's not much, but it's home for about eighty hours of my week. I'll just clean off the guest chair –"

"I'm coming with you."

"I don't plan to be long," Candace said.

"I'm still coming."

As they headed back to the elevators, Candace turned into the doorway of a fellow Assistant US Attorney with a quick knock.

"Hey, Josh, you hear anything about Palmer Ross getting new evidence on William MacKenzie?" Getting a distracted headshake in response, she frowned and muttered, "Dammit, Ross. You'd better have more in hand than your stubby little fingers."

In the elevator heading to the right floor at last, Kenna asked, "I heard you'd gone to law school, but lost track. How long have you been in the US Attorney's office?"

"I clerked here my last summer before graduation, then four years since. How about you? After you transferred – where was it you went after Fordham?"

"Hudson College," Kenna said. "They have a gallery program that fit better. I got the curatorial and art management background I needed to run a gallery."

"And are you? Where?" Candace asked as she held the elevator door for Kenna.

Kenna's bright green eyes tilted merrily as she laughed. "Right now, I specialize in velvet Elvis and unknown artists, just one undiscovered genius away from opening my own place."

Candace was walking down the corridor at a fast clip. Kenna had to quicken her pace to keep up. An inch or two shorter than Kenna and of a slimmer build, Candace glided smoothly in her heels, whereas Kenna had previously observed so many petite women walked like linemen if they were in a hurry. Kenna unconsciously tugged the front of her top to ensure she wasn't gaping the buttonholes of her blouse while the equally buxom Candace was confident she had nothing out of place. As they slowed, Kenna hid a smile, imagining the flames of an engine streaking behind her guide.

Candace stopped next to a window and slid a switch all the

way up with obvious annoyance. The window cleared and she scowled at the scene inside the interview room. "Oh, for God's sake." She rapped on the glass. The agent standing by the door cleared his throat and made a hasty retreat with a, "'Scuse me, ma'am."

Kenna leaned closer to see what had Candace so ticked off. She had the feeling someone inside the room was about to get cold-cocked by a gutsy little redhead and hoped it wasn't Will. She decided she liked this version of her old college friend.

The two women watched – one with irritation, the other curiosity – as a laconic Palmer Ross rose from his seat at the interrogation table and strolled to the door. He cracked it a few inches.

"What's up, Miz Fisher?"

"You are, Ross. Just what do you think you're doing in there?"

Ross eased himself into the hall, giving Kenna a speculative look as he turned to speak to Candace. "I am following up on leads."

"You are so full of ..." Candace scoffed. "You and I both know you've got nothing new here." She looked back through the window. "Who's that in there with you?"

Ross smirked, "Besides MacKenzie? A forensic psychologist I have invited to sit in and profile the person of interest. Consider her my lie detector."

Kenna looked back, one ear open to the conversation, to check out the woman in the room. She was young, gorgeous and wearing at least three thousand dollars' worth of Armani. Lie detecting paid well. Will's posture was relaxed, even insolent, but Kenna had lived with him long enough to know there was nothing casual about him or the way he was looking at the strawberry blonde.

"Again, and I don't think this can be overstated, you are so full of crap. That woman is a civilian, and the policies you have violated in that one, self-indulgent move, Ross, will get you written up …"

"Go ahead and try, Fisher –"

"Get her out of there. Now."

Only someone who knew him, or someone like Kenna so hyper-observant of human behavior out of an enhanced sense of self-preservation, would have noticed the redness flushing Ross' ears at this dressing down. Kenna bit her lip to hide the grin. She thought, *Score another point for Candace Fisher*.

When Ross turned to re-enter the interview room, Kenna met Candace's glance and the two shared a moment of complete, feminine accord. Shortly, the woman from Ross' interview of Will MacKenzie exited the room and looked curiously from Candace's annoyed face to Kenna's carefully blank expression.

"Okaaay, why do I feel like I'm being taken to the woodshed?"

Kenna made an amused sound in her throat thinking, *glad I'm not in your Louboutins right now*.

Candace extended her hand. "I'm Candace Fisher, Assistant US Attorney for the Southern District of New York." There was a slight, questioning inflection at the end of her introduction.

Frankie Winslow shook her hand. "Frankie Winslow. No title."

"Funny, Ross indicated you're a forensic psychologist, attending this interview in a professional capacity." Candace tilted her head as she regarded the young woman.

Frankie muttered, "I knew this was a horrible idea." She returned Candace's look and said, "Technically, I have a psychology background, but I gave it up to be a writer. Palmer asked me to sit in as background."

"Background for what?" Candace held up her hand. "Save that." She entered the interview room.

Kenna cocked her head and smiled as she studied Frankie. She said, "Hi. I'm a friend of Will's. Have you two known each other long?"

Frankie blushed a little, "No, we don't. I mean, we just met, actually."

"I meant Ross. I *know* Will's friends." Her tone left no doubt that Frankie wasn't on the list.

They turned as Will came through the door with Candace at his elbow and Palmer Ross lurking in the background. "Please accept my apologies for any inconvenience, Mr. MacKenzie." Candace turned to Ross. "Have your admin check with mine. I think I have some time Monday morning before court. Come by my office, and we'll wrap this up."

Ross leveled what he thought was a threatening look at Will MacKenzie and stepped close to Frankie. "Thank you for coming in, Miss Winslow. Call me if you change your mind about that other thing."

Frankie visibly stiffened and took a step back. "You're welcome, but my calendar is full at present."

They all watched him swagger down the hall, each with their own bemusement at his impervious attitude.

Candace waited until Ross was well out of earshot and said to MacKenzie, "Would you please excuse us, Mr. MacKenzie? I know Kenna's been waiting for you, but I need her – and Ms. Winslow – for just a bit. Is there somewhere Kenna can meet you?"

Will raised an eyebrow and locked gazes with Frankie. Leaning into Kenna, he tugged on a long, blonde curl while murmuring, "I'll catch you up downstairs, yeah?"

"Are you ill?" she said, looking up at him as if he had soiled her shoe, pushing his hand and the never-before-performed gesture away from her hair.

Knowing he'd be making his own coffee for a week, Will laughed as he walked away.

Candace smiled to herself at the differing reactions of the two women to MacKenzie and then suggested that the three adjourn to her office for a chat.

CHAPTER FIVE

In the elevator, Candace said to Frankie, "You say 'technically' you have a psychology background. My mother's a clinical psychologist, but in a different specialty – not forensics."

"I wasn't specializing in forensics either. That was all a Palmer fiction. I was working on my PhD in child psychology when I gave it up," Frankie said matter-of-factly. She'd never regretted her decision, although she sometimes wished her freelance writing afforded her enough stability to move out of the co-op she'd inherited from her grandmother.

"No kidding!" Candace was genuinely interested now. "That's my mom's specialty. Where did you study?"

"NYU."

"That's where my mom got her PhD, but my folks live in Ithaca. Still, it's a small world," Candace said. Her gaze fixed on Frankie's blue eyes.

At the mention of Ithaca, the penny dropped for Frankie. "Fisher. Is your mother Susan Fisher?"

"Yes," Candace said. "You know her?"

"She was on my PhD committee," Frankie said as they

exited the elevator on Candace's floor. "She tried to talk me out of quitting. I really loved working with her. I remember she said her daughter was in law school. She was – is – really proud of you."

Candace grimaced as she motioned them into her cramped office. "She's never seen where I work. Hold on, let me move these files." She cleared the guest chair and went to the office next door to borrow another.

Kenna, who'd been silently watching this exchange, marveled at the random old-home-week the three of them were experiencing.

"Thanks for staying. Both of you." Candace gestured for the two of them to sit and then asked Frankie, "Tell me again how you wound up in an interview room with Ross and MacKenzie?"

Crossing her arms over her chest, Kenna adopted a detached pose that oddly mirrored MacKenzie's posture from earlier.

Frankie was studying her manicure, "Working on a spec script for a 'Law and Order' reboot?"

"Ha!"

At Kenna's involuntary laugh, Frankie looked up with a half-smile and then met Candace's serious gaze. "Sorry. I did an article about Palmer about a year ago –"

"That was you?" Candace interrupted with a snort. "Ross posted a laminated copy in our break room. There's probably one on every floor at Federal Plaza. I read it. It was well written, but I could wish you hadn't made it sound like Ross has super powers. He thinks he's Teflon now." She moved some papers from the center of her desk to another stack. "Be that as it may, it still doesn't explain why you were sitting in an interview with Ross and a man – potentially a bad man – he's calling a person of interest." She shrugged in response to Kenna's accusing look.

Frankie gave her a wan smile. "Yes, that sounds like Palmer.

So he, being of a self-aggrandizing bent, asked me to sit in today. Listen, I asked him whether or not my being in there was against any rules, and he told me not to worry about it." The idea that The Senator had either suggested Ross involve her or encouraged him was still niggling at the back of her mind. She took a fortifying breath. "I know that isn't what you asked. I was thinking of turning the article into a book outline. It sounded like a good idea at the time."

Will would be a great book, Kenna thought.

"Did you learn anything significant?" Candace pressed.

"About Will? I mean, Mr. MacKenzie? No. Palmer spent most of the time reciting the contents of his file," was what she said. What she thought was, *Only that Will MacKenzie's as smooth as a fifteen-year-old single malt.*

Candace nodded, acknowledging to herself what she already assumed and turned to Kenna. "Kenna, you're friends with MacKenzie. Did he mention why Ross called him in? Anything you can tell me that might shed some light on this situation?"

Kenna glanced sideways at Frankie. Thinking about what she wanted to say, she inhaled deeply, her impressive breasts rising, and made solid eye contact with Candace, "No. No, he didn't. Is he even under investigation?"

Candace returned her look. Kenna probably knew more than she was saying, but wasn't comfortable saying more. Maybe because their lives had taken different tracks years ago, maybe because Frankie Winslow was an unknown quantity. Knowing that Kenna would be reporting back to Will MacKenzie at the earliest possible moment, Candace said with a small smile, "At this time, I am unaware of an ongoing investigation involving Will MacKenzie. Should that situation change, I'm quite sure someone will be communicating with him promptly."

"Wow. You're good." Frankie was surprised she'd said that out loud. "Can I interview you at some point?"

In the silence that followed, Kenna studied the other two. She looked at Candace. "Thanks for getting Will out of there, but I know you're a prosecutor with a job to do." She decided she would have Will's promise on this one, that he wasn't into anything illegal and wouldn't be. To Frankie, she said, "What's your story with Ross?"

Candace joined her in looking at Frankie, both waiting for an answer with interest.

"Loathe as I am to share personal information on such brief acquaintance," Frankie smiled at the irony, "When I wrote the article about Palmer, we, uh, we spent a fair amount of time together, and it became, well, personal." At the twin-appalled expressions, she went on, "I know, I know. A lapse in judgment."

Kenna nodded. She understood that concept. "So what are you, a plant?" Candace, propping her chin on her hand, was enjoying letting Kenna do the questioning for the moment.

"A plant? Do you mean like a ficus?" Frankie knew what Kenna meant. As she looked at Candace for a little appreciation for her lame attempt at humor, all she saw was another question mark. "No, I swear on my trust fund, I am not a plant."

"Did you get what you hoped for?" Candace asked.

"No, I didn't," Frankie said, "At least an hour in that room and I've no idea if there was anything to investigate, aside from Will MacKenzie's interesting choice of friends." She wondered if Palmer was capable of manufacturing charges against MacKenzie. Shrugging, she added, "I think Palmer was showing off. And here I am trying to explain why he cooked up this dog and pony show." Frankie paused and leveled a look at Candace, "Now, I have a question."

Candace gestured for her to go on.

"Why is Palmer obsessed with Will MacKenzie?"

Kenna tried to hide her eagerness for the answer as she looked at Candace.

"I wish I knew," Candace said. She returned Kenna's look, an element of concern showing for Kenna's possible involvement.

Before Candace could ask another question, Frankie looked at the other two and threw herself into the breach, "Well, if there's nothing else, it's been a hell of a day, and I'm feeling the need for a very large, very dirty martini. Anyone?"

Candace glanced at her watch. Her eyes widened at the hour. "I can't leave *now*?" It almost sounded like a question. Or a whine. At that moment, a martini sounded like exactly what she needed.

Kenna decided then and there that going for cocktails would give her a chance to see what kind of person Candace had become in the past several years, and she could size up Frankie Winslow. Two good reasons to decide if she should put on her protective sister suit for Will.

"Come on," she teased. "You know you were here at the ass crack of dawn. Come out and play with us."

Candace thought about all those years she'd been the good girl, staying inside to practice the piano when her friends wanted her to go out and have some fun. She *had* been there before seven, by God. She'd be damned if she spent another Friday night chained to her files when she could be spending some more time with these women. Maybe in a casual setting, she'd form a more complete picture of their respective roles in this little drama.

She decided. "Okay. This day has been circling the drain for a while. I'm in." She looked up at Kenna and Frankie. "I doubt I'm the only one in this room who thinks we three may have more to talk about." She raised her hands, palms out. "Unof-ficially."

The other two looked at her for a heartbeat or two.

Candace added, "You know, neutral ground?"

Frankie was a bit surprised that both women had agreed so readily, but she was game. She had plans for the evening, but the thought of spending another night at yet another boring fundraiser, eating surf and turf while some scion or other groped her under the table prompted her to say yes to drinks with these two. Could be research, could be fun.

Kenna said, "I know a guy. I know a place. It's in Midtown. If we go now, we can beat the after-work meat market." She sent a silent "sorry" into the atmosphere for standing up Will.

CHAPTER SIX

They stepped out of a cab in front of a flashy new club skirting the theater district.

"I hope you know a guy with keys. They don't appear to be open." Candace gazed up at the façade that towered three levels above them, past the stainless steel lettering backed by electric blue lights – "Swag."

"Trust me," Kenna said, opening the door into the dimly lit entry.

Frankie and Candace held back, not quite sure about the dark entrance or Kenna's "trust me."

"You go ahead and make sure everything's okay in there," Candace said, only half in jest.

Kenna looked down into the black maw, back at the other women, and chuckled before disappearing inside.

Frankie looked at Candace. "Good idea. That's how every slasher movie starts. If she screams, we run."

Lights flickered on inside, ruining the sexy ambiance, but assuring them that there was no axe wielding maniac inside the door. Kenna pushed through, turned and bowed low with a flourish. "Better?"

"Much."

The top forty song coming softly from the speakers was a stark contrast to the electric blue lights that continued through the bar and discreet corners of the club, the brushed nickel table tops, mirrored walls and glass railings all suggesting that the night life here had a pulsing, techno beat.

"Sorry, ladies, we don't open until five," said a deep voice from the shadows of a passageway behind the bar as its owner emerged. His dark hair was slicked back above arched brows and dark eyes. The suit was perfectly tailored, but mid-day casual without a tie. A shade brighter and the blue would have been gaudy. One more ring and he would have looked like a pimp. "I'd be happy to reserve you a table," he stopped. A wide grin made his dark eyes squint. "Kenna! The fuck you doin' here during working hours?" The shock of seeing her made him slide momentarily back into the family idioms he'd been trying to shake off his expensive Italian loafers.

Kenna skirted the truth a bit. "I brought a couple of girl-friends for drinks. Didn't think I'd actually find *you* here this early, though."

"Since when do you have girlfriends?" He turned the smile to Frankie and Candace and gestured towards a low table and plush club chairs, which he held for each of them as they sat. "Planning on sweet talking Henry out of my good booze again?"

Kenna flashed a toothy grin at their host. "I was going to pay. Eventually."

He adjusted his suit coat sleeves to flash crisp cuffs and sapphire cufflinks that matched the suit before extending a hand to Kenna's companions. "I'm Sal. Welcome to Swag."

Candace's mouth turned up at the corners. "Nice to meet you, Mr. Tomasi." She recognized the junior Tomasi, not only from recent headlines about his father that occasionally included "family" photos, but also from the racketeering indictment documents against Big Sally Tomasi sitting on her boss' desk right at this moment.

"Just Sal around here." He smiled again. "I'll have Henry bring you something special."

Frankie gaped at Kenna as Sal glided away. Like Candace, she'd recognized their host, and it didn't take a journalist to smell a story. "I'd suggest you *do* know a couple of guys. Are you a collector?"

Kenna curled her lip and stared back at Frankie. "What? I don't date these people." She hoped the lie buried in that statement was not showing on her expressive face.

Soon, Henry set in front of them three very big, very dirty martinis garnished with a cobalt blue glow-stick skewer spearing chunks of raw tuna and wasabi-stuffed olives. "Enjoy, ladies," He gave Kenna an affectionate pat on the shoulder and left them, as unobtrusively as he'd come. From deep in the bowels of the nightclub, staff moved glassware, tables and equipment. They laughed or sang along to whatever song popped up on someone's playlist.

"What shall we drink to?" Kenna asked holding up her glass.

"Neutral ground?" Candace said, her voice dripped with sarcasm.

"Here's to Switzerland," Frankie laughed, her glass raised. "Love the skiing. Great cheese."

Kenna gave an unapologetic shrug.

The toast was interrupted by a loud car horn blaring from Kenna's purse. "Ooh, shit! Will!" she scrambled to connect his call.

"Feckin' hell, Kenna!" Will's voice bellowed from the tiny slit of a speaker as Kenna held the phone a foot away from her ear. "First that dobber Ross takes up my whole day then you leave me waiting in the car for forty-five minutes holding my knob."

"Classy, Will. I'm with the girls."

"What girls?!"

"From the thing."

"What thing?"

Frankie whispered to Candace, "I think I want to buy a vowel."

"The FBI chicks," Kenna said with an exasperated sigh.

"Frankie and that lawyer, whatshername Candace Fisher?"

"How do you not know 'the thing,' but you remember Frankie and Candace? Do you remember *my* name, asshole?"

"Fuck off, Kenna." Will ended the call.

"Is there something you'd like to share with the class?" Candace asked, twirling her glow-stick through the icy drink.

Frankie had to force herself not to lean closer.

Kenna reached for her drink before making eye contact. "Who's askin'?" Kenna drawled. "Candace or 'that lawyer?'"

Candace raised her hand. "Fair point. Right now, it's your business." She and Kenna exchanged a look that acknowledged that future circumstances could change that.

Frankie clenched a fist in her lap to keep her own curious frustration from showing on her face. Instead, she turned to Kenna and asked brightly, "Speaking of which, what exactly is your business?"

Kenna took a long sip of her martini. "Dogs playing poker. Ford Pinto transmission parts welded into erotica," she said, making air quotes with her fingers when she added, "art." Shaking her head, she backtracked. "They actually aren't that bad." She laughed, "Well, yeah some are. And for the record, I sell it. I don't make it."

She stretched an arm over her head to point behind her. "The glass and steel piece over the bar is mine. Sal was supposed to borrow it for a few weeks, then trade out with the same artist. The customers ooh'ed and ahh'ed so much he bought it, and now we trade out newer pieces for the lounge, offices and restrooms." She directed their attention with her electric blue swizzle stick to two other intricate blue glass and polished steel pieces.

"You do this for all of Sal's bars?" Candace asked. She knew more about the Tomasi family holdings than might be comfortable for some.

Kenna paused, then nodded. "And others. Six bars, four Asian restaurants, three bankers, one lawyer, a tattoo parlor –"

"This line of work pays your bills?" Frankie asked, still curious as to where Will fit in.

"Close enough," Kenna said. "VIP seating. Free Pings. And you meet a lot of people wanting to 'invest' in art." The air quotes made another appearance.

"An art pimp," Frankie quipped, making Kenna laugh.

"Okay, it's your turn." Kenna leaned toward Frankie. "Tell me more about this article. My memory's a bit foggy around that time."

Candace gave Kenna a puzzled look. The story had been national news.

Frankie started at the beginning. Candace had read her article, but it was all new to Kenna. She told them how she'd gotten an assignment from the glossy weekly tabloid for which she freelanced to go interview the newest recipient of the FBI Medal of Valor.

Kenna listened intently. She wasn't sure if she was remembering a real story Will had read to her or an episode of some crime drama marathon during her convalescence. "He's the one who took a bullet for a judge?"

Frankie nodded. "Instead of a crime story, I got the eligible bachelor gig." She mimicked Ross' southern drawl, but added her own sarcasm, "Aw shucks, ma'am. I'm just a humble rancher's kid from Texas tryin' to do right."

Frankie bit the last piece of tuna from her pick and said around the bite, "Ironic, Palmer as the poster boy for women hoping for decent, gainfully employed single men. And I was his procurer. I'm trying to become financially independent. You're an art pimp, and I'm a celebrity whore."

"I doubt that's true." Candace put down her drink and turned to Kenna. "How did you miss that story? It was everywhere."

Kenna swallowed hard, looking from one to the other as she massaged the tender hand she'd been rehabbing hours earlier. Maybe it was Henry's magic martini. Maybe it was the emotional drain of the day. Maybe it was the earnest faces of the two women watching her nervous hands, women who weren't looking for evidence or trying to "fix" her, that made her finally talk about it.

She kicked off her shoes under the table and leaned back in the roomy chair. "I had an accident," she said, holding her hand up to show them the thin surgical scar on her palm.

"No," she stopped and squeezed her eyes together, "I had a lapse in judgment." Kenna pointed at Frankie, who raised her glass. "*This* was deliberate and ... awful. *My* lapse didn't try and woo me back with a sexy Scotsman though. He nearly killed me."

Candace sat up straight. "He what?"

Frankie had a grip on the arms of her chair.

Kenna shrugged with fake casualness. "I ended it. He disagreed. But that's how I met Will. He saved my life. I couldn't stay by myself after I left the hospital, so Will and Sal Jr.," – Kenna wiggled her thumb toward the back of the bar – "moved me into Will's apartment. I've been there ever since. He took care of me. I guess we take care of each other, now."

"Is the guy in prison?" Frankie asked, but Kenna was silent.

"I *assume* the bastard's in prison," Frankie said hoping for confirmation.

Kenna shook her head, "After it happened I didn't remember much. There were no witnesses so the police couldn't bring charges even if I'd pushed for them."

"There's still time," Candace said. "I could look into it."

Kenna shook her head. "I want to get on with my life." She flexed her hand, "PT cleared me this morning. Besides, y'all have seen enough Law & Order." She winked at Frankie. "There are so many worse cases than this. She blew out a long breath, as if she'd been holding it for months, which she had. "Wow, they were right. I do feel better."

With preternatural accuracy, Henry arrived with a second round.

The three of them stared at the fresh, pretty drinks, unable to make eye contact for a moment. Then, Frankie leaned forward and lifted her glass.

"Here's to Henry's perfect timing."

THE GATHERING happy hour crowd began to raise Swag's hum. Sal, making his rounds, stopped at their table. With his arm on the back of Kenna's chair, he spoke softly and diplomatically, "I can't have you three nursing martinis for an hour and nothing else. It's happy hour – I gotta flip this table."

"Or," Kenna said, "you can bring us some nibbles and let us be decorative for a while?" Her words earned her double fist bumps from Frankie and Candace.

Defeated, Sal nodded. "I'll send over another round, some bar food – you gotta eat – and smile for the paying customers, will you?"

The suspicious, inquisitive tension from earlier faded along with Henry's magical concoctions and Sal's complimentary cheese board and crudités. They were getting comfortable enough to be annoyed when a man approached the table. He leered at the three while slurping his drink, but he lacked the confidence of a true predator.

"*Hellooo*, lovely ladies," he crooned, swaying. "How about I buy us another round, and we all get to know each other?" He clearly hoped that at least one of the three hot women was drunk enough to appreciate his smooth moves.

Candace dragged her disinterested, whisky-colored gaze from his overly-shined oxfords up to his crooked tie and blood-shot eyes before laconically replying, "I don't think so."

"We'll pass," Frankie added in a bored tone.

Kenna shooed him away and kept her attention on her new pals. "As I was saying..."

The dejected lothario decamped to his friends at the bar.

Kenna grinned, "Five bucks says he tells his buds we're lesbians."

"No bet."

BEHIND KENNA, there was a slight altercation. Barely glancing around, she ignored what was no doubt one of the happy hour's over-indulged patron's summons home for supper, secure in the knowledge that none of the fray would be allowed to reach their table.

Candace and Frankie had a direct line of sight to the kerfuffle at the bar and watched intently over Kenna's shoulder. Sal, moving like a boxer, grasped another tall, dark and hand-some – if a bit smarmy – guy by the lapels, blocking the other man's view of their table. Their host's eyes were narrow, angry slits that distorted his handsome features into the dangerous persona attributed to his family by the media. His mouth formed a hard line as he spoke, and the women didn't need to hear the words to know that Sal was vehemently warning the newcomer away from them.

"What the hell is so interesting?" Kenna said, untucking her feet from beneath her bottom to rotate toward the action.

"Suits wrestling," Frankie said, all the while thinking Mr. Smarmy looked familiar.

Candace knew from the organized crime case currently active on her boss' docket that the interloper was another member of the Tomasi *compagnia*. Lorenzo Barzini, from the photos she'd seen numerous times. This "neutral ground" Kenna had chosen got more interesting by the minute.

Kenna turned to see what was so fascinating. She spun back around, firmly planting her hands on the table.

"Time to go."

"Fine with me," Candace said. "It's getting really loud in here, and I'm not really in the mood for more drunken, not to mention lame, pick-up lines." She moved her empty glass away and gathered her handbag.

As if on cue, Sal squatted next to Kenna and held up her discarded shoes. "I can't babysit you all night. I called Will to come take you home."

Kenna snatched her shoes and her purse and rose in a single motion. "I can't believe you, Sal! We're already on our way out." She waved to Candace and Frankie, who were in departure mode. "Hurry, Will's gonna get here and ruin everything." Kenna's thus far hidden southern accent broadened with the surge of irritation and adrenaline.

"Your tab?" Sal called wryly to their rapidly retreating backs.

"Oh, we are *so* even for this," Kenna shot over her shoulder. His laughter only fueled her irritation.

At the door, Frankie asked, "Why don't you want to wait for

Will?" Personally, she wouldn't mind bumping into him again, accidentally of course.

Kenna looked at Frankie, almost feeling sorry for the impending fall. "I saw y'all first. He'll swoop in and take over like he always does."

"Shall we, then?" Candace said from an open taxi door.

Wide-eyed, Kenna looked at Frankie, and her mouth turned down in an impressed *Would-you-look-at-her?* expression.

"The lawyer gets shit done." Frankie laughed and scrambled across the back seat of the cab.

Candace and Kenna followed, realizing they had switched bags at some point in the rush to get out of Swag. A laughing bag exchange followed with mutual admiration for their similar tastes.

"Where to?" the cab driver asked in a surprising American accent.

"Just drive," Kenna said, looking out the back window, certain the next set of headlights would be Will careening around the corner.

Frankie leaned forward and gave him an address in Gramercy Park.

Candace whistled. "Who lives there?"

Chewing her lip, Frankie confessed, "I kind of do."

"How do you 'kind of' live somewhere?" Candace asked. She gave Frankie a piercing look. *What's she hiding?*

"Oh that's easy," said Kenna absently. "You don't really want to be there, but it beats sleeping under a bridge or eating ketchup soup to pay rent on a dump."

Candace slowly turned to look at Kenna. "And I have one for you too, Miss Campbell. How do you 'kind of' have a southern accent? And how come I've never heard it before?"

"That *was* a Reese Witherspoon, *Sweet Home Alabama*, switch," Frankie added to Candace's query.

"You caught that, huh?" Kenna scrunched her face, mentally kicking herself for the lapse, then crooked her fingers for them to lean in and whispered conspiratorially. "I'm not a native." She gave them a nod and wink, then sat back digging in her purse for nothing in particular.

The silence that followed lasted long enough for the cab driver to check in his mirror and ask if they were having a nice evening. He received absent nods and thumbs-up in response.

"What's going to happen when Will gets there and you've vanished?" Frankie asked, looking back into a sea of cars.

"Nothing."

"*Nothing?*" Candace gave Kenna a look of complete disbelief. "I don't get the impression that Will MacKenzie just lets things go. Not when it comes to you."

"Don't worry about it." Kenna flicked her hand at the mental gnats of worry and the inevitable argument with Will.

"SAL!" Will stalked toward the man, shouting as he made short work of the distance from his car to the door of Swag. "*Sal!*"

Sal gestured for two barely twenty-one-year-old girls in body-con dresses to enter the club before turning to respond. "You missed them."

"Did you tell her I was coming?" When Sal only shrugged, Will shook his head. "Fuck, Sal. I got a club to run too. *Your* club, remember?"

"And I'm not worried about that." He put an arm around Will's shoulder. "You and Kenna still just friends?"

Will stepped away from Sal's arm. "Since when do you care? Is there something you need to tell me?"

Sal's hands went up. "Just asking. Interesting crowd she's hanging with though. One of them knew me. Cop?"

"Bonny red hair?" Sal grinned, and Will said, "Assistant US Attorney. I got pulled in today. Remember that Fed who was poking around a few weeks ago, looking for shite on you or your old man?" Sal nodded. "Ross thought I'd flip under the hot lights." Will jerked his thumb towards the street. "That attorney was ready to cut his baws off. Guess Kenna found a kindred spirit there." They both laughed. Kenna had a sharp tongue, but, as far as they knew, she wasn't a castrator.

"Will MacKenzie." The effusive, loud tone and false cama-raderie emanating from a few feet away made Will's teeth clench.

"Barzini," Will said with minimal civility. He'd had enough of this guy for one day, and that encounter had been only a photograph.

The brutally handsome, slightly oily, man Sal had fended away from the girls' table earlier draped his arms around Sal's and Will's shoulders. "Cousin, when you gonna get Willie Boy here to let me bring some ladies around to Spoiled?" Will slung off the arm, and Barzini grinned lasciviously. "We could make some nice scratch outta that place."

Sal started to speak, but was cut off by Will. "Fucker! Who're you calling Boy? You don't speak to me."

"I'm just bustin' your balls, man."

Will had two fingers in Barzini's face, "Sal hired me to run a straight club and make money. In. That. Order. No drugs, no whores, no cops. No trouble. You stay the fuck away from my club and my balls."

Sal shrugged, "You heard the man, Cousin."

Barzini slicked back his hair with both hands and snarled, "Fuck you both," and turned for the door.

"I can't put a finger on it, Sal, but I hate that fucking roaster," Will lit a cigarette. "If he comes in to Spoiled again, I'm tossing him in the street. Your cousin or no."

"Management reserves the right to refuse service, Will. You won't have any trouble from me if you do," Sal assured him. "Still pissed at Kenna?"

Will sighed and took another long drag. "Nah. She had her last therapy for the hand today. She seems good."

Sal nodded. "Yeah, real good."

CHAPTER SEVEN

Davit Lazarashvilli, alias David Lawrence, paced in his luxuriously appointed compound, commensurate with the status of his family name, the befouling of which he would never admit responsibility for. He curled his lip to think of how he'd spent far too many days in squalor. Never of his own making, of course.

God, how he'd hated his father, a prominent Turkish judge, who had seen him educated at Eton and Oxford. David never acknowledged that he was like hundreds – thousands – of typically lawless children of the aristocracy. He was accustomed to fine things and the privilege that mitigated his worst juvenile crimes down to petty offenses. Car theft became "loitering." Drug distribution – "minor in possession." Attempted sexual assault – "public intoxication."

When his social deviancy grew more violent, public and embarrassing as he reached his twenties, His Honor had cut off financial support, although Mother slipped him some *lira* whenever he became too inconvenient. *She was such a gullible fool*, he thought with a sneer. The car accident that killed them both had been ... unfortunate.

He was proud of his natural entrepreneurial ability that led him to use his inheritance to hire and arm his band of scavengers harvested from military deserters, gangs and the desperate poor. Often dressed as soldiers or UN troops if they could steal the uniforms, they had moved through war torn areas of Eastern Europe, pillaging at will and discovering the lucrative world of the modern slave trade.

When the war crime hunters came, he moved to Africa, but found too much opportunistic competition there. Competition and the man responsible for his greatest financial losses and physical ruin.

Lawrence blamed one man above all others for the bullet wounds that had severed his manhood from his body. Wounds that had soon festered and begun to rot away his urinary tract, his bowels, and the flesh of his lower abdomen and thighs. It took him many months to recover, and longer to torture the information from local informants, but he soon had names and locations. UN aid workers, their security teams, and most importantly the *Others*, the SAS-led Allied Joint Operations bastards. Sometimes in blue helmets, sometimes dressed as goat herders, more often completely invisible until the bastards started shooting men in the groin over something as minor as the rape of a whore.

Who were they to decide who was a "war criminal" and who was a revolutionary? It was war, everyone was a criminal.

Today, however, it was his flow of income that had been interrupted. Again. Another shipment of his particular product had been intercepted, and he could smell Chaerea's influence on the interception. Lawrence barked for Hans.

"Hans" was not *his* real name either, but in all the years he'd been a paid follower of Lazarashvilli, through many aliases before David Lawrence, Hans never corrected the boss. He enjoyed the perks of being the right hand man, including the occasional free samples of the merchandise, too much to risk his position over something as trivial as a name. And, ah, what a lovely sample was the beauty he'd had to leave behind a locked door. He especially relished the human chattel that tried to fight back.

Waves of refugees from multiple war-torn regions, poverty to the east and out of Africa were a virtual buffet for their particular brand of human trade. Yet still, demand always exceeded supply. Even the starved, scarred and used could be sold to someone. Thirty-two billion dollars a year, and that was only the best guess that humanitarian watch groups could estimate. Over three quarters of a million human victims bought and sold annually. The few slave traders who were caught and brought to trial had a less than ten percent conviction rate. The odds were vastly in their favor.

The boss fancied himself a dealer in high end, high priced, preferably Western-appearing and English language capable product. Hans really didn't care. Everyone was fuckable and sellable. With chaos on every doorstep around the world, who cared about the nameless and faceless?

"HANS!" Lawrence screamed on the heels of his first summons, as the door opened and Hans' muscular shoulders cast a shadow over the floor. "Did Chaerea bite?"

"Not that we can tell, Boss. He was in Cairo last week but didn't ask questions or speak to anyone about the information we slipped to him," Hans answered in his thick Ukrainian accent. Unlike Lawrence, he had not had the aural clues of his mother tongue educated out of him.

"He did something," Lawrence spat, waving a crumpled piece of paper, "or I would not be losing men and money with every shipment!"

"He hasn't been on an interception team in months," Hans reminded Lawrence.

"You think he suspects a trap?"

"Doesn't he always?" Hans asked, cautious as one would be in close proximity to a live landmine. Lawrence hated to be reminded of his failed attempts on Lucius Chaerea's life. Those opportunities had grown fewer and fewer since the Colonel's "retirement" and relocation to the United States.

"He's ignoring me, Hans. He's waiting for a grand gesture. An engraved invitation perhaps." Lawrence tapped his chin with a finger gnarled from a break that had healed badly. "What draws the wolf out of his den?"

"Blood? Food? Sex?" Strategy was not Hans' strong suit.

"No. The cries of wounded rabbits. We must find his rabbit."

"Since the passing of Mrs. Chaerea, he's had no one –"

Lawrence leveled a frustrated look on his slow-witted employee. "I don't need you to state the obvious. I need you to step up your surveillance and *find me a fucking rabbit!*"

CHAPTER EIGHT

"What?!" Kenna popped out of the chair with wild eyes and wilder hair.

As soon as he'd opened the door to his apartment, Will saw the glow of the television in his otherwise dark living room. Wrapped in a quilt, Kenna was curled up in his big chair. Whatever black and white movie she'd found to keep her company while she waited for him obviously hadn't been good enough to keep her awake. He'd dropped his keys on the table with a resounding clatter.

"Asshole. Did you *have* to do that?"

Will chuckled and popped the tab on a Coke he'd found in the fridge. "What're you doing?"

"Watching a movie." She reached up and took the can out of his hand, had a sip and passed it back.

"You do that with your eyes closed now? And where the hell were you all night?"

Kenna tucked herself back into the quilt, and turned her focus back to the muted TV. "Hanging out. Girl stuff." *Way too much to drink and way too much sharing*, she thought.

"Hanging out where?"

"Frankie's place. You could fit three of these apartments in there."

"She's got money?"

Kenna squirmed and scrunched up her face. *Frankie Winslow is lucky she got a big ass apartment instead of a padded room after life with that grandmother of hers.* "More like payback, but drunk utterances are privileged. Do I go around asking you what guys talk about over the urinals?"

"I don't talk over the urinals," Will said, incredulous and offended.

"Really? We talk between the stalls."

He chuckled. "Privileged? Drunk utterances? Just how much did you rub against that lawyer?"

"Don't be a perv!" Kenna kicked the air in his direction.

He took another deep swallow and watched her face in the gray-blue glow. She was holding something back, and he wasn't sure if he wanted to pry the lid off it right at this moment. "What girl stuff? Like makeup? Hair? Or boys?"

"We're not twelve."

"Yeah, so? What girl stuff?"

Kenna massaged her hand under the quilt. Will noticed and pointed at the action, wiggling his hand for her to show him. "You loupin?"

"English, please?"

"Pain, Kenna. Are you in pain?"

"A little. They asked about it." She pulled her hand out and placed it in his.

"What'd you say?" Will gently prodded the scar, hoping he sounded only half as interested as he actually was in her answer. Any discussion of the cause, with anyone, would be a step forward. Satisfied when she didn't flinch or gasp, he let go.

"Too damn much. You came off as the hero of the story, I promise," Kenna smiled up at him.

"Hero my ass. Probably did you some good to get some of that shite out of your head." Before she could respond with the litany of excuses, he waved his hand. "Never mind. You were waiting up. Why?"

Relieved at the topic change, Kenna sat up straight. "You need to tell me what yesterday was all about. Why did some pencil-neck FBI agent think you had anything he wanted? What are you doing?"

"Christ, Kenna." He looked at his watch and blew out a breath before plopping down on the couch. Ten minutes ago, all he'd wanted was to kick back and watch the footie match starting in half an hour on the other side of the world. "How the fuck do I know why any of those fuckers do anything? Did you ask your new friend, the lawyer?"

"I'm asking you. Are you mixed up in something for Uncle Sally –"

Will interrupted. "Sally is not your uncle."

"Don't change the subject. Is Sally the reason you take off for three or four days without a word? You know, I really don't need another snow globe or a shot glass you picked up at some random airport gift shop. Just tell me what you're doing for them so I'll know how much bail money to keep under my mattress."

"Go to bed, Kenna." He got up and started down the hall, unbuttoning his shirt as went. "I promise, I'm not doing anything for them." Let her make of that comment what she would.

"I'll remember you said that!" Kenna grabbed the quilt from the chair, headed for her own room and then remembered the slip of paper in her pocket. She tossed the scrap with Frankie's number on it onto the table next to his keys. "And, by the way, I got you a present. You're welcome!"

CHAPTER NINE

"She's here? I'll be right out," Candace said into her office phone. She glanced around her tiny office and grimaced yet again over the fact there was barely enough room for herself, a laptop, and her stacks of paper, let alone a visitor. Still, she grabbed the files piled in her only guest chair and put them onto the floor next to her desk.

Candace's face broke into a big grin when she saw Kenna, holding a brown paper-wrapped parcel, at the receptionist's desk. Kenna looked cool and collected in a printed pencil skirt, the design pulled right off Tut's sarcophagus and wrapped around her hips. The skirt was paired with a plain white, three-quarter-sleeve, v-neck tee.

"Hey! Twice in as many weeks. People will begin to think you're a material witness or something." She gave Kenna a quick hug. "Come on back to my hovel, I mean office. Would you like a cup of coffee or a soft drink?"

"No, I'm good," Kenna said, admiring the tailored slacks and silk shirt Candace was wearing with three-and-a-half inch heels. "I had something I wanted to see if you'd hang in your office or somewhere out here, if you hate it." She lifted the flat parcel.

"What? Oh! Let's see." Candace waved Kenna to the empty chair and accepted the package, neatly lifting the tape from the folded edges to unwrap it.

Kenna snorted. "You can tell a lot about a person by the way they open presents, either ripping them open or lifting the tape to do the big reveal. You did say you're a control freak – I guess that extends to neat freak too."

Chagrined, Candace gave her friend a half-smile. "Yeah, that's me, appearances in this office notwithstanding. Sorry for the mess."

Kenna looked around the little space noting that, while there were files and papers stacked everywhere, they did seem to have a sense of order about them. She also noticed that the only window was a narrow slit with a spectacular view of the featureless office building next door. Yes, Kenna'd chosen well.

As Candace lifted the painting from the wrapping, Kenna said, "A son of a friend painted it, and it's too good to try to sell through the gallery next to the velvet Elvises. But he's still an unknown, so I didn't think there was much chance the Senator would let Frankie hang it in the mausoleum." She looked around Candace's office. "From what I'd seen of this place, I thought maybe you could use some color, and he'd get some exposure at the same time by getting one of his pieces hung in a public building."

"Wow! This is stunning – lush and romantic." Candace held the painting reverently and fell in love with the bright color, the Impressionistic view of a couple under a red umbrella, walking in a late summer rain, through leafy trees starting to take on fall color. "Kenna, I can't accept something so valuable." Candace sadly placed the painting on top of the papers on her desk. "Federal employee stuff, no gifts of any value."

"Okay. It's not a gift. It's on loan from the private collection of Kenna Campbell." She stood and went behind the desk to look at the painting with Candace. "I especially like the way he's used a palette knife to add the layers of color and texture. It's reminiscent of Afremov, don't you think?"

Candace looked sideways at Kenna and noted the authoritative tone. She said, "You're talking to someone who knows what she likes, but doesn't know from – who'd you say? Afremov? I'm not surprised you know your stuff. Still, I'm impressed, and yes, I will explain it as a loan. Or, you can let me buy it. Either way, you can tell the son of your friend that his piece is 'displayed in the offices of the United States Attorney for the Southern District of New York.'" She hugged Kenna again. "Thank you!"

Unaccustomed to affectionate displays – and it was clear Candace was a hugger – Kenna hesitated before returning the embrace. "You're welcome. I brought a hanger and a hammer if you want to hang it. I'm thinking over that useless window."

Laughing, they hung the painting over the window and stood back to admire their handiwork.

"What an improvement! I love my new view," Candace said. "The least I can do now is buy you lunch. Are you free?"

"Not free, but cheap for my friends." It felt wonderful to say that and know it was true. They were friends.

Palmer Ross was entering as they left the Federal Building. His suspicions about what Candace Fisher and Will MacKenzie's bimbo might have to talk about were on high alert. He'd hang around after his meeting to catch Ms. Fisher and get answers.

Candace barely had her purse put away after returning from lunch before he pounced.

"Darlin'! Where ya been? I've been waiting for twenty minutes." Ross assumed his customary lounging position in Candace's office doorway.

She eyed him skeptically before answering. "Lunch. It generally happens about this time of day. What do you need?"

Ignoring her question, he asked one of his own. "Who'd you have lunch with?"

"And that falls squarely in the none-of-your-business bucket. What do you need?"

Ross' face hardened, but he kept the lazy smile in place. "I saw you leave with MacKenzie's girlfriend. It raised some questions, like, 'what could these two people have in common?' Oh, wait. That would be Will MacKenzie. Or, what do they have to talk about – or do – that they have to leave the building? I'm thinkin' to myself, 'maybe they're meeting with MacKenzie.' Or, how about this? Is Candace Fisher goin' behind my back to get information about MacKenzie, or hide it, when she knows I'm buildin' a case?"

Candace rolled her eyes, "You. Are delusional. And possibly paranoid. Kenna Campbell is not Will MacKenzie's girlfriend. Not in the way you mean anyway. She's a girl, and she's his friend and, thanks to a wild coincidence that wouldn't have happened if you hadn't brought Will MacKenzie in for your little puppet show, I've renewed my old friendship with her too. And, it must be said that I have not met Mr. MacKenzie anywhere but outside your interrogation room.

"Not that it's any of your concern, but Kenna and I simply had lunch together. We have a lot of catching up to do. Will MacKenzie wasn't there, wasn't invited any more than you were, or Harry, the homeless man on the subway grate in front of this building was, and his name never came up. MacKenzie's that is, not Harry's. Satisfied?"

Ross ambled over and leaned on her desk, bringing his face close enough that she pushed her chair back, her revulsion clear on her face. "No. I am not satisfied. And if your name, image or voice comes up on any of my surveillance, we'll be having a very different conversation."

At that outrageous statement, she stood and leaned back

across the desk, getting in his face as he had hers. "You had better take care with your unfounded accusations against an officer of the court and the U.S. government. Your surveillance – all of it – better have probable cause and been approved by someone in this office and a real federal judge, or you couldn't be more right. We will be having a very different conversation. Are we done?"

Ross smirked and pushed off her desk with a wink. "For now." He looked up at the new art behind her. "Nice." And then he left.

"Creep," she muttered to his retreating back.

"STOP HERE," Lorenzo Barzini said, rapping his ringed knuckle against the plexiglass partition of the cab. He'd ditched his own silver Corvette Zo6 in the parking garage, knowing Kenna would recognize it too easily.

"Let me pull over."

"Don't you fucking move." Barzini cut off the cabbie, stranding the taxi in the middle of the street.

"The fuck is she doing here?" He noted the Federal Building and surrounding support offices as he watched Kenna smile and hug the hot redhead from Swag. "Bet the bitch turned snitch."

Kenna stuck out in the sea of business suits. The clear, warm, fall day made an overcoat unnecessary. Her bright patterned skirt and untamed blonde waves were a bullseye for him in the proverbial concrete jungle. His fists clenched possessively as he watched her walk toward the street. When she stopped suddenly and slowly looked around, searching the faces and cars, he slumped down in the back seat. Her eyes passed right over his taxi.

Horns behind his cab started to blare. "Fuck! Drive, but not too fast."

Kenna spun on the balls of her feet at the sound and watched the taxi that had been blocking traffic pull away slowly, then turn the corner in front of the Starbucks she'd been swilling lattes in a couple of weeks earlier.

I'm losing my mind, she thought, but hailed a cab instead of taking the subway back to the gallery.

CHAPTER TEN

"Ohh! You look nice," Kenna said as she put her computer on the sofa cushion beside her and turned to watch Will adjusting his cuffs and fingering his hair. "Where ya going? Who with? Do I know her parents?"

Will didn't look over at her. He leaned closer to the mirror and said quietly, "Frankie. I'm taking her to that duck place."

Kenna scrambled over the back of the sofa. "What do you mean 'Frankie'? *My* Frankie?"

"You," – he tapped her chest – "gave me her number. Remember? Don't look at me like that."

"That was weeks ago. I didn't know her then. Now when this goes south, I'm down one friend." She spread her arms out wide. "It's not like that bank account is overflowing you know."

Will may have been insulted if she didn't look so disappointed at the prospect.

"I promise, I won't fuck it up that bad. And I'll bring you a doggie bag."

She followed him to the door. "Full *entrée*. The noodles I like and extra duck skin crispies." She was still talking when he reached the stairs, her voice rising, "And don't put out on the first date. She'll think you're easy."

———

FRANKIE SPENT a ridiculous amount of time obsessing over what to wear, before heading downtown to meet Will. His invitation had been surprisingly quick after their first meeting. Finding a free evening had taken a bit longer. She still didn't know much about him, though she'd had two Sunday brunches and one early bird trunk sale spree with Kenna and Candace.

As the cab turned onto Mott Street, she saw him illuminated by the red, yellow and green light from the restaurant's sign. The taxi pulled up, and as Frankie paid the driver, Will flicked his lit cigarette into the street. He reached for the door as she opened it. Her forward momentum out and his attempt to be the gentleman caused an old-fashioned "meet cute" collision.

"Hey," he grinned.

"Hey."

"That was fun. Can we do it a few more times?"

She was staring at his mouth. "You have to feed me first."

"Good idea."

With his hand on her lower back, Will guided her toward the entrance of the Chinese restaurant regularly described as a hidden gem for duck. The *maître d'* greeted him by name, gathered leather-bound menus and led the way to the back. "Will you have a carry-out order this evening, Mr. MacKenzie?"

"Yeah, with the extra crispy things," Will rumbled, distracted by the curves walking in front of him.

Frankie had opted for a simple black dress, but the skirt was tight enough to accentuate what she considered to be her best feature, other than her eyes. She had nothing on the Kardashians, but she did all right. As he followed her to the table, she could feel Will's eyes tracking the sway of her hips and knew she'd made the right choice. She also would have sworn she heard him growl.

What century is this Frankie? That should not make you tingle. But it did, and she smiled as she slid onto the tufted leather banquette of the back booth.

When Will was seated across from her, Frankie tried to study the menu while she surreptitiously studied her date. He was wearing a very well-tailored navy suit. *Definitely Italian. Probably Zegna.*

The collar of his crisp white dress shirt was left open and he'd dispensed with one more button on the shirt than most men would have dared. The cuffs of his sleeves weren't buttoned either. The studied negligence gave him the overall look of someone who couldn't be contained by their clothes. She imagined that it took a great deal of time in front of the mirror to look so casual.

A waitress appeared at the table and asked if Will wanted his usual.

"Thanks, lass."

Frankie got the distinct impression that if she weren't there, the woman would be taking Will's order from his lap. "What's the usual?"

"Two fingers of Macallan's," the waitress answered. "And for you? White wine spritzer?"

"Really? Vodka martini, straight up, very dry, three olives. Thanks."

Will raked his teeth over his bottom lip and nodded. The waitress departed in a cloud of Chanel No. 5, which annoyed Frankie as it interfered with her ability to figure out what her date was wearing.

After drinks were delivered, Will watched, fascinated, as she squeezed an olive like a lime over the top of her drink before popping it into her mouth. "I have a confession to make," she said.

"Yeah?"

"I'm not really a forensic psychologist. Palmer should not have said that."

She thought she saw his eyes narrow slightly. "No shite. Why would he do that? What were you doing there?"

Frankie's glass paused on its way to her mouth as her eyebrow arched. "Kenna didn't tell you?"

"No, but she passed on your number, so whatever it was, I guess she didn't think it would be a deal-breaker."

"Wow. Okay." Frankie took a healthy swig of her martini, happy for reasons she couldn't name that her new friend apparently trusted her. Still, she felt like she needed Cliffs Notes to figure out how those two communicated.

She filled in the blanks for Will with the same information she'd given the girls regarding Palmer Ross' motivation for having her in the interview.

Will's large hands mauled a roll from the basket on the table and he roughly slabbed butter on it while trying to sound casual. "So, you're really writing a book?"

"Yes. Are you mad at that piece of bread?"

"What? No. I'm just hungry." He'd thought Ross was a pain in the ass before, but now he really didn't like him. "Let's order."

Over dinner, they talked about usual first date stuff like favorite movies, music, coffee and Scotch, and discovered they shared an appreciation for both Quentin Tarantino and British gangster flicks. When it was Frankie's turn to ask a few questions, Will did his best to give her one word answers whenever possible.

"How long have you been in New York?"

"A few years."

"What made you decide to come in the first place?"

"Fresh start. Change of scenery."

Frankie remembered Palmer's recitation of Will's activities in the UK and could well believe he came to the States for a new playing field. As she mulled over how the bits and pieces she'd learned through Palmer and Kenna fit into the big picture called Will MacKenzie, a bottle of wine they hadn't ordered arrived. The *maître d'* leaned over and whispered something to Will, who looked around the room until he spotted a man at another table with a raised glass. Frankie raised an eyebrow.

"You bring me to a restaurant that specializes in duck, and you order a steak, so we didn't come for the food. The place is full of who I can only assume are your wise guy friends. What is this? A test? Do you bring all of your dates here?" Under the table, Frankie clenched her fists.

"What're you doing with *me*? Slumming? Working?"

"Working?! For whom? You think I'm wearing a wire?" Frankie's eyes flashed a challenge as she leaned closer to the table and taunted him. "Do you wanna frisk me?"

Will sat back in the booth, stretched his long arms across the top of it, and gave her a smirk. "Thought about it, but that would be cheating."

She stared at him for a long minute, then asked, "What does that mean?"

He took his arms down and mirrored her posture so that their faces were mere inches apart. "When I put my hands on you, it'll be because you want them there."

You said 'when.' Not if. Any timetable on that? 'Cause now is good for me. She gulped and hesitated before she murmured, "Oh."

She had the feeling he knew exactly what she was thinking as their eyes remained locked, and he signaled for the check.

CHAPTER ELEVEN

CAIRO, EGYPT

Three men sat in mismatched chairs at one of the many tables crammed together on the sidewalk outside a small café in Cairo's Khan el Khalili bazaar – an American, an Egyptian and one who could be whatever he chose.

Discarded cigarette packs and food wrappers littered the street. Most of the surrounding tables were occupied with backgammon sets, teacups and hookah pipes. This one was only distinguished by the small, black USB drive sitting in the center.

Lucius Chaerea appeared relaxed, lounging as much as he could with his long legs stretched under the table, forcing the CIA agent across from him to sit with his tucked under his chair. Chaerea flicked the ashes off a cigarette burning unsmoked in the hand dangling loosely at his side. The man beside him spoke fast in thick, Egyptian-accented English.

"This, this is the exact copy of the files," the man said, tapping enthusiastically on the USB drive. "All of the names of the Geoscience Global employees and how much they will ask for the ransom. Of course, they will be sold to ISIS for prisoner trades no matter what they are paid. It's good, yes? I tell you I'm your man."

"Well, Colonel?" the CIA agent asked, tilting his dark glasses down to look at Lucius.

Lucius straightened. He leaned both elbows on the table and laced his fingers together, his eyes fixed on the memory device. "No."

"No?" The Egyptian man asked throwing his hands in the air. "How can you say that? You haven't looked –"

Lucius turned his head to look at the man for the first time since taking a seat at the table. "You're lying, Firas."

The CIA agent stretched and scratched his head with both hands. "Sorry, Firas." He rose to leave, as did Lucius.

"Wait? Who is this man to say I'm lying?" Glaring at the agent, Firas pointed at Lucius accusingly.

"Someone the CIA trusts a fucking lot more than you. Maybe the Russians will bite for you," the agent said.

"Wait, wait. Sit please," Firas said, patting his hands in the inch of air above the table. "Please, sit. Sit. I promised you the names. Here they are." He held out the USB like a supplicant. "All the names Hossam Eldeen has of foreign contractors coming in the next six months."

"How'd you get them?" the agent asked, taking his seat, but turning to extend his legs into the walkway. Eldeen was a new fly in the ointment. A gang leader turned radical devotee.

Firas shrugged and waggled his finger in the air. "No, no. You cannot ask." He forced out a laugh. "If you knew my secrets, why would you need me?" He tugged on his shirt and wiped at the sweat on his neck with a dingy handkerchief.

"Why, indeed?" Lucius said, but he sat.

A silence hung over the table, Firas held his breath while the agent picked up the device and rolled it like a quarter over his fingers. "You have something better, Colonel?"

Firas started to jump up from his seat, but froze, his arms held away from his body, when he saw the flash of a red dot on his chest.

"You'd better sit down, Firas," the agent suggested, his tone pleasant. "The Colonel's men don't appreciate anyone making sudden moves around him."

An hour later, Lucius and the CIA contact were in the back seat of a deceptively run down Range Rover on the way back to the operative's hotel.

"Fucker. I almost didn't recognize you with the beard. How do you look like some Arab street vendor one day and the fuckin' Duke of Wellington the next? And how did you know Firas was bullshitting with that USB?"

Lucius scratched at his dark beard. "I didn't until he started trying to sell it. Don't they teach you how to spot a tell?"

"What tell? And if you say his lips were moving –"

Lucius laughed. He'd always been able to pick up on lies and deception. Some of his superiors had believed it to be a gift, others attributed it to his ability to detect subtle changes in speech or manner. He tapped the shoulder of his driver and took the envelope held over the seat back.

"Here's your list. The real one."

"You going to tell me how you came by this?"

"While Firas was getting caught trying to steal it from Hossam Eldeen's home computer, a friend of a friend hacked in. That's why this one is free. Your guy's fuck up was my guy's free pass." Lucius smiled remembering the clandestine meeting in the back of a limo in Muscat and how Mike Chapman's colleague Layla Gazale had manipulated Firas. The informant would never know how he'd been played ... maybe that would be useful in the future. He gave himself a mental shrug.

The car stopped at the Meridian Hotel where the CIA agent was staying. As he opened the door to climb out, he turned. "Free? Until you need a favor. If I see you, I won't know you."

"You won't see me," Lucius said as the car door slammed.

The agent laughed and slapped the roof, shaking his head as the car disappeared into traffic. "Scary fucker."

CHAPTER TWELVE

The incessant, shrill beeping of the garbage truck backing into the alley dumpster two stories below interrupted what was already a fitful sleep. Frankie woke with a start, flapping her hands near her face, trying to bat away the sound.

She looked down at the arm draped across her middle and followed it to where it was attached to the well-muscled shoulder and the smooth, broad back of the chainsaw sleeping next to her. Frankie muffled a laugh with her hand and debated whether it was too early in the relationship to smother Will with a pillow. *Good thing he looks like that. Definitely, too soon.* With a sigh, she snuggled further under the covers and closer to Will, letting the clouds of sleep enfold her once again.

Ten seconds later, her eyelids snapped open. She never slept well in a new or foreign environment, but it was neither Will's snoring nor the city sanitation services that had her staring at the ceiling at the ass-crack of dawn. *Will. I'm in Will's apartment. Kenna!*

This wasn't the plan. It was only their second real date. She hadn't even told Kenna, or Candace for that matter, about their first one. Sure they'd had fun ... a *lot* of fun, but that's all it was. If he called, great. If not, pffft. Who was she kidding? Of course he'd call, which was how she ended up ditching her sweats, and the article she was working on, for a pair of sky-high stilettos on a Tuesday night. Will MacKenzie wanted to take her dancing, so she went dancing.

By the time they left Marquee, sweaty and stuck together despite the chill in the air, the fact that his apartment was only a few blocks away – and empty he'd assured her – was all that mattered.

Frankie lay there chewing on her lower lip, plotting a graceful exit before Kenna could surprise them. Will had said Kenna stayed in her loft at the gallery sometimes. He wished she wouldn't, but he'd installed the last two locks on the loft's door himself. Finally, it was a full bladder that made her decide to get up. She extricated herself from beneath Will's arm, found her discarded silk blouse, tiptoed to the door, and inched her way out into the hall.

After some rudimentary freshening up, Frankie ventured into the kitchen to see if there was any coffee. She found the beans as well as one entire shelf dedicated to what appeared to be every flavor of Pop-tarts known to man. *Ugh. Who still eats that stuff?* She was about to search for the coffee grinder when she took a good look at the imposing piece of stainless steel machinery taking up more than its fair share of counter space. She snorted, "He has two mugs, two forks, two plates and a $2,500 coffee maker." She opened the fridge in search of some juice or bottled water. All she found was some half and half, nearly as many take-out containers as she had in her own fridge, and several bottles of Yoo-Hoo. "What the –"

"I wouldn't touch those if I were you."

Frankie nearly dropped the bottle in her hand as she spun around to find a bleary–eyed Kenna sitting at the kitchen table, knees tucked inside a baggy NYU t-shirt and her fine blonde hair sticking up like she'd slept with a Tesla ball. "*Merde!* Where did you come from? You scared the crap out of me!"

"I live here."

"Well, yeah." Frankie took in Kenna's just-out-of-bed look. "I know. Um ... were you ... how long have you been here?"

"About a year and half." Kenna's exaggerated sleepy expression was starting to crack. She clearly enjoyed her friend's discomfort.

Frankie narrowed her eyes. "You know what I mean."

"I was sleeping. Until 'Oh, God, Will! Right there!'" Kenna swooned in her chair, head back, legs splayed out under the table. "'Christ, Frankie! Do that again!'" She sat up and looked Frankie in the eye. "Should I go on?"

"That won't be necessary." Frankie had gone rosy pink from her décolletage to the tips of her ears. "Thanks for the memories, though."

"You sure? There's a whole barnyard full of sounds I haven't gotten to yet. Even with the pillow wrapped around my head. I was going to call Candace and give her color commentary, but I figured one of us should get some sleep, and she works such long hours, you know."

"Will said you were at the gallery, or else I wouldn't ... we wouldn't ..." Frankie slumped into a chair on the other side of the table. "I was going to tell you."

Kenna got up and started to make the coffee, expertly using the machine that had left Frankie so intimidated. "Why didn't you? He does bring me the doggie bags." She showed Frankie the foil swan from the night before.

"I'm a coward?" Kenna shot Frankie a look over her shoulder. "Now, I know how the few boys who got that far felt when they actually met The Senator."

"Give me a break," Kenna said.

"It's true! I know how you feel about Will. I didn't want to say anything until there was something to say. I mean we've been out twice. I like him. We're not planning too far ahead." Frankie cleared her throat and ran her fingers through her hair. "We're having fun."

"So how come you didn't go to your place?" Kenna leaned against the counter and resisted the urge to cross her arms over her chest. She was sleepy, not judgy.

Frankie's eyes went round. "Oh, no. I couldn't do that!"

And just like that, Kenna's guard was back up. "Why not? Will can cross the tracks as well as you."

"That's not it at all! I just ... do you think he's ready for all ... that?" If she found her family surroundings suffocating, why would anyone else be comfortable there?

Kenna set mugs on the table with a shrug. "He might surprise you."

Will came into the kitchen scratching his bare chest. "What'm I not ready for?" He picked up Frankie's mug and looked at the two of them over the rim.

Frankie and Kenna looked at each other and said simultaneously, "Nothing."

Will rolled his eyes and blew out a breath, "It's too early for this shite. I'm going back to bed."

CHAPTER THIRTEEN

F all in New York flew by. Under Candace's tutelage, they had managed a fire-free Thanksgiving dinner. Christmas was almost familial, and New Year's Eve had been the best in years, despite Will outing Kenna's date from the marriage closet days before the ball dropped. Frankie and Will both seemed happy with their no-strings arrangement. Kenna didn't question how or why she'd found this peace. Instead, and probably for the first time in her life, she accepted the universe's gift of friendship.

A month into the New Year and balanced precariously on the top rung of a ladder, Kenna regaled Sal Jr. with the finer points of New Year's Eve as she reattached the sculpture pieces above the bar in Swag. She had insisted she remove the installation prior to and reinstall it after Super Bowl Sunday, when a massive TV had hung in its place above the bar.

Sal Jr. held the ladder steady and tried not to notice that her ass was in his face. He'd always put Kenna in the off-limits category, but, damn, he was only human. Henry had bragged about his ladder holding skills after the sculpture's removal the week before. Sal wasn't about to let that happen twice.

"You should have come out with us," she called down. "Candace and I were kissless at midnight. You could've had a twofer."

"My date may have objected," he said and then changed the subject before she asked. He scowled at his choice for New Year's Eve companionship. He could almost hear Kenna offering him antibiotics in his head. "You know I could have done this myself."

"I know." She looked over her back and smiled down at him. "But I haven't seen you since Christmas. Thanks for the boots." She turned her foot in the air, showing off the butter-soft, leather-clad calf.

Sal wrapped a hand around the boot shaft and squeezed. "You only got the one pair. Uncle Antonio was a little disappointed. He held several pairs for me. You were supposed to get something for wet weather too."

Kenna adjusted the last piece to her satisfaction and started down the ladder. "I have wet weather shoes."

When she stopped a few rungs off the floor and turned to face him, Sal flipped his eyes up from her small waist and flared hips and tried not to stare at the other curves inches away from his face.

Kenna kissed his forehead. "You got them for me last year, and these were expensive enough, without the back-of-the-truck discount."

"Got what?" he asked, ignoring her comment on the semi-legal "found" merchandise to which he often had access.

She ran her fingers through the thick mass of dark hair, from his soft widow's peak to the crown, intending to suggest he stop covering the gray. Sal closed his eyes and the ladder creaked as he gripped it tighter and stiffened his arms. Realizing her actions could be considered flirting, Kenna snatched her hand back and scrambled down the last few rungs of the ladder. She wasn't about to tell him how he could be *more* handsome. His ego was healthy enough.

"So, did you make any money on the game?"

Sal smoothed his palms over his hair. "I don't bet." Kenna rolled her eyes. "I don't bet on the Super Bowl. It's a sucker's game. Ask my cousin Tony. He's into the Old Man for fifty."

"Tony Barzini? Fat Tony? Fat Tony your cousin?" Kenna had turned into a ball of kinetic energy. He watched her vibrate in front of him. "He owes your father fifty thousand dollars and can't pay a dime, can he?" She was all but giggling.

"I'll be sure to tell him how heartbroken you are over his trouble."

Kenna threw her arms in the air, whooped, and then threw them around Sal's neck. He caught her and couldn't help smiling at whatever had her so excited.

"You tell Fat Tony not to do anything stupid and hold off the Old Man."

"You going to tell me what's going on?"

Kenna let him go and grabbed her purse. She wrestled her way into her coat, flailing until he grabbed the empty arm and held it for her. "Just keep everybody still for a couple of weeks. Okay?"

"Okay," he agreed.

Sal was still watching the door she'd flown out of when Henry nudged his shoulder.

"So?"

"So, what?"

"So ... you know. The kid?" Henry winked and jerked his head to the door. "That was some pretty good ladder holding you did today. She likes you."

"Maybe," Sal said and rapped his knuckles on the bar. "Maybe."

CHAPTER FOURTEEN

Over the past five months, Marco's in Tribeca had been their Sunday meeting place for breakfast, brunch, or lunch or whatever you called anything between ten and three. On an unusually bright morning in February, Kenna, fresh from mass, breathlessly slapped the *Times'* Style section down on the table and declared, "I have to get into that party."

"I have to get to the Prada trunk sale," Frankie popped off, poorly, but hilariously imitating Kenna's Southern drawl.

Candace, the picture of cool, sipped on her drink and grinned. "Why that one?"

Leaning conspiratorially towards them, Kenna tapped the stock photo of society pillars, Wallace and Althea Henneby, from the previous year's ball. "Three months ago, this ice bitch bid up to one-twenty K on a painting. It sold for one-forty." She sat back quite self-satisfied.

"And?" Frankie nudged her under the table with the toe of her favorite suede boots.

"And, the winning bidder was none other than Fat Tony Barzini, who is up to his neckless head into Big Sal for fifty grand. I know he'd take that in cash, easy!" Kenna shrugged out of her coat.

"Yo! Vinnie the Weasel. Speak English," Frankie said.

Candace used her teeth to pull an olive off her garnish pick as she watched the verbal tennis and patiently waited for Kenna to make sense.

Kenna sighed, her cool wise guy act died a slow death as she sank into the third chair. "Sal Jr. told me his cousin Tony was pretty desperate for cash. He lost it on the Super Bowl. Anyway, if I could sell the painting to Henneby for eighty thousand, my admittedly generous commission, plus what I have saved ..." She became almost wistful. "I could have first and last month's rent on this great gallery space I want by summer. Maybe even have some things on display."

"Sal Jr.?" Frankie confirmed. "You sure you want to use that friendship this way?"

"Sal would never let me get my hands dirty. This is just about a painting and his dumbass cousin – his Uncle Angelo's kid, not Carmine's - who needs money," she said with absolute confidence. Candace noted the distinction between Angelo and Carmine Barzini, but didn't find it all that comforting.

"And Will? He's okay with this?" Frankie prodded. While it was perfectly fine for Will to associate with Sal Jr. and his extended family in legitimate ventures, he was not so liberal in his thinking toward Kenna's friendship with Sal Jr. or her contact with his family.

"He'd crap kittens because it's a Barzini. And he's not wrong, the whole lot are," she swallowed bile and shivered involuntarily, "awful. But I can handle 'awful' for this."

"'Awful' could be the least of it, actually." Candace inclined her head and sipped again to hide a smirk. "I take it you've met Mrs. Henneby."

"I saw her at the auction," Kenna mumbled around a goat

cheese-stuffed olive. "And apparently ..." Impersonating a 1940s movie butler, she exaggerated her arched brows, looked down her nose, and spoke through her teeth. "Mrs. Henneby does not accept unsolicited appointments."

Frankie snorted, covering her mouth with a napkin. "You sound like my mother's secretary."

"They breed them in the Hamptons."

"If The Senator and I were speaking this year, I could probably manage some invitations. But, not so much." Frankie tried to sound flippant even though the strained relationship with her father was a constant source of emotional and financial stress. "Maybe you could crash as part of the wait staff?"

"Frank! I can't carry reheated Pings take-out Kung Pao from the kitchen to the table without leaving half of it on my boobs. It's why I eat over the sink," Kenna said. Looking over at Candace, she anticipated an easy jab at Frankie's and her own lack of culinary skills. Candace was not joining in on the joke, but swirling her fork, waiting for them to pay attention. "What?"

"Oh, nothing," Candace sang. "Just, I will be attending that party and sitting at Wallace Henneby's table." She relished the moment with a Cheshire Cat grin.

"Your plus one?" Kenna asked hopefully.

Candace grimaced. "It's too late for that. But you could come for cocktails. I'll introduce you as an old friend. Simple."

CHAPTER FIFTEEN

S*imple,* she'd said back when they started cooking up this scheme a month ago. Candace snorted. She should have known the planning and plotting would reach epic proportions.

They knew how desperate Kenna was to get her own place where her knowledge and passion could flourish, and they wanted it for her. Now, with a panicking Kenna on the phone, she happily dialed Frankie for a conference call.

"We Are Family" blasted from the nightstand. Frankie scrambled out of bed to find her phone. She squinted through the eye that was mostly awake to see Candace's name as she headed in the direction of the kitchen. "'Sup buttercup?"

"Kenna's on the ledge. I'm conferencing."

"Where is she?" Frankie was already measuring out coffee grounds.

"I think the gallery," Candace said.

"What's wrong?" Frankie asked through a yawn.

"She just said that she needs to go over the plan again."

Frankie groaned. She'd sucked it up and called her father's

social secretary only to find out he was not attending the Henneby event. So, using her tabloid connections, she'd managed to get a press pass to cover the who, what, and who-are-you-wearing for a freelance society piece. "Okay, coffee's in progress. Get her on." She groaned and stretched again, trying to wake herself up.

"*Hello!*" Kenna's voice confirmed Candace's diagnosis. If their friend wasn't in full-on panic mode yet, she was circling the block.

"Oh! Sorry. What's wrong, honey?" Frankie asked, genuinely trying to soothe her friend.

"You've got your dress, yes?" Candace asked.

"It works. But it's old."

"Vintage," they said in unison. Kenna knew this, but nerves had a way of making one forget even the simplest principles of fashion.

"Frankie, what about that black Carolina Herrera your mother sent over Christmas?" Kenna asked.

Both women laughed in her ear. Frankie's mother, who was herself built like a socially acceptable twig, had a habit of sending her daughter samples that her friends, the designers, had pressed upon her at various fashion shows or she had purchased at a charity auction. The dress in question was fresh off the runway and had cinched Kenna's ample cleavage to her chin. "*Okay!* Okay. It's a bit snug."

"So, you want us to bind your breasts to fit you into it?" Candace said, still chuckling over the fashion debacle.

"But it's new," Kenna wailed. "Doesn't new trump ...?"

"*No!*" Frankie and Candace said at once.

"*Your* dress is vintage Valentino," Candace assured her. "Have you noticed how much vintage marches up the red carpeted steps of the Met's Costume Gala every year?! They'll think you're another one of Wintour's waifs."

A beat of silence. And another. Then laughter erupted over the lines.

Kenna snorted, "Waif, my tiny ass."

"All better?" asked Frankie.

"Yeah. We still on for mani-pedis at two?"

The call over, Kenna crossed herself. She knew the dress was perfect. She had even gasped when she saw herself in it the first time. "Needy much, Kenna?" she muttered, petting the signature satin bow on the dress.

Uptown, Frankie poured a cup, grabbed her tablet, and shuffled back to bed.

Candace turned on her computer, stared at the screen for a few minutes, and then shut it down. Looking at the fluffy ball of tabby fur at her feet, she said, "How about a mud mask, Fuzzbutt? We want to look pretty too."

CHAPTER SIXTEEN

In his home office and base of operations, Lucius had been awake and working for hours. Just past eight, he was already in his shirtsleeves and a loosened tie. Squinting, he adjusted the blinds over the windows, then turned to resume his pacing across the Persian carpet. The rug was a gift from a very grateful-to-be-alive Saudi prince. Staying alive or keeping someone alive wasn't overly difficult if you knew the bullet was coming. Today, he'd learned of another being chambered, figuratively speaking. Every source confirmed an assassination was being planned. Now, it was his turn to fit the puzzle together and find out who, where, how, and when. Certainly, there were others with his connections and information. Very few bothered with the why of such plots, but he embraced it. By understanding why, the rest of the pieces fell into place.

A job in security had not been his goal when he left his official duties with the Special Air Service. Information was his commodity and, as a former Prime Minister once complimented, "a certain moral ambiguity towards those deserving of justice." As part of an SAS unit deployed in Bosnia, Serbia, and Afghanistan, he'd honed his skills in intelligence gathering, asset acquisition and management, strategic precision strikes, and negotiation, if possible or warranted.

He methodically turned through the photographs, coded texts, and notes hastily made in his elegant hand, rearranged them on the desk, paced, then paused to arrange again. As the fourth son of a moderately wealthy sheik, the subject wasn't particularly outstanding in his father's business ventures or as a philanthropist or philanderer. Nothing about this man seemed to earn him notice. Or death.

Was he meant to be the next Archduke Ferdinand? The spark that razed the globe? And what, if anything, should Lucius do? This question plagued him as often as any other. Should he stop every act of violence whispered into his ear? If only his world were that simple.

There were always rumors, intercepted emails, recordings of phone calls, and personal accounts of overheard conversations. There was always someone calling for a new government. Few wanted changes achieved through diplomacy. He wondered how the Western world so soon forgot its own evolution through violence?

Settling behind his desk again, he pushed aside the intelligence reports to consider the engraved invitation beneath. For months, Wallace Henneby had been urging him to attend the annual fundraiser. Lucius suspected there was an eligible female on the other end and had resisted – even politely refused – to be drawn in. Yet, for reasons he couldn't explain, he felt an internal pull toward this night. He had no other obligations, and another night of international intrigue felt too empty.

He flipped the invitation over and over with one hand. With a sigh, he dialed the RSVP contact. Late and ill-mannered, he knew he would be forgiven.

Istanbul, Turkey

DAVID LAWRENCE SWALLOWED his bile and the violent urge to eviscerate his nurse. In her defense, she had not been hired for her skills, but rather for her breasts, her youth and her inability to speak English. The chronic complications associated with the colostomy and urostomy lines, drains and collection bags necessary for him to void his ruined body were often more than her education or his dignity could manage. On the worst days, she would cry as she cleaned him and anything else fouled by the process. On the easy days, he could be dressed and appear practically normal, save the slight limp caused by massive scarring on his abdomen, groin and thighs.

Like most of her predecessors, she would leave within a month. A generous salary was enough to attract applicants, but never enough to keep employees. Few could tolerate his rages. Fewer still could handle the disgusting sexual advances that came with the discovery of the fact that his mind was as mangled and dysfunctional as his body.

Lawrence closed his eyes, allowing the memory of his revenge to soothe him.

The refugee woman barely made a sound as his men took their turns. Bored, he glanced over his shoulder as the last and most violent, Hans, finished. Despite his best efforts, she only whimpered for him. This was not her first gang rape, Lawrence mused. It would be her last. He had to give it to the Sudanese warlords. They trained their people well. Screaming women brought people running, and running would-be-rescuers made easy targets. So, they would wait for the mistress of this shack.

He almost admired the dedication of his real target. As a United Nations aid worker, she'd lived in squalor trying to save people who would most likely die before they reached a safe border. Or starve once inside a refugee camp.

She was scooping water from a leaky boat with a kitchen sieve. Even in the dark, he recognized her instantly. Tall and lean, her dark hair braided down her back. He'd watched her for weeks. She wasn't sweet like the missionary women. Sofia Chaerea was all discipline and efficiency in her work.

Lawrence felt a phantom surge in his groin as she approached her temporary dwelling.

Even now, he could feel his non-existent cock harden remembering Sofia's horrified face as she'd stepped through the flap entrance and had seen what and who was waiting.

She fought, God bless her she fought like a tigress. Even with her hands bound, she kicked and spat and tried to scream out. He was afraid Hans had killed her with the punch that eventually knocked her unconscious. But a stream of piss in the face had amazing restorative qualities.

He could still see her face when he bent over her. "Mrs. Chaerea, you need to know. This is not about you."

She was quickly stripped of her trousers and panties, the small white cotton garment stuffed into her mouth. Lawrence knelt between her legs, held spread on the floor by his followers and fellow deserters. Hans had chosen to remain close to her head, holding the underwear in her mouth with his meaty hand. She tried to close her eyes.

"Look at me, Mrs. Chaerea." A cold blade pressed against her throat, and she opened tear-filled eyes. "Much better." He praised her with a sweet smile.

Lawrence pulled a gun from his hip and pointed to the woman his men had just used. Curled up into a ball in the corner, she refused to move or open her eyes. Sophia groaned in pity for her friend. "I promise you will not suffer her fate." He trailed the muzzle of the gun down her body, sliding the barrel between the folds of her sex. "Only one of us will be using your cunt." He waited, stroking her with the cold metal until she was shaking and gagging behind Hans' hand.

Leaning over, he put his face inches from hers and thrust the barrel inside her. With his mouth by her ear, he whispered, "Your husband will learn to make sure his target is dead." Then he pulled the trigger.

CHAPTER SEVENTEEN

"I t seems I only get a chance to catch up with you at these annual affairs," Sid Rosen said. "How've you been, Candace?"

"Oh, fine," she flicked a hand airily. "A new US Attorney was appointed, and there are some growing pains in the office, but we'll struggle through."

"You know – I tell you this every time I see you – I'd love for you to come to Rosen Weitz."

"Or Henneby Industries," Wallace Henneby interjected as he walked up to them. He turned to Rosen. "Why she'd rather toil away in a cubicle –"

"I have an office," Candace retorted with a grin. "More like a phone booth without the delightful view, but it has a door, at least."

Henneby gave her an arch look. "— than work in an environment where she's appreciated ..."

"Not to mention compensated," Rosen added, piling on to Henneby's inducements with a rumbling chuckle.

Candace held up her hands in surrender. "All right, all right. I get it. What's more, I'm gratified." She felt a warm presence at her shoulder and turned to look up into smiling blue eyes. "Hello."

"Hello."

The dark blond man, who looked damned good in a tux she noted, turned to Rosen. "Sid, sorry I missed the partners' meeting this afternoon. I had an outside appointment." Not missing a beat, he held out a hand to Henneby. "Sir, I'm Thom Cooper. I've been hoping to speak with you this evening to thank you and the Foundation personally, once again."

A few inches taller than Cooper, Rosen placed a paternal hand onto the young man's shoulder and said, "Wallace, do you remember Thom? He was one of the Foundation's scholarship recipients about nine, ten years ago. He's just made partner at the firm, currently working in corporate and has shown a real talent for mergers and acquisitions."

Henneby, at least thirty years senior to Sid's new partner, murmured that he did, indeed, remember Cooper, congratulated him on his promotion and thanked him for coming to the gala. He mused, *It's hell getting old. Every year these kids get younger and younger.*

Rosen gestured toward Candace. "And this is Candace Fisher, another scholarship recipient. I'm sure there was some overlap at Yale with you two. Are you acquainted?"

Candace and Cooper spoke at once, "No. Unfortunately ..."

They laughed.

"Where are you working?" Cooper asked.

"I'm at the US Attorney's office downtown. White collar crime, as they believe that's the safest place for a female."

"Wallace and I are competing to see which of us can lure her away from all that glamour."

Cooper looked at her with a speculative gleam. "Would it help if I sang the praises of Rosen Weitz?"

Candace smiled. "No need. Two more flattering offers I could never imagine."

"Maybe over lunch? Or drinks after work one day?"

She returned his speculative look and her smile widened. "That. Sounds delightful."

As he slipped her a business card, he leaned close to whisper, "Call me." At that moment, Althea Henneby sailed up to their little group, interrupting the fledgling flirtation.

"Wallace," she said, "the Richards just arrived, and I know you wanted to speak with David about sending the Wyeths with his collection on the tour."

"Momentarily, my dear. Let me introduce you." He reached his hand to Candace. "I believe you've met Candace Fisher, one of our scholarships. She'll be joining us at dinner. And this," he gestured to Cooper, "is Thom Cooper. Another scholarship. He works with Sid."

"Mrs. Henneby," Candace murmured.

"Ms. Fisher. How nice to see you again." Althea inclined her head as her cool tone and gaze passed over Candace and focused on Cooper. She held out a graceful hand adorned with a spectacular, but tasteful, emerald ring. "Mr. Cooper. It's a pleasure to meet one of the Foundation's recipients. Wallace and I always look forward to this event and the opportunity to get better acquainted with so many bright young people."

Cooper held Althea's hand in both of his and gave her a lazy smile. "A pleasure, Mrs. Henneby."

"Please. It's Althea."

Candace gave a mental eye roll over the batting eyelashes and jumped only a little bit when her cellphone buzzed in her evening bag.

A hundred feet away, Frankie's bejeweled clutch buzzed. "BATHROOM 911!"

She looked across the ballroom to see Candace standing in

the midst of Henneby's inner circle and reading the same message. Candace, looked up and around, made eye contact with Frankie and mouthed, "What happened?" Frankie only shrugged. In unison, they gestured towards the exit leading to the nearest restroom. Candace made her excuses and headed in Frankie's direction.

Frankie tucked her notepad into her clutch and signaled her photographer to keep snapping. Without breaking stride, she nabbed a full tray of canapés from a passing waiter. "Who's the hottie?"

Candace was moving quickly in her four-inch heels, hoping not to be missed by their host. "Hottie? What hottie?"

"Don't play coy with me, missy. The hot blond in the Prada."

"Oh, him." Candace caught the caustic look Frankie shot her and laughed. "He's a lawyer. Works with my friend, Sid Rosen."

"Lawyers – present company excepted, naturally – are supposed to look pasty and flabby with some stage of male pattern baldness setting in."

"Apparently, not this one."

As they neared the women's restroom, Candace whispered, "Did she get cold feet?"

"Wardrobe malfunction?" Frankie replied, rapping lightly on the locked bathroom door.

Candace's mouth dropped open when a half-naked Kenna cracked open the door. "Malfunction may be an understatement."

"What took you so long?" Kenna hissed, frantically tugging on the top of the offending Lycra shaper. "I'm so sweaty. It's like trying to stuff biscuits back into the can."

Frankie rolled her eyes and held out the tray of appetizers. "I stopped by the kitchen to make you these."

"Sorry. Hey! Is that salmon?" Kenna stuffed a canapé whole into her mouth.

"Careful, you'll pop those Spanx, Pillsbury."

"Take a spinach one for your teeth," Candace teased.

"Oh, y'all are funny! *Help me!*" Kenna swallowed hard, yanking and hopping around to get back into her underwear.

Candace grabbed one side of the torture device while Frankie set her tray by the sinks and began pulling the other side. "I just know I won't be able to get through the night without belching." She tried to imitate Scarlett O'Hara, but wound up sounding like Kenna.

"No shit, but I had to pee," Kenna grunted.

Candace straightened and smoothed the elastic. "Here's a silly question. Why didn't you go potty at home?"

"I did. Got nervous," Kenna shrugged, a little embarrassed.

Frankie gently pulled the dress from its resting place over the stall door, catching the dangling price tag. "Fifteen hundred dollars? You didn't tell us this part. How'd you get it?"

"The American way. I charged it."

"You'd better stop sweating, or you'll have saved the tag for nothing," Candace said. "We can pull together some cash. You know that." Frankie nodded in agreement.

"I can't ask that. Seriously, what am I going to do with this thing after tonight? It's not like I'm going to another one of these things next week. Or next year. Besides, if this works, I can pay American Express and keep the dress for sentimental reasons. But don't tell Will. He'll flip if he thinks I need money."

Frankie winked. "Your secrets are safe with us."

Candace said helpfully, "Lift up your boobs."

"This is as high as they get," Kenna cupped herself and hoisted them anyway.

"No one will know it's a Valentino if they can't see the damned bow," Frankie reminded her.

They helped her repair her hair in an oh-so-fashionable messy bun at the nape of her neck. Neat and coiffed was a waste of precious time and energy. No matter how much spray or how many pins or passes with a flat iron, the mass of loose blonde curls always managed to fall and look tousled. She was grateful the undone look was so popular.

Frankie smoothed the Carolina Herrera gown over her statuesque curves and grabbed her handbag. Candace fluffed her coppery curls, fingering back the loose tendrils that had gone astray and adjusted her own bust to maintain the modesty of the strapless, princess bodice, straightening the ruching put askew while spotting Kenna during her underwear gymnastics.

Kenna stood for a moment and looked at their reflections, half expecting the magic mirror to out her as the one who didn't belong. It didn't. They had always shared a sense of style and taste. Standing between her friends, she felt a double shot of confidence. She fit with them. Oddly, but she fit.

Candace caught Kenna's eyes in the mirror. "Shoulders back."

"Tits out." Frankie grinned.

Kenna squeezed their hands before they left her. She took several cleansing breaths, counted to a hundred and moved towards the grand ballroom.

CHAPTER EIGHTEEN

L ucius entered the ballroom in a halo of cold March air and the remains of cigars on the balcony, unconcerned with the attention he and his fellow aficionados brought upon themselves. As much as he avoided notice, it was impossible to cloak his presence tonight. He was accompanied by a former District Attorney from New York whose name appeared on many shortlists for everything from Director of the FBI to President, two retired generals one of whom served as Vice Chairman of the Joint Chiefs of Staff to the last administration, the senior vice president of Henneby Industries' Arms Division, and the honorable Senator from Kentucky who provided the cigars.

As he talked casually with his companions, Lucius' hawkish eyes swept the room, pausing only long enough to catch the subtle nod from his man indicating the room remained secure.

His gaze moved on uninterested until it snagged on the curvaceous, pale blonde who stood poised at the top of the stairs. He watched, fascinated, as she raised her chin and started to speak, softly it appeared, to no one. His eyes narrowed suspiciously, suspecting that she was speaking to someone via a remote earpiece. He watched her perfect mouth carefully, reading her lips. An infrequent smile tugged the corner of his mouth. *"Good evening Mr. Henneby. So nice to meet you."* He easily followed her repetition and line of sight to his friend and host, who was conversing with a group of eager young attorneys a few yards away.

His appreciation grew as he watched the young woman smile and say "hello" to complete strangers as if they were old friends. The confused looks, insincere smiles and "oh, how nice to see you too's" clearly amused her and seemed to bolster her courage as she moved through the crowd. Her girl-next-door beauty and bright smile didn't hurt either. Blending in wasn't overly difficult in a city where most people pretended to be something they weren't. They were too busy maintaining their own façade to notice hers. Lucius noticed. Nature teaches beasts to know their own.

He took in the details of her face and form. Her features, both delicate and lush, hinted at an innocence her manner and carriage denied. Her green eyes blazed each time she scored a point off one of the swells as she approached on her trajectory to Wallace Henneby. The dress, obviously once intended for a more slender woman, accentuated her pin-up girl silhouette. His fingers tingled as he imagined the feel of her small waist and the curve of her hip swaying under his palm when she walked. He would later say it was as if someone had brought dozens of candles into the room.

She smiled at a petite redhead – Miss Fisher if he recalled correctly – evidently her ticket in. *The accomplice,* he thought.

"Kenna?" He watched with amusement as Miss Fisher feigned happy surprise at seeing her "old friend." *She will have to hone her theatrical skills if she hoped to make it as a high-powered lawyer in this town,* he mused to himself.

Another uncharacteristic smile threatened to break through

his normally unreadable features. Like a child watching other children play, Lucius felt an urge to join the game, sidling up to the edge of the playground until the ball rolled his way. He finished his Calvados, the apple-infused brandy he preferred with his cigars and which Wallace Henneby always made available at these functions for him, and moved toward the Henneby table.

"Candace! How *are* you?" Kenna affected a double take and halted for hugs and gushing. "It's been so long. You look gorgeous, as always," she said, hoping she wasn't overplaying the role.

Candace cleared her throat. Wallace and Sid were already rising to attend the new female at the table. Mrs. Henneby couldn't be bothered and didn't deign to acknowledge the newcomer.

"Wallace Henneby, Sid Rosen – this is Kenna Campbell. We were at Fordham together. Art history, right?"

"Excellent memory." Kenna offered her hand and her best Scarlett O'Hara smile first to Sid, then turned the charm onto Wallace. "A true pleasure to meet you both."

Just then, a towering figure loomed at Kenna's side, invading her personal space. The light touch on her elbow made her jump and jerk her head up. *Busted!* she thought, looking up into the man's expressionless face. Only security guards and vice principals had that look. Panic flashed momentarily in her eyes.

"Lucius!" Wallace took the interloper's hand in a warm embrace. "I wasn't expecting you. When we met last week, you said you had other commitments." He didn't ask when Lucius had slipped in. The man rarely just walked in the main entrance.

"Fortunately, for me," the man's grip on Kenna's elbow tightened as if the reply were more for her than Henneby, "my plans changed." He turned to look down at Kenna. "I believe this is our dance."

Too surprised to formulate an immediate objection, she just stared. Blinking, her panic was replaced by a quick, calculated alteration in her agenda. He was impressed with her adaptation. Arching her eyebrows, she smiled a little too innocently. "Of course. How could I forget? It was nice to see you, Candace." Unwilling to give up the ruse just yet, Kenna fought to keep her composure as she and her friend exchanged obligatory cheek kisses and promised to "get together soon."

With a parting nod for Wallace, the man called Lucius led her to the parquet dance floor as the first piano notes of "The Nearness of You" drifted from the stage.

Henneby smiled, a gnarled finger crooking under his bottom lip. *Interesting*, he thought. He couldn't remember the last time he'd seen his young friend speak to a woman out of more than courtesy, much less seek her out. And never for a dance.

As HE LED the young woman to the dance floor, Lucius watched Candace Fisher from the corner of his eye as she gulped a flute of champagne and simultaneously heard the clatter of a tray close by. *A trio?* He was thoroughly entertained by this series of events, so this time his grin was genuine. Lucius guided Kenna closer to the spill. Over the top of her head, he eyed the flustered waiter, paparazzo and a strawberry blonde guest frantically scooping up the spill. He waited, wondering which was the third? As expected, the woman, Conspirator Number Three, looked anxiously towards the dance floor. Lucius winked at her, then spun Kenna away, but not before catching the guilty flush on Three's cheeks.

He appreciated that Kenna was smart enough not to try

whatever this scam was alone. This crew was no physical threat to his friend. That left only one other reason. *It's always about money.* He looked her up and down, more closely this time. Classic black dress, imitation jewelry, but nothing ostentatious enough to draw attention or inspection. And the shoes? He cocked his head for a better look. Those were the real thing.

Kenna felt his gaze like warm water being poured over her. The pleasant feeling more than the inspection angered her. Like it or not, she was used to being looked over. She widened the gap between them. Flight was not an option. Fight it is. "You're staring. Is there something you wanted?" She tried to sound irritated.

He gently pulled her back to him, and she couldn't suppress a shiver.

Lucius paused and took a breath before answering. The tip of his tongue flicked the corner of his mouth. Kenna's stomach tightened in disappointment as she anticipated a lascivious response. "Perhaps, I was enjoying your game and wanted to play." His voice was a deep purr. The accent as generic and genuine Western European as hers was, for tonight, generic American news anchor. She sighed in relief that he didn't say something crude about her boobs or mouth and relaxed into his arms.

Over six feet tall, he was lean and fluid. Maybe as tall as Will, she couldn't tell. He filled too much of her space to be objective. Even the way his hand held hers was a study in graceful strength. Long fingers gently curved around hers and splayed at her waist. She wasn't a practiced dancer, but he was easy to follow and surrounded her with his presence. Every other person was pushed to the edges of her awareness.

Kenna soaked in the details of him like a sponge. He smelled of cigars and alcohol. Not scotch, bourbon maybe? From beneath her lashes she studied his face. He wasn't handsome, not like Will or Sal Jr., but striking and far too appealing for her comfort. Dark slashes of brows and thick lashes framed piercing hazel eyes, the moss green feathered with dark honey-gold. If he knew she was examining him, he didn't acknowledge it and continued to glide across the floor. The sharp angles of his jaw and narrow nose reminded her of ancient Greek and Roman busts. She guessed him to be close to forty by the sprinkling of gray at his temples and the slight crinkle at the corner of his eyes.

Kenna no longer attempted to hide her perusal. She was never going to see him again, so why not get a good look? Narrowing her eyes, Kenna noticed the smoothness of his olive skin and the shadow of a beard. She suspected her Greek or Roman comparison wasn't too far off. Her gaze lingered on his mouth. Firm, not too full, slightly crooked and very tempting. Unconsciously, she bit her own tingling lips.

His tuxedo was a classic cut. She'd have bet her favorite Jimmy Choos that it was a Tom Ford. With a mind of their own, her fingers petted the perfect seam on his shoulder and moved to the collar, curling back before actually raking through the close-cropped hair at the nape of his neck.

It was then she noticed just how closely he was holding her and how easily she leaned into him. Kenna scowled, mentally shaking herself. This was not a date. There wasn't a glass slipper or kiss at midnight. It was time to get out of this mess.

Feeling her tense, Lucius tightened his hold and looked down into her wide green eyes. "Have you finished your examination?"

Blushing, she looked away and made a half-hearted attempt to step off the floor. "Thank you for the dance."

"The song is still playing," he murmured as he moved them toward the center of the floor. "And I was rather enjoying your inspection." He didn't confess to conducting his own. Or how much he enjoyed the way her curves fit so perfectly against him when she wasn't trying so hard to put daylight between them. Most of all, he quieted the near primal instinct she stirred in him to protect her from whatever situation she was about to get herself into.

Sighing in resignation, Kenna looked up. There were other paths to Wallace Henneby, and despite being nervous and cautious, she wasn't afraid of this man making a scene or threatening her. She decided, on a breath to seize this Cinderella moment. "Lucius ...?" she said, dropping her acquired non-accent for her real one, a delicate Southern drawl.

He paused for a beat, his name sounded like honey dripping from her lips, then resumed the dance. "Chaerea," enunciating each syllable for her, *ker-EE-ah*. His head tilted in inquiry, although he'd overheard her introduction earlier.

"Kenna Campbell. Professional blonde," she said giving him a little head toss. "Just Ken to people I know well."

"I doubt you are *just* anything, Miss Campbell. Kenna," he said definitively. No diminutive nicknames for her. "What is your business with Wallace Henneby?"

"My own." She stiffened and tried again to put some space between them, but he held her fast.

"I could have you removed, possibly arrested. Doesn't that earn me some measure of confidence."

She laughed. "Not one bit." He felt the tremors of her mirth in every bone and almost smiled, again.

"Do you play poker Miss Campbell?" She shrugged. "Not very well I suspect." He chuckled at her offended frown. "You haven't the liar's face for it. You've decided to finish this dance and find another approach to Wallace Henneby. Possibly, I could be of some service."

Suspicious, Kenna stopped dancing and dropped her arms. "Why?" The few other couples dancing stared, as did some guests close to the floor. Lucius seemed unmoved or hardly aware of the attention.

"Very simply, I'm curious."

"I doubt there is anything *simple* with you Mr. Chaerea. Again, thank you for the dance."

She truly considered taking advantage of his offer. Wallace Henneby obviously knew him and seemed pleased to see him. That would make for a better opening than, "I almost met your wife at an auction three months ago." But at what price? Giving him an apologetic smile, she shook her head and shrugged. "I can't accept your help."

He caught her hand before she could escape. "You have accomplices in the press and among Wallace's guests. Why refuse me?"

"How do you know that?" She looked around for Candace and Frankie.

He smiled – he'd never felt the urge to smile as much as he had in the last fifteen minutes – and with that gesture wiped years from his face and completely disarmed her. Stroking the inside of her wrist he leaned over, his breath hot on her skin. His lips were a whisper away from the delicate shell of her ear. Goose bumps covered her arms. Closing her eyes, she swayed forward. Lucius' nostrils flared, catching her clean floral fragrance and something he knew on a carnal level was simply *Kenna*. He breathed, slowly, prolonging the moment. "I ... pay attention."

Kenna's eyes drifted back to the dance floor, and for a moment she wished she could stay and just dance with him. Feel strong arms around her and a warm heart beating beneath her ear. "You called my hand, Mr. Chaerea," she said, almost breathless. "I may not be a very good poker player, but I know when to fold." The disappointment in her voice was real and raw and seared him when she said with a touch of sadness, "It really was a nice dance."

He had a brief, mental image of pulling her close, cupping her stubborn chin in one hand, threading his other through her silky blonde hair and claiming her mouth in a kiss.

Kenna held her breath. The intensity of his look made her brace for ... something.

Lucius reluctantly dropped her hand and offered her a slight bow. "Indeed. Good night, Kenna."

CHAPTER NINETEEN

Mike Chapman sat back and stared in amusement at the email he'd pulled up on his monitor. He'd long thought he couldn't be surprised by anything anymore, but this was rich. He scratched his chin, the gold stubble sounding like sandpaper as he re-read the email. Now, why did a U.S. Attorney – make that *Assistant* U.S. Attorney – need a background check on Lt. Col. Lucius Chaerea, Ret.? He picked up his phone and sent a text.

Hey, Colonel. I've got a request for a background check on you from an Assistant U.S. Attorney named Candace Fisher. Referred by a former JAG I knew back when. How'd you like me to handle it?

While he was waiting on Lucius' reply, Chapman did a little digging of his own. Candace Fisher, 28, had been at the U.S. Attorney's office since graduation – in the top ten percent – from Yale Law four years ago, her cases mostly white collar, finance sector. Fordham undergrad. He looked over her college and law school transcripts. Huh, Phi Beta Kappa at Fordham. *Scary smart.* Father an architecture professor at Syracuse, mother a clinical psychologist specializing in children with learning disabilities. Married for 34 years, living in Ithaca. Her brother, employed at a tech company in Cupertino, was married too, with two children under six. Sister in law, Laura, was a stay-at-home mom, but held a degree in environmental science from Stanford, where she'd met Kyle Fisher at a volunteer day event.

So far, everything was so vanilla, he was stumped at how her simple path could have crossed Chaerea's labyrinthine, if not subterranean, trails. He looked into her finances. Nothing stood out. Bank deposits matched with her salary and some dividends from some conservative investments. Taxes filed by early February every year. Again, they aligned with her income and expected deductions. Digging a little deeper, he found no offshore accounts. She lived in a rent-stabilized building near NYU and didn't own a car. He looked at her credit cards. She paid off her credit balances nearly every month. There were a few blips each month for largish purchases at upscale retail stores.

Fisher had never been married. She'd shown up as part of a group a few times in the society pages attending charity functions. *Man, she was a pocket goddess!* Long coppery hair, impressive rack, but otherwise tiny. He zoomed in on a color photo from last year's fundraiser for the Henneby Foundation. He stared long at the twinkling cognac eyes and sunny smile.

CHAPTER TWENTY

C andace and Frankie signaled Kenna over, the first round of hot coffee and something to snack on already on their table at Marco's. Their respective late nights were evident only by the empty coffee carafe and low-heeled shoes. A pre-Barney's-sale strategy brunch six months ago, quickly became a standing date on their weekly calendars. Kenna being the only one with a Sunday morning commitment, they always patiently waited until she arrived to order drinks stronger than coffee.

"How was mass?" Frankie yawned, caught their waiter's eye and held up the empty carafe to ask for a refill. He nodded and brushed off protests by other hung-over brunchers as he made his way over with a tray of pastries. Three beautiful regulars who tipped well and never complained were his top priority.

"Weird." Kenna sipped the coffee. The warmth seeped into her.

"Weird how? Communion line limbo?" Frankie pointed her index fingers into the air making Kenna snort her next sip.

"Ow!" she protested. "Goon. No, I could have sworn I saw Lucius Chaerea when I came back from communion, but when

I turned and looked after mass I didn't see him." She shuddered visibly as an eerie feeling swept up her spine.

"The way you jumped at the gala when he crept up on you, I thought maybe he was a friend." Frankie drew out the word and pushed her pert nose out of place with her index finger, aping the universal gesture for a mobster or wise guy. "You really do have a type, you greedy bitch."

Kenna shook her head while gesturing to the bartender for three of the brunch special cocktails. He grinned and gave her a thumbs-up – three spicy, bacon Bloody Marys on the way.

"Mr. Henneby sure knew him. Scared the crap out of me. Don't suppose you know anything about him?" She looked expectantly at Candace.

Candace smiled around her bite of croissant. "I didn't, but I did some poking around last night. It was late, and today is Sunday, but ..." Her words trailed off as she pulled her tablet from her purse and touched the screen. "He's interesting."

"I suppose if he were a serial killer you'd use a stronger word," Frankie said, buttering her own bite of pastry. "Whatever. He makes me nervous. All night, after you left, he was watching us. Like we were gazelles on the Savanna."

Kenna frowned, not so much *that* he watched, but she didn't like the idea of him watching her friends like they were dinner. Was she just the discarded stuffed mushroom cap? And the fact that she was bothered was even more disturbing. She felt like she was on some emotional hamster wheel. "So, do you think he's dangerous?" Just saying the word gave her a small frisson of arousal and another spin on the wheel.

"That's what we wanted to know last night, even if we thought you might know him. Type, remember?"

"The whole time you were on the dance floor, we were trying to get your attention," Candace said.

"But he kept spinning you around like Rhett spinning Scarlett in the Virginia Reel," Frankie added.

"Not to mention, you can see over heads better than I can. I couldn't exactly stand on a chair and wave a semaphore." Candace rolled her eyes at Frankie.

"Not that she would have noticed." Frankie feigned a swoon and nudged Kenna with the tip of her boot.

"As it was, the waiters thought we were ordering drinks. So, hangover notwithstanding, it wasn't a total exercise in futility," Candace said with a laugh.

"Hey!" Kenna waved her arms pointing at herself. "Focus, please. What did you find that's so interesting?"

"Well, the *most* interesting thing is, there's almost nothing I could find out about him. And I don't mean things I haven't clearance for. I mean nothing, zip, nada, zilch," said Candace.

"How is that possible?" Frankie, the writer, was no longer nervous, but curious. Her mind was already mentally ticking off possible sources she could access.

"It's not. In fact, it's impossible to not have some kind of electronic footprint unless you *know* someone or *are* someone who erases such things." Candace waited, letting that morsel dangle in front of her friends.

Kenna pinched the bridge of her nose. "I'm sure there is some witty, clever explanation for your cat-that-ate-the-canary grin, but I don't do hungry and clever at the same time. Spill, Red."

"Look, however awkward Lucius Chaerea's attention was, it got you Wallace Henneby's. Frankie can verify this. Wallace was in my ear all night. He asked about you, how we met, the gallery, your family."

Kenna blanched. "What'd you say?"

"Just the basics," Candace soothed. "Mostly about the gallery. I think I could follow up and give him more on the painting. We can say you remembered it after meeting him. See what happens."

"I will so owe you for this." Kenna blinked wet eyes.

Candace put her arm around Kenna's shoulders, noticing that she didn't stiffen or end the contact abruptly like she used to. "What are you going to call the new gallery?"

"*Mine*," Kenna said, stuffing her rising hope down with an obscenely large bite of cream cheese Danish. "Ffflucuis?" she mumbled for "Lucius," as a few flaky crumbs trickled down onto her chest.

"Kenna Campbell, always keeping it classy," Frankie teased.

Kenna swallowed with a gulp. "I hear you've had bigger in your mouth." She left the question of "bigger what" hanging in the air.

"Lalalalala," Candace patted her hands against her ears. Her shoulders shook with suppressed laughter and mild disgust.

Frankie flicked a non-existent smudge of lipstick at the edge of her mouth with a pinky, then showed Kenna another digit. Of course, that was the same moment their obscenely gorgeous bartender and the primary reason they'd started brunching at Marco's set the Bloody Marys in front of them and grinned knowingly. "Can I get you ladies anything else? Something with syrup?" The deep Welsh timbre and dazzling smile never failed to strike something wanton and feminine. All three turned crimson.

"Luscious," Candace managed to say, her meaning having nothing to do with Lucius Chaerea. The Bartender, as he would forever after be known, laughed and moved away with a quick wink.

Candace tipped her head around Kenna to watch his exit, "Someone should take him home."

"Speaking of taking men home, before we forget to talk about this." Frankie poked Candace in the arm. "What's the story with Mr. Tall, Blond and Not-at-all-lawyer-like last night? It looked like he was into you, then he turned the high-beams onto Mrs. Henneby ..."

"What's this?" Kenna came back from daydreams of Lucius with a snap.

"Seriously hot. Ice blue eyes, well-tailored Prada suit." Frankie knew her designers like some women knew the differences among chocolates.

"Yeah, yeah. You said something in the bathroom," Kenna recalled.

"Nothing much." Candace interrupted with a shrug. "Just a new partner at Sid Rosen's firm. I was introduced last night, just before your sartorial emergency in the ladies room. He made some noise about lunch or a drink after work, gave me his card, then Althea Henneby swanned into the conversation and that was that."

"I guess for a certain type, she's attractive enough," Frankie sniffed. "Certainly well-preserved. She has a lot in common with my mother. Hell, they're probably old friends ... or mortal enemies." Frankie drifted off. "It's always one or the other with her."

Kenna giggled and sang softly, "Lawyers in love ..."

"Stop!" Candace laughed and swatted her. "I'll spot you he's cute, but I'm too busy to chase men. Let's get back to your Lucius."

"Yes, let's!" Frankie slurped on her straw.

Kenna placed her fingertips against Candace's temples and intoned, "You vill tell me vhat you know. You vill tell me *now*."

Frankie snapped her fingers. "Boris and Natasha, right? You're about to make big trouble for Moose and Squirrel."

"Bite me, Frank." Kenna leveled a pointed look at Candace. "Proceed."

"I wasn't kidding. I had a devil of a time finding out anything at all about him. You'd think he was some kind of Cold War spy or something. He has a passport from Great Britain. He pays taxes on a residence here, but the street address is not available. It takes some serious horsepower to keep your address out of the public tax rolls."

Frankie mused, "Takes a while, but I could file an FOIA request."

Kenna shifted in her seat, tucked a stray curl behind her ear and toyed with the delicate gold chain and crucifix around her neck. Candace and Frankie felt the rising interest coming off her in waves. Moths went to flames, Kenna dove headfirst into shadows. If they'd thought it was just nerves or surprise that kept her so focused on him as they danced last night, today they were certain. If the mysterious Lucius wanted to, he only need set the hook.

"I can't for the life of me figure out the connection to Wallace," Candace continued. "Anyway, I sent a text last night to one of our friendlier FBI contacts – not Ross obviously – and within an hour he texted me the name of a specialist who's a contractor to one of the more obscure clandestine services. Not really expecting anything for a few days, I reached out to this Chapman person, and this email was waiting for me this morning." She turned her tablet for them to see the email. Kenna and Frankie leaned over the table to read, then looked up as Candace began the Wiki version.

"Turns out, Lucius Chaerea retired from the British Special Air Service as a Lieutenant Colonel about three years ago. He had an illustrious career, advanced quickly and at a young age. When everyone else was fully engaged in Iraq and Afghanistan, then Captain Chaerea deployed to Somalia. There is a wife listed as deceased. That, my dears, is all. Information about his deployments, actions, honors, whatever, in the non-classified military records comes to a screeching halt. For the last decade and more of his career, he doesn't appear anywhere that Chapman could find, or would find – I got the impression he knows more than he's telling and this is a clean version – until Lucius retired from active duty. What came after? We're back to nada." She chuckled. "I even Googled him because, why not? Nothing. No. Thing. How does he do that? Even my niece, Kaitlin, comes up on Google, and she's two!"

Kenna sighed and sucked the last bits of red from a strawberry. "I wonder what's wrong with him? Probably wanted for war crimes or something."

Candace arched a brow. "Just the opposite, based on Wallace's reaction."

"Oh, well. It's not like I'll ever see him again." Kenna's disappointment was palpable. "Bet he doesn't stroll over to Hell's Kitchen for tattoos and Pings. Ever."

Frankie twisted her body to get in Kenna's face. "Maybe you should consider movin' on up, Weezie." Kenna laughed. "No one said you had to stay down there and defend the last ungentrified block in the city, you know."

"So, you want me to keep looking?" Candace asked.

"At this point, I'd rather sell some art than deal with a relationship."

"So don't have one. But you need to get laid." Frankie rolled her eyes. Candace laughed, and Frankie glared at her. "You, too!"

"Don't start with me, Frank," the other two said at once.

CHAPTER TWENTY-ONE

A ll morning, Candace had successfully avoided FBI Special Agent in Charge, Palmer Ross, refusing to take his repeated calls. Their working relationship had deteriorated over the past six months from bare professional courtesy to marginal tolerance to militant avoidance since she'd shut down his petty attempt to railroad Will MacKenzie for offenses unknown. Frankie had dated Ross once, and Candace and Kenna had yet to ferret out what had ever possessed her to do it other than her father, the Senator, liked him. Candace looked fondly at the smiling couple framed on her desk and silently thanked them for never putting her in that place.

That momentary lapse into sentimentality was all he needed.

"You got anything new for me, Honey?" Ross leaned casually against the door jamb of her office.

She gave him a hard look. "And there it is again. Your misogyny is showing, Ross. That's pretty bold when you're talking to an attorney, may I say. Anything new about what, exactly?"

He sighed with exaggerated patience. "About MacKenzie

violating Homeland Security or, hell, immigration regs by entering this fine country with a violent criminal record and running an establishment that sells alcohol and God knows what all for known organized crime figures. That."

"No, Agent Ross. I've told you, so many times now I can repeat it in my sleep, I am not your law clerk researching legal precedent for you. I'm busy with real crimes and the longer you screw around with this, the less I believe there's anything more than your paranoia and ego involved here. If Will MacKenzie has broken the law, bring me your evidence. Then we *might* have something to talk about."

He grinned, "I figured with all the time you spend around him and his friends ..." His easy Texas drawl did nothing to hide the insinuation behind his comment, nor did he intend it to.

"Do you have any idea how many violations of privacy rights that statement implies? Never mind, of course you do." Candace turned back to her computer screen.

"Honey –" She interrupted with a disgusted sound, but he kept on. "— privacy is a luxury of peace. We are at war here."

Candace retorted, "What's worse for you, Agent Ross? That you can't nail MacKenzie or that Frankie is? The better you and I have gotten to know each other recently, I can't say I doubt her judgment."

"Don't you worry about ole Palmer." He tapped his chest and drawled with a sneer, "Frankie's just takin' a walk on the wild side. I'll get him. Thugs like him can't keep clean forever. And then, well, Frankie'll see who's the better man."

Mercifully, Candace's phone rang. The LED display showed Wallace Henneby's personal number. "I have to take this Agent Ross. In private." She fixed her unwanted guest with a dismissive glare. "Candace Fisher," she said as she answered the call.

Ross rolled himself upright, smiled as if they'd been

discussing the weather, and moved on down the aisle to the next "honey."

"Candace?" Wallace said, apparently for the second time.

"Oh! Forgive me. Someone was just leaving my office. How are you, Wallace?"

"In fine fettle, thank you. Your message said you had something to tell me about your friend, Miss Campbell?"

"Yes. This is a little outside my bailiwick, but over brunch last Sunday she recalled seeing Althea at an art auction before Christmas –"

Henneby interrupted her, knowing he would more likely get the truth if he could look her in the eye. "I think this subject is better discussed in person. Would you be able to join me for an early dinner? We haven't visited in a while, and you can tell me more."

"Absolutely."

Dinner plans set, Candace hung up and looked again at the photo of her parents. She thought about Frankie and the Senator and the mother that left her to the tender mercies of an abusive, alcoholic, blueblood grandmother. She thought about Kenna, growing up and fighting for survival on the fringes of Big Sally Tomasi's empire. Overwhelmed with a moment of homesickness, she called her childhood home upstate.

"Hi, Dad," she said, her voice thick with emotion. "No, nothing's wrong. Just wanted to hear your voice. How's Mom?"

<hr />

AT THE RESTAURANT filled with the pre-theatre crowd, Candace broached the subject. "Wallace, I'm no more than a middle-man here." Seeing his open expression, she continued, "Kenna mentioned that she'd watched Althea bid almost to the max on this painting. Kenna's in a position to facilitate a sale at a much-reduced price and just wanted an 'in' to offer it to you and Althea in the event there's still an interest." She looked a bit chagrined. "I apologize for our theatrics if that's caused you to question my sincerity."

Henneby gestured to their server to refill their wine glasses. "Candace, my dear, we've known each other long enough for me to know the tenor of your integrity." He smiled warmly. "I also remember some of the machinations I've undertaken in my day to pierce the establishment barriers and to attain my objectives more directly than conventions allowed." He sipped his cabernet and, for a moment, his mind turned to a time or a place far from their table at Charlie Palmer's. He returned to their present and looked up. "If you vouch for Miss Campbell, I'll be happy to listen."

"Thank you, Wallace. I'll let her know she can call you?"

He patted her hand resting on the table. "Of course. Now, tell me what's going on with you."

Home at last, Candace kicked the door closed behind her and dropped her computer bag inside the tiny entryway to her flat near Washington Square and NYU. Her large, orange tabby bumped his head against her shin before winding between her feet.

"Fuzzbutt, please. Just thirty seconds to bolt the door, 'kay?" That done, she rolled her forehead against the door. "My God. I'm whipped, and it's only Tuesday."

She toed off her shoes and looked down with a jaundiced eye at the cat who was now meticulously licking the toes on an extended hind leg. "Right. You're hungry, and you smell the halibut I had for dinner on my clothes." Candace scooped up her discarded sling-backs and made her way through the apartment. "Tough. Human first."

Hair up in a hurried ponytail, socks sagging around her ankles and her brother's old Stanford rugby jersey swallowing her slight frame, Candace poured herself a glass of wine and tried unsuccessfully to stare down the cat sitting primly next to his food bowl and looking at her with slitted eyes.

"Something is wrong with this picture when my social life is so pathetic that the only dinner date I've had with a man in the last six months is with Wallace, and we talked business." She emptied a can of chicken bits into the empty dish. "Or that I spend the two waking hours I have at home each night carrying on one-sided conversations with my cat." Fuzzbutt rubbed appreciatively under her scratching fingers and tucked into his late supper. "You're welcome."

Candace set her wine glass on a stack of evidence reports covering the little dining table and opened her laptop in the two square feet she'd designated for its use. She had at least an hour's worth of work ahead to make up for the time she'd taken to meet with Wallace. "Fuck my life," she muttered and started on a motion to compel production of what she hoped were the incriminating corporate emails she needed to prove the guilt of another mid-level manager at a jumped-up hedge fund that had been playing fast and loose with its clients' investments.

The cat, replete with chicken, leaped into her lap and curled into a contented ball. Idly, she stroked the silky ears, "I hate them. I hate them all. And that applies in spades to Palmer Dickhead Ross and Charlie Numbnuts Hannigan." Sharing with Wallace stories about the passive-aggressive head of her department had just served to remind her of how miserable Hannigan had made her job since he'd joined the US Attorney's office a few months ago. Not that she'd ever particularly enjoyed the sheer mass of paperwork involved in building a case and trying white-collar crimes, which was all they assumed a female prosecutor was good for.

Wallace had assured her there was a place for her in his corporate legal department if she wanted to make the move, but she didn't think that would be much better than her current situation ... the devil you know.

At two in the morning, she shut down the computer and headed to bed for a few hours before she had to jump up at six to start it all again. The cat gracefully soared from the floor to the high antique bedstead that was one of Candace's few indulgences to what she hoped would one day be a comfortable, if not elegant, lifestyle. She allowed Fuzzbutt to spoon against the back of her legs. Before she fell into a dead sleep, she murmured, "At least I can look forward to a positive report to Kenna later. Then, it's all up to her."

CHAPTER TWENTY-TWO

I f Lucius could ever be described as distracted, this was it –
an unscheduled appointment, small talk, picking at non-
existent lint. Wallace hid his amusement as he poured
coffee. Lucius never talked about the weather, but now he'd
mentioned the absence of the sun twice before their coffee
arrived.

"How was Tuscany?" Henneby asked, gently opening the
door for personal conversation.

Lucius sighed deeply, contemplating the dark contents of
his cup. "I didn't go." He looked up.

Wallace didn't hide his surprise. Lucius' pilgrimage to his
childhood church and parents' graves during Easter had been a
non-negotiable entry on Lucius' calendar since he'd met the
young man as a Lieutenant Colonel years before. It occurred to
him the reason could be professional. Evil didn't recognize fixed
entries, even Lucius'. "Nothing serious I hope."

Lucius rose and moved to the window. The trees were just
beginning to bud, signaling the season change. "No. Perhaps I'll
go in June when the vines are leafing." He left the thought of,
perhaps not alone this year, unspoken.

He wasn't prepared to confess his delayed trip was because of a woman. Lucius had almost missed Kenna passing him during communion the morning after he'd foiled her plans at the Henneby gala. Since then, he'd continued to attend the same Sunday services at St. Patrick's, despite the near impossibility of any kind of casual encounter during Lenten and Easter services. The Cathedral had been so packed on Good Friday he'd barely been able to turn his head, much less reconnoiter the room for a woman he'd met once.

Clearing his throat, Wallace tried a new approach. "Luc? The young woman you danced with at the gala? Miss Campbell. Do you know her well?"

Lucius slowly looked over his shoulder, expressionless. A stranger would think he'd never heard the name before. "You aren't acquainted?"

"Not particularly. Only through Candace Fisher. Definitely a favorable recommendation." Wallace sipped, enjoying the moment before dropping his real information. "I have an appointment with her tomorrow. She manages an obscure gallery, and according to Candace, has a painting she thinks I may be interested in."

"Are you? Interested in the painting?"

"Possibly. Althea has persistently encouraged my support of the arts. I only asked as you seemed to know the young lady, and I rarely go into a sales pitch without knowing my opponent."

"You're certain art is all she is selling?"

"You suspect her of seduction and extortion?" Lucius' jaw flexed. Wallace grinned. "I'm flattered."

There was a long silence. Wallace waited, imagining the gears turning behind the marble façade of Luc's features. "I suspect everyone, Wallace."

"If your schedule allows, why don't you join us tomorrow?" Wallace hid a sly smile behind the rim of his cup. Lucius wasn't the only one capable of concealing his thoughts. He could not, however, resist a slight dig. "You will sleep better knowing her true motives, and it saves you the trouble of contriving a ruse to be here."

Lucius coughed down his latest sip. "I'm that transparent?"

"It's a pleasant change. Young men need to be surprised occasionally." The light flashed on Henneby's desk, signaling the arrival of his next appointment. "One-thirty, tomorrow."

CHAPTER TWENTY-THREE

W ill was away again, which meant two things to Kenna: he and Frankie were not in the next room, and Kenna could attempt a decent night's sleep without ear plugs or having to muffle the sounds of passion whenever Will happened to bump into Frankie in the night. Here, she felt safe enough to sleep without a dozen locks on the door like she did at the efficiency over the gallery, her home away from home.

Nerves over her upcoming meeting with Wallace Henneby notwithstanding, Kenna managed to get dressed and get to work without throwing up. By noon, she was not so confident. How does one sell a painting one doesn't own to a man whose party one had crashed weeks earlier? And do it quickly? Fat Tony, the current owner, may be in desperate need of cash, but he wouldn't be forever. His impatient bookie might make art sales moot before Kenna could arrange the sale.

She stepped from the cab in front of the Henneby building twenty minutes early. Along with the frantic butterflies, she felt a rush of excitement. The same rush she felt when looking at a new artist's work or the occasional rare find at an estate sale. Or the thrill of socking away a little more into her savings and being a step closer to having her own gallery space.

You could always pick up some work from Sal Jr., she thought. Hostessing at one of his clubs could bring in serious tips if she were willing to deal with the clientele. Kenna shuddered and swallowed the rising bile as faces from the past swam in her memory. No, even the lure of fast cash and the relative safety of Sal's friendship wasn't enough to send her back into that world. Well, not after this deal went through anyway.

She hadn't been awakened by her own screams in over a year. The paranoia and panic attacks were only bad memories. She repeated to herself she was normal. She was sane. She was about to be an art dealer and, one day soon, a gallery owner. The details of her own gallery were clear in her mind as the elevator doors opened into the hushed reception area of Henneby's private offices.

"I'm so fucked!" she hissed under her breath.

Mounted on the mahogany paneling, across from the elevator, was a fabulous neo-classic scene from the American Revolution. She recognized it instantly as a John Trumbull. Probably the same one sold two years ago by Christie's. The briefcase Candace had loaned her felt like it was filled with rocks instead of high gloss prints of the Jackson Pollock knockoff she was peddling.

"Miss Campbell?" the receptionist asked politely.

Kenna took a deep breath and smiled. "Yes. I know I'm early."

"That's not a problem. Mr. Henneby is waiting. If you will follow me."

Already? Damn! She'd counted on a few minutes to settle her nerves and maybe pray a rosary. She hardly felt her legs as she followed the assistant to the looming carved doors. The woman must have offered to take her coat because Kenna was handing it over and straightening her favorite gray pinstripe skirt. It was just like the one she'd seen Veronica Lake wear in some film noir on late night TCM. It always made her feel a bit *femme fatale* and smarter than the ubiquitous power suits strutting around New York. The door opened and Kenna had a flash of a drawbridge lowering with a fire-breathing dragon inside.

"Mr. Henneby. Miss Campbell is here."

"Thank you, Helen." Wallace was already at the door taking Kenna's robotically offered hand. "Please come in, Miss Campbell. Can I offer you some tea? Coffee?" He placed a gentle hand under her elbow.

Kenna began to feel her anxiety ease under his kindness. "Tea plea—" She jerked to a stop, her mouth a perfect "O." Lucius Chaerea had risen from his chair. It took her a moment to recognize him under the new dark beard and longer hair. He had, however, magically sucked the air from the room, or at least her lungs.

"Colonel!" she barely whispered. Until that moment, she'd not realized how often she referred to him in her head as Lieutenant Colonel or Colonel Chaerea, or how much she'd hoped to see him again. Just not here, or now.

"Miss Campbell." He grinned, acknowledging her inadvertent use of his rank, and bowed slightly. He may have taken her breath away, but for him, she'd ushered in the light. His mind instantly snapped a photograph and slipped it in with the others he'd hoarded in his mind from the gala and the chance sighting at the Cathedral the following morning. Now, his mind catalogued for easy retrieval the image of her soft pink blouse that matched the flush in her cheeks, the gray skirt accentuating her curves and that fleeting look of pleasure when she first saw him.

Although brief and discrete, she felt his eyes roaming over her. The pleasant discomfort this generated was enough to put some of her spine back together and, as she set the briefcase on the small coffee table where Wallace was pouring tea, her initial surprise became irritation. This was the second time he'd intruded on her attempts to woo Wallace Henneby. Kenna ground her teeth and forced what she hoped was a look of professional serenity onto her face.

Lucius took the seat to Wallace's right, leaving only the chair across from them for Kenna. From beneath her lashes, she shot daggers at him for delegating her to the hot seat. A bit childish she admitted, but it steeled her for her next move. One she couldn't believe she was about to make.

"Sugar or lemon?" Wallace asked.

"Milk, if you have it. Thank you." Kenna sat smoothly into her chair crossing her ankles and doing her best to ignore Lucius. *He's not here. He's not here. He's not here. No ruffled feathers on me ... Liar.*

Smiling benignly, Wallace handed her the delicate china cup. He held his amusement inside. Any two people so intent on pretending to be indifferent were certainly not. Although curious about the painting, he was far more interested in the non-verbal interplay happening between his guests.

Deciding to get this show on the road, Wallace said, "Candace briefed me about the painting you are selling."

Kenna took a deep breath and set the untouched cup on the table in front of her. "Mr. Henneby, did you choose the pieces you have in your office?"

Lucius' cup paused halfway to his mouth. Wallace leaned back in his own chair. "Let's say I was consulted. My wife is the expert. Before I married Althea, I was an indifferent collector."

"Do you have a more alternative, less traditional collection? In your home or as investments?"

"No, we do not."

She couldn't help a quick look at Lucius and hoped the sinking feeling in her stomach didn't make her look green.

Kenna shrugged and didn't try to hide the disappointed smile. "I'm afraid I've wasted your time. I assumed if Mrs. Henneby was bidding on the piece ..." She shook her head. "She could have paid any price, couldn't she?" The last was said more to herself.

Wallace held out his hand gesturing to the case. "May I see the photographs while you tell me about the painting? Before you pull the offer off the table."

Kenna stood to pass the folder across. Both Wallace and Lucius moved to the edge of their seats, looking from the images to her. She remained standing. *He may not buy, but show him you know your stuff.*

"As you can see, he's a fan of abstract, trying quite obviously to combine Pollock and Kandinsky." She didn't hide her personal dislike of the painting.

Lucius lifted a close-up and squinted at the signature of backwards letters. "The artist is 'Dog'?"

Kenna rolled her eyes. "He thinks it's clever. A cheap shot at religion. His real name is Andrew McMillian."

"Would *you* recommend this as an investment?" Wallace asked. His genuine interest in her opinion filled Kenna with unexpected pride. She flushed.

"I suspect his work will have a popularity surge in the next few years. Existing pieces will become collector items." They still looked curious and attentive, so she kept talking. "Andrew is a heroin addict and thinks it's the only way he can create. If he lives another three years, it will be by the grace of God. And, like it or not, the art community fawns over its dead. Death means instant, if short-lived, success for the deceased. Even bad art is appreciated for a while."

"You think this is bad?" Lucius asked, turning the photo toward her.

"It's ..." she began, pausing, before going on. "I'm hesitant to belittle any creative endeavor or the courage needed to try. However," she said, scrunching her nose and closing her eyes as if the painting itself pained her, "I find it derivative and unoriginal." Then she laughed. "I also nearly failed art appreciation because, and I quote Professor Allen of Hudson," – she mimicked his faux French accent perfectly — "'Miz Campbell, *you* are a *snob*.'"

Lucius smiled, believing he'd caught her in another deceit. *Which is it – Fordham as she and Candace had portrayed her credentials or Hudson?*

She had to force herself to focus back on Henneby who was also smiling broadly.

"If the piece has investment potential, why is it for sale?"

Kenna bit her lip and clenched her hands behind her back as she studied her shoes. Not that any good broker wouldn't know heroin-addicted artists or seedy collectors trying to class themselves up by spending too much on pretend works of art, but she felt the cloud of her not so legitimate associations move into the room. Wallace politely ignored her fidget. For Lucius, it was like a red cape to a bull. The simple question made her too nervous.

"The current owner is in a financial bind." Two sets of brows raised, and Kenna plowed forward. "I doubt his bookie will take payment in canvas and oils." Lucius leaned back, his arms folded over his chest and legs crossed. The crease so perfect in his trousers it didn't even buckle at the knee. She hated the scrutiny and the way she could imagine him moving the puzzle pieces of her life around. Judging. Putting her in the same class with Fat Tony and Big Sally.

"Forgive me, Miss Campbell, I presumed you or the gallery possessed the painting," Wallace said.

"No, sir. I just happen to know it can be had for half the

auction price and one of the wealthiest women in Manhattan was bidding on it before Christmas."

"And you were hoping to make a generous commission?" Lucius accused and immediately regretted it when she shot him a glare tinged with hurt more than defensiveness.

Kenna scooped up the file and its contents and tucked them back into the briefcase. "Only a fair one, Mr. Chaerea," she said softly, meeting his intense look with one of her own.

"Thank you for seeing me, Mr. Henneby. I won't take any more of your time."

Kenna held out her hand. Despite Lucius' suggestion that she was only after a commission, which she was, and she was never one to back away from the truth, Kenna didn't feel too defeated. The plan had been a long shot from the beginning.

Wallace and Lucius rose, both a bit surprised at the sudden end to the meeting, an end not initiated by either of them. "If you find something else, Miss Campbell —"

"I'll keep an eye out, Mr. Henneby," she lied, never expecting to see him again and turned to the door.

"Allow me to see you out, Miss Campbell," Lucius said, quickly making his farewells to Wallace.

Just like the night of the Henneby gala when he'd insisted on a dance, Kenna couldn't formulate a plausible reason to refuse. They collected their coats and rode in silence to the building lobby. The elevator felt small even though just the two of them occupied it. Kenna had to remind her lungs to push air in and out. He stood close, encroaching on her personal space. Moving away would have felt like running, so she stared at the satiny mahogany walls and forced her body not to shiver.

She remembered the feel of his hand on the small of her back and the crinkle at the corner of his eyes when he laughed during their dance weeks ago, the way he'd smelled. The same maleness, without the lingering headiness of cigars, now infiltrated her senses. An involuntary smile turned up the corner of her mouth. One needed to be practically in his arms to catch it, and she found both the subtle scent and the fact that it was not shared with everyone else very appealing.

With a slight tilt of his head, Lucius studied her. She didn't flinch or even seem to notice. He wondered what thought caused her to smile. He wanted to reach out and tuck a stray curl behind her ear. To feel the silkiness of it wrap around his finger. Kenna flexed her fingers around the handle of the brief-case. He recalled her discomfort in Wallace's office. The discussion around the owner of Dog's latest work made her too nervous. Every instinct cried out to find out why that was so and keep anything from ever making her feel that uncomfortable again.

Kenna power-walked out of the building, then stopped and took a large cleansing breath. The cold spring air cleared her head.

"May I offer you my car, Miss Campbell?" Lucius was at her elbow, gesturing to the open door of the sedan on the street. He could see her about to refuse. "Consider it my way of apologizing for doubting you and offering you an opportunity to ask me anything the Misses Fisher and Winslow were unable to discover."

Kenna's head snapped up in shock, her cheeks red with embarrassment, her heart thumping, a guilty response to being caught. Lucius' smile was only a little smug. She nodded a wry acknowledgment and walked toward the car, somehow feeling she owed him the penance of accepting the courtesy in light of her supposed offense.

Before climbing in, she turned to him. "How did you know?"

He smiled more broadly, leaning towards her just enough to invade her space – again – without being threatening and fixed his eyes on hers. "I pay attention."

"I've noticed, but that doesn't answer my question." She felt his deep chuckle in the most feminine part of herself.

Once the car pulled into traffic, she turned to him, expecting an answer. He was leaning into his corner of the back seat, one arm propped on the back. Long elegant fingers draped over the edge inches from her shoulder.

Chaerea's driver looked in the rearview mirror. He had the most piercing, soulful green eyes. "The address, miss?"

Kenna gave the address of the gallery and watched him look to Lucius for a nod to proceed. A heavy silence settled over them. The car had traveled about six blocks when Kenna finally spoke.

"Does this really work for you?"

"Pardon?"

"This?" She waved her hand between them. "The awkward-silence-until-the-other-person-becomes-so-uncomfortable-they-start-rambling-and-tell-you-their-life-story thing."

"I find it quite effective."

"I find it quite rude. Fortunately, I happen to be a fan of silence." Kenna sat back, imitating his relaxed posture, and focused out her window and on her breathing. She could swear her heartbeats were echoing in the quiet car.

Knowing she would not share his amusement, Lucius placed a knuckle to his lips to stop a grin and cleared his throat. "You called me Colonel," he said, beginning his answer to her question of how he knew she and her friends had been checking him out. "I have only introduced myself as Lucius and only Captain Griffin," he gestured to the front seat, "or those I have served with use the title. None of them are in the US just now. Furthermore, while Miss Fisher and Miss Winslow did nothing intrusive or inappropriate, in my profession we err on the side of caution. When inquiries are made, even discrete, innocent ones, I am informed."

Kenna looked over at him and smiled. "Can you really blame me? You disrupted my plan, and I don't like surprises. We did try simpler methods, but you are un-Googleable." She grinned. "Unless you actually *are* a first century, eunuch assassin."

He laughed, deep and resonant. "I've been called many things. Un-Googleable is a first. Is there anything you wish to know that the ladies did not uncover?"

She thought for a moment and reached half way to his cheek before pulling back and stroking her own chin. "Why the beard?"

Lucius scratched the dark thick scruff covering his cheeks and most of his head, wondering how much to reveal. "I travel a great deal. The beard is more accepted, even trusted, in some parts of the world."

"Are you leaving or returning?"

"I leave tomorrow."

"Oh." Her brow furrowed. To her surprise, she was disappointed.

The regret in her voice warmed him. He couldn't remember the last time anyone was disappointed at his parting or might actually rejoice in his return.

"Kenna?" There it was again, the deep purr of his voice pouring over her. "Will you join me for dinner?"

The car rolled to a stop in front of the tattoo parlor below the gallery where she worked. The window shade moved imperceptibly. Kenna looked out at the decaying buildings, seeing the seediness as though for the first time. "Thank you, but I can't. *Pretty Woman* was just a movie, Colonel."

"Pretty Woman?"

"Julia Roberts ..."

"I'm familiar, but fail to see the connection. We are neither tycoon nor prostitute."

She wanted to point out the window and explain. *I work in a gallery that is one velvet Elvis away from a Tijuana flea market. My closest thing to family is a mostly former gangster. My last relationship was a gangster who damn near killed me. I crash society parties to sell paintings I don't own for wise guy gamblers about to be crippled by wise guy bookmakers. You wear Tom Ford like it's an old tennis shoe, travel the globe doing God only knows what and have friends like Wallace Henneby.*

She opted for a simple, "People like us don't date."

He reached out for her hand letting his thumb caress the scars running along the underside of her fingers. "I leave for three weeks. Have dinner with me when I return. If you still have objections, I shall not intrude on your life again."

Three weeks was a long time. *He may forget*, she tried to tell herself, knowing in her gut this man never forgot anything. She could feel the pull. The need for contact and affection was a heavy aching weight in her arms and chest. If she leaned over and hugged him now, would he wrap her in his arms until it subsided? A familiar lump rose in her throat. She had dear friends who she knew loved her, a job and a warm place to live, but Kenna's soul was lonely. She looked at their hands. Hers seemed so small in his. Then she looked up to find the ever-present veil was gone from his face. Lucius knew her ache. She saw it. He was lonely too.

She nodded and swallowed hard.

"Say it, Kenna. Tell me." His murmur was a caress.

"In three weeks, I will have dinner with you."

"Thank you."

On cue, his door opened, and Lucius stepped out, extending his hand for hers. The spell was broken, both of them cloaked once more in their protective layers. He pulled her close and fitted her to his body.

Kenna placed a hand on his chest. "Be safe."

He chuckled. "What makes you say that?"

She pushed playfully away and walked toward the gallery stairs. "You're not a Bible salesman, Colonel," she said, looking back over her shoulder, one foot on the bottom step showcasing every curve she was blessed with. She couldn't resist flirting. After all he was leaving for three weeks. It was safe ... ish. "If you were safe, I'm pretty sure I wouldn't find you so attractive."

She could hear him laughing as the door closed and the car pulled away.

Two days later, the first note arrived. No stamp or postmark. Simply her name in an elegant masculine script, on heavy pale gray stationery, with a **C** pressed into an old fashioned red wax seal. Kenna carefully separated the wax from paper.

"How far away the stars seem,
and how far is our first kiss,
and ah, how old my heart."
-- William Butler Yeats
Luc

CHAPTER TWENTY-FOUR

"Why are they still dressed?" Davit Lazarashvilli asked, pursing his nose in disdain at the row of women lined up in the shipping container that now sat in the center of a large warehouse.

They had been deprived of everything but the sounds of a semi-truck and their own voices, smells and fears for three days. The meager light buzzing above in fluorescent tubes burned their retinas. Their eyes, some wide in shock or fear, others narrowed and suspicious, followed Lazarashvilli as he paced in front of the opening at the small end of the container. The women paralyzed by terror clung to the women watching Lazarashvilli with wary loathing.

"Leave their clothes in the container and burn it," he said over his shoulder to an armed guard who threatened the women with his weapon, grabbing at their clothes and pointing to the ground until they understood.

Lazarashvilli spun when the whimpering began. The move pulled his dual ostemy lines. Pain shot through his groin and into his thighs. "Shut them up!"

The women were, for the most part, stoic. The strong ones

understood at once, though they didn't know the words. A few covered the mouths of those on the brink of hysteria.

Lazarashvilli closed his eyes, took a deep breath and found his calming place far away from the tedium of human cattle. He sensed Hans behind him. "You have something for me?"

"Not much," Hans said warily, "could be something."

Lazarashvilli held out his hand for the envelope. Inside was a black and white photo of a tattoo parlor and a black car with a driver standing with his face to the camera.

"What is this bullshit?" Lazarashvilli asked, and flung the photo at Hans. His irritation made more obvious by the appearance of his Eastern European accent over his painstakingly acquired English one.

"This is Chaerea's car. The man is Chaerea's driver," Hans offered as explanation. "He made the photographer before he could get a shot of Chaerea or find out why he was there."

"Where did he go after?" Lazarashvilli said through clenched teeth.

"We don't know. We have never been able to track him to his house. Just random offices and the UN, but never the same place twice. Never the same route. Seldom the same vehicle." Hans tried to hide his respect for the illusive Chaerea.

Lazarashvilli turned his head and glared at his second in command. "Perhaps when we catch him, you can suck his cock." Hans wisely did not respond.

The women had been herded from the container like sheep driven from a pen, through the alley to the chute, and now stood against the long side of the container. They kept their bodies turned with arms and hands crossed in futile efforts to preserve their modesty. Lazarashvilli swept his arm toward them, "Why do they *always* do that? Such a waste of my time."

As he looked down the line, there was one, there was always one, who stood out. She wasn't the prettiest, she didn't have large or firm breasts, but what made her eye-catching was her straightforward stare and refusal to cover herself. She didn't even look toward him as he approached.

"This one," Lazarashvilli said.

Hans pulled her out of line and turned her to face the others. Hans grinned and folded the photograph, slipping it into the pocket of his black combat pants. He did enjoy the demonstration part of product intake. He hoped she was a fighter.

Lazarashvilli smiled, almost benevolently, to the group, and pointed to his model. "Like *this*." He even stood up straight and motioned his hands up and down his body, mirroring her lack of self-consciousness. When they didn't move to imitate Lazarashvilli or the woman, Hans and the other guard moved in and forced them, jerking arms down, turning shoulders to face forward, grabbing their faces and holding them up, until everyone was at last mimicking the required posture.

Lazarashvilli clapped his hands to draw their full attention to him. Bringing one finger to his lips, he shushed them, tapped the side of his temple close to his eye, then pointed at the lone woman. "Pay very close attention."

Their eyes darted from Lazarashvilli to the woman and back. "You may proceed," he ordered his man.

He didn't need to watch Hans' demonstration. He'd seen the breaking-in many times. Lazarashvilli watched the line, resignation and abandoned hope dropping like bridal veils over each face. Satisfied there would now be full compliance, he straightened his cuffs and the buttons on his double-breasted suit and walked out of the warehouse.

CHAPTER TWENTY-FIVE

"How's the manuscript?" Kenna asked as she probed the apple bin for the least bruised fruit, sniffing them like the elderly woman beside her was doing.

"A better question is why are we buying food? We don't cook." Frankie tucked her backside in just in time to avoid being butt-swiped by a runaway toddler and cart.

"I need stuff in the loft. I think the Kung Pao is beginning to pickle my brain. Where's the cookie dough?" She looked up at aisle markers, so unfamiliar with this market she really didn't know where anything was.

"Cookie dough? What happened?" Frankie's stomach churned remembering her one and only encounter with Kenna's brand of self-medication. She'd found Kenna crying on the sofa in Will's apartment after she learned her New Year's dream date – a young, newly promoted police sergeant – was married. "No one needs Prozac if they have cookie dough and tequila," Kenna had said that night. Frankie's stomach had vehemently disagreed for almost a week.

"Nothing. It's just in case. We can text Candace and do

drinkies after. I have something to show y'all." Kenna began to squeeze bread. This she knew how to choose. "So, manuscript?"

"Under the bed with the others." Frankie sighed long and then brightened. "But I have a new feature series. It was Will's idea."

"Oh, yeah?" Kenna screwed up her face. "What about?"

"Quit making that face! It's not about sex." The apple lady gasped and sped by them, tsk-ing as she went.

"Oh, thank God." Kenna leaned dramatically against a severely misplaced display of adult diapers, the back of her hand against her forehead.

Frankie shook her head. "No one buys the act, Prudence."

Kenna shrugged. "But it's funny. What's the story?"

"Horse racing." Kenna turned in slow motion to give Frankie her full attention. "The season starts in a few weeks. You know the Triple Crown races and all that. My editor liked the idea of having the point-of-view of a novice. He thinks it puts a new spin on the sport. Anyway, he gave me the green light. It's not exactly *new*, but doing these kinds of features every few years boosts interest."

"And this was Will's idea?" Kenna asked, as if the idea were a suspicious brown lump on the rug.

"I know, right? We were lying in bed, my latest book rejection in shreds, and he just threw that on the wall."

"He did, huh?"

"What? *Whaaat?*" Frankie's shoulders went up as she raised her arms in a dramatic shrug.

"Nothing. Nothing. I'm happy for you and proud of Will for showing interest. It's damn near grown-up relationship type stuff. Just," Kenna said and put her hand on Frankie's arm, "be careful."

Frankie pulled back. Her tone sharp. "Be careful? You do

see the irony here, right? How's the art deal with Fat Tony going?"

Even though that long shot had died weeks earlier in Wallace Henneby's office, Frankie had a point. How many times a week was she in one of Sal Jr.'s places and around his clientele?

"Yes, I know. And I know that whatever is going on with you and Will is different, for you both. But I know these people. I also know how you research. You won't be content with pretty hats for very long, and beyond the betting windows are people who won't just whisper and ruin your reputation." Kenna massaged her right palm with her left thumb and shivered.

"Something slither over your grave?" Mollified, Frankie gave her a hip nudge.

"It's nothing. Just a cramp."

"Just a cramp that you get every time discussion dances close to yours and Will's acquaintances and employer." Frankie didn't force her friend into eye contact and politely turned away while Kenna mentally shoved her baggage back in the closet.

Kenna looked unenthusiastically into her basket. Apples, bread, cheese. "That's good enough," she said as she moved toward the check-out.

Frankie pulled out her phone and began tapping out a message to Candace. "What's this you want to show us?"

Swinging her cloth grocery bag, Kenna grinned over her shoulder. "You'll see." *Either the most romantic gesture ever or an epic level stalker.*

"I HOPE THIS IS GOOD," Candace said, practically falling into the booth where Kenna and Frankie had been waiting for almost an hour. "It's been a day."

Frankie pushed the waiting martini closer to Candace, then gestured to Kenna like a game show hostess. "You're on."

Kenna blew out a breath, her cheeks flushed with excitement. She set the stack of pale gray envelopes with red wax seals onto the table with the gentleness she might use to show them a rare Faberge jewelry box. "The first one came two days after the meeting with Mr. Henneby. A new one every two or three days since."

Frankie and Candace reached out, each taking one off the pile and opening it as carefully as Kenna had presented them. They looked at Kenna, then back to the pages in their hands.

Frankie cleared her throat. "'Bitter winter, but with you here, we needed no fire; flames leapt between us.' Wallada. Obviously, he was watching the same dance we were."

Candace opened her page. "I have a Whitman. 'This is the touch of my lips to yours ... this is the murmur of yearning.' This is some serious old-school courting."

"I'm not sure if it's stalker or sexy," Kenna said, looking hopefully at her friends.

Frankie counted the stack with the tip of her nail. "Ten?"

"Eleven," Kenna said holding up a long envelope. "This one is on hotel paper, I think. He cut the top off, though."

When she didn't offer that one up for perusal, they each took another from the stack.

"Did he give you a poem in that one?" Candace asked with a sly glance. Kenna blushed.

"I'll take that as a big, hell yes."

"It doesn't contain the word Nantucket, does it?" Frankie teased.

"No!" Kenna said on a laugh. "It's kinda sexy though."

"Honey, they all are."

In the beat of silence, they stared at her, waiting. Kenna unfolded the sheet of paper from a hotel room pad, the top of which had been cleanly cut away, leaving only lines of neat, slanted script. "'Kiss me again, rekiss me, kiss me more, give me your most consuming, tasty one, give me your sensual kiss, a savory one, I'll give you back four burning at the core.' Uhm, Louise Labé."

"Maybe it's my finely tuned writer's instincts, but I think he wants to kiss you." Frankie fairly swooned.

Her brow furrowing, Candace turned the envelope in her hand over and over. "Courier delivery?"

Kenna's mouth became a fine line, and she shook her head. "Nope. Under the door. Sent with Ping's delivery. Sitting on my desk one day." They laid the notes back onto the table with excruciating care. Now suspicious of things that, perhaps, they shouldn't leave fingerprints on. "Yeah. Either grand romance or ..."

"Stalker that loses his shit when you want to break it off." Frankie finished the thought they all shared. They contemplated the stack of notes in silence.

After a moment, Candace shook her head and said, "I don't see it. Not in Wallace Henneby's circle. I'm not talking mere sphere of acquaintances. He knows your Colonel, and Wallace didn't treat him casually."

"He obviously doesn't want me to know where he is." Kenna held up the cut edge of her page, pinching the top corners with each hand. "Who is delivering these? I never see anyone. And I *notice* creeps." This affirmation of her ability to spot pickpockets, perverts and predators was painfully Shakespearean – "the lady doth protest too much." No matter how often she declared her instincts infallible, she could never change history, never go back and see the danger to herself until the violence was loosed upon her.

"What about the driver you told us about? Mr. Soulful Green Eyes."

"What was his name?" Kenna mused and squinted into the light overhead searching for the answer. "I can see the eyes. The name is gone for now, but I got the feeling he never leaves the Colonel. I sure got the no trust vibe off him."

"When is Lucius supposed to be back?" Candace asked.

"He said three weeks. Seventeen days ago."

"Counting much?" Frankie caught their waiter's eye and twirled her finger for another round.

"What else am I supposed to do?" Kenna forced herself to sit up and not whine. "Write back to nowhere? Google matching verses? Because I'd have to Google. Ten notes and I knew who Walt Whitman was. Seriously, I thought he was some kind of cop or spy. What if he's a professor or something? Artistic types are too needy. I can't do needy."

"Relax, he probably had to look these up too. Maybe he didn't know what to say, so he let the poems do the talking," Frankie said, nodding at the notes, not completely convinced, but trying to stem Kenna's insecurity.

"Let's give him five more days for travel and jet lag to tip the scales between either romance or restraining order. Meanwhile, you enjoy the one-sided conversation," Candace said.

Kenna nodded and drained her glass. "What are you doing this weekend?"

Candace flopped her head back against the booth seat. "I'll be under the wheels of justice."

"I thought you had a date with that guy from the gala."

"Raincheck. If I date, I don't get to sleep." She rolled her head to look at Frankie. "You?"

"I think I have that beat. Hold on to your olives, girls," Frankie said, making Kenna and Candace sit up in anticipation of some grand adventure. "I get to make the annual pilgrimage to the accountants tomorrow!" Her faux enthusiasm dissolved into utter boredom. "'Hello, Francesca. Would you consider investing your trust in, blah blah blah.'"

"That's why I barter," Kenna said. "That and my money has one purpose."

Frankie tilted her head as if the proverbial bulb had just clicked on, although she and Candace had privately discussed how to bring up the topic of Kenna's financial planning before. "Do you realize how many people you know who would love to invest in your gallery? Or who know people who know people?"

"And how many would advise against using all of your own savings?" Candace said with closed eyelids.

"And how money makes people think they can control you," Kenna said. "I'll take my chances."

From her tone, they knew this was not yet a topic open for discussion. They also knew she was a long way from having enough saved to even begin. Later, when the reality was upon her, they could gently broach the subject again.

CHAPTER TWENTY-SIX

Kenna tried to concentrate on the mass, but the readings were little more than white noise today. Lucius' last note, slipped under her door yesterday, practically hummed in her purse. Unlike the others, this one had been *his* words, *his* voice. A real letter. A conversation. A piece of himself in paper and ink. She'd tucked it into her purse this morning, thinking that she'd show the girls, but as the morning passed, a possessiveness came over her. She'd shared his small notes with pride at being so thoroughly courted, despite the undercurrent of suspicion, but this one was different. This letter was intimate. Hers.

She completely missed the homily and came out of her trance only from habit to rise, kneel and recite liturgical responses. The Lord's Prayer hardly pulled her mind from the small vineyard described in Lucius' letter.

"Let us offer each other a sign of peace," the deacon said.

Kenna smiled and offered her hand to the family sitting in front of her. She gasped audibly when she turned to the pew behind.

"Peace be with you," he spoke low.

"You're back." Kenna smiled, surprising them both with her open joy at seeing him. *How was it possible to miss him so much? I hardly know him, but it feels like I've known him forever.*

He held her hand in both of his. The congregation, a distant blur around them, murmured their offering to one another. Warmth seeped through her, and Lucius felt the sun on his face.

"Peace be with you," he said again.

"Peace be with you," Kenna whispered, then turned to face the altar. Reluctant to let go of his hand, she stretched her arm behind her.

Lucius had never felt such true communion away from his childhood church. He'd first seen her in prayer weeks earlier during Lenten celebrations, divine providence after their auspicious meeting at Wallace Henneby's event. He sat through a second mass when he'd seen her climbing St. Patrick's steps. Even as distracted as she seemed today, he felt closer to God praying with her near.

After communion, she didn't return to her seat, but moved to an empty pew in the back. Lucius followed, kneeling beside her. Not close enough to touch and, with hands folded, they knelt hyper-aware of each other. Kenna took a deep breath. She couldn't remember the last time anyone knelt with her in church. Not beside her, with her. Emotions she didn't recognize swelled inside, making her chest feel heavy and her eyes burn with momentary tears.

Head bowed, she studied his hands – long, elegant, strong. She resisted the urge to slip hers between them, but she smiled at the idea. *This is going to hurt,* Kenna thought. Her smile turned from hopeful pleasure to resigned defeat in seconds.

Lucius smiled when she smiled, and frowned when her look turned suddenly. He wondered what thought caused the change. He marveled that her face hid nothing, while he possessed the natural and learned ability to reveal nothing.

Outside the church, Lucius positioned himself a step below her so she would not be squinting into the infrequent appearances of the sun. "I trust you don't object to my imposition this morning. You *are* a creature of habit." He squelched the tactician's voice and decided to save the cautionary lecture about the dangers of predictability and routine for another time.

"I don't mind." Kenna hid a wide smile by biting her lip and smoothing the front of her sunshine-yellow maxi dress, worn beneath a cropped black leather jacket. The dress was a summons for spring to hurry. "When did you get back?" *I forced myself not to expect you for two more days.*

Lucius scratched his fuller, but neatly trimmed beard, "Late last night."

"You got some sun," she said.

It was not quite a question, but an opening he had to ignore. He knew she was drawn to the mystery. Most women were. He knew she wasn't just flirting when she'd said she might not be so attracted to him if he were safe. He didn't know how well she would embrace the brutal truth of his life.

He looked up at the cloudy spring sky. "I should have brought some back for you. As a souvenir."

"Commemorative plates are easier to get through Customs." Another subtle probe into his whereabouts.

He smiled. "I will remember that next time."

"Next time? Are you leaving again soon?"

Was that concern? Disappointment? Old fashioned curiosity? He wondered. "I cannot say exactly." He tilted his head to catch her eyes. "I've been debating the advantages of perhaps delegating some of my duties."

So you can stay here. Kenna flushed at the thought. "I'm not the one to give advice on that. I never delegate. Of course, it's just me at the gallery. Uhm," she said and glanced at her watch. "I need to get going. I'm glad you're back." She realized she truly was.

"My car?" he asked. Kenna knew without looking that the black sedan would magically appear when Lucius moved toward the street.

"I'm only going a few blocks. Brunch with the girls."

"Ah, yes," Lucius said with a grin, "the Accomplices. Allow me to walk with you." He offered his arm.

Who does that?? "Uhm." Kenna blushed at her suddenly absent vocabulary, and bit her bottom lip. "It's ten blocks."

He grinned. "We'll walk ten blocks, then, if you wish."

She rewarded him with an exasperated eye roll, one they both knew was not genuine, for she flushed again and smiled. "I'm sure there is some cardinal rule about turning down a free ride in the city. Right next to free drinks or shoes." She pointed to the car with her small clutch and slipped her free hand into the crook of his arm.

The drive to the restaurant was quiet. Not the suffocating silence of their first drive weeks before, but the comfortable sort between two people happy simply to be in each other's company.

Don't get too comfy. This is a temp job. Kenna scowled.

"Is there a problem?" Lucius had been thoroughly enjoying watching her. From the way she was continually tucking the errant curl behind her ear, he knew he unnerved her. Now, an unpleasant thought crossing her expressive face interrupted his pleasure.

Kenna fumbled for a reply and settled for a mundane complaint over the truth that he was on the brink of breaching her defenses. "Just typical traffic. Shouldn't they be home in the burbs on Sunday?"

Their driver today, was not as startlingly handsome as

Captain *Griffin* – *that* was his name. This man had skin the color of the dark Belgian chocolates she'd gifted herself on Valentine's Day. Like Lucius and everyone around him, Kenna thought, he had the same bearing, equally at ease kissing you or killing you.

"I can move us along, Lucius." His voice was as dark and rich as the chocolates. Kenna wondered if she was mistaken about the nature of his connection to the Colonel since he'd used his name instead of his rank.

She was embarrassed by her juvenile frustrations, even if they were manufactured, and a bit thrilled at the prospect of having traffic moved out of the way on her whim. Lucius' mouth turned up as he read her expression. "Well?" The decision was hers.

"Thank you. I can be patient for another block or two."

"Four." The driver now turned fully around and raised an inquiring eyebrow to get direction. "Lucius?"

"The lady says she can wait, Mac."

With a nod, "Mac" turned back toward the street. Before she realized what she was doing, Kenna had popped her head over the front seat at his shoulder. "If you wanted to, how exactly would you move this mess along?"

Mac's bright white grin spread the width of his face. "I knew I was gonna like you." He grabbed her fingers, planted a hard kiss on them and didn't wait for Kenna to sit back or even glance at Lucius for the green light. He punched forward and over two lanes. His skill in escape and evasion turned traffic signals into suggestions not necessities. Cabs and cars alike honked, drivers cursed, but everyone moved out of the way.

Lucius was ready when the jerky stop and start jostled Kenna back into the seat. Strong hands clamped around her waist and pulled her safely back and much closer than she had been. He smiled.

She laughed. "You did that on purpose."

"Would that I had that much control over the universe, I would have done it sooner, I think."

"You think so?" she lowered her chin and looked up at him with arched, doubtful brows.

The arms still around her tightened. "Indeed."

"Colonel, are you flirting with me?" She cooed, and her real accent was thicker than she usually allowed. Lucius liked it. A lot.

He leaned over, lips close to her ear, hoping for a repeat response of their first meeting and got it. She shivered and stilled in anticipation before he spoke. "Is it working?"

The car stopped abruptly in the middle of the street in front of the restaurant to more honking and fist shaking. Kenna smiled. "I think Mac wins this flirting round." The door opened, and she took Mac's large, meaty hand to climb out. "You're a doll!"

He winked and flashed her another of his dazzling smiles. "Anytime."

———

"Oh, my god! That car nearly hit a cab!" someone by the windows yelled, obviously a tourist. The natives simply raised the volume on their conversations to be heard over the horns and yelling.

"Probably Kenna Duck Dodgering through traffic." Candace craned her head around just in case it was an actual incident.

"You taught her that move," Frankie said.

"Me? That is all you, cutting between cars without getting splashed or swiped and without breaking a heel." Candace mimicked Frankie's Upper East Side intonation. "Pedestrians win. Just smile and wave."

Kenna burst through the doors of Marco's, panting when she reached their table. "He's here. Be nice."

"Be nice?" They asked in unison. Kenna made a frantic pointing gesture at her chest, contorted her face in a gruesome, comical smile. Their curious, pretty faces peered around her to see the crowd parting for Lucius Chaerea.

"I'll be right back," she said as she dashed off before introductions, leaving Frankie and Candace staring up at Lucius.

"Ladies." He offered a slight nod and took the seat intended for Kenna. "Forgive my intrusion, I won't stay long. Coffee." He shot the order over his shoulder to the waiter who had appeared instantly. "I thought as The Accomplices and Research Team we should meet," he said, his tone clearly indicating that was the title he'd given them. He offered his hand. "Lucius Chaerea."

They looked at each other and shared a non-verbal agreement to "be nice." Frankie took the offering first. "A pleasure, Colonel," she said, using Kenna's preferred moniker. "Frankie Winslow."

"Miss Fisher." Lucius smiled at Candace.

"I think you give us too much credit as a research team, Mr. Chaerea. There isn't much to search, but you know that, of course."

Lucius leaned back as the waiter set the coffee in front of him. Every move was smooth and deliberate as he crossed his legs, lifted the cup and smiled over the rim before sipping. "Of course. What would you like to know?"

"Isn't this a conversation you should be having with Kenna?" Frankie asked.

"It is. And I intend to and many more. However, my intentions matter little when faced with such lovely and devoted guardians. May I suggest we hurry. I doubt her call of nature is genuine or lengthy enough to allow for small talk."

"Out of curiosity, Mr. Chaerea," Candace said. "Why hand-delivered notes? Why not call her or text her or use email?"

"Call it a touch of romance."

That was the correct answer. The one Kenna wanted and the one they wanted for her, but, as they fully absorbed the implications of the question, Frankie and Candace leaned closer.

"Or, it could mean you don't want her replying or hitting 'call back' where someone else might see or hear." Frankie watched the granite veil drop over his features.

"Are you married or living a double life, Lucius?" Candace struck, surprising him by dropping the "Mr. Chaerea."

"You know I'm widowed." Their silken wall of protection made him want their approval all the more and raised his opinion of Kenna. He knew what kind of woman inspired such loyalty. "My communications served two purposes. First and foremost, I thought she would like them. Second, I could ensure consistent delivery. Something not always possible with travel. My intentions toward Kenna include neither secrecy nor deception. She is ... a light." This last he spoke low, reverently, and his face brightened when he saw Kenna approach.

"Sorry, there was a line. Didn't you order croissants?" She looked at the foodless table like a child opening a gift of socks for her birthday.

Lucius stood. "I believe your breakfast approaches. And I must leave you for now. Miss Fisher, Miss Winslow, it has been a pleasure." He cupped Kenna's cheek and kissed the opposite one. "I will call you about our dinner."

Under the table, Candace nudged Frankie with her toe and mouthed "museum" while not too subtly jerking her head towards Lucius.

"Ken likes to go to the museum on Sunday afternoons," Frankie blurted.

Kenna's head swung around at the lie. What she liked was to lie around reading trashy vampire romances, watching old movies and ordering Mr. Pings before falling asleep by ten. That was before Lucius.

"Well, *that* was subtle," she drawled. "Luc?" The saccharine sweet, singsong way she drew out his name fooled no one. "Would you like to join me?"

He smiled appreciatively over the top of her head. "I'm nothing if not opportunistic and don't wish to intrude further on your brunch." *Or deny the three of you time to thoroughly discuss me.* "Shall I return after, or would you prefer to meet there?"

"Meet." "Return." "Come back." Kenna, Frankie and Candace spoke in unison.

Kenna smiled over her shoulder, only to be met with pastry-filled grins from the table. "I've got this, thank you."

"No problem," Frankie muffled around a mouthful.

When she looked up, Lucius was grinning too. "You look like the Cheshire cat." Kenna tried to sound irritated at all three of them. "The Met at two. We'll find out what you like."

"Until two, then. Ladies." He winked and was gone.

Kenna plopped into her chair. "The hell? Frank, are you blushing?"

Candace burst out laughing at them both. She pointed her fork at Kenna and said, "Hope you shaved your legs this morning."

"I didn't, thank God. He's great, and I'd like to get some quality time in before I ruin it with sex."

"A little fuzz never ruined hot monkey sex." Frankie wiggled her brows.

"Your Colonel looks like he could do hot monkey sex. An extended session, in fact," Candace mused as she slathered jam on her croissant.

"Here, Cheeta. Have a banana," Frankie laughed.

"*Stop* saying hot monkey sex!" The nearby tables went dead quiet. Kenna rubbed her face with both hands.

"Stop that." Candace yanked one hand away. "You'll smudge your make-up."

"What are you so worried about? He *likes* you," Frankie said. "Sally-Field-at-the-Oscars likes you. Sex with him won't ruin anything but your lipstick and hair."

"He might turn gay ... or ... or ... or start crying because he's decided to go back to his wife. Or?" Kenna shuddered and swallowed the bile in her throat as she contemplated the dire possibilities. "Never mind."

Candace grabbed the seat of her chair and turned to face her friend. "First, you don't have the magic wand to turn anyone gay, and that waiter slash actor you dated? The only thing straight about him was his teeth."

"They were beautiful teeth," Kenna said with a sigh.

"Second," it was Frankie's turn. "You knew the *po*-lice man was a temp anyway. He was cute, carried a gun and had a hero complex. Boxes one, two, and three, check check check. It was inevitable that he'd go back to his wife." Frankie paused and said, "Although the crying was excessive. And *Or* is history. So, don't be doomed to repeat it."

"Did you just come up with that?" Candace nudged Frankie's elbow. "I like it."

"Nah, it's been cooking. Did it sound profound?"

"We need drinks," Kenna said, and three arms shot in the air to signal their favorite tall, dark and he-should-be-an-underwear-model bartender.

———

WITH A BOTTOMLESS CUP OF COFFEE, three mimosas and

ninety minutes of girl time under her belt, Kenna squinted into the afternoon sun as she and her two friends left the restaurant.

"The clouds cleared." She covered her eyes.

"It's a good omen," Frankie said. "Go look at pretty pictures with your pretty man."

"He's not pretty." Kenna subtly scanned the line of cars and cabs looking for Lucius' car even though she'd said she'd meet him at the museum. A small part of her half-expected, half-wanted, to see him there on his white horse or black or whatever-the-hell that car was.

Candace looped her arm through Kenna's. "No, but he thinks *you* are, and that's all that matters. Stop looking for his car. You told him to meet you, silly girl."

"Who said I was looking?" Two sets of eyes rolled. "So, shoot me. I was lookin'." They hugged, and broke like a team huddle for subway stops.

"What are the odds, do you suppose, she buys a disposable and shaves in a sink?" Candace asked Frankie.

"Fifty-fifty." Frankie laughed.

CHAPTER TWENTY-SEVEN

Kenna hailed a cab outside the subway exit.

"Lady, it's two miles up Fifth," groused the cabbie who was not particularly interested in such a small fare.

"Yeah, and I have a date in five minutes. Pleeeease. I tip better without having to beg. Four minutes."

Lucius was leaning against the columns flanking the Met's main entrance into the Great Hall. She almost didn't recognize him. Gone was the perfectly tailored suit with distractingly perfect pocket square. He wore a silver-gray dress shirt with the faintest pinstripe and well-worn jeans beneath a three-quarter length coat that only accentuated his long, lean legs. The collar was open just enough for her to get a peek at the corded muscles of his neck, with its soft buttery hollow and a hint of dark curls. Something told her it was deliciously soft. *Stop that!*

Lucius didn't rush to meet her. He too was taking inventory, or at least a closer one than he'd permitted himself during mass. He wasn't sure he liked the loose-flowing style of maxi dresses with the sometimes matronly shapes or oddly misplaced designs. As Kenna walked toward him, his opinion was rapidly changing. The sunshine yellow was a delightful contrast to the formal black cocktail dress from the Henneby Gala or soft colors he'd seen her in before. The high waist accentuated breasts he knew would fit perfectly in his hands, and the cropped black leather jacket hinted at an edginess he intended to explore further.

Smiling when she reached him, she pointed at the guide pamphlet in his hand. "Anything special you want to see?"

He leveled his eyes on her. The corner of his mouth twitched, and he swallowed hard.

Kenna blushed and unnecessarily adjusted her jacket and the folds of her dress. "It's actually been a while," she managed to say, and the double entendre available in her statement made her begin to sweat. She refused to look up at him now. "Let's see what's in the new collections guide," she rushed to add.

"As you wish." He held the door for her to pass.

Kenna froze and looked up. "*The Princess Bride?*"

"Is that a painting?"

"Never mind," she said and visibly shook herself. "I forget not everyone speaks in movie quotes."

"And you do?"

"Not as much as I like to pretend I do. I usually remember the perfect quote three days later. The crap that flies out of my mouth in the moment is never so clever."

"I'll reserve my judgment on that." He spoke just at her ear. Not familiarly close, they were in public, but enough to remind her of the sensation of his whisper on her skin.

Kenna cleared her throat, twice. "Let's do The Director's Tour. It covers the high points, and we can see most of the collections, if we want. You want the audio guide?"

"That rather defeats the purpose of getting to know one another, doesn't it?"

"Rather keeps me from spouting off about pretentious crap too," she muttered, but not quietly enough.

He laughed. "I think I can handle a spout or two."

He bought their tickets, and they checked their coats. Kenna hesitated, but figured shivering a bit was better than sweating profusely in the jacket. She led the way through Egypt and the Americas. Where she knew the art, Lucius knew the history. The symbiotic conversation took on a rhythm of its own. In the Armory, she didn't need to read wall plaques. Lucius described the military and practical purpose for all the artifacts and provided battle stories to illustrate.

"And I thought I would be the docent today," Kenna said, smiling.

"Are you impressed?" he asked.

"Are you trying?"

"Oh, indeed." He gave an exaggerated bow and offered his arm. A chivalric gesture made in front of a knight's shining armor.

She took his arm, and they strolled through European and Medieval statues. As they passed a scroll, she spoke as if the writing had just reminded her of something. "Thank you for writing to me. I think it was my very first real letter."

"My pleasure," he said as he placed his free hand over hers in the crook of his arm. "And the notes?"

"Your quotes were beautiful." She tried to sound casual. They had all been about one subject, kissing, and she was not opening that conversational floodgate. "I like reading in your voice better, though." *Oh yeah, that's SO much safer than talking about kissing.*

He stopped in front of a long tapestry and looked down at her. She wasn't lying to him. His stream-of-consciousness letter about his breakfast, his parents and the tree outside his childhood bedroom window had been her favorite. He recalled the feeling that had overwhelmed him when he wrote to her from his remote location. The need to pour himself onto the page and into her mind, if he failed to return and be a wisp of a memory for her, had been urgent. He was doing it now. As much as he was memorizing every pale, stray curl around her face, the exact emerald green of her eyes, the sweet, tender curve of her neck, he was willing his face, his scent, his touch into her consciousness.

Kenna stood mesmerized. The moment lasted less than a minute, but it felt like time had stopped. She could have sworn she was floating, her feet didn't touch the floor. Her eyes flickered between his, trying to read him, to see into the green-gold depths. "What is that look?" she asked, and it was gone.

"Tea?" He looked away, down the gallery, toward the Petrie Court Café entrance.

"Uhm, sure. We just have one more gallery to see."

As they sat by the windows with steaming pots of tea before them, a silence fell between them. Kenna wondered what he was thinking. *Is he bored? Is the silence good or bad?*

"You don't really come here on Sundays." It was not a question.

Kenna shrugged, appreciating the not so subtle help from her friends. "I used to with my Dad. Every Sunday we'd do a different gallery or collection. I think he was bored to tears, but I loved it, so he brought me."

"Why have you stopped?" He leaned forward, genuinely interested.

"He died right before I started college." Kenna sipped to force down the lump in her throat. She looked out the window.

"I am sorry." Lucius' gut knotted for her and at himself for opening a delicate wound.

"Thank you, but it was a long time ago." She tried to smile to ease the crease between his brows.

"I was on my first deployment when my Papa was diagnosed with lung cancer. He was never a smoker." Lucius smiled nostalgically. "Save the occasional celebratory cigar, he confessed to my mother. She always knew." He drew a slow deep, deliberate breath. Kenna could almost see the words forming in his mind before he spoke and knew this was Lucius' norm. "They thought it was pneumonia. Within a month of his diagnosis, he was gone."

"You didn't get to see him?" In her gut, she already knew the answer.

"War is," he paused again, "chaotic to say the least."

She touched his arm. "Were you hurt? Was that why you couldn't go home?" Her face was drawn, part of her hoping she could change the outcome in the retelling.

Lucius took her hand, putting the horrors of where and why he was unable to be at his father's deathbed out of his mind. "Not that time. The mission would have been irrevocably compromised, and months of preparation lost, were any one of us to be pulled out. Command opted to inform me after completion."

"Oh, Luc. I'm so sorry." Her voice cracked. Her pain for him was fresh, and the sincerity of her sympathy moved him more than he expected.

"They were right to do so." He kissed her fingers. "We got the bad guys." He turned her hand over and gently touched the scar on her palm. "And what battle were you in?" he asked playfully.

She slowly balled her fist and pulled it away. "Just an accident. Wrong place, wrong time."

A dark shadow passed over his features. This was no delicate wound he'd touched, nor was it, he feared, accidental.

Kenna did a one-eighty, mentally and physically. "Let's save

Oceania and Modern Art for another day. It's beautiful out. I'd like a walk in the park."

"Last call, is it?" he asked.

"Well, no. I just," she stammered to silence. "What would you like to do?"

"You," he pinned her with a look, "promised me dinner. This was an added pleasure."

Kenna squinted, giving him a practiced side-eye once over. "I think you're cheating."

"I am shameless, but in this, guiltless." Lucius raised his chin and his voice, adopting an excellent generic American accent. "Luc, I will have dinner with you." He quoted her exactly, including pause and inflection.

"Nathan's from a cart?" Kenna grinned.

"No." Lucius stood and held her chair. "I know where we can have a lovely carbonara."

They took their time meandering back through European statues and Medieval art to the Great Hall.

"Do you have a favorite in all this?" Lucius asked with a gesture that encompassed the entirety of the museum.

Kenna tilted her head in thought as he helped her into her jacket. "Honestly, it changes all the time. I love the religious Renaissance and see something new every time I look at a Van Gogh. What about you? Anything?" While he'd known history, she hadn't noted any particular affinity for style, artist or period.

"I've seen the Sistine Chapel, the Mona Lisa, the Fountains of Rome." He opened his hands almost apologetically. "I admire and appreciate the skill and dedication required, but I have never been lost in the brush strokes."

"It's okay, Colonel," she said, smiling, "not everyone is." Lucius made a "humph" sound of surprise and curiosity. "What?" she asked.

He was looking through the gift shop window. "I like that one."

"Which one?" There were a dozen reproduction posters, and *objets d'art* on display. She chuckled. "Five hundred paintings and you like something in the gift shop?"

"I do. That one. With the gold leaf and red."

Kenna glared at him. Irritation rolled off her. He was pointing through the window display past the souvenir mugs, stuffed Sphinxes and t-shirts to a poster on the back wall from the previous season's special showing of a Gustav Klimt collection. Klimt's *The Kiss*. The elephant in her room bellowed.

"Fine!" she snapped. Turning to face him, her back ramrod straight, fists in tight balls at her side. "Let's get this done. Your little notes did the job. Just kiss me and get it over with." Kenna tilted her chin up and closed her eyes tight. Her lips a thin rock-hard line.

Passersby stopped and stared at Lucius. The rushing noise of blood in her ears drowned out the beehive hum of patrons in the vast entry. Gently, Lucius placed his hands on her shoulders. Then drew them up to glide over her neck, her pulse leapt under his fingertips. He felt her lean towards him. He lowered his lips to her forehead. "Soon," he said against her cool skin.

CHAPTER TWENTY-EIGHT

Kenna opened her eyes. She was standing alone in the center of the Great Hall. People were staring, a few smiling sympathetically. She thought she heard a teen mutter "Burn!" as he passed. It took her the longest thirty seconds of her life to register what had happened. His hands on her shoulders, on her neck. His body so close she could feel the heat coming off him. Then ... nothing. No soft yet firm lips on hers. No arms closing around her to pull her against his lean body. No rush of adrenaline or delicious pooling of heat.

She looked around, as if some tour guide were about to appear and explain the tableau. She saw Lucius holding a door open, studying the tiles beneath his feet. In one motion, Kenna cocked her head, popped her hip, sucked her teeth and tapped her foot. "Soon?" she said to no one and walked to the open door.

As he waited, Lucius began, for the first time in more years than he could remember, to doubt his instinct. *Is she angry? I should have kissed her. Hell, I should have kissed her the first night I saw her.*

Passing him, she dipped her head to make sure she made full eye contact. "Soon?"

"Soon," Lucius replied.

"Soon, he says." She strode out the door. Sashayed, more accurately, talking to no one and everyone. "Soon. I may not be offering again. *Colonel.*"

Lucius cleared his throat to cover the grin he knew she would not find amusing, and followed her around the Met to a path through Central Park. As he walked half a step behind her, it occurred to him how often his reaction to her was filled with humor and unguarded.

Arms crossed, Kenna maintained a cool air and brisk pace, too confused to even pinpoint her true feelings. She wasn't really angry or embarrassed. In fact, she'd liked the tender forehead kiss and his minor display of contrition for the gawkers.

"An apology would be good right about now," she snapped and cringed at the bitchy tone.

"If you wish, I fully accept," Lucius drolled.

Kenna spun, teetering, only to be caught around the waist and held tight against him. Gaping like a fish, she looked up to see his broad smile. She imagined this was the face his mother had seen when little Lucius presented her with a frog, and laughed at herself.

"You're right. It annoys me, but you're right. I was rude and … well, you fluster me!" She wriggled to loosen his now unnecessary hold. "I'm not going to fall."

"Just making certain." He slipped his arms away, but grasped her hands in his and brought her fingers to his lips. "Where would you like to walk?"

Anywhere, Kenna thought. It was so easy, talking to this man. She'd thought about the night they met more times than she would ever be able to count. How, knowing he'd made her as a crasher, she'd never felt he meant to intimidate her. Quite the opposite. She'd felt safe and protected when they danced. She'd played the meeting at Wallace Henneby's office over and over in her mind. Lucius had never revealed her secret.

She thought about the way he'd knelt beside her during mass, the way he'd shared the pain of losing a parent without pity; his ability to tease her, how he refused to be manipulated by her. Never did he embarrass her or make her feel he was testing her. Kenna found it hard not to like him intensely. Who was she kidding, she'd liked him from the first smile.

"Kenna?" Lucius pushed a stray curl behind her ear. God, he'd wanted to do that for weeks and was not disappointed as the loose strand wrapped around his fingers before he pulled his hand away.

"Huh?" She blinked. "Sorry. I drifted."

"Someplace nice?"

Kenna shrugged and gave him a soft smile. "Not terrible. What did you ask me? Oh yeah, walk." She looked around to find her bearings. "Listen, Colonel." Lucius leaned back from her, reading her tone, body language, averted eyes, and frowned in anticipation of the brush off. Reading him too, Kenna squeezed his hand. "I'm not trying to weasel out of dinner or our afternoon. It's just, I'm not really prepared for a dinner out." For a *real* date, she would want to soak and scrub, primp and polish. Put on her favorite perfume and find the red lip gloss she'd lost New Year's Eve.

They were nearing the south entrance before he spoke. "Might I offer a suggestion?"

"I'm listening."

Without breaking stride or looking down, he laid out his alternative. He'd felt more comfortable negotiating a hostage release in Somalia. Her skeptical side-look was akin to live fire. He made it short and sweet.

Kenna started to protest. If he noticed, he didn't pause, just kept walking and talking, as calm as if he were giving her his plans for a haircut. She wondered how often he'd used this steady delivery to get his way. He was quite convincing. When he had finished, he stopped and looked down at her. Kenna's breath caught. The perpetual mask was gone. Lucius was unguarded and was looking at her with the hope of a child asking another to come outside to play.

"If I agree, there is one caveat."

"Ahh, the counter," he said, eyes flashing with the thrill of it.

"Not quite. You let me buy next time. I don't cook," she said.

Lucius' mouth twitched, pleased she was anticipating more time with him. "Agreed. Any other addenda?"

"No, but I reserve the right to add as we go."

CHAPTER TWENTY-NINE

K enna thumped her head against the window when they turned onto Embassy Row. *This is not happening.* Mac grinned at Lucius in the rearview mirror. She breathed easier when they turned again down a connecting street to slightly more modest homes. The gated entrance and underground parking earned Lucius a puzzled look, letting him know she would eventually ask about the need for so much security.

The question came soon enough. They stepped off the elevator onto a second-floor landing and Lucius leaned over the bannister to speak to yet another well-armed man below.

"Rainsborough, Miss Campbell will be my guest for dinner tonight. You are free to go. I will drive her home."

Kenna peeked around Lucius. The man he called Rainsborough was stern-faced, but so handsome she stared. *Good grief, was that a job requirement around here?* A dark auburn goatee accented a firm mouth and lean features. When Lucius spoke her name, Rainsborough's eyes had shifted suddenly to her. Kenna flinched. Where Mac had warm chocolate pools, and Mr. – *Captain* – Griffin's green had been soulful, there was nothing inviting in Rainsborough's dark depths. Perhaps it was the combination of his demeanor, shoulder holster, weapon and military bearing, but Kenna stepped back, putting Lucius between herself and this man.

"Yes, Colonel," was the low reply. Kenna stole a final glance over her shoulder and could see the top of his head. He was still standing in the same spot. She knew he wouldn't move until Lucius' residence door closed, and they were safe inside.

"He's pleasant. When does his shift end exactly?" Kenna whispered.

Lucius smiled over his shoulder and answered, "About half an hour ago."

Kenna slowed her steps. "Why is he here?"

"I had not dismissed him." He added, "His personal convictions, not conditions of service."

"What are the conditions of service?" she asked.

"Don't let me die." He laughed at her stunned expression.

"Good lord! What do you do?"

He only winked. "Would you like a tour?"

She gave the room and uninterested once over. It was generic male living space. Big on audiovisual, small on personality. "Who's your designer?" Kenna mentally kicked back disappointed judgment. Not everyone needed or hacked out a personal space the way she'd done.

"I couldn't say. The home was furnished. Only my study and bedroom contain my personal belongings."

Kenna swallowed hard and pretended the whisper of invitation wasn't ringing in her ears. "It's very nice. Masculine."

"Thank you." Lucius extended one hand to her and gestured towards the rooms off the open living-kitchen area. "Come, I'll show you where I live."

Her hand was small and soft in his. Although his nails were immaculate, there were callouses on his palms and some of his fingers. She rubbed her thumb along the rough patch on one of his, but decided not to ask him where he got it, yet.

Kenna's heart pounded as they walked down a dim hall. The double doors at the end could only be the master suite. While part of her was screaming and running for the exit, her hand gripped his tighter. Lucius smiled and turned into his office. Late afternoon sun filtered rose-colored light through the balcony door window panes.

She studied the brilliantly woven rug as she crossed to the wall of bookshelves. The plush wool under her feet told her of its authenticity. "You are going to ruin this if you don't stop pacing," she cautioned. "The binding edge has been replaced once."

"My faults are many." He sat at his desk, a massive piece with intricate inlaid wood designs, while she looked around the room.

Kenna examined his books, letting her fingers lightly dance over the tomes, rows of literary classics she suspected may have been read, but not here and not these pristine reproductions. She paused at a worn copy of Sun Tzu's *The Art of War*, casually tucked amidst the Tom Clancys with their creased bindings and dog-eared pages. She raised a brow as she looked over her shoulder to find him watching her. A piece of his puzzle slipped into place.

Lucius shrugged in reply. Watching her move did for him what watching fish in an aquarium did for others. The sway of her dress, the tilt of her head, a furrowed brow or amused smile created a soothing rhythm of motion in his sanctuary.

Finally, she turned, her hands hidden, clenched behind her. He didn't need to see proof she was anxious.

"Why didn't you kiss me? Too public?" This last was more of an issued challenge than a question.

Lucius took a long, deep breath and let it out, studying her before answering. Looking down, he straightened the already squared crystal ashtray on his desk. "Kissing you would be akin to drinking salt water."

"Make you crazy?" she teased.

He looked up, piercing her with his stare. "A thirst never satisfied. Driven mad with want for more."

"Oh," she whispered. "Will you ever kiss me? A real one?"

His long elegant fingers touched his lips. Kenna could almost feel them dancing over her skin.

"I will," he promised.

"Good," she said, trying to sound as matter-of-fact as he. She spun back to the engrossing contents of his shelves, this time noticing the collections. Antique coins, bullets, small firearms, miniature metal cars in shadowboxes.

"How did you get me the notes?" she asked, changing the subject.

"You remember Captain Griffin."

"Why him? I mean, why not just put a stamp on the damn things? I got the impression he was never far from you." *And not overly fond of me either.*

Lucius inhaled another deep breath. He was not naturally a liar so much as he had a natural gift for revealing nothing or only as much as he intended. "Many reasons. Most importantly, I trust him. With my life, when necessary." And with yours, went unspoken. He dared not tell her she couldn't know where he'd been nor could he risk anyone discovering her or his attachment to her.

"With your life? Can he dodge bullets?"

"Not quite. He *is* one of the best marksmen I know and exceedingly proficient in hand to hand combat."

"Trusted is a short list for you, I imagine." The fact that he'd revealed two people he trusted with his life in a matter of minutes niggled at the back of her mind.

"Indeed, it is."

"One of the best, hmm?" She looked back at him from where she stood perusing the contents of a curio cabinet, this one protecting rare and exotic knives, and he nodded. "In my experience, the Captain Griffins or unpleasant Rainsboroughs of the world don't simply give their loyalty to rank, *Colonel*," she said, putting emphasis on the title. "How's *your* aim?"

"Sufficient unto the day," he answered. His voice was quiet, cautionary.

"No," she said softly, gently and with a touch of pity. "You made your bones. And then some."

Lucius lowered his gaze to adjust a rolled cuff. When he raised his eyes to her again, the granite veil was back in place. It wasn't a look of subterfuge – it was ... blank. "I do not like to consider myself a man of violence."

Kenna crossed the room to him and leaned a hip on the desk.

"You just lied to me." It was his turn to raise his brows, either in amusement or as a challenge for her to continue. Kenna took the dare. "I may not be a good poker player, Colonel, but I can spot a tell."

"I don't lie."

"Everybody lies. Omission is a lie. Concealment is a lie. You and violence are intimate friends." She picked up a heavy miniature hound. "Violence. Pain? Fear? Chaos, maybe?" she mused, then set the paperweight deliberately out of place on the immaculate desk. She suppressed the shudder running through her. The implication of her speculations thrilled and terrified her. The muscle in his jaw ticked. "That would certainly explain the order. Control." His mouth moved with a hint of a smile at her taunt.

He leaned back in the chair, palms up and parted his knees. An invitation she accepted and slid onto his lap in one fluid motion, as if they'd danced this dance hundreds of times. Kenna laid her hand over his heart, the steady thump pulsing through her fingers to the deepest part of her. Lucius' hand rested on the curve of her hip.

Want sizzled through her. She knew it wasn't simply his kiss she craved or her unfulfilled desires. She'd felt it before – in the museum, in his car, the night they met. The instinctive pull to ease her aching loneliness with him, in him. Kenna leaned forward and brushed her lips over his. She stood on the cliff's edge, unable to alter the inevitable, desperate to jump into the abyss.

"Do you ever lose control, Colonel?" she whispered as her breath mingled with his and her voice shook. The vows she'd made once never to do so, never to lose herself or attach her happiness to another, seemed vague and unfamiliar as his steely arm closed around her waist. She wanted him to give in to the passion or, at least, to return the rolling need churning in her and take her to that elusive place where bliss replaced her fears and memories.

She'd kissed first. She'd asked the question. He was freed of constraints. Lucius tilted her chin up. His hazel, hawk eyes locked with hers. "Never," he whispered back. His kiss leisurely, he coaxed her lips apart to delve into the sweet warmth of her mouth. His body responded violently, proving the lie in his denial.

The emptiness she'd patched with friends and faith and art and denial broke open. Kenna knew sexual attraction. She knew what it was like to want and be wanted, but this was different. This was more. She was too afraid to try and name it. Too certain of its eventual end. Too starved for it to resist. Greedy and selfish, she let the emptiness flow out of her into him and filled the space with Lucius.

CHAPTER THIRTY

Sunshine! She tasted of sunshine and honey and the sweet fruits he'd picked from the vine as a child. With her in his arms, Lucius could feel the Tuscan sun on his face. The world was painted in golden light again. Gone were the shadows he'd come to know, to embrace and to master. Her trembling drew a low, deep moan from him. Then, suddenly, he tasted salt water, tears. He cupped her face, jerking himself back to search her face.

"No." Kenna buried her head in his shoulder. She kissed his neck, along the hard, strong angle of his jaw back to his open, astonished mouth. "Please." She kissed his mouth over and over, trying to soften the hard set of concern in his lips. "Please don't ask me. Just kiss me. Don't stop. Please, Lucius. Please."

He would ask her later he promised himself, but, for now, he slid his fingers into her fine mass of curls and feasted on her kiss.

Any intentions – even fleeting ones – of restraint, patience or first date propriety were lost in the churning sea of want. There was no sense in pretending the desire had done anything but grow since that first fateful night. Under different circumstances, it may have been sated then. How different would these last weeks have been? Or perhaps not have been?

A gentle tug on her hair bared her neck to him. Lucius' warm breath, teeth and tongue on her skin sent a shiver through her, and he smiled. Feeling the grin, she pulled back to look at him. Her eyes were still moist, but no longer filled with sorrowful relief. There was more. Desire set aflame, he would later recall.

Her slender hands cupped his face. "Your beard is softer than I thought it would be." She continued to pet his cheek as if counting every gray hair sprinkled among the black.

Lucius sat motionless, allowing her to trace the line of his jaw first with her fingers, then her lips, then across his forehead and down the knife's edge of his nose. Soon enough, her gaze dropped to the column of his neck and the open collar of his shirt. Her shiver now a constant tremble on his lap. He chuckled when she licked her lips, but tipped his head back and got a jolt of his own when her teeth scraped against his skin.

"Kenna," he growled, the warning and restraint thick in his voice.

He rejoiced when she laughed at this newfound power, nipped at him again, a kitten playing with a lion, and rewarded her with another feral noise. His instincts told him that, with other men, she'd never been relaxed. His prickly Kenna would always be on edge with intimacy. Her ease with him seemed to delight her. As it did him. She'd been bold enough to kiss him, to demand he kiss her back. She'd bravely revealed her desire for him. Kenna, burst out laughing.

He found it infectious and laughed too, deep and guttural. "Share the joke?" he asked.

"Oh, God, no!" Kenna howled and reddened. The more she tried to stop, the harder she laughed. Finally she managed, "Candace. Frankie. Monkeys. You don't want to know."

"Well, this is a turn of events." Lucius splayed his hands on her hips. Those nimble fingers moved subtly, each telegraphing a promise of pleasure.

"Why? They say this is supposed to be fun." There was an undercurrent of bitterness to her jest. "Of course, *they* is probably some guy living in his mother's basement slamming Rockstar and eating Hot Pockets all day."

Lucius rose, gently forcing her to her feet and out of that rabbit hole. "Interesting as these visuals are, come with me." Taking her hand, he nibbled her fingertips. "There is a time for desktop liaisons, but not for our first."

Kenna suddenly flushed and dipped her chin. He caught it between his thumb and forefinger, lifting her onto tiptoes before covering her mouth with his. His patience at an end, he led her from the study and down the hall to the master suite.

"Dragging me off to the proverbial dragon's lair?"

Lucius stopped and whirled on her. His features were stern. Kenna blinked. "Did I offend –." He tried, but she was so adorable he couldn't suppress the tug of a smile beneath his beard. He bent and hefted her onto his shoulder. She let out a "whoop!" and peals of laughter echoed off the wood paneled walls.

A playful smack on her backside and, "Quiet back there," only made her laugh more. In twenty feet, he set her lush and breathless body upright in his bedroom.

Lucius sat on the edge of his bed, and caged her between his lean thighs. When Kenna seemed to be fighting her hair away from her face, he tenderly tucked the electrified strands into place. She stopped trying and stilled, giving him his turn. Her mane tamed, he traced his fingers down the sides of her neck, along the delicate ridges of her collar bones, over her shoulders, turning his long elegant fingers to brush the backs of them against the sides of her breasts and finally coming to rest on her hips.

"I didn't shave my legs," Kenna confessed.

Lucius leaned down and reached under the hem of her dress, gliding his hands upwards from calf to thigh over peach fuzz, bunching the material at her hips. "I'll survive."

"Not wearing sexy panties either," she said, a trace of nerves in her voice. "I didn't set out this morning to seduce anyone."

Lucius leaned back on his elbows. The swell behind his zipper was obvious. He cared little about clothing soon to be on the floor. "Show me."

"What?"

He grinned and gestured with two fingers. "Show me these alleged non-sexy underthings." A part of him wondered if she would disrobe for him or become reserved and shy.

Kenna narrowed her eyes, then stepped away from the bed so he could see her from head to toe. A gauntlet had been thrown, and she had to answer. "You'll have to imagine the music, I suppose. Maybe a little saxophone bitch note?" She grinned and tugged the smocked top of her dress, pulling it down to reveal a strapless lemon yellow bra that perfectly accentuated her full breasts. Lucius shifted appreciatively.

Showing her new-found freedom and confidence, Kenna did an exaggerated shimmy to get the elasticized top over the curve of her hips, finally dropping the whole thing into a puddle on the floor.

Pale pink, cotton briefs with tiny green flowers. Luc sucked his teeth, raking his eyes over her. "Pink. I believe a redefinition of sexy is in order."

She smiled brightly and pirouetted. Gasping to find him standing close to her when she completed the spin. "Your turn?" she asked, her voice shaky.

"No."

The kiss came fast, hard and possessive. Kenna gripped the front of his shirt while his hands roamed over her. A flick of the wrist sent her bra to the floor. Lucius slid his hands into the waistband of her tighty pinkies, pulled her against him and kneaded her ass, practically lifting her off the floor. A few tugs, then another shimmy and kick sent the panties flying.

Kenna slipped out of his grasp and moved to mimic his reclined position and cool demeanor on the bed. She crossed her legs and smiled up at him, but tiny muscles in her belly quaked and her teeth threatened to chatter with nerves.

"Well, Colonel?"

He laughed. Loud and long. Unbuttoning his shirt for her, he tried to recall the last time he'd laughed until his sides ached, or smiled so freely, or wanted a woman's soul as much as the body laid out before him. He closed the distance and leaned over her, his arms braced on the bed.

"You're not finished," she teased, and trailed a cool finger through the mass of dark curls on his chest.

"Soon." He kissed along her shoulder and neck, making his way to the lush valley between her breasts.

"You keep using that word. I do not think it means what you think it means." Kenna barely managed a husky whisper and sad Inigo Montoya Spanish accent. Her body arched involuntarily to his mouth.

Teeth scraped over a rosy peak. "You keep switching accents." His mouth closed over her nipple and silenced any snappy comeback.

As HIS MOUTH and hands explored her, a part of Kenna knew with miserable certainty this was the beginning of the end. She was determined to soak in every scent, touch and taste of her time with Luc. The inevitable heartbreak might ruin her, but it would be worth it. It already was.

Lucius' fingers reached her inner thigh. Kenna drew in a sharp breath and stilled. He kissed her lips, continuing the lazy circles on her skin. "Problem, love?"

"No," she breathed, shaking her head. Rosy pink flushed her cheeks.

He smiled again and bent to her ear. "I've imagined this. Are you as soft, warm and wet as I've dreamed?" Those long fingers stroked once, then slipped between her silken folds. His head dropped to the bed beside hers. "Sweet Christ, Kenna!"

She loved knowing she tested his considerable control. There was no rush. No early meetings or morning after awkwardness to avoid. She moved in perfect rhythm with his fingers.

"I could be content with this for a very long time," his voice was gruff and strained.

Skilled as his teasing strokes were Kenna was not so content. She slipped her hands inside his open shirt, hungry to touch him as intimately. She kissed his chest and tasted the saltiness of his skin. "Luc?" she asked as she tugged on the waist of his pants. "Can we save the slow seduction for next time?" She blushed at her own impatience and refusal to play coy or innocent with him.

He laughed again. The deep rumble coursed up her spine. A shiver made her move beneath him. Together they shoved his shirt to the floor. He sat on the edge of the bed and kicked off his shoes, then stripped jeans down long lean legs. Kenna's mental mathematics regarding her bubble packet of protection were halted when he opened the bottom drawer of his night stand to retrieve two, yes two, foil packets. She wanted to weep. He didn't even ask if she were on birth control. There was no question of who should be protecting her. He simply did it. As he had the night of Wallace Henneby's party, he had her covered. The feeling, at least in this context, was so foreign to her it must have shown on her transparent face.

Lucius paused and his brow furrowed. "Are you okay?"

"I'm fine." She blinked herself back to the moment and scooted to the center of the bed. "I'm just not used to ..." She hesitated and raked her eyes over him. His body responded enthusiastically. "Never mind." She smiled as she asked, "Can I help?"

He returned her full body once-over, with interest. His heated gaze started with her full, teardrop breasts, then moved to her narrow waist and flared hips, lingering on the small mound of tummy she continually held in.

"You are my deepest fantasy," he breathed and the ache in his shaft spread to his thighs. "But, I think not. I would be unmanned should you touch me at this moment."

It was Kenna's turn to laugh, head back, tresses bouncing. "Why, Colonel," she said, allowing her full Southern accent out. "I do believe that's the sweetest compliment I've ever had."

She was still giggling when his hot tongue licked her. A violent tremor ran through Kenna. He looked up at her flushed face and flicked again, just a tease and taste.

"We will explore this more thoroughly," he promised and rose to cover her body with his.

Kenna trailed her hands up his arms, bending her knees to brush against his flanks. "I don't think I've ever done this in the daylight."

Lucius kissed her tenderly and brushed the wispy hair from her face. "My darling Kenna. You are the light." Dipping his mouth to hers, he pressed his hips forward and buried himself in her warmth.

Her entire body seized around him. Kenna's back arched and she couldn't catch her breath. For the first time in her life, her body responded without consulting her brain. The synchronized ebb and flow of Oscar-worthy Meg Ryanesque moans and hip thrusts in her repertoire were unavailable.

"Luc!" she wailed, almost in panic at the loss of control.

He didn't stop moving, but with a clenched jaw rose up and looked into her eyes. "Kenna, if you're going to stop me, do it now."

Incapable of speech, she locked her legs around his hips, raised her arms over her head to take a white-knuckle grip on the duvet and thrust up.

He needed no further encouragement. The protective urges he'd harbored transformed to possessive hunger. She'd asked to skip the pleasantries of tender seduction, and his body obeyed. Lucius barely heard her sounds of pleasure through his own primitive fog.

Kenna began to shake, biting her lip as her body careened out of control.

"Let me hear you!" he growled. "Let go, Kenna."

CHAPTER THIRTY-ONE

cents of garlic, pancetta and onions were a siren song drawing her out of the warm cocoon of Lucius' bed. Motown drifted like smoke through the centralized sound system. Kenna stretched. Her body felt loose and not entirely familiar. She didn't remember falling asleep. In fact, she was surprised because she never fell asleep. Well, not often and certainly not easily in a man's bed. She was always the one waking first and slipping away. She smiled and pulled the comforter to her chin, inhaling deeply Lucius' warm, lingering scent. Lying there, she could still feel his fingers gliding like a whisper up and down her spine, hear his steady heartbeat and soft murmurs as she'd drifted to sleep. Kenna cringed. What could he possibly be thinking? He'd been cuddling, masterfully so, and she'd fallen asleep. Wasn't that the guy's job? On a long exhale, she recalled the enticing scents from the kitchen and decided that wounded egos didn't cook dinners. Her stomach growled in anticipation.

With the duvet wrapped around her, she headed to the bathroom at the other end of the suite. "Well, hell!" she hissed, discovering after a few minutes of wrestling, she could not drag the whole of the down comforter with her into the toilet. "What's he going to do? See me naked?" Kenna rolled her eyes at herself and dropped the mass on the bedroom floor.

Lucius had watched her sleep. She'd looked so peaceful. Not the reaction he typically engendered in others. When he'd tugged the covers loose to pull over her, Kenna had muttered incoherently, snuggled closer, entwined her legs with his and smiled in her sleep. She'd also clamped a vice around his heart. The mere thought of her leaving with the dawn was suddenly unacceptable.

He'd stifled a laugh when her stomach rumbled. With a stealth usually reserved for much darker intentions, he'd slipped from her arms. He had promised her dinner.

Hearing stirrings from his bedroom, Lucius turned down the volume on his sound system and cocked his head. He politely waited until the water was shut off to take her a glass of wine. Kenna didn't hear him come down the hall or see him lean against the doorframe.

She'd managed to wrap a sheet around herself and stood contemplating the wardrobe selections draped over the arm of a chair. Lucius had placed both her dress and his discarded shirt there. Kenna's stomach growled.

"Oh, *that's* sexy," she said to her belly, sarcasm dripped from her words, and she placed a hand at her middle. "Let's do that for Luc. Next time with feeling."

"Dinner is ready when you are." Kenna jumped at his voice. Lucius smiled and held up the wine glass. "Your stomach and I spoke earlier."

Kenna blushed and held out her hand for the wine. "I'm sure you did."

Lucius crossed the room to bring it to her. He kissed her temple and picked up the gray shirt he'd worn earlier. "Allow me," he said, holding it open for her.

Kenna juggled the wine glass while slipping her arms into the shirt sleeves and maintaining a grip on the cover around her. Lucius suppressed a smile and studiously buttoned the front placket without brushing his fingers across her breasts. Tempted as he was, he knew that would lead back to the bed, if he were lucky, and Kenna was hungry. He planned a long night in his bed to succumb to temptations.

She let the sheets fall around her feet and looked up through her lashes. Maybe she wasn't so hungry after all. Her stomach quietly tightened, threatening to make its objections to that thought very public. Kenna gulped the wine hoping to pacify one hunger at a time.

Lucius' shirt covered her to mid-thigh. He didn't offer her the pink panties, but took her empty glass and guided her from the bedroom into the openness of his living quarters. A marble-topped island housing a wine vault on one end and a prep sink at the other filled the center of his kitchen. The small commercial oven and cooktop, sink and refrigerator were built into the kitchen's two walls.

With a long chef's knife, Lucius pointed to a bottle of wine at the end of the bar. "Help yourself." He turned to the stove and lit a burner for the final preparations of a meal that wafted enticing aromas throughout the flat. He'd dressed in a dark t-shirt, the emblem long ago worn or washed to a shadow on his chest, jeans frayed at the pockets, and nothing else. Barefoot, chopping parsley and humming off key to The Temptations, he was his essential self. And completely irresistible. Kenna knew she was being let in on a very big secret.

"That smells wonderful," Kenna said as she poured, needing some conversation to break the swoony spell that kept trying to creep over her. In the bedroom, she hadn't bothered to taste the wine and almost moaned when it filled her mouth this time. It was rich and full, but not too dry. "*This* is wonderful!" She stuck her nose right into the glass and inhaled.

"Thank you," he said as he sipped from his goblet. "It's mine."

"Yours?"

He reached for the bottle and set it down, the label facing toward her. It was a simple elegant design. A calligraphic "C" she recognized from the red wax seals on his love letters set above a pencil sketch of a small farmhouse set among vineyards.

She traced the letter with a manicured nail. "I'm impressed."

He slumped and clutched at his chest. "Oh, thank God. My father told me it would impress women someday."

Kenna froze for a moment before realizing he was joking. "You're terrible." His shoulders shook as he stirred his sauce a final time. "Is this your home?" She squinted to study the image behind the initial.

"Yes. Or it was when my great-grandfather planted the first vines."

He turned off the flame and moved to stand behind her, cupping his hands around hers on the bottle. Without thought or plan, they took deep breaths and leaned into each other, fitting together like two missing pieces of a puzzle. Each could feel the heat coming off the other, and the air between them crackled.

Lucius pointed to the farmhouse. "There have been two additions to the main house. The first was a summer kitchen, the second three bedrooms upstairs. And over here," he said, pointing to a clump of trees, "there is an oil press. My father added an olive orchard in the sixties."

"No grape-stomping barrels?" Kenna tilted her face to look up at him. Their eyes met. One of them need only lean in for their lips to meet as well. Kenna blinked and leaned away instead. "You know, like on *I Love Lucy*?"

"There is a community press in the village. A cooperative." Lucius set the bottle aside and began the process of gently tossing ingredients with the pasta. He had to do something with his hands besides touch her, especially when she tilted those lush lips up so invitingly.

"How do they know whose wine is whose?" She took another deep swallow, counting in her head to slow the thumping of her heart.

"They don't always. A few growers reserve some pressings for a private label. Usually only a hundred bottles or so for the family to use."

Kenna stared at his back, holding her precious glass of his family's wine to her chest. "Thank you," she whispered.

Lucius heart almost burst when he saw how she treasured his gift. "You are most welcome."

For another long moment, they looked at each other. Each of them imagined the future. Lucius saw her bathed in the Tuscan sun, chasing children with her bright blonde hair through the orchard. Kenna clung to the moment from her opposite end of the spectrum, memorizing the way he was looking at her now so she could recall it later when there would be nothing behind his eyes.

She gorged on carbonara, bread and wine and then completely trashed the order of his CD and movie collection, such as it was. Westerns and Motown. Trashed only in the sense she put everything in alphabetical order, where Lucius had them in order of preference. He would have cut out his own tongue before correcting her.

"Not what I expected," she said holding up three copies of a John Wayne classic, *The Searchers*. "Why three?"

"It's a favorite. I don't recall how I acquired them. Purchased while stranded in a hotel, I would venture to guess."

"I think I saw it on TV once," she said and set the discs back onto the shelf. "That's the one with Dean Martin?"

"You're thinking of *Rio Bravo*," he said. Kenna giggled, and Lucius realized she'd been teasing him. Still, he continued, "*The Searchers* is about a man who has someone taken from him." There was a shift in his voice that made her look up. The emotionless mask was in place again, and an icy chill ran down her spine. "He follows every trail. Every whisper. Every rumor until he finds her. He never stops looking. Then, he kills the one who took her."

"He must have loved her very much," Kenna said. Her voice was soft and distant.

"His niece. I imagine the climax would have been much ... bloodier had it been his woman." The change in his voice was subtle. His muscles coiled imperceptibly. An unvoiced warning to a non-existent threat or, perhaps, a remembered one.

Kenna looked away as a small part of her wondered who would look for her? Frankie and Candace? Absolutely, and the thought made her smile. Will? She grimaced. Will would turn the city upside down. When Kenna looked at Lucius again, his always-guarded expression had been replaced with a possessive hunger she felt like an electric shock to her chest. She instinctively stepped back.

"What were you just thinking?" Lucius followed and snaked his hand around her waist.

Kenna stammered, "Nothing. Just, well, wondering who would look for me? I mean I know Frankie and Candace would. Hell, Frank would crack her family name like a whip, and she hates people who do that. Candace would have that little mani-cured finger drilling into every chest in town." She chuckled.

Then, she shrugged. "Of course, Will would. It wouldn't be very pretty, but he'd find me too."

"Will?" Lucius' face became impassive, but his hand tightened its hold.

"Oh, yeah. My friend, Will." Kenna nervously massaged the scars in her palm. "He's with Frankie. But, you know, I kind of live with him. Sometimes. It's not as weird as it sounds." She opened her mouth to keep explaining, but cut herself off and looked everywhere except at Lucius. The Will conversation would lead directly to her scars and the grim memories she'd completely forgotten to resurrect in Lucius' bed. That path would usher in looks of pity and delicate handling on his part and resentment on hers. Kenna refused to spoil this moment. It would end soon enough. No need to hurry the inevitable.

Lucius felt her emotional wall as much as if she'd walked into another room and closed the door. While he easily justified his own barriers and secrets as necessary for her protection, Kenna's were not so easily dismissed. They were living, breathing obstacles. She'd allowed him through her defenses tonight. Being separated from her after today was no longer an acceptable option.

The silence grew uncomfortable and she wriggled from his hold. "I should go."

"You should stay." He raised her hand to his lips and kissed the scar. He knew instantly he'd made a tactical error. Kenna stiffened and pulled her fist away.

"I'm going to get dressed. Please, call me a cab," she said, reluctant resignation plain in her voice.

"I'll drive you," Lucius said gently. "I promised Rainsborough."

Kenna smiled and seemed to brighten. "Call me a cab. And tomorrow you can send me an obnoxious arrangement of French tulips. White ones. Then, tomorrow night you can call and we can talk while I eat leftover Chinese in my fuzzy socks." She grabbed one of his copies of *The Searchers*. "And watch your movie."

"Kenna. I would very much like you to stay."

She smiled. It was apparent to her that he was used to getting his way.

"I would like it too, but we'd just end up having mind blowing sex all night." She rolled her eyes and sighed dramatically. "And that's just not fair to all those poor souls relegated to cold showers and bad internet porn tonight."

Lucius nodded, laughed, then cupped her face. "Obnoxious arrangement." He kissed her slow and deep, a final assault on her defenses.

Kenna felt her resistance crumbling and pulled away. Touching her lips, she said, "You don't play fair."

He ran the pad of his thumb over her bottom lip. "No, I do not. Remember that." He dipped his head and softly kissed the column of her neck, finding the tender spot below her ear. He tried to keep the urgency from his voice, control the feeling that was too close to fear if she were to leave. "This is not a zero sum game, Kenna. You don't lose if I win. I promise." His mouth covered hers again, the gentle sweep of his tongue over hers pulled her under.

Lucius broke away, just far enough to look into her eyes. "Say you will stay."

"You agreed," she started to protest. *Why am I fighting this? I want to stay more than I want to breathe right now.*

"I agreed to obnoxious bouquets. Tell me, Kenna." *I will beg, if she demands it.*

She didn't. Reaching up, she mirrored his hands on her, cupping his face in her palms. "I'll stay."

CHAPTER THIRTY-TWO

E llis Griffin sauntered into the ground floor foyer of Lucius' home and offices just after ten Wednesday morning. He carried a delicate china cup by the rim and sipped the steaming brew without adjusting his grip to the fragile handle. Although his steps were virtually silent, Mac caught the movement and looked up from the tablet in his hands.

Mac had been on duty since seven. His suit coat hung over the back of a wingback chair. Griffin could smell fresh air, which meant Mac had recently completed an outer perimeter check.

Griffin took another sip. "Has he given out today's itinerary?"

Mac grinned and looked toward the closed resident's entry door at the top of the stairs.

"No. I got what everybody got. He's cleared his calendar for the day." Mac referred to an in-house message the Colonel had sent out earlier. "That's three days in a row. Yesterday, we had a pre-dawn grocery delivery of kid's cereal and milk."

"Kid's cereal?" Griffin's brow furrowed at the oddity.

"The one with Tony the Tiger on the front," Mac explained

with a chuckle. Griffin just looked up the stairs as if he could see through walls.

Mac's wide grin faded as Griffin turned back with a stony look. "You okay with that?"

"The Colonel's breakfast selection –"

"You know what I mean, man," Mac said. "You okay with *her?*"

"Without a background check –"

Mac cut him off again, spreading his palms wide and tilting his head. "Griffin, come on."

Griffin sipped again and swallowed hard. "Have you heard him laughing?" Mac nodded. "There are a million scenarios in which I can save his life. There isn't one in which I can make it worth living. Whether I'm 'okay with her' is irrelevant. I'll relieve you in an hour," he said as he disappeared into the offices beyond the stairs.

"Luc, I have to go home. Today," Kenna said, laughing when his arm tightened around her in reply.

She couldn't remember the last weekday she'd slept until after ten in the morning. Surely someone had noticed her absence from real life the last three days. Candace and Frankie had extracted sworn promises of details later after being assured her stay was voluntary and that she'd check in daily. As impressive as Lucius appeared, they were all about safety first where their friend was concerned.

Kenna squirmed until she could flip around to face him and knew by the scent of coffee on his breath that he'd been up and had come back to his bed before she woke.

"It's time." She spoke to him like she was trying to convince a child to leave the park.

"I've already cancelled my day," Lucius mumbled against her forehead.

"Then you have a free day. I have a life and a job and my own clothes. And shampoo. And razors."

"We can have all that brought in," he said, smiling. "And we solved the razor issue." He emphasized his point by gliding a powerful hand over her silky-smooth legs – thanks to his meticulous care, skillful hands and single blade razor.

Heat began to swirl anew in her belly at his touch and the memory of his long fingers holding the razor like a delicate flower as he swiped shaving cream in long strokes from her calves, thighs and beyond.

"Mascara!" Kenna scrambled away from kisses that were headed down her neck. "I haven't had my face on in three days. We need to come up for air." *I need air and distance before I start thinking this shit is real life.*

Lucius threw back the covers. He was half dressed in jeans and swept his shirt off the foot of the bed. He'd expected her to bolt the first morning and now braced himself for the declaration every time they finished a meal, a movie, a passage from a book or revived themselves from the effects of afterglow.

"Get dressed and I shall return you to the real world, for now." He lowered his head and gave her a sinister look. Kenna's laugh was a bit forced, he realized.

She stifled a deeper, more frightening panic that he might not let her go.

Lucius' fought the near-painful reality of acquiescing to return her to her life and work outside the protective walls of his home. He'd known from the first he would have to shield her from the part of his world occupied by violence and the enemies he'd collected over his perilous career. He hadn't expected to discover her *own* demons riding hard on her heels.

The first night, when Kenna's dreams had jolted her out of

the bed, she'd laughed it off as a hazard of waking in a strange man's home. The second night he'd watched, still and silent as she soothed herself through muffled whimpers and pleas. Last night, he found her curled into a ball clinging to the edge of the mattress out of his reach. While Kenna had snuggled against him affectionately, brushing off the incident as chills, he felt the pounding of her heart and spent tears on her cheeks. *If these are her dreams in my sanctuary, what torments her when she is alone?*

Lucius had coffee and a croissant waiting for her when she emerged from his master suite.

"You're going to spoil me," she said, wrapping her mane of hair up into a bun with the easy skill of long practice.

"I am trying," Lucius said. With a gentle tug, he loosened one of her curls and allowed his fingers to trail its length down her silken throat.

Kenna gathered her few belongings and sighed. "Walk of shame. You think your staff will remember the dress?"

Lucius kissed her forehead, "They will, and you will never feel judgment from them."

———

Double-parked in front of Will's apartment building, Lucius ignored the honking cars maneuvering around them as he opened her door. "I'll walk you in."

"No, it's okay. You might come out and find your car keyed or graffitied." Kenna rose on tiptoes to kiss him, her borrowed copy of *The Searchers* gripped in her hand. "Don't forget my flowers."

"Never," Lucius said, tucking the curl he'd liberated behind her ear.

White French tulips that wept over the lip of their vase

were delivered almost before she had her hair blown out and was dressed for work. Kenna eagerly cracked the red wax "C" and ripped into the gray stationery.

"I will kill the son-of-a-bitch who wakes me up from this," she said, holding the card over her fluttering stomach.

"Longing chains me." -- *Wallada*

Luc

CHAPTER THIRTY-THREE

Mike Chapman strolled into the inconspicuous brownstone just a few blocks away from Embassy Row. He didn't bother removing the ball cap or even flashing credentials. The door buzzed open before he had the chance to ring. When he'd first met Lt. Colonel Chaerea in Afghanistan, he'd found the man's ability to read and know people disconcerting. Being recognized and admitted before having to ask was impressive, but just part of the man's protocol.

"Rainsborough." Chapman acknowledged the stern man seated at the ground floor desk. "Am I waiting down here or can I go up?"

"He's in the office," Rainsborough said and cleared his throat with obvious meaning.

"Seriously?" Chapman asked with feigned innocence even as he reached into the holster at his back.

"You know the rules, Chapman."

"And you know I had to try. I *was* armed around the Colonel for eight months in the Sudan. I'm the exception to the rules." He kept grinning his boyish smile, aqua eyes twinkling, but turned over his weapon without rancor.

"Then you know there are no exceptions in the residence."

Chapman chuckled. "Always the hard ass, Rainsborough. Griffin and Mac around?" He was suddenly all business. "I think you all are going to want to hear this."

Rainsborough pressed a button, and both Griffin and Mac appeared from a door behind the staircase.

"Chapman." Mac flashed his wide grin. "You selling Girl Scout cookies?"

"Better," Chapman called, his long stride eating up the Persian runner that carpeted the upstairs hall to Lucius' office door. "Big fat gopher poked his head out of a hole on my golf course."

Mac bunched his fists and rolled his massive shoulders in *Caddyshack's* gopher dance moves while singing, "I'm all right. Nobody worry 'bout me."

Lucius opened the door to his office. "Let's play through gentlemen," he said, gesturing for all four men coming toward him to have a seat inside.

Chapman flopped down on a large leather sofa, parking a size thirteen trainer on a faded, denimed knee. Mac took the opposite corner. Griffin, lean and graceful, an impressive facsimile of Lucius, sank into an armchair. Rainsborough remained by the door, and Lucius leaned on the desk.

"Tee up," Lucius said.

Chapman leaned forward, elbows on knees. "Remember a few weeks ago when your girlfriend and her buddies were playing Nancy Drew?" Everyone nodded, Mac chuckled and even Lucius managed a cautious turn at the corner of his mouth. "Well, because we have search alerts on you and everyone on your team, their Googling and poking sent up red flags. Of course," he said, shrugging, "I put a tag on you that would trace back to whoever might be 'researching' you." He made air quotes.

Lucius folded his arms over his chest and shot a look at Griffin. "There was to be no tracking of Kenna."

Chapman's hands went up. "Nothing like that. We just kept the parameters open in case there was more digging on you."

Everyone waited. Even the air conditioner seemed to grow quiet, sensing something ominous in Chapman's tone.

"This morning, we got a hit. And it wasn't your girlfriend. It took my man until an hour ago to trace the IP addresses. I mean this guy was pinging off everybody around the world more times than we could count, but it kept coming back to an Istanbul IP address before winging off –"

"Lazarashvilli," Rainsborough broke in.

"But ..." Griffin mused.

"Yeah." Chapman cocked his head to Lucius. "'Nothing matters before the but,'" he echoed one Chaerea's often stated truisms. "We finally pinned him." He and Lucius locked eyes.

"Where." It wasn't a question.

"An internet café on the Lower East Side. Half a block from Mr. Ping's Chinese Restaurant."

Blood froze in Lucius' veins, but not a single man in that room could see the sheer terror this revelation inspired. Kenna had kept him at arm's length for a few days, and it took great personal restraint not to bring her into the safety of his home right at that moment.

Chapman reached for a folded piece of paper in his back pocket – a grainy image from airport security – and, shaking it open, handed it over to Lucius. "One more thing. Homeland Security facial recognition got a hit on this guy coming into JFK last night. Known associate of your David Lawrence, aka Davit Lazarashvilli. They have his luggage, but he was in a car and gone before they could get him."

Lucius stepped silently around his desk and spread the paper on his blotter. Gazing at the image now lying on his desk,

Lucius' long fingers tented in thought with an imperceptible tremor. "Thank you, Mike." Chapman warmed at the familiar, but rare, use of his given name. "I assume you are willing to go on the clock until further notice." He held up a hand before Chapman could protest. "This is too big for a favor, and I can't change anything without letting them know we know. This could be a diversion. The friend of our friend may be in town on business, and rattling my cage could be a distraction from the real purpose." He dearly hoped so.

"I'll reach out to the Feds and NYPD in case they're trying to ship women in or out," Mac volunteered. A nod from Lucius and he was out the door.

"Rainsborough, cover safe houses and shelters. Tell them not to wait if anyone disappears. Don't worry about immigration. We can help with that, if it keeps them off an auction block."

Chapman drummed his fingers on his tightened thigh for a moment as he analyzed the tension rolling off Lucius. "Well, I guess I'll get back to it."

"Mike," Lucius said, nodding his head in agreement with his internal counsel, "add Kenna to your watch. Keep your distance, but if Laz or his men have her scent or get close ..."

"I know what to do." He took this order seriously, but part of him rejoiced that, for the first time in his memory, the Colonel was so crazy about a woman that he was openly worried.

"And Mike?"

Chapman stopped in the open doorway and looked at Lucius.

"Keep a watch on Kenna's friends as well. Candace Fisher and Francesca – Frankie – Winslow."

"Got it." His memory brought up the image of Candace Fisher beaming at the *Times* cameraman. *No hardship, there.*

CHAPTER THIRTY-FOUR

Frankie was trying to hold her mirror steady enough to reapply her lipstick. Whether it was her nerves making her hands shake or the fact that her cab driver seemed to have made it his mission to find every bump and pothole on Broadway, the result was a lopsided raspberry pout that would look more at home on a Vegas hooker after a stag party. "Not exactly the look I was going for," she said to her reflection. As the taxi jerked to a halt, she gave up and snapped her compact shut.

"You say something, lady?" the cabbie asked through the dingy partition.

"Yeah, I asked if Dramamine was included in the fare."

"Huh?"

"Never mind," she said and swiped her credit card.

She dreaded the annual, year-end financial tête-à-tête that waited for her at the end of the bumpy cab ride. Not that she had to do much more than sign a few things for the accountants. Other than the Upper East Side apartment, Frankie shunned her trust fund and the strings that were attached to it. Even this string was enough to make her stomach cramp. While Senator

Winslow had never been plagued with conscience over missing school plays, awards nights or even graduations, he never missed this opportunity to see Frankie, a fact that reminded her, once again, why she chose not to eat from his silver spoon.

They were all waiting for her when she arrived at the offices of Chandler & Everett. Donald Chandler, the senior partner, was the executor of her grandmother's estate. In Frankie's mind, her grandmother would always be The Evil Old Witch. Through the glass wall, Frankie could see the five dark suits, Chandler and George Everett, tax attorneys, two of their junior lackeys and, of course, The Senator. Frankie rolled her eyes. Who exactly was he trying to impress by being there?

"Francesca." Senator Winslow met her at the door and bent to kiss her cheek. She could almost believe he was happy to see her.

"Hello, Father." She gave him a bright smile and managed to keep her tone light. "Why the troops? It's just a tax return."

"Oh, we had another matter before this. Gentlemen." He gestured to the door, and the junior suits gathered their papers and left the room.

Frankie looked around at the remaining sets of eyes that wouldn't meet hers. She shrugged and claimed the chair at the head of the long conference table, a tiny victory for which she gave herself mental props. It seemed no matter how independent she tried to be or how intelligently she wrote or directed her own life, when she was around either of her parents, she was thirteen and constantly on the verge of petulance again. The Senator moved to a new seat since she'd usurped his.

Everett cleared his throat. "Just a few things, Frankie. Your income this year was significantly more —"

"Wait." Frankie cut him off. "Sorry, George, but just like last year and the year before that, my income – apart from the trust – isn't up for public discussion."

"That's what we need to discuss, Frankie," Chandler inter-jected. "Investments made on behalf of the trust, along with your income," he paused to see if she was going to stop him from revealing anything of her earnings to the Senator. Frankie nodded for him to continue. "To keep your return from raising any red flags ..."

As he went on about tax deductions, retirement accounts and charitable contributions, Frankie studied her father. He looked almost happy, rather than the power-fueled high she was used to. He appeared relaxed and listened patiently instead of drumming his fingers until there was an opening for him to impart his infallible wisdom. She wondered if he were seeing someone, or possibly he'd winged a political protester with his car on the way into the city.

"Any questions, Frankie? Frankie?" Chandler was focusing on her.

"I'm sorry, Donald." She mentally rejoined the discussion. "You and George have managed this without any input from me since I was twenty-one. I trust that whatever you do now will be fine." She narrowed her eyes when her father smiled. "What's that smile about?"

"Nothing, Francesca. I'm simply glad you have no objections."

"Just a moment, may I see that again?" She waggled her fingers for the blue folder and focused this time. She was relieved and even more suspicious when there was nothing to be suspicious about in the contents. "Forgive me." She patted George's hand. "I was afraid I'd missed something."

"She was afraid I was trying to manipulate her through the trust," Senator Winslow said flatly. Both Chandler and Everett found something interesting in the papers under their noses.

Frankie sighed and met her father's stare. "You can't really blame me for that." When he said nothing, she opened her purse. "How much?"

Checks and returns signed, they all rose. Chandler and Everett affectionately kissed her cheek as they moved toward the door.

"I read the first installment of your racing series," Everett said. "It was good. Really good. You're doing very well with your writing." Frankie blushed and, in a moment, found herself alone in the room with her father.

"Yes. Interesting piece. What inspired you?" Senator Winslow didn't bother to hide the sour tone of his voice. The happy aura in the room faded quickly.

"Actually, Father, Will suggested it." She tilted her chin in defiance. "Candace and Kenna are going with me to the Meadowlands for some hands-on research. Don't worry. I promise not to blow the entire trust fund on a long shot." His sardonic smile made her want to kick something.

"Will? I see."

"You knew before you asked. Why do you even bother?"

"I'm only concerned about your well-being, Francesca. He's beneath you."

"It's America, Father. All men are created equal. Isn't that what you tell your constituents when you're campaigning for re-election?" Frankie wished she didn't sound defensive.

"Grow up." He knew just how to rankle her. "That man has one foot in prison, and you know it. Think of your career." The Senator's expression was hard, his face turning red.

"I just told you the series in the *Times* was his idea. He's thinking about my career more than you ever have."

The Senator continued as if he hadn't heard her. "What if, God forbid, there are children?"

"Children? That's a bit of a leap. Who said anything about children?"

"You can't think I will ever allow him to tarnish my family's name or Mother's legacy."

Her *legacy*? Frankie silently fumed. She didn't have time, nor was she in the mood, to discuss her paternal grandmother or whether her "legacy" deserved the luster her father claimed. She stood and gathered her things. "You're more concerned that the Vice President continues to take your calls."

Before he could respond, she held up a hand as she started for the door. "Don't bother. I'm tired of this dance."

CHAPTER THIRTY-FIVE

A t the Meadowlands, Frankie, Candace and Kenna climbed out of the cab into the bright Saturday morning sun.

Kenna shaded her eyes and looked around at the beehive of activity. "Shit. I *really* hate the track." Too many memories of weekends or skipped school days spent with her father at a track. Good memories, if she were honest. It was the tickle of grief and thoughts of *what if he'd lived* that followed those memories she hated.

"Hey, this is research and I need the help, so suck it up, buttercup." Frankie looped an arm through Kenna's.

Candace gave a little hop and rubbed her hands together. "I'm gonna get a racing form and study up on the pretty horses and the little men who're riding them today. I've got a hundred bucks burning a hole in my pocket."

"Don't blow it all on one race," Kenna said with a snicker.

Frankie handed them passes for their tour of the barns. She'd arranged for a brief interview with the head trainer for a string of thoroughbreds that had been sent over from Ireland for the US racing season. The three women lingered as they strolled the aisles between stalls, plucking apples from small tubs placed here and there to feed the horses. Each giggled nervously as the velvety lips snuffled the fruit from their palms. They watched the grooms braid thick manes and brush their charges until the coats shone like satin.

They chatted up jockeys, admired the silks they would wear in their races and watched the process of the jockeys' weigh-ins.

"Good God," Frankie muttered. "When I have to weigh, I take everything *off* – shoes, earrings – not pick up every damned thing I plan to wear and work with that day."

Candace and Kenna watched with some awe as Frankie asked knowledgeable questions of the trainer, following up his occasionally evasive answers with subtlety but persistence. This was the first time they'd seen her at work.

"Frankie's the real deal," Kenna said under her breath and whistled softly.

"She always downplays her talent. But we knew she had this, right?" Candace replied. She hoped like hell she hadn't overlooked the extent of Frankie's gifts. She loved her. She didn't want to think she might have underestimated her.

After an hour or more of background gathering and with Frankie's research mission accomplished, they adjourned to the clubhouse. As they walked through the growing crowd, they ignored the leering looks the three of them always garnered whenever they were together. They didn't notice the watchful blue-green eyes following their every move.

Sipping a draft beer, Mike Chapman leaned against the bar and angled his body to keep the three women discreetly in view. Wow. The photos of Candace Fisher he'd looked through back when she was investigating Lucius did *not* do her justice. She was diminutive, as he'd discovered, but there was a vibrancy that made her seem taller and more commanding. The three women were all stunners, but she more than held her own. *Pay attention, bud,* he cautioned himself. He was here for a reason.

In a corner booth of the clubhouse, Lorenzo Barzini held court. Shorty, Lorenzo's sidekick since grade-school, saw Kenna and the girls first. He whistled low and nudged Barzini. "Ain't that your ... uhm, ex?"

"Move." Barzini shoved his way out of the booth and straightened his tie. Sal Jr. wasn't here to get in his way this time.

"Come on, man. She's old news, and your Pop – " Shorty bit off the rest of his warning under the icy glare.

"Fuck her *and* the old man." Barzini strolled over to the women and, fixing his hooded gaze on Kenna, leaned against the tall table beside Frankie, "Got a winner picked, Gorgeous?"

Frankie started and an instinctive smile began to curve her full lips. Then she recognized him. He was handsome in a thuggish way, just as she remembered from the night at Swag.

"FUCK OFF!"

A racing form flew over Frankie's shoulder, bounced off Barzini's chest and fell to the floor. Frankie whipped her head around. She'd heard Kenna drop an F-bomb before, of course, but never with that kind of rage behind it.

"Come on, Sugar. I'm just helping your friend here." He kicked the form toward Shorty.

Kenna shook, her face flushed and hot. Frankie backed away from Barzini as Candace pulled up beside Kenna, shoulder to shoulder. Kenna hissed, "Get away from her. Get away from me." There was a cold fury in Kenna's voice Frankie and Candace didn't recognize. Frankie moved to stand at Kenna's other side.

Shorty tugged his boss' sleeve, "Lorenzo, come on. This is trouble we can't afford." He refused to look at the women.

Candace and Frankie made eye contact, one mouthed, "What does that mean?" and the other, "What trouble?"

"In a minute," Barzini shrugged off his toady and closed the gap of personal space between him and Kenna. "Haven't changed a bit, have you?"

The first punch was low and fast to his middle. The second drew blood. Not a knock-out strike, but a busted lip. It was enough. "I've changed a little." Kenna massaged the scar on her palm. Her knuckles grew hot where they'd made contact and she watched blood dribble off his chin onto the expensive suit.

"You fucking bitch!" Barzini spat blood on the floor.

"Heard it." She locked her knees to keep them from banging together.

Candace stepped between them. "I think you'd better take the suggestion and stay away from her, Mr. Barzini. Clearly, close proximity to her is not good for your health."

Barzini swung his angry glare in her direction. Shorty moaned at hearing her using Lorenzo's name. "Fuck, fuck, fuck," he chanted under his breath.

Frankie put one arm around Kenna's back, the other on her elbow. *Where's security?* she thought. It happened so fast it was plausible only the four of them even knew what was happening.

Not quite. Suddenly there was a tall, broad-shouldered man between Barzini and the women. "I recommend you gentlemen leave."

"Who the fuck're you?" Barzini snarled. In his fury, he was incapable of seeing he was outmatched on every level.

"The lady's manicurist. I think you chipped her nail," Chapman answered amiably as he went through the motions of dusting off Barzini's jacket lapels.

Shorty offered Barzini a wad of napkins and tugged on his arm to urge him toward the door. "Come on, man." He recognized the threat, both from his bosses and this man if Barzini were to continue this confrontation with Kenna and draw the attention of authorities of any kind.

Dabbing his lip, Barzini pointed at Kenna. "Remember. *You* walked in here." He and Shorty disappeared through the crowd.

Kenna stared at their backs, then shuddered violently and sagged against Frankie and Candace. "Yeah. Wrong place, wrong time. Story of my life."

They all jumped when Chapman spoke. "Are you hurt?" He clasped Kenna's hand to gently check the fragile bones and examined her knuckles.

She yanked it back. "I'm fine."

"I hate to sound like Barzini, but I have the same question," Candace said. "Who *are* you?"

He smiled widely. "Mike Chapman, Miss Fisher." He turned his grin to Frankie. "Miss Winslow. Perhaps we could all find a seat?" He herded them towards the open seating and signaled a waiter.

Frankie pointed at herself and her two friends. "Three vodka martinis. Dirty."

"Nothing for me," Chapman said, knowing he wasn't really invited to join them anyway.

The women sat for a minute, just staring and trying to remember to breathe. Chapman sat back and waited for them to calm down. All the while, his eyes surveyed the room and the people in it. Just because the asshole had gone didn't change the reason Chapman was here in the first place.

"You punched him," Frankie said with admiration. Her inner author was already penning the story for Will.

"Where'd you learn that?" Candace asked.

Kenna shrugged and said, "YouTube."

Candace and Frankie snorted in shock tinged with awe.

"Whatever. They should have told you not to hit the hard parts." Chapman gently lifted her hand to check for swelling.

"Put some ice on it as soon as you can, and if it's swollen later, you should get it x-rayed," Chapman advised. He smiled warily because he knew there'd be hell to pay from Lucius if Kenna were hurt on his watch.

Kenna looked up as she retrieved her hand. "Really, who *are* you, and why are you here?"

"Just standing in for a friend and, bonus, enjoying a day at the races," Chapman replied, but his amiable tone did little to reassure any of them.

"A friend," Kenna said and looked hard at him. She took in the ash blond hair that was cut short enough to keep the curls from looking girlish, the hard planes of chest and shoulders that spanned the chair he dwarfed. "Who can't be here, so you are?"

"Well, for whatever reason or whomever you're standing in for, thanks for the help, but we'll take it from here." Candace dismissed him. The last thing they needed right now was a big guy oozing testosterone, flexing his – impressive, she had to admit – muscles, no matter how agreeable the façade.

Chapman leveled one last look at her to impress upon her the gravity of their situation before getting up to leave. He said, "Keep your eyes open, ladies."

"Wait," Kenna called to his back, but he didn't turn and was soon lost in the crowd. "Hell's bells. He was following us. Is Lucius having me followed?" Her mind went to Lucius because everything about Chapman reminded her of the other men she'd seen around her Colonel.

"Honey, you don't know that. And if he is, I have to believe Lucius is just looking out for you. He seems like the type to protect what he cares about," Frankie said.

"Damn, I just got it. Remember when I researched Lucius after the gala? Yeah, Mike Chapman's the name of the guy I asked to help." Candace, agitated, ran her fingers through her hair. "Okay, before we zero in on your Colonel and this Mike person, can we talk about what just happened here? You just went off your rocker, in public, on a man, who, were it not for his flunkie, looked like he would gladly return the punch. With interest."

There was a long silence. The dull roar of the track faded around them. Finally, Kenna held up her right hand, the long scar bright where she'd been rubbing it under the table.

"He would have. You'll recall my lapse in judgment." She made air quotes. Not that either of them needed reminding of the short version she'd told them the night they met or shared in greater detail in the months since. "Better known as Lorenzo Barzini, who's now sucking on the inside of his mouth."

Frankie mused, "Now I know why you never told Will. He'd have killed him."

"And if that guy – minion – was here for Luc." Kenna's chin quivered as she said, "He'll never look at me again without seeing Lorenzo's fingerprints."

CHAPTER THIRTY-SIX

"**S**tupid fuck!" The backhand landed across Lorenzo's face, reopening his busted lip as swiftly as the words flew from his father's mouth.

Carmine Barzini flexed his hand and combed his fingers through thick, black hair that had yet to show threads of silver even though he was over sixty. He looked down at his mirror image holding a bleeding mouth and trying not to moan in pain. His lip curled in disgust.

"I told you to stay away from that girl," he said, his voice calm now. "You were dumb enough to leave her alive. I cleaned up that fucking expensive mess once. Your uncle won't be so understanding if there's another."

"I didn't –" Lorenzo started to protest, his stomach clenched at the thought of Uncle Sally's brand of disappointment.

"Shut up! You saw her and walked up to her friend, and Kenna kicked your ass." Carmine turned to Shorty. "Who was the guy?"

"Dunno, Boss. Some boy scout," Shorty offered obediently.

"Did you know she would be there? And don't you fucking

lie to me," the elder Barzini said, preparing to take another swipe at his son.

"*No! I swear, Pop.*"

Carmine crossed the room to distance himself and so he could see both men when he asked the next question. "Have you been following her?"

Lorenzo's aching head jerked up. He snapped his eyes to Shorty, then back to his father before answering. Carmine closed his eyes and was shaking his head before the first word was out.

"I swear, I just seen her around. She's in Sal Jr.'s bars all the time."

Shorty shuffled his feet and scratched the back of his neck, looking everywhere but at his boss.

"'Try again," Carmine said softly.

Lorenzo didn't say a word.

"Your uncle and cousin have a soft spot for this girl, and she's keeping her mouth shut. She's not some whore or junkie you picked up. I can't protect you if she changes her mind."

Carmine came back to his son, tenderly taking him by the arm and guiding him out of the chair. "I've got a meeting in Florida next week. You come with me. Get some sun, let this blow over."

Lorenzo nodded like a truant schoolboy being comforted by his mom in the principal's office.

"Go get cleaned up." Carmine patted his son's back, then whispered to Shorty. "If this happens again, it's on you."

"Yes, Boss," Shorty said, following Lorenzo. He waited until Barzini was out of sight to wipe the sweat off his face.

CHAPTER THIRTY-SEVEN

"**D**on't come in!" Kenna yelled, panic pitching her voice high enough to make Will wince and push through her body weight to open the kitchen door.

Kenna prided herself on her inability to cook anything but coffee and grilled cheese sandwiches, and yet his – their – kitchen, usually immaculate under her care, was strewn with battle remnants. Bits of onions and breadcrumbs appeared to have been tossed like confetti over one counter. Tomato juice dripped over the edge of a cutting board he was sure had never been used until today. Green herb bundles were obviously in mid-chop when he'd interrupted, bits of green clinging to the knife on the floor.

He didn't even try not to laugh. "What the fuck are you doing?"

Kenna turned away, blushing so intensely her cheeks burned. "Nothing." She picked up the fallen knife and dropped it into the sink.

"This is hardly nothing. *You're* cooking. Sort of." He plucked a piece of bread from a bowl, sniffed it suspiciously and popped it in his mouth. "Why're you acting like I caught you watching porn?"

Kenna jerked around. "Would you go *away*?"

Truth jumped up and bit Will right on the butt. "It's a *man*!" He laughed until he had to sit down, all the while fending off her protests and the occasional slap or kick to his backside. Gasping for air, he sat grinning. "Fuck feminism!"

"Fuck you," Kenna mumbled, before spinning around wielding a wooden spoon. "You're my guinea pig, smart ass."

Will instantly straightened, a feigned seriousness at the threat. "Seriously, what the fuck, Kenna?"

"It's not what you think."

"Oh, it's exactly what I think, so start talking. And don't give me any bullshit. Your face can't lie. And I know *that* face," he pointed at Kenna, "better than you do."

He was right. Will had changed dressings and ice packs. He'd threatened hospital staff if they dared to show any shock or dismay or give Kenna a mirror in the weeks after the night he found her. Will had nursed her through pain and drug-induced euphoria. He'd given sanctuary, sympathy and tough love when necessary and never once pushed her for answers once she'd refused to talk to the police.

Kenna, in turn, had never judged his motives for helping her, a virtual stranger. She'd done arguably the hardest part by simply accepting the gift, and she'd been a friend, even a silent confessor when he needed it. Sometimes, she was drugged and served as a mute witness. Sometimes, she just lay still and silent in her sickbed, listening to his words flow over her. He knew her face. He knew what Lucius had discovered at their first meeting – Kenna was a terrible liar. Excellent with secrets, though.

"Not lying, I promise. I kind of met someone." Will raised a skeptical brow, and Kenna pushed on. "He's not gay, married or anything else." Will got her meaning. Whatever else this guy might be, he wasn't a gangster. "He is Italian. I think. The accent comes and goes."

"The two of you should get on brilliantly then."

She ignored the jab and kept talking, relieved to not keep this new relationship from Will and terrified he would find something wrong with Lucius.

"He's got a nice place. He cooked for me," she said, omitting the fact that it was several meals, some of which were breakfasts.

She decided to spare Will her assessment of Lucius' mystery and attractiveness. "And he'll probably be gone by the Fourth of July. You won't even need to run this one off, but I don't want to jinx it before it starts."

Will avoided the subtle self-deprecation. "One! I ran off *one*. He was a cop, and he was married. And how is telling me a jinx?"

"It just is," she whined, as if that explained everything.

"You know it's a sin to be this superstitious," he said as Kenna crossed herself, and smiled. "What're you making?"

"Panzanella salad?" she said.

"You asking or telling? You hate that stuff. Soggy bread, right?"

"I liked his and wanted some, so I thought I'd try it." Kenna slumped against the sink. She held up two fingers wrapped in bandages he hadn't noticed before. "Not doing so well, actually."

"Why don't you just ask him to make you dinner again?"

"He's out of town on business."

Will's face was one big question mark.

"I don't know exactly what he does, yet. Hey, I don't know what you do on your business trips either, and I still like you, so don't give me that look."

Will took off his jacket and threw it out of the danger zone. "You got a recipe?"

"You don't cook, either," she said, but pointed to the tablet with "Easy Panzanella" in bold letters across the top of the screen.

"Yeah, but now I'm hungry, and you only have eight more fingers to slice."

As they ate amidst the mess, Will set his fork down, a new question dawning on him. "Does this guy have a name?"

CHAPTER THIRTY-EIGHT

L ucius placed the report's summary sheet squarely on top of the sheaf of papers in the middle of his blotter, rose and paced to the window where he stared unseeing at the view of the East River.

"I naïvely hoped that having you keep an eye on Kenna was just *pro forma.*"

Chapman narrowed his eyes trained on the back of Lucius' head, now sporting longer, unkempt hair. He'd also come back from this latest mission with a dark beard, telling Chapman a great deal about the part of the world Chaerea had spent the past few weeks in.

"A – you're never naïve. B – your instincts are rarely wrong. We knew there was someone putting out feelers that had focused on Kenna."

"A man can hope."

"The source of the feelers is still an unknown, and there were no approaches. I stake my rep on that. But that event at the track is not trivial. You'll pour over the details, but there's clearly *history* between Lorenzo Barzini and Kenna. He's not just muscle for Salvatore Tomasi, he's a nephew with a long, long sheet full of assault, attempted murder, illegal weapons, petty drug charges. Most dismissed because the victims refused to cooperate."

Chapman paused to formulate his next words. "Not jumping to conclusions here, but there is the open assault case last year that put Kenna in the hospital. She couldn't – or wouldn't – identify her assailant, but she'd been dating Barzini for months before that and never again after."

Lucius' back stiffened, and his hands curled into fists. Her *"accident."* When he turned to face Chapman, his face was rock hard, the muscles in his jaws clenched so hard Chapman imagined he could hear the molars crack.

"Never again. Truer words." In truth, the words that were coursing through his brain were *I'll kill him. He touched her. He'll die for that.*

"I haven't gone deeper on Kenna. I wanted to get your direction on that," Chapman said.

Lucius thought for only a moment. "No. She's entitled to her privacy. I'll wait for her to come to me. Unless Barzini makes that decision for us."

CHAPTER THIRTY-NINE

———————

W ill hit the button to lock his car as he passed the gray sedan parked at the curb. Despite the absence of a wide-shouldered goon leaning against the hood, his gut did a flip as he took the stairs two at a time to reach the door of the gallery. After rolling his eyes at the crap that passed for art, he took the next set of stairs up to the loft space Kenna called an apartment. The first thing he saw wasn't Uncle Sally, but some guy in an Italian leather jacket holding a massive bouquet of white tulips. First thing he *heard* was a girlish giggle coming out of Kenna.

What the fuck is this? he thought. What he said was, "Hey."

Kenna, obviously hypnotized by the flowers in front of her, hadn't seen him come in or heard him on the stairs. She whipped her head around at the sound of his voice. "What are you doing here?"

"You're still open for business, yeah? Thought I'd pick up that velvet dog's breakfast Frankie had her eye on."

"Fresh out, sold the last one yesterday. Still looking for a place to hide the money." Kenna cringed. She would have preferred to coordinate Will's introduction to Lucius without the heavy dose of sarcasm and snark the two of them used to communicate.

"So? I need a reason to come see you?" This was, in fact, a rare visit, and one he'd had the best of intentions in making. He'd been out of town since their cooking experiment and had been concerned at her obvious attachment to this new man. Whenever she ventured into a relationship, no matter how he tried, Will couldn't stop his mind from returning to the night he'd found her, broken and bleeding. If she could misjudge one almost fatally, she could mistake another.

It was obvious he'd interrupted something. Every instinct told Will this guy was dangerous. He poked a molar with his tongue and shifted his glare to Lucius, who had politely turned his back to their awkward greeting to set the flowers on Kenna's small dining table. When he turned to face Will, his eyes were hooded, his expression unreadable. Both men looked to Kenna, waiting for introductions.

Kenna sighed. "Lucius, this is Will MacKenzie. Will – Lucius Chaerea."

Lucius recognized the name mentioned on those rare occasions when she couldn't keep herself from revealing pieces of her life. His posture relaxed slightly, and he extended his hand. Will too, recognized the name. For his part, Will's suspicions were nothing, if not heightened, in his discovery that this was the man who'd cooked for her. He'd envisioned someone much more ... ordinary.

For Kenna's sake, Lucius tolerated the suspicious once-over he was getting, although he was ready, even eager, to relieve her army of self-appointed guardians of their duties. The two men stood staring at each other. The light finally dawned on Kenna that her question of why Will had shown up at her loft took a back seat to where he'd been this past week.

"Wait," she said to no one, thrusting her hands out in front of her. She pointed at Will. "Where have you been? Have you called Frankie? It's been three fu ... full days?" Kenna stumbled over her words trying not to curse in front of Lucius.

"Perhaps, I should go," Lucius offered. Will turned and gestured with an open palm to the door.

"You. Stay," Kenna ordered, turning to give Lucius a stern glare. "There's a vase on the shelf over the sink." She pointed to the notched-out space of a kitchenette. "I'll be right back."

Dragging Will by the sleeve, she headed down the stairs. This was not the reunion with Lucius she'd tried unsuccessfully to convince herself not to look forward to.

Once they were in the gallery, she closed the door and turned to Will. "Your timing sucks, you know that? Where were you?"

"That's the guy? Who is he?" Ignoring her questions with his own.

His suspicious tone raised her defenses. "I told you about him."

"Fuck that. You said you met someone named Luc. That guy isn't a someone. He's dangerous. It rolls off him. He's not a cop – you're not that stupid." He also hoped – no, he *knew* – she wasn't stupid enough to pick up any of Sally Tomasi's strays, and this guy sure as shit, wasn't anyone's flunkie. Will strolled to the window overlooking the street and the gray car below. Neon signs flashed "Tattoos" and "Palm Reading" on the lower floors. "What is he? A spook?"

"Paranoid much? He's a nice man who brings me tulips." For Kenna, that act alone should have told Will that this one was different. "That okay with you?"

Will had been her watchdog for too long to give in that easily. "Not if he's anything like the others, flowers or no."

"He is nothing like –" Kenna panicked, refusing to give a name to Will. "You don't know him. He makes me feel – safe."

"Right, and your record on that is out-fucking-standing. What's he do?"

Kenna turned away and said nothing. Re-arranging a display of carved figurines, she hoped he would leave this subject alone. She was happy being in the dark and a little ashamed she found the mystery of Lucius so alluring.

"Well?" Will demanded. When she still didn't answer what he considered a reasonable request for information, his expression soured. "You've no idea, do you?"

"He doesn't know everything about my business either." It was a childish answer, and she knew it.

"Oh, well then." Will threw his arms in the air, his Scottish burr thickening. "Just tell me how you see this playing out. Some slick fucker makes nice, brings you roses, excuse me tulips, then when he stops making nice, I'm supposed to ... what? Remind me."

"Quit trying to ruin this just because I didn't ask your permission."

"Of course, you didn't. You never ask anything, just jump off and hope there's water under the fuckin' bridge." Will's head fell back, realization slapping him in the forehead. "That's it. You know what he is. You think you can fix this one and not get your head bashed in."

"Stop it, Will!" Kenna's eye twitched, her hand clenched around the mug of cold coffee on her desk.

"No! Even if you survive, I can't put you back together again. And don't even think about throwing that." He pointed to the mug. "You're not half blind and doped up anymore."

"Just *stop!*" She set the mug down hard enough to splash some of the cold coffee onto her immaculate desk. "He'll hear you," she hissed.

"Bravo! Oh, my God, that was brilliant!"

Startled, both Will and Kenna turned toward the sound of

the effusive praise. A dark-haired woman in her late forties adjusted a purse strap on her shoulder to delicately clap the fingers of one hand against the palm of the other. "Oh, tell me there's more! When do you open? Are there tickets left?"

"What the fuck?" Will muttered.

Kenna smoothed her skirt and tried to adopt a business-like air. "Can I help you?"

The woman looked from Will to Kenna and back again. "Isn't this part of Hooven DeKuyper's new show?"

"Whooven who?" Will's face was pure confusion.

Missing just the barest of beats, Kenna smiled. "Yes, yes, it is." She gently placed her hand on the woman's shoulder and turned her to the door. "But I'm afraid it's not ready for public viewing yet," Kenna said, her smile still firmly fixed as she gently guided the woman out. "Please, come back on the twelfth." Even after the confused woman had disappeared down the stairs, Kenna continued to hold the door open. "You can leave now too."

"This isn't over," Will said as he left.

"This isn't over," Kenna imitated his voice and threw the bolt. "Asshole. I probably lost a customer over that."

She needed several cleansing breaths to calm her features and make the climb up to her loft and Lucius.

ALONE IN THE APARTMENT, Lucius stuck the flowers into the vase as he inspected her space. Her kitchen appeared to be nothing more than a broom closet with the door removed. Open shelves above the sink held an array of mismatched thrift store china and kid's cereal. The stove couldn't be more than twenty inches square, vintage mint green and topped with a rough-edged piece of granite. He knew it was real stone, not a faux laminate because he lifted the edge to see if there were actual burners under it and estimated the slab weighed about thirty pounds. Lucius wondered if Kenna had hefted it up two flights of stairs by herself? With a boyish grin, he opened the oven door expecting to see cobwebs and smiled wider at the small safe inside. *Fireproof*, he thought.

Remembering her keen interest in his audiovisual collection, he crossed the room to study her shelves. He smiled again, her stolen – borrowed – copy of *The Searchers* sat on the top of the stack that included *The Maltese Falcon*, *Touching Evil*, *Casablanca*, and a veritable who's who of film noir. When he moved the front stack of DVDs aside, he was surprised to find *Cinderella*, *Sleeping Beauty*, *Beauty and the Beast*, *Princess Bride* and every other princess movie made. His Kenna liked happy endings.

The converted loft was long and narrow. Living and sleeping spaces cleverly separated by salvaged doors hinged together to form an accordion partition. Her dining table and chairs rescued from a 1950s diner. In fact, everything seemed re-purposed. A coffee table made of books and wooden vegetable crates sat in front of a slipcovered sofa and two mismatched chairs re-covered in vintage cream floral damask, probably remnants of vintage fabrics as well. Nothing matched, not even the bone china set on the table. One rescued piece led to another. The apartment an extension of the gallery, of Kenna. Lucius smiled at that. Something about her mismatched delicate china and real silver set on starched linen place mats, on that red-topped diner table, reaffirmed what he already knew. Kenna found beauty in everything. She valued the cracks in porcelain, chipped paint and tarnished finishes. The broken and forgotten were given a place to belong. She knew the flaws made things and people real.

Lucius couldn't make out the words, but the volume of

shouting below had him looking toward the door. His eyes narrowed on the line of locks that bolted her in at night. The thought of their necessity offended him. The certainty of their inadequacy chilled him. *This will not do.*

He sat on the slipcovered love seat to wait for Kenna. Chapman's report had only reinforced the idea he'd been contemplating since the first night Kenna spent with him. Being in her space, her cobbled-together statement of independence, he knew it would be a fight. She would rebel against needing the comfort and protection of his home. Seeking heavenly guidance, Lucius raised his head and caught his breath.

The ceiling of the loft was so high it could have accommodated another story. The maze of exposed duct work painted black made it cavernous. Industrial chic. It was Kenna's modification that had him transfixed. A jigsaw of reclaimed windows, some with elaborate stained glass designs, old doors, some with windows others solid, aged wood. The entire length and width of the room was sheltered under this mosaic of architecture, suspended by sturdy cables and bolts in the exposed rafters above.

Kenna stood in her door watching him, pride welling in her chest. "If there's an earthquake, I'm screwed."

"Darling, it is magnificent," he said without lowering his eyes.

"Nah, just a solution to a problem," she said. "I couldn't keep the temperature sane in here with that monster high ceiling. How'd you know I was here?" He hadn't been startled by her reappearance at all.

"It's art," he countered. "And I heard your heels on the stairs."

"I never thought so," she lied, looking away when he turned a curious look to her. "You know anyone in need of a ceiling?" she asked playfully.

"It's perfect where it is," Lucius said. "Why downplay this? You may not sculpt or paint, but what you do is art."

Kenna opened her mouth, intent on self-deprecation, then looked up again and smiled. "Thank you. Have you had lunch?" She tapped a section of old pressed tin tile hanging on the wall, which was both decoratively and practically covered in food menus affixed with refrigerator magnets. "Pings will be fast. They want to meet you."

BACK ON THE STREET, Will grumbled something about Kenna not being nearly as tough as she thought she was as he slid behind the wheel of his car and thumbed the speed dial on his phone. If he'd gone to the gallery because he'd thought it would be easier to deal with Kenna in person, the last few minutes had shown him the folly of that notion. "Aye, right." He ran a hand through his hair and waited for Frankie to pick up.

"Hey baby," she purred into his ear. "Where are you?"

"Here."

She knew he meant the city. She also knew that's all she was going to get on the subject of his latest four-day absence. Beyond that, she knew it was useless to ask. For as long as she'd known him, Will sometimes found it necessary to go off by himself for a few days. He didn't offer any explanation of where he went or what he did there, and Frankie didn't press.

"Oh, good. Close enough to touch."

For his part, Will didn't know what he was supposed to expect. If he was surprised by her light tone and the lack of recriminations, he sure as hell didn't let on. "Do you have plans?"

"I think I do, now."

Will looked in his rearview mirror, gave himself a lopsided grin and turned the engine over. In a much better mood, he nosed the car into the creeping, honking morass of late afternoon traffic and headed to Chelsea and Frankie.

AT THE END of the block, the dark-haired woman typed a coded email into her phone.

To: dlawrence@dlenterprise.co.uk
    From: smith@gmail.com
    Re: Curator position
    Unable to locate lost jaguar piece, but new, unknown artist was on FULL display. Curator is a possible auction asset.

ISTANBUL, TURKEY

"Boss," Hans said, walking into Lazarashvilli's office. "Email from New York." He handed over a single sheet of paper.

Lazarashvilli was perfectly capable of checking his own email, but having them brought to him by a servant was another perk that proved their servitude. He read the email and leaned back in his chair, an amused grin distorting his mouth. Was it possible Lucius Chaerea had a rival for this woman's attention? Now that was interesting.

AN HOUR LATER, Will met Frankie at the door of his apartment and quickly relieved her of the Dean & DeLuca bag that carried their dinner. With one hand, he dropped the bag into a chair along with the purse he'd taken from her shoulder, while the other pulled her against him.

No one bothered to say, "Welcome back," or "I missed you." It wasn't their style. This was their style. Mouths and tongues collided while fingers flew over buttons and fumbled at zippers as they moved toward Will's bedroom.

At dusk, Will stood at the bar separating his kitchen from the living room, poking through take-out containers. Frankie, her skin still damp from a shower, came up behind him, wearing his robe and a smile. Her hands snaked around his hips and into the top of the jeans he'd jumped into, but hadn't bothered to fasten.

"Who's Lucius Chaerea?"

Damn, that was quick. "Just a guy," she said with her lips pressed to his back. She'd been expecting the question, but thought the "afterglow" might last at least until after dinner.

"That's what Kenna said both times I asked her. And that's shit." He turned around and offered her a bite of cold noodle salad.

"Okay ..." While Frankie chewed, she tried to figure out how to describe just exactly what Lucius was to her friend, especially since she, herself, wasn't all that clear about it. Kenna worked very hard at pretending that Lucius was no one special, despite the way her eyes lit up whenever she or Candace could get her to talk about him. "He's not just 'a guy,' he's ... he's Kenna's guy."

Will scowled, but Frankie smiled. If she let him, he'd not only continue to pepper her with questions about a man she knew little about, but would manage to work himself into such a lather he'd have to go back over to the gallery to demand answers. It might drive Kenna nuts, but to Frankie, Will's protective instincts, especially toward the woman she'd come to love as much as he did, was one of his most endearing qualities.

"You might as well get used to it," Frankie led him to the couch and pushed him down so that she could straddle his lap. "I, for one, think she's pretty smitten."

"Smitten?" He said the word like he'd never heard it before and was unfamiliar with the concept.

"Yeah, smitten. You know," she said, her warm breath raising goose bumps as her lips found his neck, "the way I am about you."

Will untied the robe and slipped his hands inside, over her thighs, and around her hips to her ass, kneading the soft pliant flesh of his favorite part of her anatomy. "Is that what you are? You're 'smitten?'"

Frankie raised her head and looked him in the eye, suddenly afraid she'd said too much.

"Yeah, I mean ..."

"What?"

They'd always played fast and loose with their relationship or whatever this was. They didn't talk about their feelings. Neither of them would dream of admitting that in the six months since they'd met, neither had felt like seeing anyone else. It hadn't been a conscious choice, it was just the way of it.

She could admit, if only to herself, that Will's shadowy past, and his connections to some of the more nefarious, bold-faced names found on the front pages of the *Post* gave her a tingle. But it was his efforts to overcome all of that and to be his own man that really intrigued her. He was different from all the bloodless heirs-apparent that she'd grown up with. The kind of man her father expected her to marry. Frankie couldn't think of anything more boring or anything she wanted to do less.

"What?" Will asked again.

"Nothing." She put her head on his shoulder and burrowed into the warmth of his body. "You want to keep talking, or you want to take me back to bed?"

CHAPTER FORTY

"Well, well! Look who skipped mass." Frankie wiggled her brows at Kenna's messy topknot, yoga pants and t-shirt with a faded out logo, obviously from Lucius' closet.

"Did you at least drive by and wave at St. Patrick?" Candace asked with a grin. "This is what? The third marathon of debauchery between mysterious trips? I've lost count."

Candace wasn't wrong. Crimson-faced and smiling, Kenna squeezed her eyes shut and rubbed her temples with the heels of her hands. "He asked me to move in."

"Whoa." Candace's coffee cup paused halfway to her mouth. "That was fast."

Kenna threw her arms out wide and looked around for support from the patrons. "*Thank* you! That's what I said."

"And your Colonel had a perfectly reasonable, logical, well-thought-out list of reasons why," Frankie punished her croissant with knife and butter.

"I hate when they do that." Candace stabbed a bit of melon with her fork. Then admitted, "Like I would know."

Kenna replayed Lucius' arguments for them. Candace and

Frankie walked the tightrope of agreeing with his assessment of her security situation and supporting Kenna's need for independence. After the altercation with Barzini at the race track, they had worried he was following Kenna and tried to find reasons to check in with her on the nights she spent in the gallery loft. The mention of the door locks had Frankie nodding. "Will's exact words were, 'If you need twelve fucking deadbolts, it's never going to be safe.'"

"You and Will talked about my locks?" Accusation hung in the air.

Frankie shrugged and bobbed her head. "He just mentioned the number of locks. A few times. *I* didn't bring it up." Her fingernail tapped the table between them. "And I reminded him that you are smart and capable of taking care of yourself."

Kenna rolled her eyes. "He'll never believe that, but thanks for trying."

"If you're here, does that mean the Colonel relented?" Candace asked, not believing for a moment the answer would be yes.

"When he's home, I'll stay there. That's as far as we got."

"So, you have a drawer or something?" Frankie said.

Looking down at her fashion statement, Kenna grinned. "I should probably put something of my own in it, huh?"

CHAPTER FORTY-ONE

"She's late." Will paced like a caged tiger in front of Spoiled's wide front window as he looked out onto the street. An unlit cigarette dangled from his lips and vibrated with each anxious step.

Their Day at the Races celebration, capping off Frankie's successful and popular four-part *Times* series, had seemed like the perfect start to summer. Along with Spoiled's regulars, they'd invited colleagues and friends and reserved the VIP lounge for themselves. Will had mounted more big-screen TVs in the main bar so everyone could watch the races. The bar hummed with the festive vibe, as even the hard-core patrons embraced the theme with feathered fascinators for the ladies and sport coats and straw hats for the men.

"She'll call if it's too much," Frankie placed a calming hand on his arm. "I'm surprised her therapist didn't suggest this sooner." Curious, she looked up at Will.

Will toyed with the cigarette and shook his head. She wasn't sure if that meant no suggestion was made, Kenna refused or if he couldn't handle it.

"I'm going to look for her," he pulled a lighter from his

pocket as he pushed through the growing crowd, headed for the door. Kenna plowed through the entrance into Spoiled with equal determination.

"Sorry I'm late." She opened her mouth to offer up some excuse, but it died on her lips. Late was not her norm. She'd been building her courage, circling the block in a cab for the last twenty minutes.

"We're in the VIP lounge," Frankie said, leading the way.

Will gripped Kenna's elbow and guided her toward the stairs up to the large room with deep cushioned velvet couches, half-moon shaped leather banquettes and big screen TVs. They both found something more interesting to look at as they passed the long main floor bar and its polished brass railing.

"Pick a hat and get a drink." Frankie raised her arms like Vanna White, to the colorful array of hats in all shapes and sizes displayed on one of the tables.

Kenna heard the clink of glasses. "How far behind am I?"

"Just one, Miz Scarlett," Candace called back, mimicking Kenna's Southern drawl.

Kenna grinned and stuck an elaborate blue-feathered hat onto her head before flopping down beside Candace. "How long did it take you to convince Will to host this shindig?"

Frankie passed her a Mint Julip. "Not long. This is better anyway. Prime viewing from anywhere in the bar, smoking lounge so no one litters the sidewalk –"

"Upper East Side apartment under wraps." Candace broke in.

Frankie shrugged. "That too."

"Will knows you have money and that Daddy's a US Senator," Kenna said.

"I'm not comfortable there. Besides, there's knowing a thing and having your nose rubbed in it. One issue at a time."

Kenna fell silent and pensive as she studied the swirl of ice and mint leaves in her drink.

"You okay?"

"I've got this," Kenna said, a bit shaky, touching her silver cup to Candace's.

"And we've got you."

A FEW RACES in and Spoiled was thrumming with excitement and side bets. Kenna was at the VIP lounge bar getting a fresh julep when Will made his quarter-hour pass-through.

Will pulled Kenna into a tight hug as he groaned, "This is making me crazy." She knew he was serious because the brogue surfaced.

Kenna smoothed the lapels of his suit. Frankie had insisted that if they couldn't get to Kentucky, they would at least dress the part. Spring dresses, festive hats, and a suit for Will. Kenna suspected that that particular mandate was because Will in a three-piece made Frankie weak in the knees, not to avoid fashion *faux pas*.

She also knew it wasn't the pomp making him twitchy. Like her, he was beating back the memories of the last time they had been in this place together. Pretending he didn't see her battered face superimposed over the one looking up at him now. Will paced, flexed his hands in and out of fists and took the same unlit cigarette in and out of his mouth so many times it was bent.

Kenna went for the less complicated source of his stress. "The horse racing story was your idea. Suck it up." She leaned in to his ear. "From which orifice did you pull that idea anyway?"

"What the fuck does that mean?" Will did not whisper.

"Nothing. Not. A. Thing." Kenna raised her hands.

"No, no. You've got something to say, let's have it."

"I don't want to pick your nits," she drawled with exaggerated sweetness. "It's just interesting, that's all."

Frankie and Candace watched the juvenile exchange from across the room.

It never failed. Will and Kenna would give each other a lung, if needed, but they never passed up the slightest opportunity to needle each other. It was a well-established habit long before the fateful day Frankie and Candace became fixtures in their lives.

"Interesting how?" Will loomed into her personal space.

Unintimidated, Kenna pushed against his chest. "You've been with Frankie for what? Six ... eight months? Have you given a fat rat's ass about her writing or anything that wasn't specifically about you before? I find it interesting you picked horse racing. Why not boxing or Fight Club? Or are they too straight? *Oh!* I know, let's get her to do a bio on Uncle Sally!"

"Don't call him that." His finger was in her face.

"Whatever. Anyway Sal Jr. said –"

Will cut her off. "You need to keep clear of Jr. and the old man. Nothing but trouble there, and you know it."

"Oh, please!" Kenna pointed to the man standing in the cigar lounge smoking a cheroot. "He owns this bar, and he lets me decorate the others."

"But I run it. And I know what fingers are in the pie."

Frankie rounded the corner of a sofa. "Truce. We gave you one round to let off the steam, and that's it for the day. If I thought it would work, I could recommend someone, and you could start couples counseling." They gave similar nasally sounds of disapproval.

Will pulled Frankie possessively close to him and kissed her. Kenna turned away, giving herself a mental kick for the stab of envy their obvious affection inflicted. She missed Lucius who was away on another business trip. Another ten days living in ignorance about where he was, what he was doing and to whom. He'd given her an approximate return date, but no assurances.

The afternoon passed with side bets no one intended to collect on, a tutorial from Will on racing forms and trivia from Frankie on nearly every horse, rider, owner and trainer in the race.

"Research much, Frank?" Kenna teased.

Candace tilted her head back and forth, examining Frankie. "I'd like to know where she puts all that data. Her head's normal human size. A Watson computer couldn't possibly fit." Julep-fueled giggling followed.

Will rose, shaking his head, but smiling. He did enjoy being allowed into these hen fests. "I'm going for a smoke."

"Oh, wait. Wait." Frankie jumped up and dashed behind the bar. They all stretched their necks to see over the bar top. She stood bearing a humidor like the crown jewels. "Ta Da! Cubans." Three blank faces stared back, unimpressed with her big reveal. "Em-bar-goed Cubans," she stressed.

"Yes!" Will tossed his pack of cigarettes on the bar.

"Oh, well, in that case." Kenna rolled her eyes. "Because we don't want any of those *legal* stinkweeds they're now foisting on the tourists in here."

"Pretending I'm not an officer of the court," Candace said, smoothing a brow with a pinky finger.

Frankie opened the lid, and the air was instantly infused with fragrant tobacco. Kenna closed her eyes and inhaled. "Mmm, my Colonel," she murmured.

Warm lips brushed over her ear. "You summoned?" Lucius' hands slipped down her arms.

Kenna jumped and spun around. She forgot to temper her joy in public view and threw her arms around his neck. "You made it back!"

He smiled and held her close, welcoming the chore of keeping her balanced on tiptoes. "I promised I would."

"You *said* you'd do your best," Kenna reminded him, her fingers stroked the sprinkling of gray at his temples. She'd interpreted his promise as a gentle way of not raising her hopes.

Cigar in hand, Will leaned against the bar, watching the exchange and tried to reconcile this woman with the Kenna he knew. The closest thing to public affection he'd ever seen her show was to kick him under a table or the girlfriend hugs she, Frankie and Candace freely exchanged. Despite the gut level warning Will felt with this new guy, the man was obviously all about Kenna.

Lucius kept his arm around Kenna as he leaned toward Will and extended his hand. "Will. Nice to see you again."

"Chaerea."

"Ladies. I hope I'm not intruding."

Candace and Frankie shared a look that said, *"as if,"* before answering,

"Not at all."

"Of course, you aren't."

He tilted his head, seriously appraising the colorful tulle and feather concoctions adorning their heads. "Lovely hats."

Will squinted at Frankie's blush, but he ignored it and asked Lucius, "What can I get you?"

"Just water for me, thanks. Jet lag."

No one else noticed Kenna's jaw tighten slightly behind the smile still trained on Chaerea, but he did. *We will be talking about that.*

Will picked up the humidor and offered it to Lucius. "Don't ask me how she managed to get her hands on them, but Frankie says these are the genuine article." He waited while Chaerea rolled a cigar appreciatively between his fingers and inclined his head toward the glass wall of the otherwise cedar-lined cigar room. "Shall we?"

Lucius knew the invitation was intended as more than a collegial smoke with the man. He looked at Kenna and dropped a kiss to her forehead. "Absolutely."

Will threw a perfunctory "anyone else?" over his shoulder, but all three women saw what Lucius had. Will wanted time to assess Lucius without the filter of Kenna's affection. Frankie and Candace flanked Kenna. "Nah. We're good."

———

SIDES ACHING and gasping for breath from laughing at their bourbon-induced, cigar-phallic humor, Candace, Frankie and Kenna ignored the latest uproar from the main bar below. That is, until they saw Will and Sal Jr. fling open the doors of the cigar lounge and race down the stairs.

"Something really lit a fire under *them*." Candace followed their path to the front door with a smooth roll of her head.

Frankie half rose to see over the railing to the floor below. "Throwing someone famous out, you think?"

"What? Who's on fire?" Kenna said.

"Another julep for the queen of observation," Frankie said, circling a hand over Kenna's head.

In that moment, the crowd parted enough to allow Candace and Frankie to see a wild-eyed Lorenzo Barzini yelling down a bouncer and then turning his wrath on his cousin and Will. The throng quieted to a dull roar, the better to watch the free show, so they both heard Barzini when he shouted, "It's a free country. You can't keep me out!"

Candace turned a wide, sunshine smile to Kenna. "Just a couple of drunks."

Frankie curled her lips inward, making her lush mouth a firm line.

Kenna slowly lowered her silver cup and spit a perfectly seasoned chunk of ice back inside. "What's wrong with y'all?"

She stood and leaned over the rail to look down on the confrontation, now a verbal and physical battle at the main doors. Candace and Frankie leapt to stand beside her. Kenna's legs softened like melting ice pops.

"Oh, God, no. Not now. Please, not now." Everything came rushing back. This time with witnesses. Her friends, her *family*, were here to become part of her worst nightmare. She frantically looked toward the glass wall of the cigar lounge as Lucius turned his ever-watchful hawk eyes from the fracas to her. The horror on Kenna's face catapulted him into action. The cigar forgotten, he moved toward her, long strides closing the distance.

"What is *wrong* with him?" Candace said, a rhetorical question because it was clear Barzini was under the influence of something. His arms flailed away from muscled hands trying to shove him toward the door.

"Coke high," Kenna said flatly.

Below, Barzini continued his erratic attempts to throw off Will and breach the threshold of Spoiled. Spittle flew from his lips as he sneered.

"You'll never keep me out. I christened this shit hole the night I taught your little fuck toy a lesson." With preternatural accuracy, he found Kenna watching from above. "Maybe it's time for another."

Kenna couldn't hear his words, but the effect was as if he'd snarled them into her ear. Her stomach lurched. She backed away from the railing into the hard wall of Lucius' chest. Caged by the comforting arms of her friends, a twelve foot drop and Lucius' overwhelming presence, her breath caught and beads of sweat covered her forehead and arms. Her tremors traveled from her body into the people encircling her.

"Kenna?" Frankie gripped Kenna's arm.

Kenna snatched her arm away, her tunnel vision riveted by the tableau below.

"Steady," Candace said and laid a gentle hand on Kenna's arm.

"*Stop touching me.*"

"You've got it," Candace gave her a last comforting pat and moved to stand in front of her.

Lucius clenched his jaw. He was usually the one in command of situations and, in this moment, he had control over nothing. Another side effect of his relationship with Kenna: accepting that over which he had no jurisdiction.

His punch line delivered, Barzini laughed and gave a two-handed flip off to Will and Sal Jr. before straightening his jacket and strutting out of the club.

Will turned to Sal Jr. "You motherfucker. You knew. You *had* to know."

"Hey, for a while, I thought it was *you*. *WhatamIgonnado?* He's my cousin." The excuse sounded as weak aloud as it did echoing in his head.

"*Yer whinging?* You jobby fuckin' bawbag!"

"Jobby?! Bawbag?! The fuck?"

"Ball sac, you sack o' shite." As Will's temper got loose, his Scots got thicker and he had no fucks to give that he was yelling at his boss. "Legit or no, yer still Sally's laddy buck."

"You don't know my position here!"

"Yeah, fucker. I do."

"You don't." Sal looked down to hide his pained expression. "*She* made me promise never to tell."

HOODED EYES WATCHED as the two men quite obviously in charge ejected a third in mid-rant. *Fascinating.*

He turned his gaze back to the mezzanine where Lucius Chaerea stood with the little blonde and her friends, all four focused on the action at the door.

His objective this night had been to observe the woman who was, apparently, now the focus of Chaerea's very personal interest. *It was serendipitous that the man himself had appeared.*

A chink in Chaerea's armor? She was surrounded by protectors at the moment, but that wouldn't always be the case.

LUCIUS HAD HURRIED Kenna out before her panic attack caused her to faint. The crowd seemed to have forgotten the whole affair as soon as Barzini was gone. Candace refused the offered flame, but put the cigar between her teeth like a small female version of James Cagney. "I'd pay money to be a fly on that wall. How much will she tell him, do you think?" She referred to Lucius' surgical extraction of Kenna from the club.

"Who knows? Could be a full disclosure or smoke and mirrors." Frankie mimed a delicate puff off her stogie and wondered how long she should wait for Will to remember she was still upstairs. While she had Candace to herself, she said, "Speaking of smoke blowing and pricks who gaze endlessly at their own reflection in mirrors, is Palmer still poking around Will?"

"He tries. What a pain in my ass." Candace, exhaustion in her voice, leaned back against the velvet cushion and adjusted the angle of her saucy little fascinator. "When I left law school and took this job, I thought I'd be bringing justice because, you know, Justice Department? Instead of getting the bad guys – like Barzini, just as a for instance – I'm up to my neck in paper. Or

I'm fending off jerks like Ross. You know what really pisses me off?" Her slender finger jabbed the air between them. "I can't remember the last time I had a real date that didn't involve business of some kind, and now an asshole mobster has hijacked my day at the races."

CHAPTER FORTY-TWO

"Breathe," Lucius said. He pressed his hand between her shoulders and forced Kenna's head to her knees. He whipped through the traffic heading north on Riverside Drive. His maneuvering skills rivaled Mac's. There was no immediate destination other than away from the club. Away from Barzini. He'd even had the fleeting thought that he could have her on a plane and hidden safely away in his family home in Tuscany before anyone realized she was gone.

Kenna flailed her arms like a marionette fighting its strings as she tried to sit upright.

"Breathe." Lucius ordered, again.

She swatted feebly at his arms. "Stop touching me!"

Lucius' molars ground together, that was the third or fourth time she'd demanded someone's hands be removed from her. She was allowing neither comfort nor aid. He slowly pulled his arm away and grasped the steering wheel.

Kenna didn't register that Lucius no longer held her head between her knees so when she flipped her hair back, she slammed into the seat. The out of control motion slung her hand against the window and cracked her knuckles. "Shit!" she said, shaking her throbbing hand violently.

Aware of every breath she took, Lucius drove up the highway, listening for regular intervals of inhalation and slow exhales as evidence she was calmer. His peripheral vision monitored the relaxation of her shoulders and the receding tremors in her hands.

When she finally managed a controlled breath, he unlocked his jaw to speak. "You need to tell me about that man."

"It doesn't have anything to do with you."

"After today, it does. Your confrontation at the Meadowlands may have been coincidental –"

"I *knew* it!" She interrupted him, slamming her palm against the dash to punctuate every word. "I knew it! That was *your* minion. I didn't want to believe it. I'm so stupid. Will said you were a spook." She rubbed her hand and whined, "Ow."

"That is not the point," Lucius said with an eerie calm.

"It's *my* point. You spied on me. Ohmygod." She clasped her hands to her head. "The letters. Hand delivered by your pets. I'm not believing this. At least Barzini has the balls to stalk me in person."

Lucius jerked the wheel and threaded his car across lanes of traffic into a parking lot. The tires screeched when he whipped into the first available space. "I can't do this and drive."

"Do what? Explain to me how you're different."

The look he gave her pierced her with shame. She wasn't being fair, but she was too scared, angry and humiliated to care. She'd been unmasked. Her deepest wound had been ripped open.

"Where's my bag?" She reached for the door handle, only to be stopped by her seatbelt and Lucius' hand on her wrist.

She shot him a withering look and tried to jerk away. He didn't let go. "I'm sure your friends will return it."

"Let. Go."

"Are you planning to flee through the park?" His hawk-like eyes scanned the area. The last rays of twilight shimmered on the river. For a moment, the city was bathed in the softness of peach, pink and purple. Gentle shadows would soon be endless pits of darkness or stretches of neon-lit chaos.

"No," she said without conviction. "I need air." Kenna felt the panic rising in her again. "Let me out. Now!"

Lucius let go of her arm and opened his door, hoping she would allow him to get around to the passenger side. He cursed under his breath when Kenna flew out her door as soon as his foot hit the pavement. She hurried toward the little-used stairs that led to the ivy-covered arches of Freedom Tunnel. Lucius took the time to secure his car before following. She could sprint down the crumbling concrete steps into the park, or worse, find an open gate into the tunnel. No matter, he was faster and accustomed to the hunt.

She knew he would follow, but Kenna needed a moment to get herself together, to steel her frustration and anger. *He had me followed. He's been spying on me.* She repeated the words over and over to herself, the new mantra fueling her diversionary tactic while she negotiated the steps in the fading light.

From the top of the stairs, he called down to her. "You may as well stop. I can catch you here or in a hundred feet. The choice is yours."

"Predatory, *Colonel?*" she spat over her shoulder. A cyclist slowed for a moment to give her a questioning look, but shrugged and peddled on when she shot him a "what are *you* looking at?" glare.

Kenna took a few steps, then turned and looked up at Lucius ready to pounce from the top of the stairs. Streetlights glowed behind him, concealed his features and turned him into a looming shadow gliding down to her.

"You had me followed," she accused. "How could you do that? On what planet did you think that was ever going to be okay? Seriously?"

With measured steps, he reached level ground, closing the gap between them, but he didn't touch her. "I am protecting you. And could have prevented that situation long ago had you simply been honest."

"Simple? Honest? Are you *kidding me*?" She flung her hands in the air. "Mr. I-don't-lie. Your whole life is one big secret, but I'm not allowed mine? Go to hell."

"Been there."

"Don't! Don't you dare make me feel sorry for you because your wife died or because you have a few scars." Kenna stepped closer, her fists in tight balls, her arms crossed. "And don't try to convince me you're saving me. From the first dance, *you* have been the real threat."

He turned and with both hands grabbed the iron gate of the tunnel arch instead of her. The underlying truth in her angry rant shot cold fear through him. He shook his head.

"What?" Kenna pushed his shoulder. "Why are you shaking your head? Tell me I'm wrong."

"You're wrong," he said, so low she felt more than heard the words. Lucius held fast to the rusted bars and looked over his shoulder. "What is your history with that man?" He'd drawn his own conclusions based on Chapman's report and her dream-induced clues, but Lucius needed to know what happened as much as she needed to purge it.

"*History*," she spat, tilting her head to get into his face, "and none of your fucking business."

"Damnit, Kenna!" He slammed his fist into the gate. It rattled, and the hinges squeaked open.

He saw the flinch pass over her upturned face. "Am I next?" she challenged.

"What?" Lucius cupped her face with his hands as if he were holding spun sugar. "How could you think ..."

Kenna grabbed his wrists, intent on pulling his hands away and escaping the deep pain in his eyes – pain she'd caused and something more. A love she wanted and had refused to accept, so great was her fear of losing it.

He squeezed tighter, slowly sliding his fingers into her hair, gripping and pulling her head back. Lucius' mouth crushed hers. Kenna moaned a protest that died as her lips opened and her tongue slashed against his.

Their bodies crashed into the iron bars, Lucius' back taking the brunt of the force. The fencing clanged in its footings. He pulled his mouth away, intent on getting to the truth before they were beyond talking. "Tell me."

Shaking her head, Kenna forced his mouth back to hers. She didn't want to talk or think. She wanted to lash out and, as unfair as it was, hurl the weight of her pain onto someone else.

She nipped at his lip with her teeth, and the sting startled him. Lucius flicked his tongue over the tender spot and tasted the coppery tang of his own blood. Dipping his head, he tenderly kissed the column of her neck, and with the light brush of his lips, he forced away the near violent urge to punish her in return.

Kenna punched at his back, even as she bent her head back offering, begging for more. "Don't! Fuck me or fight me, but don't you dare make love to me!"

As Lucius bit into the tender flesh below her ear, he gripped her ass with both hands and lifted her to him. The bottom of her dress rode up her thighs as her legs locked around him. A few strides carried them through the open rusted gate into the sanctuary of the dark tunnel.

Cold stone dug into Kenna's back. Lucius' rock hard length pressed against her soft, pulsing center, unerringly grinding the tender nub through layers of clothes until she whimpered under his brutal kisses.

Lowering her feet to the ground, he knelt and stripped her panties down her legs, narrowly avoiding getting kicked as she tried to sling the garment away. He cursed as he stood and tucked them safely into the pocket of his jacket with one hand as the other opened the fly of his jeans. Kenna reached for him, but he caught her wrists and pinned them to the wall above her head.

"Don't move."

She didn't listen, but reached for him again and pulled at his clothes in desperation. Lucius hissed when her nails raked his hard flesh.

He locked a hand around both of her wrists and held them against the wall over her head. "I said don't move." He freed himself with the other, all the while feasting on her neck and mouth. One moment his tongue was in fierce battle with hers; the next, he was throwing her off her combative mission with sizzling licks and lingering kisses on her neck and shoulders.

Kenna wrapped a leg around his hip, the other barely balanced on the uneven gravel. Her mind and body reached for oblivion. Lucius roughly jerked the hem of her dress up to her waist. His shoes scraped in the gravel when he thrust his hips, driving the air from her lungs.

Kenna's heel dug into the back of his thigh to pull him closer and give her leverage to meet the driving force of his body plunging into hers. All she felt was his mouth on hers, the fierce length inside her and the delicious pressure building. Heat flooded through her limbs and there it was, the moment she'd been seeking where nothing mattered but them. The cry that broke from her lips was a shattered wail of pleasure and anguish. As soon as it began, it was over.

Lucius braced his hand on the wall, allowing hers to fall to his shoulders. He ground his teeth as the muscles in his back and thighs seized in release with her. Kenna wrapped her arms around his neck and buried her face against his chest.

Fatigue overwhelmed him. Thirty-six hours of being awake and vigilant, then on a plane to get home, combined with the events of the last hour had siphoned Lucius' remaining strength. He let her foot slip to the ground and propped his forehead against the cool stone above hers.

"We must go," he managed.

Kenna nodded and straightened her clothes. "You can take me to the gallery."

"I have neither the energy nor the inclination." He buttoned his jeans. "This is not a debate or a democracy. I'm taking you home."

They drove in silence to Lucius' house. Kenna shivered beneath the sport coat he'd given her. She wasn't cold. Everything she'd tried so hard to keep locked down for so many months was determined to escape her body all at once.

"Would you like some tea? Something to eat?" Lucius asked, leaning against the frame of his bedroom door.

Kenna sat on his bed. One of his t-shirts swallowed her, her shower damp hair clung to her neck and back. She looked so fragile in that moment, it made him feel powerless.

Kenna shook her head no as she picked at a thread on the shirt hem.

"I'll be on the sofa if you need anything," he said.

She nodded but still didn't look up. Lucius shifted, but didn't leave.

Kenna finally raised her eyes and managed a choked whisper. "I need time."

It was his turn to silently nod. *Time for what?* he wanted to ask. Patience had always been his secret ally, and tonight he needed it more than ever before.

"When you're ready then," he said softly.

Kenna managed to dam the tears until his back was turned.

Lucius paused and turned his head just enough so she would hear him clearly. "I didn't need a name or face to know this man existed. I've seen your wounds. I've lain beside you when you dream. There are no secrets, Kenna."

CHAPTER FORTY-THREE

L ucius stilled as the soft padding of her bare feet on the hall floor reached him.

"Are you awake?" Her voice was so soft had he been asleep, he may not have heard her.

"Yes," he said, just as hushed. As tired as he was, sleep had not been possible.

Kenna stayed in the shadows, just out of reach of the flickering light from the television. *The Searchers* played, though Lucius had muted the volume.

"You could have turned the sound up," she said.

He didn't reply, but she thought she heard a shift from the sofa cushions, as if he'd turned his head toward her.

"I'd been seeing him for about six months." Her left thumb unconsciously massaged the barely visible scar on her right palm.

Lucius started to rise.

"Please, stay there. I can do this easier if you're not looking at me."

She saw his head nod once and then disappear into the shadows of the sofa.

"I saw the proverbial writing on the wall. Calling to ask how my day was going became wanting to know where I was twenty-four seven. My skirts were too short or too long or too tight. I was too boring in bed." Lucius grunted his dissent and that somehow helped her go on with the story. "But it was our last date that did it. He sent my steak back. *Mine!*" She laughed without humor.

She tucked her cold fingers under her arms and shifted her feet. They were getting cold too, and she was starting to shiver in earnest now.

"He *always* treated waiters like shit, but somehow sending my half-eaten, perfectly cooked dinner back, while I sat there and did *nothing*, was my fish-or-cut-bait moment. I envisioned how things would go. How it wouldn't be long before everything I said and did would be him pulling the puppet strings, not me, and decided I had to end it.

"So, I asked him to meet me at Spoiled." She took a deep breath. "I hadn't been back there before today."

Lucius sat up and swung his legs over the seat of the couch. He still wasn't looking at her, but stared straight ahead, nodding. He appreciated the significance attending that party had held for her.

Encouraged by the gesture, Kenna continued. "Anyway, I had the whole speech worked out. How I knew he wasn't happy. How I didn't want to be the reason he couldn't find someone who made him happy. It all sounded brilliant, rational, self-deprecating enough in my head."

"He didn't follow the script," Lucius clenched his fists on his knees to force himself to stay still and listen.

"He did for about a minute. I thought it was over and started to walk away. But he'd brought one of his sidekicks, a witness who'd seen *me* break it off."

The image of her turning away from Barzini was so vivid,

Lucius envisioned he could shout out a warning to watch her back.

She paused, and when she started the story again, her voice shook. "Then he asked me who I was fucking. I'd never heard that much hate in a person's voice before." Now her flat tone matched Lucius'.

"He grabbed my arm and slung me into the bar. Sal Jr., at my insistence, had put in that long beautiful brass rail." Kenna let out a harsh humorless laugh. "Son-of-a-bitch left a bruise across my back like I'd been hit by a car." She shook her head. The whole series of events still sounded unreal to her ears.

Lucius' body tensed as he imagined the shock and pain arcing across his back instead of hers.

"When I didn't answer, that's when he slapped me the first time. It's not just in the cartoons, you know. You *do* see stars."

His stomach lurched. He'd seen bodies beaten and broken, and the visual of Kenna's ordeal was too vivid and only beginning.

"I think he said something, but it may have been my imagination. I don't know how many times he slapped me. Seriously, who open-handed slaps a thing over and over like that?"

Lucius recoiled at her use of "a thing."

"He stopped long enough for me to drop my hands. Never drop your hands, Kenna," she added the aside to herself. She chuffed out a breath when she saw Lucius' silhouetted head nod in agreement.

"I guess his palm was tired, so he went at the other side with the backhand." Kenna unconsciously touched her hairline as she itemized the damage. "Did I mention he wears a big sapphire ring? Seven stitches on my forehead."

Lucius recalled the silver thread of a scar that cut through the fine blonde strands just above her temple.

"The next one cracked my nose. I almost passed out. Things

get a little fuzzy after that, but I remember seeing the paring knife by the bar sink."

Lucius sucked in an audible breath.

"I don't know how I got to it. I had to have jumped and grabbed it. Dumb move." Kenna muttered to herself as she rubbed the old scars on her hand. "He grabbed my wrist and smashed my hand against that damn brass rail until I dropped the knife."

A pained groan escaped from deep in Lucius' chest. He'd had enough broken or cracked bones to know the pain that she'd endured. He wasn't sure how much more he could listen to. Each detail was more agonizing to him than the last.

"After that, I've got nothing other than what the ER report says and the few things Will let slip out. Anyway, he started punching at some point. There were too many cuts and cracked facial bones for just slaps and backhands."

She traced over her left brow, "They super-glued my eyebrow!" she added with startling and discordant gaiety. "How cool is that?

"Anyway, that's where Will found me in the morning. Wrapped around a barstool. Shoe prints on my stomach, thighs and back." She paused for a breath. "Ferragamo."

Kenna's tone softened, and Lucius heard the soft smile in her voice. "Will didn't know me from Adam, but he carried me to the ER and sat vigil. He wouldn't let Sal Jr. in for two days, thinking it was him who'd done it. But then, Sal was suspicious of Will. The detectives barred both of them from my room until I could talk well enough to make them believe it wasn't either Will or Sal."

She smiled, and for the first time, tears pooled in her eyes. "Will was unbelievable. The first thing I clearly remember was hearing him dressing down hospital staff in that Scottish brogue because there was blood in my cath line. Apparently, that's not uncommon when someone plays soccer with your kidneys."

With that, Will MacKenzie became the holder of a debt Lucius could never repay. He reached out to her over the arm of the sofa. "Please, Kenna, I will close my eyes if I must, but I can't do this with you so far away."

Kenna shook her head and choked back a sob. For worse was still to come.

"They came to see me one night. Big Sally and Carmine Barzini. I was too drugged to know much, but when I checked out of the hospital my bills were paid, my student loans were gone and the gallery has a perpetual petty cash reserve for the months I can't make ends meet. They bought me ..." She swallowed hard. "And I was cheap."

She straightened her back and took a deep breath. "I never told you because I was selfish. I wanted you for as long as I could hold on to you. Luc, you look at me like ... like it's the first time you've ever seen the sun." She coughed out something between a laugh and a cry and fought to keep from weeping with anguish. "You don't see the bruises Will sees or the discount sale tag. All that's lost now."

He felt more than heard her backing away down the hall and leapt to his feet, vaulting over the back of the couch. Kenna yelped when his hand locked around her wrist and he began to pull her around the room, turning on every light and lamp in the place as they went.

Standing in the bright center of his home, Lucius cupped her face and turned it up to his. His heart was pounding in his chest, his breaths shallow and ragged. "Look at me. Look at my face. What do you see? I am in anguish for that woman I never knew. Horrified this man still feels any right to the same air you breathe and despise the danger that he still is to you." Lucius kissed the tears on her cheeks and eyes. "Look at me and see.

You amaze me." He placed a hand in the center of her chest. "Your heart, your light awakened a part of me I believed was lost."

When Kenna blinked away enough tears to see his face, she saw he was telling her the truth. His emotionless mask was gone, revealing the same smile he'd had as they danced that first night at Wallace Henneby's gala. The smile she loved.

Kenna sagged against him, and Lucius wrapped his arms around her.

"I'm so tired, Luc."

THE NEXT MORNING, as Lucius sat in a chair outside his bedroom reading Chapman's dossier on Lorenzo Barzini, his phone dinged with Kenna's tone. Peeking in to see if she'd been awakened, he spoke softly. "Chaerea."

"Will MacKenzie. Is she sleeping?"

"About ten hours now," Lucius said, moving away from the door.

"Don't let her go over twelve, or she'll have a migraine. Just hot tea and some kind of clear soup when she wakes. She's going to ask for pasta or Pings, but those just come back up. She'll probably sleep for another twelve hours straight after."

"Thank you, MacKenzie, for every –"

"Don't thank me yet. I'm not done," Will said. "Coping mechanism, they call it. Fucking shrinks."

Lucius gave a curt nod as if Will could see it. "Anything else?"

"She'll pick a fight about some bullshit, split-hair issue. Don't engage," Will said. He continued using language the therapists had used with him. "Don't reward unproductive dialogue." At

Lucius' chuckle, Will smiled. "Let me guess. That warning is a little fucking late."

"We survived," Lucius said.

Will snorted. "Unh huh. Got all your limbs and crockery?"

There was a pause that stretched into awkward silence.

"Oh, after a day's sleep, *make her* shower and use soap, get dressed and get out."

"I'll have her call you as soon as possible," Lucius said.

"Yeah, soon. Frankie and Candace too. *They* know she's safe." Will's emphasis was not lost to Lucius. "But they want to hear her voice and all that."

"Understood." Lucius sucked his teeth before changing the subject. "Barzini."

"Fuckin' dobber's in the wind," Will said almost instantly. He'd been expecting the question. "If the old man finds him, it's over." There was another long pause. "I'll let you know if I hear anything."

"Thank you."

Lucius ended the call, his eyes fixed on the door to his bedroom. *Lorenzo Barzini would do well to run to his father's justice.*

CHAPTER FORTY-FOUR

K enna was quite pleased with her recovery time on this melt-down. Less than a week and she'd given all the therapists and PTSD gurus a mental middle finger. She didn't need their magic potions or emotional vomit marathons. Sleep and Campbell's Chicken Noodle fixed everything. Everything, but this.

She'd literally lost a few days after the disastrous racing party, but had finally convinced Lucius she was well enough, stable enough and secure enough in his affections to return to the real world.

Kenna stared at the clickbait on her iPad, her wet eyes struggling to focus. She'd wished for this. Prayed for it. Even created elaborate scenarios where she'd caused it.

Mob Boss Scion Found Dead In Abandoned Car

"Bastard! Could have at least died in a pool of his own piss from a drug overdose, but *noooo*. He passed out in his car. Probably drunk and never knew it happened." Hot, angry tears streaked mascara down her cheeks.

"FUCK YOU!" She hurled magazines, books and anything else that wasn't nailed to her desk across the room. Her low, wailing scream echoed off the gallery walls. Even in her mania, she managed to stop her arm from slinging her iPad and dropped it to the floor. A small spider web of cracks appeared in the corner of the screen. Her pretty, antique desk chair shattered when she'd swung it like a baseball bat against one of the gallery's support columns.

On the street, Lucius heard the sounds of battle. His long legs took the stairs two at a time. Ellis Griffin was close behind, weapon in hand.

Kenna screamed in fright when the gallery doors exploded open. Their grim faces belonged on Berserkers in chainmail, brandishing broadswords and slaying dragons, not the ghosts she was fighting.

She had forgotten the Colonel's concession to her return to work was that he would pick her up in the afternoons. "Get out! *Get out!*" She spun away from their astonished faces. "Oh, God, please leave." She clung to the column she'd just attacked with the chair. "*Please!* Please, go away."

Without a word, Ellis retreated soundlessly down the steps. Lucius picked his way through the debris, stopping a few feet behind her. "Kenna?"

"Leave me alone." Her hands curled into fists, desperate to fight back another emotional nosedive.

"I cannot do that. What happened?"

"Nothing." She sagged against the column and attempted to wipe her face clean. A handkerchief appeared in front of her. She hadn't heard or felt him move around her.

"Let us not have this discussion again." There was nothing forgiving or gentle in his voice.

Her head jerked up as she snapped her teeth closed on a

curse. Kenna rolled around the square post, her back to Lucius, her answer barely audible. "The son-of-a-bitch is dead."

"I've seen the news."

Kenna dabbed her eyes and gave a sheepish nudge to the splintered chair at her feet. "I guess I thought it would be more."

"More?" His eyes wide, he wondered what her definition of more than dead might be.

"You know, something humiliating and painful. And slow."

"Who knew you had a torturous streak, love?" He had the audacity to wink at her when she handed him his handkerchief.

"I'm serious." Kenna blew out a breath, kneeling to begin the task of plucking toothpick-sized pieces of wood off her floor. "I suppose it's enough to know he's on a rotisserie in hell."

Lucius removed his suit coat and draped it over another chair he was certain was part of an exhibit. "Or ice, if you believe your Dante. Come here." He took her hand, brushed the wood scraps from her palm and sat her in the seat now serving as his coat rack. "You sit. I'll sweep. Broom?"

Kenna did as she was bid and pointed to a narrow school locker in the corner.

As she watched in fascination, her Colonel, sleeves rolled up, swept and tidied the detritus of her fit of temper and frustration. The bright search engine homepage was still visible on her screen. Kenna picked up the tablet and read the story beneath the photo and headline.

Slowly, she raised her eyes to Lucius, still busy with his housekeeping. Words from the article floated around him like a dark cloud, familiar words from her own ordeal – *Contusions on extremities. Fractured orbital. Fingers broken or missing. Kidneys ruptured. Injuries consistent with brutal assault and torture.*

Her mind was racing. *Sal Jr. or any of the Tomasis would*

have had him overdosed or drowned and dumped the body. Will?
Not his style.

There'd be a bullet somewhere.

"Did you do this?" she whispered.

THREE DAYS BEFORE, Kenna had slept through a third call from this blocked number. Suspicious, Lucius had assumed Barzini was attempting to harass her and picked up the fourth time. Silent, he held the phone waiting for the caller to speak.

"Chaerea?" Sal Jr., had asked hesitantly.

"Kenna is not taking calls," Lucius said.

"I figured. Wondered how long before you'd answer a blocked number."

"You have my attention, Tomasi. Speak quickly."

"I know where my cousin's hiding out. He's got a woman –"

"Isn't this something your family would rather deal with?" Lucius asked.

"They cut him loose. Kenna'd kill me if MacKenzie got busted on an assault or, worse, murder. He'll be looked at no matter what happens anyway. Got a feeling you don't have that problem. I owe her."

Lucius took a long breath and looked across at the slow rise and fall of the blankets over Kenna as she slept. "Where is he?"

CHAPTER FORTY-FIVE

Kneeling beside Lucius on a sunny, summer Sunday morning, Kenna offered up her moment of silence, grateful for the relative calm in her tribe. Lucius' and Will's two-pronged assault against her keeping the loft above the gallery had relaxed as the weeks following Barzini's death passed without incident. Not even a lost tourist dripping gelato on her floors disturbed her bubble of contentment.

Lucius' trips continued, but with less frequency and duration. She marked the passage of time by his homecomings and the blissful days she was in residence with him rather than days or numbers on a calendar. Kenna blushed as the previous twelve hours of welcoming him home flashed in her mind. Lucius gave her a questioning look as they sat back in the pew.

"Don't ask," she mouthed, blushing deeper as the seat vibrated with his chuckle.

He didn't need specifics. One topic above all others caused such an enticing glow, and the fact she was having such thoughts during mass amused him immensely.

"I vote we start Midnight Mass in the summers and do our drinking at one," Frankie pressed the cool glass of her gin and tonic against the column of her neck.

"We do drink at one," Candace fanned her face as they sat waiting on Kenna for their weekly caucus. "This is miserable. The garbage is self-basting in this heat." She shuddered. "And let's not contemplate the rats tanning themselves on the heaps of trash. Why is there always a waste management strike in the hottest month of the summer or when there're two feet of snow on the ground?"

Kenna pushed through to the table. Beads of perspiration, formed in the short walk from the car to the door, shimmered around her hairline. "Fan me!" she said, her arms were over her head hands flapping toward her armpits.

"That's attractive," Candace said laconically as she waved the menu in a few big sweeps toward Kenna.

Plopping into her chair like a scoop of melting ice cream sliding off its cone, Kenna shrugged. "There are just some things Luc will *not* do."

"Who'd-a-thunk the Colonel was vanilla," Frankie mused.

"You might as well spill it now," said Candace, after their server had refilled their water goblets for the third time. The heat was making them drink it down faster than the frosty gin and tonics. "You're not really present this morning. By now, you should have noticed The Bartender is wearing that blue shirt you love because it matches his eyes."

"Or the dark man fur you can see peeking out of the vee where it's unbuttoned," Frankie added with a waggle of elegant eyebrows.

"What are you two babbling about?"

"We can't do it all," Candace said. Although, there was enough female attention at the bar, he didn't actually need more from their table.

"Keep up, Ken. You're a drink and a leer behind," Frankie pointed out.

Kenna scratched her head beneath the loose bun, dislodging stray curls that clung to her neck. The gesture was a nervous delaying tactic more than a physical necessity. "I need a favor," she finally said. Her averted eyes and almost embarrassed tone stopped Frankie's and Candace's forks mid-air.

"Ooh-kaay." Candace drew out the word and lowered her bite of crabmeat omelet in slow motion.

Both women stared at Kenna. Concern and curiosity swirled around their little table. Kenna looked from one to the other.

Unable to stand the silence, Frankie blurted out, "What?"

Kenna rubbed her face and drew a deep breath. She'd spent many sleepless nights since Lorenzo Barzini's death worrying over this decision. Finally, she said, "I need to borrow ten thousand dollars to pay back my student loans."

"I thought that was handled," Frankie said.

"It was." Kenna played with a fingernail. "I didn't figure the vig on this one." She used the slang for interest on money owed to a loan-shark. "It's too high and too permanent." She shrugged. "I need to cut the cord. I kept their secrets, and I could have ruined everything."

"I'm guessing, since you're asking us, you haven't talked to Luc about this," Candace said.

"He knows they paid for the hospital, rehab and the loans." They being Carmine Barzini and Salvatore Tomasi Sr., who'd visited Kenna in the hospital and then her debts were gone. "I suspect he'd say they got off easy paying for it all. Or, he'd go to some secret safe behind a bookcase or something and hand me the cash."

"I vote for door number two," Frankie said.

Kenna nodded in agreement. "Some days, I can convince myself they owed me. Most days, it's just cash on the nightstand of my life." The humiliation of being bought, more than being assaulted, had kept her hiding the truth of the assault from everyone.

"Are you sure keeping Luc out of the loop is the best plan?" Candace asked. "If we're learning from mistakes and secret keeping."

"Baby steps," Kenna replied. "Using Luc's money would feel like switching sides of the bed. I will tell him, but money makes people weird." They had heard her views on money and control before. She was making a huge exception in asking her friends for a loan, but they were women, more like sisters, and she wasn't sharing a bed with either.

"We disagree," Candace said, gesturing from herself to Frankie. "And so will your Colonel, but you know we're in."

"Thank you," Kenna said. She was terrified. This would deplete her life savings and probably leave her unemployed, but she would be free of any obligations to the Tomasi family.

There was a moment of dissent when Frankie offered to dip into her trust fund for the whole of Kenna's debt or just the ten thousand she was short, but Candace and Kenna insisted the loan be split. It was the best way to allow Kenna to keep some control over her circumstances.

"I guess this means you'll have to do that smart business model thing and find investors for the new gallery after all," Frankie said.

As painful as the idea of giving up her nest egg was, being

free of Big Sally once and for all, while not sacrificing her morality or sanity at the altar of secrets, was worth more years of scrimping and saving. She'd have to learn to trust others to support and share her dream without hidden strings attached.

CHAPTER FORTY-SIX

M ike had been keeping his eyes and ears open, especially when Lucius was away. Not quite a bodyguard. Not exactly a spy. Not that he minded. Eyes on Kenna Campbell usually meant a peek at Candace Fisher.

Today's status update meeting was in a small diner not far from the Tribeca hot spot where the girls brunched. The rear booth where they sat, across from the diner's long counter and stools, was inconspicuous and small. They each had clear visibility of the front door, the street and the combination fire-exit-delivery-door beyond the restrooms. Grilled meatloaf sandwiches and fresh pie were added bonuses. When Lucius arrived after delivering Kenna to Marco's, Mike rose to abdicate his seat facing the front to the Colonel.

"Sit." Lucius slid into the booth seat facing the rear exit. He grinned at Mike's quizzical look. "Don't get used to it, Mike. Coffee," he said over his shoulder before the waitress could get around the end of the counter with her pad and pencil.

Their initial suspicion of Lazarashvilli's presence had yielded no fruit and there were no indications he had a hint of

Kenna's and Lucius' relationship beyond the coincidence of internet activity close to Kenna's gallery. Despite being on several watch lists, Lazarashvilli was not a high priority for international intelligence agencies. Still, no one in Lucius' organization was foolish enough to let his guard down.

In the wake of 9-11, petty war criminals and human trafficking took a back seat to terrorists, foreign and domestic. These men knew Lazarashvilli wouldn't come out of hiding simply to check out Lucius' acquaintances, but, as he'd proved many times over the last few years, he was keeping tabs, and his lust for revenge had not diminished.

Lazarashvilli was forever searching for bait, tempting Lucius to hunt.

He'd made a game out of luring the Colonel out of his carefully preserved privacy. He blamed Lucius for the fateful shot that left him so physically deformed he couldn't enjoy the pleasures of his product, nor the small dignity of relieving himself.

In the last month, three known associates of Lazarashvilli's had been seen. The first in New York, another in London, then the third in Cairo. Now, there had been another sighting back in the Big Apple. One instance had made Lucius put precautionary eyes on Kenna and give notice to his extensive network in the intelligence community. With two, someone was detained and questioned. Three times, and now twice in his back yard, reminded him there are no coincidences.

"Tell me again." Lucius ordered, now in full Lt. Colonel Chaerea mode. He placed the folder containing a written report and several photos on the seat beside him.

His arms folded across his chest, his eyes closed, Lucius leaned back in the booth, his food forgotten as Mike began. The written report was thorough. However, there was always more to any story than simply the facts, and that was what he sought now. *That* was where Lucius excelled, in that place beyond facts.

"It didn't start out as anything for you. We were checking a security alert for another client. There's a Russian, ah, social club a few blocks over. We didn't really think the attempt was from the outside. There are some computer traces my guys are monitoring, but it never hurts to kick a few anthills. So, we strolled over for a little *borscht.*" He put the cap back on his head, took it off to scratch his scalp and wedged the cap back on. "Now, Colonel, I've never seen this one in person before. Only remember seeing his headshot pop when we did that thing in the Sudan. I wasn't even sure it was the same guy. It took us about fifty passes to clear up the photo enough to be sure."

"Was he with anyone?" Lucius' eyes remained closed. Mike imagined he heard the clicking of gears.

"No, sir. He sat alone, eating."

"Drinking?"

"Just coffee."

Lucius' eyes opened, and he leaned his forearms on the table. "What made you notice him?"

Mike nodded. They were on the same page. "The alone part. If he were trying to hide in plain sight, he'd have been part of the crowd. Not this guy." He pointed to the photos. "He wasn't too concerned with discretion and didn't seem to be waiting for anyone. Conspicuous in his isolation."

"Intending to be seen," Lucius added.

"Yeah, looked that way to me," Mike agreed. "Seen by you though?"

"Maybe," Lucius said. "Let's take a stroll. Pick up some *pastila.*" The mention of the traditional Russian fruit confectionary told Mike exactly where they were going.

Mike pulled his phone from his pocket. "You calling your team, or do you want me to put one together?"

"No team. We will be too many or not enough," Lucius said.

"Colonel, I don't recommend we go in alone," Mike said, showing his unease. They were mutually respectful colleagues and, occasionally in battle situations, had been damn near friendly drinking buddies. The Lt. Colonel might not be accustomed to getting such direct opposition, but Mike wasn't about ceremony or politeness right now.

"We're only going to see and be seen. He wanted my attention. He's got it. Relax, Mike. No one is going to shoot me without the go ahead from Laz, and we won't be there long enough for that."

"Could be kill on sight," Mike said.

Lucius rose and dropped enough cash onto the table to cover both meals. "Laz will not be satisfied if I am shot and he doesn't get to give the order."

CHAPTER FORTY-SEVEN

A week later, Kenna stood in front of the massive doors of the Tomasi family home in the Bluff Area of Fort Lee, New Jersey, across the Hudson River from Manhattan. Standing there transported her back to the days after her father's death when she'd been packed up and brought to these same doors and ushered inside by a social worker. Into the big, dark-paneled room where Sally and a family court judge explained that she would live here now, and Uncle Sally would be her guardian until she turned seventeen. At that point, she would be free to stay or leave.

Too numb with grief and feeling abandoned by her only remaining parent, Kenna had nodded and carried her bag upstairs to a room that had once belonged to Sal Jr. Someone had kindly painted it in a soft cream and replaced his furniture with a collection from Pottery Barn's teen line in Tiffany Blue and black.

When she thought back to that time now, she knew from her grown up perspective that what had looked like concern for her young, broken heart was really the manifestation of Big Sally's guilt, if he was even capable of it.

The housekeeper opened the front doors of the *faux*-Georgian manor house and pulled her into the foyer with a hug. The older woman who'd served her after-school snacks now patted her hand before opening the sliding door into Big Sally's study.

"Hey, kid," Sally gestured for her to sit on a sofa with him.

Kenna swallowed hard and tried to smile back. Despite the moniker, Salvatore Tomasi, Sr. was not a big man. Much like Lucius, she thought, Sally's personal charisma took up all the space in the room. And when he smiled, it was disarming in its brilliance and apparent genuineness. If one didn't look at his eyes, it was easy to forget how brutal, dangerous and unforgiving he truly was.

"You need money?" he asked as soon as Kenna was seated on the edge of her cushion at the far end of the couch.

"Oh, no! It's nothing like that." She reached into her purse and pulled out an envelope containing a cashier's check. "Just the opposite. I'm giving this back to you. For my student loans."

The elder Tomasi didn't take the envelope and refused to acknowledge its presence. "That was a gift."

Kenna's stomach tightened. She wanted to call it what it was, a bribe. "Under the circumstances, I can't accept it."

"What circumstances? You accepted it for over a year," he said with a slight edge to his voice.

When she looked into his eyes, she had to dig a nail into the palm of her folded hands to keep from shivering under the cold stare. "I know, but it's time."

"I hear you have a man." The quick change startled her. "Did he give you this?" Sally flicked a hand toward the envelope.

"No. It's mine."

Sally drummed his fingers on the back of the sofa. "You have a better plan for that shit hole of a gallery?"

The stiffness in Kenna's shoulders melted, and she sat back

a bit against the arm of the couch. "I'd like to stay on, for commission, until I can find a home for the pieces we have on display."

"What about Al?" While Sally was the owner of record, Al's Gallery and Framing had been set up to provide income and framing work for his older brother long before Kenna came into their lives.

Kenna pulled a folded sheet of paper from her purse. "I found him a place. In Pennsylvania." She waited for him to take the printed email, and when he ignored it, she placed it on top of the envelope. "It's an artist's community. He can work with skilled craftsmen, build as slow or as fast as he wants."

"These those religious nuts?" Sally's handsome smile curled with disgust.

Kenna closed her eyes and sighed. "Some of the craftsmen are from religious communities, but he will not be indoctrinated or asked to convert."

"And they're ok with him being ... different?"

She was thankful he didn't call Al a retard or idiot or dummy. The few times she'd stood up to Sally had been over the way he talked about Al's disorder. "I've spoken with the woman who runs things out there. They have a couple of high-functioning Autistic artists in the community. Everyone is familiar with most of their needs and boundary issues. I think it will be a good place for him." Kenna reached over and placed her hand on Sally's arm. "He'll call you every week just like he does now. And he can call me anytime."

Oddly, she'd thought getting him to take her money and not be offended would be the hard part, not what to do about Al.

"He's always been nutty for that Amish furniture." They sat together for a few moments. The cashier's check lay between them on the tufted leather like a ticking time bomb. Then, Sally pointed at her. "This guy turns out to be a bum, you come see me."

The check was still sitting on the sofa when she left.

CHAPTER FORTY-EIGHT

Kenna stood on tiptoes on the second rung of an eight-foot ladder to reach dust bunnies making their nest on the mixed media landscape twelve feet from the floor. She'd been moving this piece around the gallery for over a year. The poor old canvas had begun to show wear from improper storage long before Kenna had agreed to take over its care and feeding. At first, she'd had no real appreciation for it, but as the months passed and she changed the display, adjusted lighting, paired it with other pieces she *did* like, the scrapped together skyline and oddly placed landmarks of New York began to gain appeal. She liked the bright blue patch of Central Park and the nearly black, smoky shadows where the Twin Towers should have been.

"I'll find you a good home," she said, skimming the duster a final time over the top edge.

"Do they ever speak back?"

Kenna started and nearly tipped backward off the ladder. The duster clattered to the floor and she clung to the artwork until the world steadied itself. Looking over her shoulder, she tried not to glare at the woman staring unfazed at her from the gallery door. She'd not heard a sound announcing anyone. Usually, the stairs echoed or the door creaked.

The woman didn't move to help her down or even ask if she was okay. She stared, waiting for Kenna to collect herself once she'd eased down the ladder. Kenna felt a tickle of recognition and instant dislike for the woman.

Despite her continuous protestations that she could take care of herself, she'd found comfort in the protective bubble Will, Lucius, Sal Jr., Mr. Ping, Frankie and Candace maintained around her. She'd begun to count on Mike Chapman's visits each week, the one that she knew of, to check the security cameras or Ellis Griffin checking on her under the guise of delivering Lucius' notes, without the secrecy now.

"I'm fine. Thanks," she said, straightening her skirt and slipping on a pair of red patent leather pumps, today's pop of color beneath her signature pencil skirt in white, and her black cropped blouse. "You need a bell."

"Actually, your door needs a bell," the woman said.

The silence was irritatingly awkward. Kenna finally asked, "Can I help you?" She couldn't shake the feeling she'd seen this woman before.

"I'm looking for art." The woman, Kenna now saw, was in her mid-thirties, hair pulled into a severe ponytail and not wearing much, if any, make-up. The severity of her sparse grooming gave her a homely look as she stepped fully into the gallery and looked around. Kenna couldn't tell if the woman was completely lost, not sure where to start the search for art, or possibly didn't think anything in this gallery qualified.

Kenna smiled patiently. "Anything specific? A special occasion? Your home, or office?"

"Not for me," the woman said as if Kenna should have known that. Condescension dripped from her slightly accented voice, an accent that Kenna couldn't place right away. "I represent Mr. David Lawrence." The woman handed Kenna a card with Lazarashvilli's alias printed across the front and a phone number on the back. "He is expanding his American collection. Only original pieces, of course, anything unique or quintessentially New York."

Kenna studied the card. It reminded her of Lucius'. "And you are?"

"Smith."

Kenna forced herself to brighten and bury her initial pique. "Well, Ms. Smith, I'm sure we have several pieces your employer would find interesting."

"Just Smith," the woman corrected.

Kenna nodded, "Very well, Smith. Can you tell me more about Mr. Lawrence's preferences? Tastes? Does he prefer abstracts, modern, impressionistic?"

"He desires American. Original. Unique. Beautiful." Keeping her lips together and tilting her head a bit, Smith smiled stiffly at Kenna. Kenna wondered if she felt as uncomfortable as she looked.

"Oh," Kenna said on a sigh. "I can promise three of those. Beauty, as they say ..."

"Is in the eye of the beholder. Yes."

"How did you find us?" Kenna asked as she gestured for Smith to follow her toward the front displays.

"A simple elimination process. We find the most," Smith paused and her eyes scanned Kenna's face, "interesting items in small, hidden places."

"Fair enough," Kenna said, using a phrase she'd picked up from Candace and found it fit a multitude of occasions. She looked around, unsure where to begin. "Perhaps, if you told me more about Mr. Lawrence's other collections, I could suggest some place to start."

Smith began to pace the length of the gallery, pausing occasionally to ask about one piece or another. Kenna's attempts to describe the individual artists or other available pieces were dismissed.

Her circuitous inspection complete, Smith paused at Kenna's small desk. "How soon can you have them packaged and delivered?"

"Which ones?" Kenna noticed Smith had said "them."

"All of them," Smith said, again the tone suggested Kenna should have known this.

"*All*? Everything?" Kenna braced her hand on the edge of the desk. Her legs had turned to jelly.

"Yes. Everything."

"Is this a joke?"

"No, Miss Campbell. I am quite serious."

"Do you mind if I sit?" Kenna said, lowering herself into a tufted parson's chair she'd purchased from Overstock.com to replace the antique she'd smashed upon learning of Lorenzo Barzini's death. "That is quite an investment Ms ... uhm, Smith."

Smith reached into her briefcase and withdrew an envelope. "I am prepared to make a cash deposit and give you a cashier's check upon delivery, provided you can *make* delivery."

Kenna stared at Smith for a full minute and struggled to get her brain into gear. A hundred questions raced through her mind, and a single thought that involved doing double back flips. *This is my ticket out.* Her mental gymnast silenced the skeptic and kicked down any red flags.

Smith stood impassive, knowing instantly when Kenna's mind was made up. Her transparent features morphed from confused to determined. She was indeed an All-American beauty as Lazarashvilli had said. Blonde hair, green eyes, lovely mouth, she should be singing in Coca Cola commercials or praising floral-scented shampoo.

Kenna opened the laptop on her desk and, after a few

keystrokes, pulled up a spreadsheet of inventory and estimated values. Looking back at Smith, her wide-eyed innocence was gone. Narrowed green lasers, skilled in negotiating on behalf of starving artists, pinned the older woman.

"You understand my disbelief." She waited for Smith's affirming nod. "*We,*" she said, emphasizing the word to ensure Smith knew she was not alone in this venture, "will need half, in cash. Let's call it good faith, given the magnitude of this acquisition." Kenna lifted her chin and gave Smith her sweetest smile. Sweat trickled between her breasts and down her spine. She hoped she looked calm. She hoped Smith didn't see blood pulsing in her neck or hear the quiver in her voice.

Smith attempted to peer over at her screen to see exactly how much "half" meant, but Kenna snapped the laptop closed.

"Two hundred fifty thousand, before anything comes off my walls. And any additional labor costs. It's going to take a moving team to get all of this crated and down the stairs." She tried to take in a slow breath. She was talking too fast. Smith would see she was too eager for the deal.

"You have half a million in inventory?" Smith looked skeptical.

"I have close to one hundred artists displayed here, all on consignment. That's twenty-five hundred apiece, give or take a few hundred. My twenty percent commission and my boss gets to pay off his mortgage if he wants. So yes, Ms. Smith. I have half a million in inventory." She waited, not breathing, for Smith to take the envelope and walk out the door.

Smith placed her briefcase on Kenna's desk and reached into it for two more fat manila envelopes, twice as full as the one she'd pulled from the interior pocket earlier. On the top one, she wrote the address of a location in New Jersey where Kenna should deliver the crated art. "I will meet you there next Friday to supervise the loading onto the cargo plane, and I will have the remainder of your payment at that time."

Kenna glanced at the address and lifted the flap to look inside the fat package. Ten, ten thousand dollar bundles. She didn't have to check the other two. Kenna knew she had a quarter of a million dollars in her hands.

"I assume you have a secure place for that amount of cash?"

Kenna nodded, thinking Will or Sal Jr. would let her use the safe at one of the clubs. Lucius' house was on perpetual guard as well. Kenna drew her brows together. *What am I thinking? I can handle this.* "I have a bank." Her puzzled look asked Smith why she would ask such a question?

Again, the condescending smile. "Of course. An honest woman."

"Dishonest women aren't very happy." Kenna carefully slid the envelopes into a deep side drawer of the desk, fished the desk key from the Carnival glass candy dish that held bits and pieces, locked the desk and squinted at Smith like she was trying to read out-of-focus print. "Why are you really doing this?"

"Mr. Lawrence wanted a collection. Now he has one."

"He buys his library books by the pound, does he?"

"I wouldn't speculate on that," Smith said. Kenna thought there was a slight warning in her tone, but brushed it off as part of the miasma of suspicion she was already fighting.

"How can I contact you before Friday if there are any problems?"

"I *do* hope there won't be any. You may call Mr. Lawrence directly should something interfere with the delivery schedule."

Kenna picked up the card and examined it again. "I guess I will ..." She looked almost wistfully around her. "... start packing."

When she looked up, Smith was closing the gallery door.

Kenna paced, tapping her index fingernail against her teeth, stopping when she tasted flecks of lacquer on her tongue. *Add "fix polish" to the To-Do list.*

Her first call was to the bank to schedule an appointment to open a safety deposit box. No need to get there and find a line. The second call was to the mysterious David Lawrence to confirm Smith wasn't running a con.

———

"Everything?" Candace looked over the rim of her martini glass.

"Yep." Kenna nodded and took a large gulp of her own. She dangled the safe deposit box key from a chain around her neck, then tucked it back inside her blouse.

"That's the safest place for that?" Frankie said with a wink.

"For today."

"Safe from everyone but Luc," Candace said before she got serious. "Are you sure this is for real?" Skepticism was written across her face. "Sounds too good to be true, and you know what they say about that."

"Two hundred fifty thousand in cash is real enough. I'll believe the rest when I see it, but so far everything checks out." Kenna hunched her shoulders and dropped them dramatically, easing the tension. "I even talked to this David Lawrence guy." She nodded, her face contorted, mouth turned down into a DeNiro-esque expression. "Seems legit. Very polite. Reassuring. Asked if I had any issues with his representative."

"Yeah, what *about* this Smith person?" Frankie said. "Is she the Cher of middle men?" She was thinking of all the single-named celebrities – Madonna, Prince, Sting ...

Kenna hedged. "She was ... odd. But wouldn't you be too,

with that kind of cash and a mission to buy art." She made finger quotes around the word.

"I could only wish for that job." Candace rubbed her temples out of sheer fatigue. "So, what's your plan?"

"Pack it up as fast as I can. Al's going to have to build me crates. It's gonna be a pain in my ass to keep him from obsessing over sixteenth-of-an-inch measurements." A swell of panic hit her hard. Pushing back from the table, she sucked in deep breaths. "Oh God! I've never done anything this big. Some of these sculptures have moveable parts. Who's going to reassemble them on site? I don't have a passport to do that. I'll have to take photos and write down instructions."

"Easy there, Guggenheim," Frankie said as she and Candace rubbed her back and fanned her neck with cocktail napkins.

"You move this stuff all the time. And schlep it across town on a whim," Candace added.

Kenna's phone jingled Lucius' tone.

I'll be there in 20 minutes.

read the incoming text.

"Crap, I nearly forgot," she said, rising with flushed cheeks, flipping her hair off her face. "Date night."

"Isn't that every night?"

Kenna blushed a little, but didn't deny it. When Lucius was in town, they spent every available moment together.

She texted back,

Stay there. I'm close. Big news.

"WHAT? WHAAAAT?" Kenna stepped away from Lucius' embrace. She'd watched his face shift from pure joy at her enthusiasm, to concern, to its current state somewhere between carved stone and fury.

"Give me the card." His hand shot out between them.

"Why?" She fished the card from her purse. "I called him. I have the cash. It's not a hoax."

Lucius spoke slowly through clenched teeth. "You *talked to him?*"

"Yes, of course I did. I called immediately to see if this was for real."

"Tell me everything about this Smith person."

"There's nothing to tell. She was ..." Kenna searched for the right description. "Plain. Brown."

"What ethnicity?" Lucius began to pace, the card clenched in his fist.

"Not her skin, her everything. Hair, eyes, suit, voice, build. Plain ole brown. Medium. Average." Kenna watched him. Lucius' restless movements made her nervous. He was always so cool, patient, controlled, and now he looked like he was about to explode.

"I swear I've seen her before." Kenna closed her eyes. Her mind flipped through images until she found the one she was looking for. Lucius spun, his lip curled in a snarl. He barely managed to bring his face to some semblance of normal before she continued.

"The day Will was there. You were upstairs. This woman interrupted Will and me in mid-argument. She said she thought we were rehearsing a performance piece."

Lucius calculated the weeks that had passed and felt sick. Lazarashvilli had been that close to her for months. He could have taken her at any time. A foreign surge of fear and panic pushed at the edges of Lucius' reason. His instincts demanded he call in every resource, every favor, no matter the cost or collateral damage, to have Lazarashvilli's head on a pike by morning.

"What did – David Lawrence," he said, bracing his hands against the bar and almost gagging on the name, "say to you?"

"He confirmed Smith's story," Kenna said, using the same tone she used to assure and soothe nervous artists. "He's looking for a unique, whole collection of American originals. I told him if he were willing to wait, I could put together a portfolio of pieces that weren't so disjointed. Find him a real collection that actually complimented each other, that had some value as a whole and in pieces, but he wasn't interested."

The sound of disgust that erupted from Lucius' throat made her speak faster, as if she could convince him if she just kept talking.

"He wanted it as soon as possible. He said the disconnected nature of the pieces was exactly what he had in mind."

Lucius' hand shook as he pulled Kenna to a chair and knelt on the floor, holding her hands in his. He fought to control his pulse and breathing. He flexed his fingers to loosen the vice grip on her hands and stuttered out the first word.

"Promise ... promise me you won't call his number again. Promise me you won't do anything until I, we, can verify this through more secure avenues. Swear you will not meet with anyone or oversee transport of anything to any location."

Kenna pulled her hands free, icy fear was snaking its way up her arms into her chest. "Okay. What do I do with this money then?"

Lucius almost fell onto his rear when she agreed. Knees bent, he rested his forearms on his knees and dropped his chin to his chest, inhaling deep, calming breaths. His head slowly rose at her question.

"Give it to your artists. Right away. Keep nothing."

"My ass. I'm keeping my commission."

Lucius snarled, "Keep nothing he touched."

He was scaring her and doing so deliberately. Kenna gripped the arms of the chair and pushed herself to her feet. "Don't you dare try to scare me or make me feel threatened. I have a chance at real security here. My own gallery, something I built, something that won't vanish because of someone else's decisions. Don't you dare take that away."

Lucius looked up into her eyes, his brows drawn together in confusion and hurt. What had he been trying to give her all these months if not security and a future?

Kenna raked her hands through her hair. "I didn't mean I don't feel safe with you. But things change. People change. They move away or, fall in love or get sick. I want something that's mine, something real, not here because of the whim of someone else."

Lucius was on his feet, pulling her against him to kiss her temples and hair. "I'm sorry, love. I know you wanted this to be real. I thought I could keep you safe from everything." He would have to put aside soothing her relationship fears and focus on the real threat to her life.

Kenna tried to push away. "It still can be. Your intel might show that everything is legitimate about this."

Her hope in the face of his truth caused physical pain in his chest. He cupped her cheek and prepared to catch the tear forming in the corner of her eye. "No, it won't. David Lawrence is Davit Lazarashvilli, a man I've been hunting for ten years. A war criminal. A human slave trader." His arms tightened and he shuddered when he said, "He murdered my wife, and he found you."

CHAPTER FORTY-NINE

Seated in Lucius' private study, Mike twirled his ball cap on his finger. This was a rare invitation beyond the boundary of professionalism. He felt the familiar adrenaline rush of impending battle and looked around at Griffin to see if he shared the feeling. *"He's as bad as Chaerea. Stone-faced SOB,"* Mike thought.

Lucius walked in and closed the door behind him. "As of last night, Kenna is a permanent guest." He then relayed to them her story of Smith.

"Bold, sending someone in that close. Smart, using a woman – less threatening. Shrewd, throwing that much money at her to dazzle and stun her into ignoring her intuition," Mike said, summarizing the situation succinctly.

"Why didn't they simply take her?" Griffin asked. It's what he would have done. Then he nodded in understanding. "The taunting."

"I want Smith. Now," Lucius said. His body was as taut as a guitar string tightened to break with the slightest pluck.

"We can tap into surveillance cameras. Find her before and after she left Kenna. Street cams. Convenience stores. Banks,

ATMs," Mike said, already tapping out instructions on his phone.

Nodding in agreement with his internal counsel, Lucius said, "Let me know when you have her." He had made his decision. "I'm weary of the game. Lazarashvilli has been baiting me for too long. I believe it's time I baited him in return.

"THIRD FLOOR, last apartment on the left," Mike said in his report to Lucius. The dim interior of the car was made darker by the mood of its occupants. "You need me for this?"

"Thank you, Mike. I won't ask this of you," Lucius said, focusing his eyes on the non-descript building as if he could see through the walls.

"You're not asking. I'm volunteering."

Lucius turned and extended his hand. "This is not your forte."

Mike nodded in reluctant agreement. Extraordinary rendition wasn't to his taste, notwithstanding his years in USAF Spec Ops. He waited as Lucius and Rainsborough slipped through the doorway, which was conveniently darkened, thanks to a hoodie-wearing vandal with an aptitude for disabling security lights. When Smith approached the building, Mike texted,

You're up!

Smith cursed in English and her native tongue about the dark corridors and stairwells as she unlocked the door, anxious to be inside the security of her week-to-week apartment, such as it was. She froze inside the threshold of the efficiency at the lean silhouette sitting in her armchair.

"Please join me, Ms. Andreas. *Lera*," Lucius said, using her real name as he turned on the floor lamp beside him and indicated the chair placed across from him.

The door softly clicked closed behind her, too softly. She didn't need to look behind her to know there was another man in the room. She fought the wave of panic and nausea rising from deep within. Tilting up her chin she said, "I've been raped before."

Again, Lucius gestured to the metal folding chair he'd provided for her. "I'm certain your life has been fraught with tragedy." The sympathy in his voice bordered on genuine. "Let's not create another. Sit."

Moving to the chair, she did look over her shoulder to confirm the other man's presence. Her eyes widened at the cruelly handsome face and tall runner's build of the man standing sentry. Lazarashvilli's henchmen looked the part – brutish, bulging bulls of men, with brains in stark contrast to their bulk. This man looked like a rapier. When his eyes shifted from her to the chair and back, she sank onto the cold metal seat as if he'd reached out one of those broad hands and pushed her shoulder down.

"So, you know my name." She folded her arms across her chest and looked out the window with forced boredom. Inside, she braced for a blow from across the room.

When there was only a silence, she turned back to Lucius. "What is this?"

Lucius leaned forward, hands clasped, his elbows braced on his knees. "You have a choice, Lera. Had you come to me weeks ago, perhaps I could have mitigated your circumstances."

"I have survived torture worse than yours, Chaerea." She practically boasted, but squeezed her thighs together, her arms tightening around her in a protective girdle.

Rainsborough shifted with impatience, and Lera's head snapped around. She'd again expected an attack. The calm reserve of these men unnerved her. She couldn't hide the shudder that moved through her.

"I'm certain you believe that." Lucius sat back and sighed. He waited until she relaxed and directed her attention back to him. "Unlike your employer, I do not enjoy this. I will, however, have my answers. How they are obtained and the condition of your remains is entirely up to you."

"None of his people know about the business other than whatever we are told to do," she said.

"My interest is no longer in Lazarashvilli's slave trade." Lucius held up the last three fingers of his hand. "Three questions."

Lera narrowed her eyes at him.

"Who directed you to the gallery? Where is he now? Do you desire a priest?"

She started to chuckle, then abruptly stopped to draw in a deep breath. She smiled with not a little resignation. "Are you serious? You, Colonel Chaerea, gave him all he needed. Dinner dates. Tulip bouquets. Strolls through Central Park. You carried your little doll to him on a silver platter."

The muscle in Lucius' jaw ticked. Guilt sat like a stone in his gut. A subtle flick of his wrist brought Rainsborough into the halo of light from the lamp. Lera instinctively leaned away.

"His compound? The Phuket estate has been empty for months."

Head shaking, she said, "I don't know. Maybe he's in London."

Rainsborough stepped behind her.

"I won't ask you again, Lera," Lucius said. The temperature in the room dropped with the ice in his voice.

When she moved to jump away from the chair, Rainsborough caught her by the hair and slammed her back with a thud. The metal chair legs screeched in protest against the floor.

"Exactly like *him*," she taunted Lucius. "Never get your own hands dirty." The fist in her hair tightened, and she couldn't hold back the grunt of pain.

"I promise, Lera, you will prefer Mr. Rainsborough's efficiency to my clumsy techniques."

She shivered again as the stories of Colonel Chaerea's ruthlessness when hunting and capturing war criminals flooded her mind.

Lucius stilled, as if he knew what her mind's eye was seeing and let the legends persuade her. The silence held a more vicious grip than Rainsborough.

"Turkey," she said, resigned to her fate. "Istanbul."

Lucius stood.

"What about my priest?" Lera asked in a panicked cry. A part of her thought the delay or presence of a priest might provide some opportunity to save her life.

"You will be granted the Rite. of Committal, next to your parents' graves."

"I *never touched her!*" she screamed, squirming and clawing at the hand in her hair.

Lucius shrugged into the coat that had been draped over the back of the lone armchair and towered over her. "Thus, my mercy."

Lera's mind never registered the gun in his hand.

DAYS LATER, Lucius poured coffee for himself and Griffin.

"Anything more from Chapman?" he asked.

"Her cell was a burner, blocked number. Incoming calls only, but we expected that. Her laptop appears to have been used for emailing 'D. Lawrence.'" Chaerea nodded, acknowledging Lazarashvilli's alias, and Griffin continued. "Google searches on Kenna and the gallery and some obscure pornography. Nothing helpful." Griffin shifted uncomfortably. "She was one of Lazarashvilli's procurers, but she wasn't recruiting this trip."

"Only Kenna," Chaerea said.

"Only you," Griffin corrected. "How is she?" He looked up in the general direction of the Colonel's living quarters above.

"'The caged bird sings of freedom.' She thinks I'm being paranoid and controlling. I believe 'conspiracy whack job' and references to Gitmo were also hurled about." He smiled over the rim of his coffee cup at his Captain's raised brows. "Kenna will see reason on her own faster than my arguing can convince her. And she is staying, another sign she believes the threat, despite wishing it weren't true."

"Have you told her you're leaving?" Griffin asked without looking up from his pages.

"No. The less she knows the better."

"Colonel, ignorance won't keep her complacent."

CHAPTER FIFTY

"Are you certain this is your only recourse? There are other men who would gladly take on this task." Wallace knew he was grasping at straws, and that Lucius' decision was made, yet he couldn't shake the dark shadow he saw looming over this trip.

Lucius had long ago given Wallace his power of attorney, but this was the first time he'd left Wallace a copy of his will, which named Wallace his executor.

Wallace quietly placed his hand on the papers Lucius had given him. "Have you told Kenna where you are going or why?"

"No. As far as she knows this is another business trip." He read Wallace's silent disapproval correctly. "I don't want her to be anxious."

"She would not be alone in that, son."

Lucius braced his arms on the window frame and looked out over the city.

"She makes me smile, Wallace. Laugh. Sophia and I shared common goals of peace and justice. We had a passion for the missions. I hunted war criminals, she brought aid to the victims. We existed in the same darkness." He turned and let Wallace see the anguish on his face. "Kenna is my light. I can't let him get that close to her again, and he will keep trying."

Resigned, Lucius shook his head. "I moved here. Stopped chasing him. I passed every whisper and clue on to others. I'm the only one who can get close enough. He'll let me. Even welcome it. This reckoning has been a long time coming. For both of us. It's time."

Wallace did something he'd never done before. Despite years spent in building camaraderie, respect and paternal affection with this younger man, he'd never embraced Lucius as he might a son. Today he crossed the room, put his hands on Lucius' arms and pulled him in. Lucius faltered for a moment, then leaned into the embrace.

"Take Ellis Griffin with you," Wallace said tightly as he fought to steady the emotion in his voice. "We will protect your Kenna, but you do *this* for us."

Lucius nodded. He was suddenly ten again, being held by his grateful father when he, while playing in the rafters, had fallen from a barn loft and been knocked unconscious. Only a minute or two passed, but in those agonizing moments, his father had known a world without Lucius in it. He'd held his son so tightly that, when he woke, the young boy could hardly breathe as he promised to never be so reckless again.

"Yes, sir," Lucius said, exactly as he had before.

CHAPTER FIFTY-ONE

Lucius stared from the back seat, out over the dusty road and increasingly barren landscape, his weapon aimed steadily at the back of his driver's head. They were miles from the crowded streets and breathtaking architecture of Istanbul, but traffic was surprisingly heavy. Lucius felt lucky in that, at least.

"Allow me this," he prayed. *"Give me the strength to keep her safe."*

Finding a load of refugees being moved through the city had been relatively easy. Persuading the rescue organization on site to let him and Griffin join in the raid took more convincing. Capturing a ranking Lazarashvilli lieutenant had been pure luck.

Unobserved by Lazarashvilli's right hand, Hans – his involuntary guide – Lucius checked the rearview mirror. The rusted-out shell of an unremarkable white, two-door hatchback was still there. As always, Griffin had his back.

No one was more surprised than the ever-loyal Hans when the first explosion rocked the car. An ordinary roadside bomb. Traffic from both directions skidded to a halt, and cars, trucks and motorcycles slammed into one another. Passengers poured out of idling vehicles like ants from a wrecked anthill, fleeing the potential second blast and fires. Hans drew his weapon and pointed it at Lucius' chest.

"Tell them to stop," he snarled.

Lucius' hands were up. Smoke billowed around them and poured into the open windows. Their nostrils flared, and their eyes and throats began to burn. The two men, both veterans of war, recognized the scent of distraction instead of destruction.

"Not mine," Lucius croaked. "Rebels? Davit?"

"He has plans for you, dog." Hans coughed. "Get out. We walk."

Hands still raised, Lucius climbed from the car, imperceptibly signaling the approaching Griffin to stay back.

A hundred yards away, Captain Griffin cursed under his breath and placed his rifle back under the seat. He only needed seconds. Hans would lose most of his skull, and he could get his Colonel home. They would deal with the enemy later. Let the bastard come after Kenna the way he'd gone after Sophia. But Griffin knew Lucius would never allow Kenna to be bait, intentionally or not. He was watching Lucius' and Hans' retreating backs through the haze of black smoke when the second blast hit.

Hans spun towards the explosion. His car lifted off the pavement and burst into a ball of fire. Flames and shrapnel raced out in a circle of destruction. He could only watch in horror with the realization that his vehicle had been the target, and he was supposed to be in it with Colonel Chaerea. The gasping breath he sucked in to curse his boss was nothing but flames that consumed him inside and out.

Lucius dove for the ground. Nothing was low enough to provide cover. He tucked into a ball, hoping to minimize the target he presented. Chaos engulfed him. The heat scorched the hair on his arms, face and head. His ears throbbed from the explosion's roar and concussive airwaves, and he could feel blood seeping down his neck. Razor sharp pieces of metal rained down around him. On him. He'd looked death in the face before. Only now did it finally matter if he won the fight. He closed his eyes. "Please God ..." He saw her face. Kenna was laughing, and everything went black.

GRIFFIN CAME TO, his vision blurred and head throbbing. In a daze, he watched with some detachment as emergency responders rushed towards the scene. As flames ate through cars, trucks and people, those attempting to deliver aid slowly made their way towards him.

"Sir! Sir!" A police officer was trying to drag him out of the car.

Released, Griffin tried to pull away from the policeman and stagger towards the carnage. "Colonel."

"No! No!" The officer gripped his arm.

Griffin's equilibrium was too far gone, the heat and smoke too intense. He sank to the ground and stared in disbelief. Needed closer to the explosion to assist with the more severe trauma cases, the officer left him there.

"Colonel," Griffin rasped. Eventually, he crawled away, leaving his rifle, identification and mentor behind.

CHAPTER FIFTY-TWO

Hearing Palmer Ross' grand entrance into the office maze on her floor of the US attorney's office, Candace audibly groaned. She didn't need to hear the "honeys" or "sugar pies" or "pardners" to know he was slopping his southern sugar all over the office and would soon be in her corner of the crime-fighting world.

She had purposefully turned her back to the office door, hoping to discourage him from invading her space and digging for information on Will MacKenzie or whatever wild hare he was after today. So, she jumped when the knock came followed by a deep voice saying, "Candace." It wasn't a question, and she spun in her chair. It wasn't Ross looming in her doorway. She stared dumbstruck for a split second. This was the last person she expected to see filling the doorframe of her office.

"Mike, right? From the race track." She narrowed her eyes suspiciously at him. "Did Lucius send you?"

"You need to come with me. Now," Mike said, ignoring her question. The skin around his blue-green eyes looked tight with fatigue. There was no trace of the flirty slacker vibe she'd gotten from him at the Meadowlands.

"I don't *need* to do anything until you tell me why?"

His reply was cut off by her phone. She held up a finger and scowled when he cleared the stacked files off her single guest chair and sat to wait.

"Candace Fisher," she answered. A long silence followed in which she slowly looked up at Mike. He was looking at her with sad resignation. "Yes, Wallace, he's here. I understand. I'll call Frankie and Will." She hung up and fixed him with a look. "You'd better talk fast."

"WHERE'S KENNA?" Will demanded as soon as he burst into the lobby of the Henneby Industries Building.

Frankie rushed to him, lacing her fingers through his, as much to calm him as to comfort herself. Candace had given her the high points. Frankie, in turn, had given Will an even more condensed version. Only after she had assured him Kenna was already *en route* did he agree to meet them at Henneby's instead of going straight to the gallery.

"She's on the way."

"Who's that?" He jerked his head towards Mike, in hushed conversation with Candace.

"Mike something. He knows Lucius ... knew Lucius, and Mr. Henneby." A gentle tug drew him forward. "Mike, I'm sorry, your last name escapes me." Will slipped his arm around her waist. Frankie never forgot names.

Mike offered his hand. "Mike Chapman."

Frankie picked up on the pleasantries they all seemed to be clinging to while waiting for Kenna. "This is Will MacKenzie. Kenna's ..." she trailed off. No one had ever defined Will and Kenna. They just were.

"Family," Will filled in, taking Mike's hand. "You knew her man?"

"Yeah. I was doing some work for him related to this last trip."

Will was about to ask more about this work and trip, and why Lucius was anywhere near places with car bombs, when the front doors opened. Kenna saw them all standing there and froze.

The wind whipped around her into the lobby. When he'd called, Wallace had only said it was important he see her. Despite every instinct telling her otherwise, she'd spent the entire cab ride convincing herself this was about an art investment. The dread she'd ignored hit her like a bus and she gasped for air, refusing to step through the open door. If she stayed on this side of the threshold, whatever disaster lay inside would be averted.

"Kenna?" Will had crossed the expanse of the lobby's granite floor, and she hadn't seen him move. He reached for her elbow. "Come in here."

Frankie and Candace were behind him.

"Just tell me," Kenna whispered.

Frankie took her other elbow. "Come on, honey. Let's go on up to Wallace's office where we can talk in private."

Kenna nodded, and the five of them silently got in the elevator leading to the executive suites. Kenna remembered the last time she was in this elevator, with Lucius so casually watching the numbers tick down. The same suffocating silence descended on the cab of the elevator today. The only difference was that then there had been the undercurrent of attraction, an excitement of the unspoken. Today felt like she was underwater too long, knowing there wasn't enough air left in her lungs to reach the surface.

Wallace met them at the door to his office. He spoke to

Candace first, "Thank you." When he reached for Kenna's arm, neither Will nor Frankie seemed inclined to let go. "Please have a seat." He tried valiantly to keep his own emotions in check.

They half-followed, half-steered her to the sofa. Kenna's troubled eyes locked onto Ellis Griffin standing straight as a soldier at attention beside the window. His chiseled face was grim and marked with cuts and livid bruises, and he was struggling to marshal the emotionless façade he'd learned from Lucius. His deep green eyes burned with grief. Kenna and Griffin stared at each other for what seemed like forever, but was probably only a few seconds. He closed his eyes and whispered, "I'm sorry."

Kenna pulled her arms away from Will and Frankie and wrapped them around herself. Taking a deep breath, she finally looked at Wallace, mute in the face of what was so clearly going to be horrific news.

It was Candace who broke the tense silence. "Wallace, what happened?"

He placed his hand on a folder resting in the center of his desk and then decided the official details were best left inside. "The official report lists the cause of death as an improvised explosive device. Lucius, his driver – more accurately the man driving him – and six others were killed in the explosions. The investigation continues, but much of the evidence is destroyed in these types of attacks."

"Where was he, and was it directed at him?" Will asked. Kenna shuddered violently and looked to Ellis as Luc's voice played in her head, *I trust him with my life when necessary.*

"It's too early in the investigation to make that assumption." Mike shifted at this evasion of the truth, and Ellis grew more still, if that were possible. "The other, I don't know," Wallace answered truthfully. He never asked, and Lucius never told him specifics.

Will rose and pointed at Ellis. "I bet he knows. Or did you walk through a glass door and fall down a flight of stairs for shits and giggles?"

"Mr. MacKenzie," Wallace soothed. "The nature of Lucius' work often demanded the utmost discretion. Captain Griffin cannot reveal that information to us."

"What can we do? Does he – *did* he – have family? Are there arrangements needed? Can we help with anything?" Frankie asked.

Wallace looked directly at Kenna, unsure if she were seeing or hearing him. She'd not made a sound or movement. "As far as arrangements ... Luc had no desire for that, he had no immediate family. If Kenna would like it, we can do something privately." He swallowed hard. "Recovery of his remains may take time, so there's no urgency." He reached into the envelope and pulled out several smaller ones. On top was the pale gray of Lucius' personal stationery. "These are for you." He handed them to Kenna.

It took her a moment, but she finally reached out for them. "What are they?" Her voice sounded far away to her own ears.

"The first packet is letters Luc has left for you."

"Letters?" Kenna turned the envelope over and noticed it was thick with folded sheets. She held it with both hands, leaving the other envelopes balanced precariously on her lap.

"He wrote a new one every time he left." Wallace smiled. "He brought the first one to me around midnight after our initial meeting regarding that art piece. You had him quite smitten, young lady."

Kenna shifted and the remaining correspondence fell to the floor. Candace and Frankie immediately began picking them up, although there were only half a dozen or so pieces. Both needed something to do.

"Condolences?" Candace asked, turning over a telegram.

Her eyes widened in surprise at the name and rank of the sender.

"Luc was respected by those he served under and, I think more importantly, by those who were under his command."

"Aim high," Mike recited the Air Force slogan more to himself and Lucius than to the people in the room.

"Those should go to Captain Griffin or Luc's men." Kenna leaned away from the stack in Candace's hand. "I just dated him for a few months. You keep them, Mr. Henneby." She was looking at the unopened envelopes as if they were snakes coiled to strike.

Suddenly, Kenna stood up, startling everyone in the room. Her words came unnaturally fast and clipped. "I need to, uhm, I mean thank you for these." She flapped Lucius' letters. "And, and, and for telling me in person. I have an artist coming by the gallery. I can't stay." Her eyes wouldn't focus on any one person, but jumped around the room until finally landing on Will. "I need to go."

Kenna backed towards the door, muttering what she hoped were appreciative words and sympathy to Wallace Henneby and Ellis Griffin. She was certain they were all going to jump on her and make her sit and listen to more. When her father had died, she'd cried so much she couldn't eat or sleep. Then she had to sit and listen as Big Sally, lawyers, the judge and social services explained what a negligent father she'd had, and how her life was going to be from then on. How she had to pull herself together and move on. *It was for the best.*

In the hospital, after Lorenzo's attack, care-givers and detectives strapped her to the bed and pelted her with questions, horrid details, wanting her to say the right things, scream and cry so they could put her back together like Humpty Dumpty. Now, she saw the same desire in Wallace and Ellis. Even

Frankie and Candace were on the verge of weeping. Is that what they wanted? For her to cry and fall to pieces?

Will recognized the panic – he'd seen it before. "Sure."

He stepped between Kenna and Wallace, although the older man had merely risen in surprise. "We can finish this another time."

"Of course." The pain was plain on Wallace's face. Kenna's withdrawal and denial of the magnitude of her relationship with Lucius intensified his own loss. A part of him had welcomed the chance to share his grief with another who loved Lucius. It saddened him, for them both, that she was having none of it. Wallace directed his next words to Candace. "There are provisions in Lucius' will. Some for Kenna. We do need to discuss them as soon as possible."

"We'll call in a few days," she said, putting her arms around his neck. "I'm so very sorry, Wallace."

"Thank you, dear." He gently returned the embrace.

CHAPTER FIFTY-THREE

crid smoke burned his lungs. He knew what he would find inside the burnt-out homes in the Somali village. Once again, they were too late. He'd seen statues of ash before, frozen in a death tableau. These would not have the beauty and sterility of Pompeii's victims achieved with the passage of millennia. Charred remains lay twisted and frozen in terror and anguish. The soot clouded around his boots as he gingerly stepped through the bodies, respectful whispers of "all clear" in his ear. The team unanimously vowed they wouldn't let these horrors go unpunished. The gaping mouths cried out, screaming, reaching toward him. Louder and louder, they began to scream. The residual heat from the extinguished fire turned the hollow shell of a building into an oven. He could almost feel the flames licking up his spine.

The clouds outside opened, streaming angel wings of light across the floor. Through the echo of screams, he heard Kenna's laughter. Turning he began to run through the wreckage. She can't be here. He must find her before ...

The screams of the damned grew louder. He struggled to

reach Kenna before the flames consumed him. And her. Lucius opened his mouth to call to her. To tell her to run.

His eyes flew open. His body was on fire, inside and out. Every breath seared his lungs, and the movement of breathing caused red-hot blades to slash at his back. The screams were his. He wasn't sure if they were coming from his mind or his mouth. This was Hell. Dante had warned him. Lucius' eyes fluttered open long enough to see the gnarled, wrinkled hands of his savior before the pain sucked him back into the abyss.

CHAPTER FIFTY-FOUR

The buzzing intercom from the street entrance at Will's building roused Kenna from the sofa cushions where she'd finally collapsed. Tears, saliva and God only knew what else had created a fine layer of adhesive between her cheek and the sofa pillow.

"Go away," she croaked from her seat.

"You hear that?" Will said into the speaker as he buzzed them in.

"Breakfast, sunshine. You promised." Candace's firm tone came through the intercom. "We're coming up."

Kenna mumbled a few colorful curses, then said, "Fine." Knowing resistance was futile, she resumed her fetal position amid the used tissues and papers she'd strewn around her the night before.

Inside the door, Candace and Frankie paused in horror at the normally camera-ready apartment. Kenna and Will looked like they both needed sleep, showers and coffee, and in no particular order.

"How did this happen in fifteen hours?" Frankie moved white take-out boxes off the coffee table. Candace followed footstep for footstep, gathering the litter of hours of casual indulgence and neglect.

Will scrubbed his hands over his face and through his hair. "Long night. Give me two minutes to shower."

"Sure, we've got her," Frankie said as he landed a peck on the top of her head.

When Will was out of earshot, Candace wrinkled her nose and whispered, "Is that her?"

"I can hear you." Kenna said her face half in the pillow. "Just move it over there." She waved in no actual direction.

"Which 'it?'" Candace mouthed.

Frankie petted back the ratted mass of blonde hair from Kenna's face. Although they had expected a few dark circles, maybe puffy tear-soaked eyes, Kenna was more like one of the stray kittens featured on some heart-wrenching SPCA television commercial, with Sara McLachlan crooning about angels in the background.

"Rock, paper, scissors. Winner takes the garbage," Candace said to Frankie, hand extended.

"Fuck off," Kenna mumbled.

Frankie tugged her shoulders and sat Kenna up straight. "That's a lovely invitation, but I think we'll decline." She looked over at Candace, who was already picking up food containers and an empty cookie dough wrapper. "Where was Will during this?"

"Tipping the guy from Pings," Kenna's head flopped back. "I'll get that later."

"We've got it. Had we known you'd let this place get so ... interesting, we'd have worn hazmat suits," Candace said. Kenna looked up with a curled lip. Candace held up her hand. "I know, 'fuck off.' Where are the garbage bags?"

"Sink." Kenna pointed, suddenly grateful for their presence as fresh tears rolled down her cheeks. They were beside her in seconds. Four arms wrapped around her, the detritus of the night forgotten.

"Tissues?" Candace asked. They all needed one now.

"Gone." Kenna sniffed and raised the mascara-smeared hem of her shirt. "I ran out. Here." She tugged the shirt to a cleanish segment at the back and held it out to her friends.

"I think we can find something," Frankie said. "But first, a shower."

They half-herded, half-carried Kenna down the hall to her bedroom and the bath. "Do we need to leave this open?" Candace nodded toward the bathroom door.

As if on cue, Will stepped out, still dripping wet with a towel around his hips. He pointed at Kenna. "Use soap!"

"*I will,*" Kenna snapped, then fatigue swamped her voice again. "It was a long night." As if that explained the mini-disaster area she'd managed to create.

When the bathroom door closed, Candace and Frankie looked over their shoulders to the living room at the end of the hall. The shock was only slightly blunted by a second look.

"What happened?" Frankie said to Will.

"Like she said. Long night." The exhaustion in his voice gave away how big an understatement that was. Frankie gently rubbed his arm and gave him a nudge. "Get some rest. We'll take this for a bit."

Nodding, he kissed her. "Thanks."

"You take the food. I'll start on the cups of ..." Frankie mused as she spoke to a mug's interior, nose crinkled, "scum. What was she drinking that formed cheese on top overnight?"

Candace sniffed a gelatinous container of cold food. "I don't think she even ate this."

In fact, nothing seemed to have been consumed at all except the roll of cookie dough.

"At least, we got here before the roaches," Frankie said

putting her ear to the bathroom door. "You'd better use shampoo too," she called out. "If I'm washing dishes, you wash hair." She gave Candace a thumbs-up when she heard a water-logged "fuck off" from inside the shower.

Half an hour later, Will could be heard snoring from his room, and Candace and Frankie had Kenna clean, relatively dry and tucked away in her bed. She'd either passed out or fallen asleep almost immediately, though neither of them believed it would last very long. With mutual sighs of relief and clutching clean cups of fresh coffee, they sank onto the couch and surveyed the now environmentally safe living room.

"Okay," Frankie turned to Candace.

"Yeah, now what?"

CHAPTER FIFTY-FIVE

"Y'all didn't have to come," Kenna said in the elevator to Wallace's offices the next morning, but her white-knuckle grip on her purse told them otherwise.

All of them were feeling some sense of residual dread on the heels of their last ride to the thirty-sixth floor three days earlier.

There was an air of professional compassion about Wallace's executive assistant when she met the elevators and led them to his office door.

"Mr. Henneby is ready for you. Can I get you coffee or tea? The morning's pastries are still fresh."

"I don't think I can eat," Kenna said to Candace. Her stomach performed an unpleasant flip that was unrelated to her consumption – or lack thereof – of food over the last thirty-six hours.

"Coffee and tea, please," Candace answered.

"I'll bring some chamomile," the assistant said softly. Years of experience had taught her to recognize the potential need for the soothing brew.

"Ladies, thank you for coming so promptly." Wallace greeted them at the door.

Kenna paused when she saw Ellis Griffin in the same position by the window as he'd held when she'd left here days ago. The scene was too raw and familiar, but her perspective now allowed her to see the sphere of grief he and Wallace occupied.

Wallace cleared his throat. "I know making this journey to Midtown wasn't convenient. Maybe I should have suggested coming to you," he said with a worried tone.

Candace hugged him. "Wallace. This is fine, and a change of scene will do Kenna some good, I think."

Frankie held one hand out to Wallace. The other supported Kenna's elbow.

Wallace smiled gently at Kenna and offered his hand, palm up. "I know this is terribly painful for you ..."

Kenna had barely touched his hand before she stepped close and wrapped her arms around his neck.

"I'm so sorry," she whispered. "I'm so very sorry. I couldn't see."

Wallace put his arms around her in return. The weight of his own sorrow now lightened with her embrace and emotion-filled apology.

"Shhh." He pulled away enough to hand her his handkerchief. "Luc would not forgive me your tears."

Kenna sniffled and dabbed under her eyes as she regained her composure. She'd had her meltdown. Now it was time to cowgirl up. Wallace gestured to the seating area as the hot beverage cart was pushed through the doors.

"One moment," Kenna said, crossing the room to Ellis.

He quickly straightened and braced himself, although nothing she could do or say could be worse than anything he'd said to himself.

Kenna noted the untidy scruff covering his battered face. His eyes were red-rimmed and bloodshot and, beneath the subtle scents of soap and cologne was the distinct hint of whiskey, and lots of it.

"I'm not going to bite you, Mr. Griffin," she said, then awkwardly, with a stuttering stop and start, managed to slip her arms around his neck as well.

Stiffly, he placed his hands on her hips to keep her from tipping off her toes.

"How are you all?" she asked, and he knew she meant Lucius' men.

"Hung over, Miss Campbell."

"Gave him a proper sendoff, did you?" She smiled up at him.

"Indeed, miss."

Kenna smiled and patted his arm. "Indeed."

Armed with chamomile and caffeine, they all sat and began the task of putting Lucius' final wishes in motion.

"Now, Kenna," Wallace began. "Luc asked me to administer his affairs in an event like this. Specifically, he has made provisions for you to proceed with your gallery plans. This is not a blank check you realize. The funds must be used for property, renovations, acquisitions and the like. He believed in you and this dream and was prepared to invest a great deal to see it fulfilled."

"Why didn't he just tell me?" Kenna's chin quivered for a moment.

"Would you have accepted his backing and the conditions attached?" Wallace grinned, remembering the pride and obstinacy she'd shown in their first meeting in this office.

"Probably not. It would have felt like he was buying my ..." her voice trailed off as she searched for a word other than services or company.

"What conditions?" Frankie asked. All too familiar with financial strings, her ears had pricked at the word.

Wallace nodded, "As I said, the funds are strictly to be used for the gallery. As trustee, I have oversight over the use of the money."

Kenna wiped her eyes again. "I never knew he believed in me this much." Restricting the funds to her gallery was more a sign of faith than if he'd provided for her comforts.

Wallace gave her a winsome smile. "Luc was not one to doubt his instincts or alter his course. He made his decision, the moment he met you."

Kenna held in her hands everything she'd ever wanted and they were still empty. The gallery would never smile at her and make her think of Luc as a little boy. Art would never hold her at night or write her love letters. Financial security would never be as safe as Luc's arms.

"I'll flip burgers until I'm a hundred, if I can have him back."

CHAPTER FIFTY-SIX

"**F**uck," Will said on a groan, staring into an empty cupboard where there should have been coffee cups. The dishwasher was also empty. He would have settled for a scummy-ringed mug and scraped the coffee remnants out of it after his seven-hour flight.

The last month had been all too reminiscent of his first weeks with Kenna. He knew she wasn't sleeping, but was swilling coffee, as his empty cupboard and dishwasher attested. Calls and conversations were cut short with assurances that she was "fine" and busy keeping the construction crew working to her timetable for the gallery Chaerea had underwritten for her. He also knew Frankie and Candace had been getting the same arms-length treatment. When Will had left a few days earlier, she'd been almost normal, persuading him she would be "fine." *That fucking word again.*

He viciously scrubbed his head. Enough was enough. "Kenna?" Will called before knocking on her door. "Kenna. Time to talk about this."

Nothing. Will looked around as he remembered it was almost noon on Sunday, and she was supposed to be at brunch.

"Fuck it." He opened her bedroom door and slumped against the frame.

———

"You think she'll show?" Frankie asked. She and Candace both looked at their phones sitting on the table, expecting to see a text with a half-assed excuse from Kenna for missing another of their long-standing brunch dates.

"If not, it's time we intervene. With Will there and obvious work happening at the new gallery, I've hoped ..." Candace sighed.

"Me too. At least this made Will give me a little advance notice of his trip this time. What are your calls with her like?"

"You mean the 'yeah-yeah-I'm-great-come-by-the-building-sometime-gotta-go-talk-to-the-contractor' calls? Have *you* seen her when you're at Will's?" Candace asked.

"Not so much," Frankie gestured to the air next to her ear. "Same conversation. Cheek kisses. 'Gotta run. I'm fine.'"

"When is Will due back?" Candace checked her watch and the door again.

"Today. He said he'd be gone five days at the most. He said Kenna was always on her laptop looking at blueprints or schematics, charts ... he didn't pay close attention." It was Frankie's turn to scan the front windows for any sign of Kenna.

"I want to hope she really is diving in at the gallery and not avoiding us for other reasons." Candace rubbed her forehead to forestall an incipient headache, maybe she should take up meditating or yoga or something. She started at Frankie's cry.

"Dear God! Was she mugged?" Frankie half rose from the table to stare open-mouthed at the woman shoving through Marco's Sunday brunch crowd to their regular table.

Across from her, Candace turned and gasped. She searched

in vain for signs of trauma amidst the dirty clothes and rat's nest of hair closing the distance between the front door and the table.

The friends noted the bruised circles under Kenna's eyes, normally bright green but now dull, her hair lank and the color of old dishwater, the black t-shirt and yoga pants. Her clothes, apparently used as napkins, were smudged with food stains where she'd wiped her fingers or licked a drip of some unidentifiable substance off the shelf formed by her breasts.

As Kenna pushed her way through the late Sunday morning diners, she glared at anyone who slowed her down. Frenetic energy seemed to bounce off her as she reached the table, carefully placed a folder at her place and reached out to grab their arms.

"He's not dead. And we're going to find him. Or a body if I'm wrong," she said, vehement. "But I'm right." They gripped her chilled, trembling hands.

"He who?" Candace asked.

"What we?" Frankie said.

"Lucius!" Kenna snapped, startling their favorite bartender so that he sent a highball glass crashing to the floor.

They hadn't really seen or spoken to her in any meaningful way for three weeks. Their worry escalated each time she'd begged off or failed to show up for one of their regular Sunday brunches or weeknight "decompression sessions." Now that she'd made an appearance, their anxiety spiked to new heights. They knew she was spending long hours working on getting her gallery built out and ready for opening, but now they knew the remaining hours of her days and nights had been consumed resurrecting the dead.

Frankie said, "Honey, it's been weeks." She held Kenna's hand, her eyes wet with fear and concern.

Kenna jerked free and glared at her two best friends and declared, "He's. Not. Dead."

"What makes you so certain?" Candace asked, outwardly calm except for the pink flooding up from her chest to her neck.

Alarmed, they watched as Kenna's eyes welled with tears. Her chin trembled, and her head moved in quick twitches. She rubbed the center of her chest and said with a cracking voice, "He's out there. I have to find him. You have to help me find him."

Frankie and Candace shared a look of understanding.

"Where do we start?" Frankie asked.

Kenna laughed. "If I knew *that,* he wouldn't need finding."

Relieved for the first time in weeks, Candace laughed with her and raised her glass. "Well, then, we'd better make a plan."

Frankie picked up her Bloody Mary, Kenna a water goblet, and the three glasses came together in a toast. "A plan."

Kenna laid her hand reverently on the folder she'd placed on the table before opening it to show a thick stack of papers. "I want you guys to see this."

Candace and Frankie peered over at the documents, some photocopies, some wrinkled like they'd been wadded up and then smoothed out again. Kenna carefully removed what appeared to be a smudged mosaic of printed news articles, maps, all adorned with her own red-inked scrawls. "Do you see?"

"Walk us through it, sweetie," Candace said.

Kenna exhaled in frustration. "Isn't it obvious? Look!" She pointed with a bitten fingernail. "Three airports. Two evacuated, one bombing on the same day or thereabout since no one will tell me exactly. And ... and three car explosions, one in each city, that were ignored. Paris, Beirut, Istanbul."

Frankie pasted on a look she hoped was not one of total disbelief. "There must have been hundreds of car explosions that week."

"Thousands," Kenna said, her voice flat. "But only three with unidentifiable remains and within hours of the airport threats.

That's if I narrowed Luc's disappearance down to the forty-eight hours before Wallace told us."

"You went through all of them?" Candace asked, schooling her features to conceal the horrified distress she felt for this fragile reflection of her usually spunky friend.

"What *else* was I going to do?"

Her two friends shared a wide-eyed look that said, *Maybe what you've been telling us you were doing?*

Frankie patted Kenna's hand and said, "Well, at least we have a place to start."

"Let's start with Wallace. What do you say?" Candace said to Kenna. "I'll text him now and see if he can meet us tomorrow. Will that work?"

Kenna felt like a marionette whose strings had all been cut. She was so relieved to have someone else make a decision and loved her friends more than she thought possible.

WILL STARED at the chaos of Kenna's room for a full five minutes before the stench of rancid coffee shook him out of his shock. Before he could process what he was seeing, he gathered up cups, mugs and ringed glasses to be dumped into the sink, liberally doused in lemon scented dish soap and drowned in hot water.

Grabbing a Coke and downing half in a single pull, he turned back to Kenna's room. The walls were papered with printed stories of car bombs. Half were simply pictures with headlines in swirling or backward script he couldn't read and didn't really need to. On the bed was a map with locations circled with either stars or X'ed through. A yellow legal pad had columns listing time, date, location, known victims, responsible party – if any had taken credit – and probable motive. This last category was almost always put down to terrorist acts. A few were noted as suspected kidnapping or assassination. These, he noticed, had been underlined repeatedly and with enough force to rip the paper in places. There were parentheticals scattered throughout with acronyms he didn't recognize, like PKK, TTP and PLF – and some names he did – IRA, Hamas, ISIS and Al-Qaeda. *What the hell was she into?*

He gulped down the rest of the Coke and turned in a circle, as he came to the inevitable, yet unbelievable, conclusion: Kenna was searching for a dead man. "Oh yeah, you're *fine*."

He snatched the notepad off the bed and a grisly photo off the wall and left. He needed a shower, coffee and food before trying to stop this insanity.

When Kenna stepped into the apartment, she crinkled her nose at the combined sensory assault of lemon soap, pizza and the gentle hum of the dishwasher. Since she'd moved into Will's apartment, she'd taken over dish duty. The alternative was plastic or fingers. Not that Will didn't wash, he just found it easier to grab a handful of forks from a deli when he stopped in for lunch.

Her buoyed spirits sank when he turned in his chair. So dark and pained was his expression.

"Who died?" she asked.

"Your man, Kenna." Will placed the pad and photo on the coffee table. "Lucius Chaerea is dead. You have to stop this."

Kenna was shaking her head, like a pup with water in its ear.

"*Yes*," he said with more force this time. "You haven't slept. You're not eating." She opened her mouth to protest. "Stop!" Will rose. "I've *seen this*, Kenna. I can see the bones in your face.

I bet I could wrap my hand around your arm and still have fingers left over. That!" He pointed down the hall to her room. "Stops. To. Day."

"*He's not dead!*" Kenna clenched her fists. "I know it!"

"Yelling at me doesn't make it true."

"Candace and Frankie believe me."

"No. They don't. They might go along with you, but no one believes this bullshit."

Will had a fleeting thought that he should call the therapist Kenna had always refused to see. He'd never really pushed it. Kenna's response had always been, "I will if you will." The shrink probably wouldn't agree with Will's method here, but direct confrontation had worked to get Kenna to do what was necessary before. If he could be strong enough, long enough, for her to see the reality, he figured it would work this time, too.

"*I,*" Kenna pounded her chest with her fist, "believe it. And you can't bully me into changing my mind. This isn't hand exercises or vitamin supplements or stupid bicep curls. I'm going to find him."

"How?"

"I have to find out where he was. Then I'm going there."

"Oh, well why didn't you say so? You got a passport hidden somewhere? That's sixty days, you know. Who's going to tell you where he was?" Will pointed a finger at her. "That guy, Mike? Or the one with the face ... Griffin? Those fuckers won't tell you dick."

"I don't know how I'll get his location, but I *will* get it." Kenna stiffened and got right in Will's face. "And you can help me or get the fuck out of my way."

"First, get off your tiptoes." He waited for her to sink back to the floor. "Second, I am helping you. I've helped you every goddamned day since I found you in a crumpled, bloody heap on the floor of my club. I'm telling you the truth. You can 'fuck' this and 'fuck' that, do side work for Sal Jr. and waste your time in that shithole gallery, but *you* are not part of that. Hell, the only time 'fuck' sounds normal coming out of your mouth is when you yell at me or when you're drunk. That's not a street chick who goes hunting her dead boyfriend!" He was panting by the time he finished his rant.

"Fine. Your goddamned days of helping are done. I'll be out of here as soon as I can get my stuff boxed up."

"Don't be stupid."

"I'm stupid? *And* delusional?"

Will, unwilling to back away from the comical ploy to misdirect and throw him into a retraction, said, "*Yes!* In this mess, fuck yes."

Kenna's chin quivered as she felt her concrete certainty soften.

"Ah, fuck." Will pulled her into a tight hug.

"I'm not crazy," she mumbled her protest into his chest.

"Yeah, you are. But," he said, putting her at arm's length, "you'll do your crazy from here. And tell me what you're doing and where you're going and who you're going with."

"You'll help me?"

Will shook his head. "I'll stay the fuck outta your way, like you said. It's the best I can do, Kenna."

She gave him a quick affirmative nod. "Okay."

"Will you clean your room now?"

"What?" Kenna walked down the hall and opened the door, staring into the mess as if seeing it for the first time. "There are degrees of crazy, you know," she said.

Will responded by turning up the TV. When he heard the bedroom door close, he grabbed his phone off the coffee table.

"We need to talk about Kenna."

FRANKIE SWALLOWED hard as she watched Will stalk up the street to the café. It was usually the girl who said, "We need to talk." But he'd said this was about Kenna, which was a whole new, uncharted territory for the two of them.

He took the seat beside her, not across and kissed her upturned lips. This was a good start.

She smiled. "Welcome back."

Will skipped the preliminaries. "You've seen her."

Frankie nodded. "She finally came to brunch after ditching us for a few weeks. We've seen her better."

"I've seen her worse. You don't buy this bullshit, do you?"

"About Lucius being alive?"

Will gave Frankie a look that said, *What else could I be talking about?*

She shrugged. "I believe Kenna believes it. I believe she is going to try and find him – or a body – with or without our help."

"*Our?*" Will's brows dove into a frown. "What's this 'our' shit? I told her I'm not touching this. And I don't want you and Candace encouraging this dead man-hunt either." He missed Frankie's defiant look as he leaned his forearms on the table, pushing his coffee out of the way. His broad shoulders took up the tiny space above his chair. "Look, I've seen this before. She doesn't take care of herself. She locks herself in that room or in that gallery. Fuckin' rearranging deck chairs. The shrink said it's a coping thing ..."

"Mechanism," Frankie said, wondering when he'd decided to call in an expert.

"Yeah. Makes her feel in control." He pulled a cigarette out of the pack from his pocket, held it unlit and pointed it at Frankie. "She needs help." He tapped the side of his head. "And I don't mean you two letting her think this is going to have a happy ending. That sonofabitch is dead. Whatever the fuck his job was, it got him blown up." Will crammed the cigarette between his lips and flopped back into the chair, crossing his arms over his chest. "Typical Kenna. Whole goddamn city of men and she finds this asshole."

"How is that typical? Lucius is the only man I've known her to really date. I mean she hasn't mentioned that there's been anyone long term since she ... well, she ..."

"Got the shit kicked out of her?" Will said, his face distorting like he was forcing down bile. "There was a gay waiter she bearded. And the married cop. That lasted about two weeks."

"Doesn't sound like Kenna has a 'typical' to me." Frankie didn't want to argue, but she wasn't about to let Will paint Kenna with such broad strokes, even if it was out of anger or concern, or love.

"I mean, she gets into shit. Gets an idea or a gut feeling and runs with it. Every fucking piece of art in that shitty place was on consignment because she pimped, traded and bartered – for food, parking, shoes – then has to scramble for cash when the ConEd is overdue; or the water gets turned off. The bills are gonna come due on this too, and everyone around her will have to ante up."

"What do you suggest I do? Refuse to help her? Pretend she's not chasing ghosts? Have you considered it might be exactly what she needs? She *needs* to find something or nothing. She needs closure." Will blew out a snort of derision and tossed the unlit cig onto the table. Frankie glared at him. "Oh, you think she needs to see a professional, but you scoff at 'closure?' What do you think a therapist is going to tell her?" she continued. "Kenna needs to bury him, and if this is how she does it ..."

"Don't encourage this, Frankie."

She put a hand over one of his that was now gripping his mug and laced their fingers. "You know there is a strong chance this will be a dead end, no pun intended. No one who knows where Lucius died is going to tell her. Candace suspects he was doing some kind of military or government contract work. Everything about him is classified, including this last trip. We have to be there when she hits that wall of silence."

Will scrubbed his fingers through his hair with his other hand before issuing a resigned, "Fuck. She keeps things from me if she knows I won't like it. You'll tell me?" He looked at Frankie with complete trust.

She nodded. "No secrets. I promise. But I'm telling Kenna the same."

CHAPTER FIFTY-SEVEN

"**W**allace," Candace said, "thanks, so much, for seeing us."

"Of course, my dear. Kenna, how are you? Is there something I can do?"

"Yes! You can tell me where Luc is." Kenna's voice shook.

The expression that settled on Wallace's face was mingled regret and resolve.

"Why do you think knowing that will be helpful, Kenna?"

"Because he's not dead, and we're going to find him and bring him home."

Wallace sighed and looked down at his shoes. "Kenna, dear ..."

"*No!* He's alive. I'd know if he's dead, and he's not. I feel him!" She thumped her chest with a fist. "We've got to go get him and bring him back. He'd *be here,* if he could, so he's hurt or in trouble or in some horrible jail cell or something."

Candace clasped Kenna's arm. "Let me step in. Take a breath."

Kenna drew in a shaky breath and put her hands to her flaming face.

"Wallace, Kenna is convinced that Lucius is still alive. Frankie and I are convinced that she'll not rest until she's satisfied herself that he's safe." She gave Wallace a meaningful look. "If we're to help her, we need to go about it with a plan and as much information as we can gather.

"We all know that you and Mike Chapman, and most especially Ellis Griffin, know exactly what happened and where. If Frankie and I can take Kenna there – if we can see for ourselves – everyone will be more settled."

Kenna whispered, "Please."

Wallace turned and walked over to the floor-to-ceiling window that comprised the east wall of his office. He stood, looking out, his hands clasped behind his back for what seemed like forever. Finally, he turned and gestured to the sitting area.

Candace could see that he was collecting his thoughts, trying to decide what and how much to tell them.

He said, "If you're determined to do this, I agree that you must have as much information and all the resources you need to see it through safely. You should know that I, and the men you mentioned, have been doing some groundwork of our own. So far, we have not been able to locate Luc, whatever his condition."

"He's alive."

"I know you believe that, Kenna, but the likelihood of that outcome – and please believe me when I say that it hurts me badly to say so – is beyond remote."

"Where did it happen, Wallace?" Candace asked.

His intent gaze met hers, then he made up his mind.

"Istanbul."

Kenna leaped up. "I told you! We've got to go. Now, we know where he is, we've got to go."

"Not without a lot of preparation, young lady. I will not allow you to race off into a dangerous part of the world without knowing what you're doing or without as much protection as I can manage."

"Then do it fast, Mr. Henneby, because I'm not waiting around for a team of SEALs to plan out every minute detail."

CHAPTER FIFTY-EIGHT

"This is crazy."

"That may be so, Mike," Wallace said, "but it's the situation, and we've got to deal with it. I will not allow these women, who have no experience in this kind of thing, to go alone and unprepared.

"There's a reason Lucius and Griffin went to see what Davit Lazarashvili is after. The man's human trafficking activities are legendary, not to mention horrific. Can you imagine a more volatile situation than Kenna Campbell, Candace Fisher and Frankie Winslow walking into his corner of the world?"

Ellis Griffin snorted in disgust and paced to the windows and back. "We've got to put a stop to this. If you won't, I'll tell them they're insane and no one will allow them to move ahead with this ridiculous notion." He paused and agony passed over his face as he remembered the last day he'd spent with Lucius Chaerea. How it had ended. "The Colonel is dead. We haven't found any evidence otherwise."

Mike Chapman scrubbed his hands over his face, exhaustion plainly written there. "My team's been all over that bombing site and turned over every fucking rock we know of and haven't found any evidence either way. Not saying they're right, but I get it. Until we find Chaerea or what's left of him, none of us will rest easy."

"If the Colonel were alive, he'd have found a way to contact us," Griffin insisted. The alternative was too unreal and painful to contemplate.

"If he's alive, he may not want to be found. He might be after Laz and staying under," Chapman said.

"What *I* want," Wallace said, interrupting this unproductive debate that they'd had many times, "is for none of this to have happened, but I don't get what I want. In lieu of that, I want you two to work with the three women to teach them, at least, basic self-defense and strategy. I want you to impress on them how dangerous this enterprise is, what the risks are to them *personally,* and to lay down the ground rules of how they will follow your direction and not deviate from the plan, no matter what. Not one iota.

"What I want," he continued, "is to know for certain what happened to Luc, for these women to be about their normal lives and for Lazarashvilli to be moldering in a grave or deep under the sea. You two want the same things, I assume, and we will do everything in our considerable power to make it so."

Mike nodded. "I'll call Candace Fisher and set up a meeting with the women to lay out the plans and ground rules. Griffin and I can teach them rudimentary skills in gun safety and personal defense, and, of course, we'll go with them, but there are a thousand ways this can go pear-shaped."

"You couldn't be more right," Wallace agreed. "I'll take care of the logistics, if you'll allow me. A Henneby plane will be made available for all of you when the time comes. I'll arrange for a secure hotel – as secure as Istanbul provides, that is – and other resources in Istanbul that will be at your disposal."

"Sounds good," Chapman said.

Wallace nodded, "Griffin. Put together a list of items you will need when you're on site and I will ensure they're ready and waiting. If there's nothing else, we've got work to do."

CHAPTER FIFTY-NINE

"**K**enna!" Mike snarled. "Fight me, goddammit!" He pushed his knee against the back of her stiff leg and made her buckle, tightening the choke hold he'd been trying to get her to break.

She barked, "I'm tryin'." Her frustration was as palpable as his.

"Okay. Try again," he said. "When my arm's around your neck this way, grab onto my wrist and elbow with both hands and pull your head *down* through." He let her go through the motions and added, "Now, run like hell." She trotted away, then returned. "Better. One more time." She dutifully complied, if without enthusiasm. When she came back from her lackluster escape, he said, "Now, let's try the other one. You remember this one?" He grabbed her neck from behind in both hands.

She stood still and grabbed his wrists.

"Focus," he said, "this is Krav Maga. Think Ziva on NCIS. You know, Mossad." His patience restored, he removed her hands from his wrists and resumed the hold. "Elbow. Hard. Repeat until the hold loosens." She gave him a few light blows with her elbow. "We'll pretend you put some arm into those and go to the next step."

Kenna stood facing forward.

"What's the next step, Kenna?"

"I don't remember." She looked around the room for some kind of clue.

He inhaled deeply. "You turn around fast and slam your knee into my crotch – alternating knees until I'm on the ground. Then, run like hell."

She made a few tepid motions with her knee in his direction.

"You know," Mike mused, hands on his hips as he glared at Kenna, "Candace had no problem whatsoever with this part." He thought about how she'd said it was payback for all the calisthenics he'd made her do to overcome what he liked to call her "wimpy lawyer muscles." He was man enough to admit that he'd really enjoyed watching her do jumping jacks.

"She doesn't like you, like I do," Kenna said with a winsome smile.

His glare hardened. "Yeah, I got that. But here's the thing, Kenna. We need you to take this seriously. Your life – Candace's and Frankie's lives – could depend on any one of you following your training."

She rolled a cramp from her neck and nodded.

"Now. Again."

During a break, Mike and Ellis Griffin sat on the floor leaning against a wall in the training facility, sucking down bottles of cold water.

"How'd it go with Frankie?"

Ellis grinned. "She's a natural. I'll be bruised tomorrow."

"Candace, too, I think. Maybe a tad *too* fierce." He rubbed his inner thigh.

"She could use a bit more control," Ellis agreed.

"I'd sacrifice control for a little ferocity, to be honest. I'm worried about Kenna."

His colleague shot him a sharp look. "What's your assessment?"

Mike considered a moment before he said, "Her head isn't in it. I know her heart and spirit are raring to go, but it's like there's a cloud hanging over her mind. It's as though she can't decide if she's grieving or if she's Xena: Warrior Princess. Whatever. I haven't been able to get her to throw her weight into the training. Literally."

Ellis was thoughtful through the seconds it took him to suck down the last of his water. "I get it. I suffer from a bit of it myself. I hold out little, if any, hope that we'll find anything reassuring in Istanbul. I told myself I'd never set a foot in that hellhole again after watching the Colonel's car explode into thousands of pieces. No one could survive that. I know it."

"I won't argue with you, man, but we owe it to Kenna, to Wallace, to ourselves for God's sake, to put our best effort into this, whatever the outcome."

Ellis gave a pensive nod, then appeared to infuse his spine with renewed purpose. Kenna had used most, if not all, of her emotional and physical currency to drag them all on board with her search. She had nothing left. They had to find a way to marshal her reserves and rekindle the fight in her. "Let's get them to the firing range and come back to the hand-to-hand later. I have an idea."

AFTER WHAT FELT like hours of handgun safety training, they were finally allowed on the firing line. They started with bull's eye targets ten feet away and moved farther out in distance. Then, they graduated to targets with male silhouettes, each with a big red oval in the center of the chest. Candace liked to imagine her target was Charlie Hannigan.

At the end of the session, Candace held her bullet-riddled target over her head and crowed, "I'm good! I'm *so* good!" While Ellis Griffin made her a little nervous, she had to admit he was a good and patient teacher. He'd made her take the semi-automatic apart, put it back together, and load and unload the magazine over and over until she could do it all without hesitation. Only then had he let her start shooting, and, oh, that had been fun.

Frankie sashayed over with a smug grin. "Twelve out of fifteen rounds right through the ticker!" She brandished her target like a flag. "How'd you do?"

"Ten through the heart and three between the eyes!" Candace bragged.

"Don't get cocky," Mike interjected. "We're heading to the live fire house where you'll have to think and react in a heartbeat and won't have time to aim and shoot." He signaled to Ellis. "You three head on over. I need to run through the exercise with Kenna one more time."

Mike and Ellis regrouped after the exercise.

"Candace and Frankie have taken to this like ducks to water," Mike said. "While I wish we had weeks more to prepare them, I think they at least know enough to avoid getting killed."

"Kenna is still not fully in the game."

"No." Mike gave Ellis a thoughtful look. "You said you had an idea."

Ellis shared one of his rare, shark-like grins. "A secret weapon."

"Let's hear it." Mike's worry lifted at Griffin's confidence, and he smiled in return.

"I've observed that Kenna seems to hold back when you or I

confront her directly and physically. I don't think reticence is her nature."

"Oh, hell no," Mike said. "I've seen her cold-cock a guy fast as a snake strike."

Ellis nodded as though that bit of information filled in the missing piece of a puzzle. "It's because she trusts us, maybe likes us on some level ..."

"Or, more like, Luc trusted us, so she feels like she has to treat us differently."

"Could be," Ellis agreed. "Same thing in the end. I've asked Rainsborough to come tomorrow and work with Kenna, and the others if there's a need or there's time."

"Rainsborough ..." Mike said, recognizing and admiring the plan.

"I don't believe she's spent much time with him. Plus, he's not one to engage on a personal level, so, I believe she won't have the same restraint where he's concerned. And, he won't hold back with her because she was Chaerea's."

The plan worked so well that Kenna was ready to chew nails after a few hours of getting thrown around and manhandled by Thomas Rainsborough. Mike and Ellis watched from the sidelines, offering suggestions and critiques, but no sympathy for her bumps and bruises.

"I could cheerfully string all three of 'em up on a big old rotisserie until they're crispy and taste good with barbeque sauce," Kenna snarled at the end of the day as the three women compared notes, results and bruises. "Son-of-a-bitch enjoyed that too much."

"I'll bring the propane," Candace said.

"I'll bring the wine," Frankie agreed.

CHAPTER SIXTY

F rankie woke, leaned over to check the clock and groaned. Her body ached from the many nights she, Candace and Kenna had spent under the strict tutelage of Messrs. Griffin and Chapman, and later Rainsborough, refining rudimentary self-defense moves designed to save their lives.

She hauled herself out of bed, and every muscle screamed in protest. Frankie wondered how any of this training would save them if it killed them in the process.

"Buck up Winslow, ya wimp." She hobbled to the bathroom and a very hot shower. "At least, you didn't have a date after ... Oh yeah! Candace's blind date!" Her phone started to sing from the nightstand, and she grabbed for it. "Hey! I was just thinking about you! How'd it go? Where are you?" She leered and said in a sly tone, "What are you doing, and who are you doing it with?"

Candace laughed out loud. It felt like her first real laugh in weeks. "It was awful, just like I knew it would be."

Frankie adopted a stern tone. "That is a defeatist attitude."

"Frankie, I had to schlep all the way out to Brooklyn to meet him at this little teeny, tiny theater to see this really awful off, off, off-Broadway play. No, actually it wasn't even a theater. It was a garage. I could have gotten my oil changed at intermission." She paused. "If I had a car."

Frankie snorted.

"It was one of those audience participation things. *I got mashed banana in my hair!*"

"Oh, Candace, that is awful!" Her suppressed laughter came across the connection.

"If I ever, ever, ever fucking ever, hint that I might at some point in the future even consider going on a blind date, you have my permission to shoot me. I know you know how. And stop laughing!"

"I'm trying! My sides hurt so bad!"

"Oh, God, mine too! As if last night wasn't bad enough, I hurt all over today. Did Chapman learn that at Gitmo?" Candace winced as she shifted gingerly in her chair.

"Yeah, I'm thinking he's getting a secret thrill out of torturing us."

"Not so secret, if you ask me. I'd go to Mars to help Kenna find Lucius if she asked, but I'm glad that once we do, I won't have to see Drill Sergeant Chapman ever again."

They both got quiet until Frankie asked, "Do you think we will? Find him, I mean?"

"I don't know. I hope so. I really do. We can hope as long as Kenna does," Candace said.

"We have to. Because if he's really dead, it'll kill her."

―――

THE NEXT MORNING, Frankie was on her hands and knees looking under the bed, trying to find the other shoe that matched her outfit. When her phone rang, she jumped and bumped her head, afraid it was either Kenna or Candace wondering where she was. She blindly grabbed for it.

"Hello, Francesca." Senator Lyman Thayer Winslow's plummy, Eastern Ivy League diction caught her off-guard.

Crap. "Hello, Father. What can I do for you? I'm kind of in a hurry."

"I've gotten you an interview at Pilkington. They're expecting your call."

"What? Who?" Frankie sank back on her heels.

"Francesca, you know very well who. We have discussed your joining Philip's firm several times."

Yes, they'd discussed it in their usual fashion. He talked, and she pretended to pay attention. Philip Casey and Lyman Winslow had gone to Yale and been inducted into Skull & Bones together. Casey would agree to what his old friend asked even if he didn't enjoy the contacts the Senator and his subcommittee provided.

"Father, did you bother to read the last piece I did for the *Times*? I love doing what I do. I get to choose my assignments, and I still have time to work on my book." The last part of that remark was a stretch. She hadn't worked on her latest manuscript in months.

"Francesca, you've given this attempt at a writing career enough of your time. Where has it gotten you? Is it really the best use of your education?" His patronizing tone seeped through the phone like an oily residue.

"Not for nothing, but a job at Pilkington isn't any kind of use of my education. Anyway. I don't have time to talk now, I'm late for an engagement. I do have something to discuss with you, though. I'll call you."

Two days later, Frankie paced her marble foyer as she waited for her father to get off the elevator. When she'd called him that morning, he'd surprised her by proposing lunch at the co-op.

"Probably wants to inspect the place," she muttered. "Make sure I'm not putting holes in the wall hanging Kenna's street artists' masterpieces or letting Will turn it into a clubhouse for his 'gang.'" She stopped in front of a gilded mirror and rolled her eyes at her reflection.

Frankie jumped at the knock on the door. She took a deep breath and reminded herself this meeting was a mere courtesy. She knew the Senator would assume her invitation was about money. It was *always* about money with him and the strings he perceived tethered her to Grandmother Winslow's apartment. She opened the door.

"Father."

"Francesca." He kissed her on both cheeks and walked past her to the living room. His eyes scanned every surface.

To make sure everything was still in its proper place, Frankie thought. "Did you want to count the silver before you go?"

Her father dropped into a Queen Anne wing chair and held the crease in his trousers as he crossed one knee over the other. "And if I did, that would be my right, would it not?"

Frankie ignored his rhetorical question. "The Plaza's delivered lunch. I'll get the tray and we can eat in here."

Frankie'd convinced herself this meeting would be cathartic for her and might show her father she was a grown-up. After desultory conversation, she put down her half-eaten turkey club and dabbed her mouth with a damask napkin. She said, "I don't want you to worry, but I want you to know that I'm going away for a few weeks."

He quirked an imperious brow, and she faltered for a moment.

"I'm withdrawing some funds from the trust." There. She'd said it. *That wasn't so bad.* She gave herself a mental pat on the back. Relieved, she picked up the other half of her sandwich and took a bite.

Winslow carefully folded his own napkin and set it beside his plate before speaking. "Where are you going?"

"I'm not at liberty to say." Frankie avoided eye contact.

"I see." He kept his tone level and watched Frankie stare silently out the massive window overlooking Central Park. "Francesca, what makes you think I'm going to allow you to do this if you won't tell me what you're doing or where you're going?"

"*Allow?*" She should have expected that response. Wouldn't The Senator be surprised to know he had something in common with Will? "Excuse me, Father, but I don't need your permission for any part of this, not withdrawing the money or the trip itself."

"Then why am I here?" His well-modulated tone began to slip.

"I didn't want you to hear that I've disappeared and get a report from one of your moles at Chandler & Everett that someone is spending grandmother's money – scratch that. *My* money."

"How kind," he said. "But why won't you tell me where you're going? Did you honestly think I wouldn't have a question or two? If you won't tell me where, will you at least tell me if it's domestic or foreign travel? Will you be traveling by car, plane or cargo ship?"

She would give him one, but she wouldn't drag Wallace Henneby's name into this. That would just beg more questions she had no intention of answering. "We're flying overseas by private jet."

"May I know who 'we' is?"

"No one you know, and, no, it's not Will," she said.

"Don't be snappish, Francesca. What's all this secrecy about? Does it have anything do with your mother?"

"No, it has nothing to do with Mother." Lucinda Winslow McChesney Gilman was currently residing in Sardinia, having divested herself of husband number three. Frankie hadn't talked to the woman in more than six months, which was fine with both of them. "All I can tell you is that I have a friend who needs some help. Since I can offer it, I will."

Winslow nodded, resigned. He wasn't prepared to embrace all the choices his daughter had made and possibly never would be. He would be more at ease with this little excursion, if she'd give him details. But, if this meeting represented a chink in the wall they'd spent most of her life building, he knew that pressing her for more information was a sure way to shore it back up. He left with her promise that she'd call him when she returned to New York. For today, that promise was enough.

CANDACE KNOCKED on the doorframe of Charlie Hannigan's office and waited politely for him to look up from the pleadings he was studying.

"A minute?"

"No more than that, Fisher. This is Monday."

She tugged on the hem of her sweater, knowing that would draw his attention.

"I need some time off, Charlie. There is an important matter that requires my participation ... some travel. I've organized my pending cases and briefed James and Marianne on the upcoming appearances and necessary motions. With your permission ..."

He tilted his desk chair back and crossed his arms over his chest, resting them on his slight paunch. "How long?"

"Maybe three weeks?"

Hannigan's eyes bulged, and he tugged his reading glasses down to the end of his hooked nose. "Are you serious? You expect me to work around you for almost a month?"

Candace glowered at him. "On hours worked over the past few years alone, I've earned far more comp time than that, Charlie. Or charge it to vacation, I don't care."

"That's Mr. Hannigan to you, Fisher. And you're a professional. We expect you to put in whatever hours are necessary to get your work completed without an expectation of quid pro quo. None of us get the luxury of vacations, as you know better than anyone."

They stared at each other in a nasty Mexican standoff.

"Really," Candace snarled.

"If you need the time so badly, Fisher, take it. Don't be surprised if you come back to find someone else sitting at your desk." He looked down at the court documents before him in a signal of dismissal. When she didn't leave, and stood there silent, he finally looked back up at her with a quizzical expression.

"You know what, *Charlie*? You go right ahead and fill my spot. Consider this my two weeks' notice ... but I'll be cleaning out my office today." She spun on her four-inch heels. "Feel free to call for a security escort. I'll be out of here within the hour."

CHAPTER SIXTY-ONE

Four people boarded one of two Henneby corporate jets, a G650 based at Teterboro. Frankie and Candace had decided to tuck Kenna into a window seat toward the rear of the passenger cabin, with Frankie beside her to serve as her wrangler. Candace would take one for the team and sit with Mike Chapman. His broad shoulders filled one of the large, plush leather seats, and his legs and feet occupied all the space between his seat and the one opposite. Candace chose a window seat facing him, one that allowed her to keep an eye out for signals from Frankie. Candace looked directly at Frankie now and silently communicated how very much she owed her one.

The flight attendant passed through the plane to take requests for refreshments while the pilots made the plane ready for takeoff. After asking for a cup of black coffee, Chapman leaned his head back against the cushioned headrest and closed his eyes. Candace leveled a jaundiced look on his placid expression and pulled out a book she'd intended to read for more than a year.

Frankie accepted two glasses of champagne from the attendant and handed one to Kenna along with a little blue pill.

"Here, honey. Take this now, okay?"

"I don't have a problem keeping an erection." Kenna held the tablet up in the air between her thumb and index finger.

"Just a Xanax. You haven't slept in weeks. You *need* to relax as much as you can." *You're about to snap as it is,* was her worried thought.

"Fine." Kenna popped the pill into her mouth and shook her head to the champagne, swallowing it dry. "I'm good." She looked forward to see Chapman put on noise-canceling headphones. "Oh, yeah. He's going to be scintillating company. Poor Candace."

"She'll survive. Maybe he'll sleep the whole way." Frankie didn't realize how clairvoyant her words might be.

In fact, soon after the plane reached altitude, Chapman declined the offer of a meal, turned off the overhead light, reclined his seat, stretched out his seemingly endless legs and, headphones firmly in place, fell promptly asleep.

Candace snarled to no one in particular. "I hate people who can fall asleep on airplanes." He shouldn't have been able to hear her, but she saw the corners of his mouth turn up in a sly smile. She may have growled.

After picking over the offered meal and drinking a few glasses of wine, Kenna was still restless and unable to relax. Frankie decided to bring out the big guns and went forward to ask the flight attendant for three glasses of single malt on the rocks.

"Here you go." She handed one to Candace and took one to Kenna before coming back to take the seat across the aisle from Candace and Mike. She pointed to Candace's drink. "Want a blue pill to chase that?"

Candace tipped the glass toward her in an air toast. "Nah.

I'm good, thanks. I'll just sit here drinking and trying to focus on this lousy biography. Why did I ever think I wanted to read about the rise and fall of the Vanderbilts?"

"*Poseurs*, every one of them. Plus, you need to get a life, sister. Your charms are being wasted on your cat when they should be wasted on the men of New York."

Kenna, tuning in from a few feet away, managed a slightly dopey smile at their banter before the whiskey finally did the trick. She fell into a troubled sleep. Frankie waited a few minutes to make sure she was really out and then leaned over to catch Candace's eye. She tilted her head toward Chapman. Candace nodded and stood, straddled the denim-clad legs and leaned down to grasp the headphones. She snapped them briskly and smiled sweetly when the blue-green eyes sprang open.

"Oh, good! You're awake."

"The hell?"

"It's time for brass tacks." Frankie propped a hip on the arm of his seat and eased the headphones off his head to circle his neck. "Before we land, you're going to fill us in on what's really going on."

"Hey. You know what's going on. We're going to Istanbul so Kenna can see where Chaerea died."

Candace got in his face. "Not buying it. Why did you insist we take the weapons handling course? Why did Ellis Griffin tell *you* to chaperone us and he'd meet us there? Why isn't *he* on this flight instead of you?"

"What? You don't like my company?"

Frankie snorted. "Funny. We could have sat a stuffed bear in that seat and been more entertained." She turned deadly serious. "What's going on, Chapman? Kenna may not want to dig too deep, but if we're going to keep her safe, keep ourselves safe, we need to know what the hell we're walking into."

"I have been doing everything required, and more, to prepare you for anything that may come up –"

"Don't," Candace said as she poked a hard finger into his sternum, "treat us like fragile females. Anyone who watches CNN knows that Istanbul is becoming a hotbed of terrorist activity. This was not a bombing of an international flight terminal. This was a very specific, very singular target – *Luc*. An IED set off in a slum on the outskirts of Istanbul where there is nothing else of value. Political, economic or otherwise."

Chapman leveled a long, hard look at her, but she stared back at him without flinching. He glanced up at Frankie who, like her sidekick, gave him no quarter. He sighed.

"Fine. Chaerea went to Istanbul, the current HQ of Davit Lazarashvilli, a sick fuck who's had a hard ... bug up his ... grudge against Chaerea since Bosnia."

"Bosnia!" Frankie gasped. "That's ... how many years?"

"Too many. Not enough."

Candace went straight to the point. "Blowing someone up sounds like more than a mere grudge. Why would Luc go there to stir things up with this guy?"

Chapman weighed the pros and cons of telling these women the truth and came down on the side of more information maybe keeping them alive, especially if it sent them back home.

"Laz is a career war criminal who loves his work. In Bosnia, he led a band of deserters who enjoyed rape and made their money in the sex trafficking trade. In case you don't know it, you three are perfect trade goods – young, beautiful, fair hair and skin. You are vulnerable in New York, and now you're walking right into his backyard. You think you have street smarts. Do not over-estimate yourselves or ever let down your guard. Watch yourselves and each other at all times."

"So that's what you and Griffin are really doing," Frankie mused.

"Mainly. But if you don't cooperate, we won't be able to cover your asses every minute."

Never one to let a conversational thread dangle, Candace brought him back to the point. "How did Luc cross this guy's path?"

Chapman massaged the tension in his forehead with two fingers. "Chaerea and Griffin were SAS, hunting war criminals under the cover of providing protection for a UNESCO team. Chaerea's wife was one of the team leaders. Laz and his merry band were harassing them, getting close enough to pick off one of the young women in the team. Our heroes tracked them to a bombed-out village, and Griffin had the kill shot on Laz. Instead of the double-tap, he shot Laz in the groin, thinking he'd hit the femoral and that Laz would die quickly, but painfully ..."

"But he didn't, obviously. So, then?" Frankie prompted, gesturing in a "get on with it" circle.

"No," Chapman said, heaving a sigh, "he didn't. He laid low for a few months. Probably recovering. Plotting and scheming. He knew who was behind the attack and waited. When Chaerea's wife was on a UNESCO mission in the Sudan, he singled her out. Killed her, among others." He saw no need to share the details with these two. "Chaerea and Laz have played cat and mouse ever since."

"What's changed?" Candace asked. "Why has Luc gone after him now?"

Chapman gave her a speculative look. "Well, darlin', why do you think?" He tilted his head to the sleeping form behind them.

"Laz threatened *Kenna*?"

"Chaerea let his guard down for a while after meeting her. And you two. Griffin and I were trading off keeping an eye out and noticed one of Laz's men, and later another operative, in New York. Both seemed focused on Kenna. Where there's one

... they're like cockroaches, you know? Chaerea drew them off. Took the fight to Laz."

"So. Laz is Luc's white whale," Frankie said and drained the scotch flavored melted ice in her tumbler. "We need more of this." She got up and went to the flight attendants' galley.

"How do you know all this? You weren't there, right? You never mentioned yourself in that scenario," Candace observed.

"Hmmm," Chapman hummed as if to himself. "Does she need to know?" She pinched a rock-hard bicep, and he humored her by whining, "Ow!"

She glared and gestured rudely for him to wait for Frankie.

"Okay, okay." He held up his hands, palms out. "More recently, Chaerea, Griffin and I were all part of a joint task force in a place you most definitely do *not* need to know about. Luc and Griffin had been embedded with the locals for so long, well, I thought they were goatherds when we met. Sometimes at night, sitting in the rocks, guys tell stories to pass the time. And, in our case, to add another set of eyes and ears to the surveillance."

His look sharpened as he paused for a second. Mike clasped the hand that Candace had rested on her thigh. "Now, listen to me and pay attention. This is the closest Laz has dared to get to Luc, to someone close to Luc, in years. I'm dead serious. You three are probable targets –" Seeing their open mouths poised to argue, he raised a hand. "You are. We stay together, and *you* need to be hyper-aware."

"I get that," Candace said.

"See that you do." He pulled the headphones from around his neck and resettled them over his ears. "G'night."

CHAPTER SIXTY-TWO

The plan was simple. Explore the market, be tourists, make Kenna relax with some retail therapy, and tomorrow they would hire a car and drive out to the location Ellis had marked on the map. Maybe then, if there was nothing more than an ash stain left in the dirt, Kenna would let go of the belief that Lucius was alive. They all could painfully move on.

Their senses were assaulted from every direction. The market hummed with every language imaginable. Locals and tourists gesticulated and shouted at each other as they searched for something beyond language that created a theater of commerce. Spices, food and humanity swirled in a cloying perfume, ebbing and flowing as the four Americans moved past a tea bar and a door labeled in several languages "pharmacy." Food stands displayed familiar flat breads, vegetables, skewered meats and more adventurous fare no one dared ask about, as snaggle-toothed crones in bright babushkas yammered and laughed at the foreigners.

The silks and textiles captured the three women's imaginations. Colors seemed brighter, the intricate patterns a feast for the eyes. They draped themselves in luxurious fabrics, imagining themselves as something from Scheherazade's stories. Someone suggested a dance of the seven veils or possibly something a bit more suggestive, if the blushing and giggling were any indication. The plan was working. The tension of the weeks before, the nervous anticipation, was bleeding out of them under the market's exotic spell.

Mike followed at a safe distance. Rueful, he watched as they turned heads, a chronic condition he'd noticed in New York, especially when they were together. The attention they garnered was nothing more sinister than Westerners looking for familiar language or shop owners looking for a sale. He, too, was beginning to feel the relaxing effects of their market excursion. He admitted to himself that maybe this trip wasn't going to be a complete goat fuck.

In a dusty tunic, worn shoes and a shuffling gait, he blended into the teeming throng. He'd at first thought it was another fevered delusion. There had been so many. During the first weeks of overwhelming pain, she'd come to him, her scent wrapping around his mind, silken blonde waves caressing his burning skin, the memory of sparkling green eyes transformed into pools of sensory deprivation for him. He refused the opiate teas offered. He preferred the drug of her mirage. It was all he'd thought to keep of her when he'd placed his signet ring on the dismembered hand and crawled away from the blast wreckage months before.

The musical laughter from the silk merchant's stall had been an electric jolt to his soul. His mind steeled against any hope as his heart pounded and demanded his feet move. He knew before she turned her face. Every cell of his broken body reached out to Kenna, but she was oblivious to him.

Cautiously, he scanned the crowd. Did others see her too? Coincidences were a luxury. If she were here, it was because his disappearance had brought her. Intentional or not, his enemy would find her, if he hadn't already.

Movement behind them. A man in a baseball cap and a t-shirt proclaiming Life Is Good. Rhythmless head bobbing to a non-existent tune from his ear buds. Chapman. His shoulders slumped in relief. They had not abandoned Kenna and her friends. He slipped between the stalls to survey the rooftops. Griffin preferred a bird's eye view to street surveillance. He was satisfied and felt a surge of pride when *he* couldn't find any sign. Somehow that reassured him of Griffin's vigilance more than anything else.

He *could* simply pass by, another body in motion. But he craved one last moment, a bit longer to soak her in. The emotionless tactician in him remained silent as she approached, weaving forward and back, inching closer and closer. His fingers ached to touch her. Of its own volition, his hand rose. Time slowed. The world became a single circle of her light. He reached for it, a loose curl down her back. A familiar friend, he almost felt it wrap around his finger in a blissful moment, the first in months.

Kenna froze. A trickle of melting ice slid down her spine, and she shuddered.

"A possum trot over your grave?" Candace teased, using one of Kenna's favorite sayings.

"Luc," Kenna whispered. She stilled, her senses reaching out, seeking, as if they could find and touch the presence she felt in her soul.

"What?" Frankie gently touched her arm, their revelry shattered in one word.

Kenna spun around, her eyes raked the crowds. A few stared back at her like she'd turned green. In truth, she'd gone white.

"Lucius?" she called out. More heads turned. Some sneered, some laughed, and one moved quickly away.

"Luc!" Frantic hope made her voice crack.

"Where, Kenna?" Candace and Frankie both asked, trying to search in the direction she was looking, but there were too many people, and they couldn't see who or what she was seeing.

Kenna began to shove through the mass of humanity that conspired against her, closing in around her like quicksand. The harder she fought to follow the man she'd seen, the tighter they squeezed in around her.

"What the hell is she doing?"

Mike heard Ellis' voice through his earpiece about a half a second before he heard Kenna's cries and saw her take off in pursuit of a ghost.

"Fuck!" he swore under his breath, fighting through the sea of tourists and locals like a salmon swimming upstream to spawn. "I can't reach them."

"I've got the visual," came the voice in his ear.

"It's him," Kenna cried over her shoulder, not surprised to see Frankie and Candace hot on her heels.

Over and over she called to him. In a desperate move to extract herself from the sea of people, Kenna climbed up on the hood of a taxi. The horn blared, and the driver shouted curses at her in Turkish. Candace and Frankie reached up to steady her and urge her down. "Kenna, you'll fall."

"Lucius!" she screamed to a retreating man's back.

"Honey, come down now."

"Come back to me!" Her energy was evaporating as she began to doubt what she knew in her heart. She searched the faces around her, then back to the man walking away. *"Please,"* she called. The magic word of childhood, her last desperate attempt to make him real and standing there next to her.

High above the scene unfolding below, Ellis watched in horror as Kenna made herself and her friends the conspicuous center of high drama. He saw Mike fighting and shoving through the crush of people to get to them. He fought the temptation to use the scope on his rifle to locate and identify the man she was pursuing. His primary objective was to protect the women. *If, by some miracle* ... He wanted to believe she was right and, God, he was tempted to follow her line of sight, but he'd seen the explosion. He'd felt the heat and the ground-shaking blast of the IED and had been knocked unconscious by the flying debris. He'd clawed and crawled through the smoke, ash and destruction only to find the Colonel's ring on a charred, severed hand. He'd been the one to tell Wallace Henneby and stayed to witness Kenna's eerily calm acceptance of Lucius' bequest. As he watched her hysterics now, those months of apparent calm seemed surreal.

While Mike struggled and shoved his way through the unyielding masses to reach the women, he was uncomfortably reminded of those times in combat when instinct kicked in and he became hyperaware of every sight and sound. No, there weren't enemy combatants hiding in the shadows that he knew of. No, there weren't live rounds punching holes into walls inches from his head. It was only a feeling on which he'd learned to rely.

As he tracked them and searched every face in the market-place, questions crowded his mind. *Is she insane? Who did she see? Could it be Luc? Why would he go to ground? Is he the hunter or hunted? What does he need from me?*

No answers were forthcoming, but Mike was convinced Kenna was a sad, definitely angry and completely sane woman. Reaching Candace, he knew they, and Lucius, were in serious trouble.

"Get her down!" Mike hissed in Candace's ear.

The urgency in his voice and his fingers digging into her arms were all she needed to move.

"Frankie!" Candace yelled over the horn, driver and Kenna. "Grab her. Now!" She stretched on tiptoes to reach for Kenna's hand.

Frankie saw Mike scanning the market. "Shit. Kenna!" She yanked Kenna's ankle, not quite toppling her from the cab's hood, but succeeding in getting her attention.

That break in her concentration was all the man needed to vanish completely. When Kenna looked up again, she found no trace of him, and she began to wonder if she'd imagined it all.

Defeated, she allowed them to help her off the car. Money talks in every language or, in this case, shuts it up. The hundred lira note that appeared in Frankie's hand was all it took to silence the stream of objections and insults from the taxi driver.

Tears filled Kenna's eyes. "It wasn't him, was it?"

"I don't know, honey." Frankie put her arm around Kenna's shoulders and turned her toward Mike and Candace, who were whispering to each other.

"What is she *thinking*?" he demanded, still tense.

"First guess – she saw Lucius, unless you have a better idea," Candace said, irritated at the need to state the obvious.

"No shit. She may have just killed him, too."

"How do you kill a dead man?" Candace hissed back. Her mind was already fitting the pieces together.

"If, and I do mean *if*, Luc is alive, he has a reason for laying low. And if someone is looking for him," Mike focused on Kenna, "or you ..."

Frankie finished for him, "We just put giant targets on our backs and his."

Mike tapped the side of his nose.

"Did you see *him?*" The plea in Kenna's voice, willed Mike to say he recognized Luc.

"No, but that doesn't mean anything. This will be all over Istanbul in an hour." He held up a hand to quell the hot retort he could see forming on Candace's lips. Mike pressed the bud in his ear. "I have them. Is it him?"

"Couldn't see him. Get them to the hotel."

Mike nodded to the unseen Ellis Griffin and gathered his charges.

LUCIUS FROZE at the sound of his name in Kenna's voice. *Damn!* He knew it was careless. Hunched over to appear older and less visible, he snaked away. Snake described exactly how he felt. *Selfish idiot!* he cursed himself.

Her cries had ripped through him. The anguish and anger he'd felt was now overpowered by raw fear. *Come on, Chapman! Gag her!* Lucius ordered his colleague, as though Mike would hear and accept his telepathic command.

He dared not look back. He felt her eyes burning into him. *Keep going. She will doubt herself. They will leave, and she will be safe. She will be safe,* he repeated the mantra he'd recited incessantly for months. This was his reason for crawling away from the wreckage, for breathing in and out for weeks as his body healed, his reason for keeping still and silent, watching and waiting. Now, he knew in his soul the reason he would have to act. Lazarashvilli would know about today's events soon enough. Even if he didn't believe Lucius was alive, he would have no reservations about eliminating Chapman and Griffin in order to seize Kenna, Frankie and Candace - prime products for his most selective clientele. Nothing would lure him out of his hole more readily than the opportunity to possess, and destroy, the last remnant of Lucius' life.

CHAPTER SIXTY-THREE

"What do we do next?" Candace demanded as Mike pushed the button to close the elevator doors before other passengers could enter.

"We go to the suite and wait for Griffin. We'll all compare notes about what we saw –"

"It was Luc," Kenna's voice was a mix of joy and exhaustion.

"We'll work from that assumption," Mike confirmed, "but we need to know exactly what you saw. What was the man wearing, did he have a beard, how tall was he, what direction did he take when he left the market? We'll need every detail you can recall, then we'll make a plan. I'll make some calls. We need more resources. Whoever you saw –"

"It was Luc," Kenna repeated, this time with more force.

"Luc, then, is long gone, and if he doesn't want to be found, he won't be. We'll have to give him a reason to find us."

The elevator dinged at their floor, and Mike held his arm out to prevent them from rushing out.

"Me first. One of you hold the elevator while I check the corridor. Wait until I give the all clear."

He walked to the end of the elevator lobby and looked down

the hall leading away from the suite, then turned toward their rooms. Three bulky men trying to break into the suite saw him. The biggest drew his gun and fired at Mike, hitting him above the right temple.

Mike dropped like a felled tree at the same time they heard a "pop."

"*Mike!*" Candace ran from the elevator and dropped to her knees next to his head. The wound bled profusely. She put her bare hand against his scalp to apply pressure.

"Get back here!" Frankie held the elevator doors open.

Candace could hear the heavy footfalls rapidly heading in her direction and grabbed Mike by the ankles, trying to drag him back to the elevator. Outweighed by a hundred pounds of muscle, she made little progress.

"*Help!*" she screamed. "*Somebody – help!*"

A blinding explosion that felt like it would rip her face off knocked her away from Mike and onto her back. The ferocious, closed-fist backhand had served its purpose as a temporary communal stun gun – working long enough to force the three women into the elevator.

While they reached for a barely conscious Candace, Frankie and Kenna kicked, punched and bit, doing everything in their power to prevent being taken to the dreaded secondary location. They'd been trained to resist at all costs and shouted in rapid-fire mode:

"*Let her go!*"
"*Turn me loose, you asshole!*"
"*Where are you taking us?*"
"*Who are you, you bastard?!*"
"*People are coming for us!*"
"*We will be missed!*"

In spite of the commotion they caused and the sight of a limp Candace hanging like a rag doll over the arm of one of the thugs, the women were inexorably dragged down a service passage past hotel staff who made a great show of seeing nothing. Their abductors took them out a delivery entrance without interference and forced the women into an unmarked van.

"*Shut up,*" snarled the huge one, he pointed a semi-automatic at Frankie's face and slammed the door.

Candace regained some of her wits and joined her friends in shouting and pounding on the vehicle's side panels and doors – doors with no interior latches that could be used for escape. No one could hear them and, if they did, would do nothing to intervene in a drama that wasn't their problem.

In less than half an hour, the van, vibrating from the battle for escape – or notice – taking place in the back, passed through iron gates in a high stone wall that surrounded a three-story, flat-roofed villa. Only the upper floors had windows. Armed guards patrolled the rooftop and grounds.

When one of the kidnappers opened the rear door, a spitting, snarling, mythological creature, with three heads, a dozen limbs and filled with fear-fueled fury, poured out.

"You can drop the thousand-yard stare, asshole!" Kenna wrenched her arm away from one of their captors. "*Where are we?!*" The non-responsive, mercenary muscle infuriated her beyond bearing.

The one in charge jammed a fat finger under Candace's already swollen chin and forced up her furious face. Hot brown eyes shot fire at him as she tried in vain to pull away. "You. Quiet. Have you learn nothing today?" He gripped her by the scruff of the neck like a snarling kitten and turned her to face Kenna and Frankie. "Enough. We go inside." He didn't need to shout or threaten more. The thick Russian accent and the way he manhandled Candace menaced enough to ensure their compliance.

They were hauled through another delivery entrance and

down a hallway with doors widely spaced along one wall, then shoved into what appeared to be a sitting room. Hissing, Kenna spun to see the door slammed in her face. The sound of the lock turning was like a gunshot.

Hurt and exhausted, Candace sank to her knees and cradled her face in her hands. Seeing her shoulders shake, Frankie knelt beside her and took her into her arms.

"Oh, sweetie! Are you okay?" Worry made her voice crack.

"It's my fault," Candace muttered and raised her reddened face to look at Frankie, tears made tracks down her bruising cheek. "They caught us because of me." Her face crumpled. "Is he dead?"

"Mike?" Frankie asked, but she knew who her friend meant.

"There was so much," – Candace hiccupped a sob – "blood."

Kenna had joined them in the middle of the floor. She gave Frankie a look and tilted her head at Candace. "Of course, Mike's alive. Head wounds bleed like a stuck pig – always look worse than they are. Plus, he's so hard-headed, it would take more than a little bullet through a suppressor to penetrate that skull."

Candace gave a little chuckle. "If he lives, he's going to kill us."

Frankie laughed. "Or Ellis will."

"They've got to find us first," Kenna said. "Think. We've got to figure out what we're going to do when these guys come back. We have to stay together." They each took one of Candace's arms and stood. For the first time since they'd been tossed into this room, the women looked around and took in their surroundings.

Backs together, they noted a sofa piled with cushions, deep chairs and occasional tables that begged for soft lighting, of which there was none. In the corner next to a fake potted palm, there was a toilet and sink. No part of the room offered privacy.

Frankie pulled aside tasteful draperies to reveal a solid wall. "Well, there's the first of no doubt many mind fucks. Whoever owns this place should call my mother for her decorator's phone number."

Kenna pointed to the sink and pushed Candace in that direction. "Rinse and spit. Get a cold towel on your face." The instructions given to her at the emergency room so many months ago came back in a rush. "We need ice."

Like the van that brought them to this place, the door to the room had no inner handle, but it did have a peephole. Kenna stalked to the door and looked out. Not only was the hole turned to see *into* the room, but they had an audience. Her fist banged furiously on the door, and she slammed her scarred hand over the portal. "See that? You cowards all think you're so tough when you beat up women." She muttered, "Assholes."

Frankie said in a low tone, "Kenna. Candace." Getting their attention, she pointed out the closed-circuit cameras mounted in the corners of the room. "We've got eyes. Probably ears too."

Instinctively, they huddled together, whispering. Kenna said, "Okay. We screwed up and wound up at the second location. Mike and Ellis will look for us."

"They won't know where to look," Candace said. "I'm so sorry."

"Stop it," Kenna said. "These guys aren't amateurs, and we're not professionals." Kenna cast another disgusted look at the reversed peephole. Irritated at herself as well as her friends, she said, "So much for trusting our training. Might as well have been newborn calves getting grabbed that way with hardly a fight."

"You're right." Frankie agreed. "We were easy pickings after they took Mike out of the equation." Looking around the room, she studied the furnishings. "We've got no weapons, except our brains."

"And mine's rattled," Candace said. She focused on where they were confined. "No windows in this room, but if we get where we can see the outside world –"

"— and the outside world can see us," Kenna said, following the train of thought, "then maybe we can signal for help." She looked down at her white shirt, smudged with dirt from their struggles, and envisioned it as a flag. Or, maybe she could write on it. If she could find something to write with. She went back to bang on the door. "Hey! We need ice!" She got no response. Exhausted and discouraged, Kenna slid down the door to sit on the floor.

Oh, Luc, what do I do now?

CHAPTER SIXTY-FOUR

G riffin got off the elevator and found Chapman sitting and holding his bunched-up t-shirt to a bleeding head wound. Griffin pulled his weapon and rushed to his fallen colleague, searching up and down the hallway for threats.

"They're gone," Mike said in flat tones. "Took the women down the elevator."

Griffin knelt beside him. "How bad is it? Can you stand?"

"Flesh wound," Mike said. "I think. I need to get a fresh shirt, and we need to head out." He winced and moaned as he staggered up. "Mother of all headaches."

With Griffin's hand bracing his elbow, they navigated the hall to Mike's room that adjoined the women's suite. In a matter of minutes, Mike had washed off much of the blood, pulled on a fresh t-shirt, slapped some gauze and tape across the still bleeding wound and crammed another baseball cap on over the makeshift bandage.

"Let's go," he said, coming out of the bathroom. "They're less than ten minutes ahead of us."

Griffin folded his arms and took a nonchalant pose in front

of the hotel room door. "Thoughts on where they may have been taken?"

Mike had to give Griffin credit for thinking tactically instead of instinctively, but he hated not being able to run right after them. "We start with hotel staff. Dragging three struggling, yelling, women through a five-star hotel in broad daylight – someone had to see them."

"Then that's where we start."

———

Candace stood at the little sink, squeezing water out of her towel. Kenna joined her and whispered, "How's the lip?" She turned Candace's face to examine it, careful not to use too much pressure and exacerbate what Kenna knew was throbbing pain. She noted the broken blood vessels beneath the skin. The initial angry welt had swollen and deepened to a livid, purple bruise from her chin to under her eye.

Candace's lips were numb as she spat blood into the sink. She gingerly wiped her puffed mouth with the towel. "That's how," she said, tonguing the gash inside her cheek and reaching in a finger to test the looseness of her teeth. Frankie leaned against the wall next to the *faux* palm and flicked the fronds in disgust.

"Did you catch the accents?" she murmured.

Candace lowered her voice and said around her distorted mouth, "Russian? Maybe Ukrainian."

She and Frankie shared a look that recalled to them both what Mike had told them on the plane.

"You need to rinse again," Kenna said. "And don't fall asleep."

"I'm not sleepy," sounded like "nah fleepy." "I'm *pissed*," sounded like "'m *piffed*."

"Good!"

Kenna prowled around the room again. "Maybe we could bust the legs off this table."

"We don't have the element of surprise." Frankie nodded to the black orbs in the corners.

"I don't like feeling like a victim, even fo. So," Candace said, with some difficulty.

They were in the process of tipping over one of the tables when the door flew open. The huge mercenary who'd first hit Candace and had been the only one to speak to them directly looked around the room, amused.

"You." He pointed to Candace and jerked his thumb towards the door. He sighed, exasperated when all three backed away and reformed their three-headed Gorgon.

"We're not going anywhere!"

"There're people looking for us right now."

He stalked to them. "Come now or –"

"Or what? You'll hit me again?" Candace hissed, wincing.

He shook his head and leaned in close to her face. "I shoot your friend."

"We're not much use dead." Frankie said.

His smile was a grimace. "I don't care about your life." His accent so thick they barely understood him.

The gun pointed at Frankie was all the incentive Candace needed. She stepped away. "I'll be back. Don't give up."

Reluctantly, they parted. Kenna and Frankie were left standing in the room to wait. So much for staying together.

A chill slithered over Kenna. Twice, Frankie had had a weapon pointed at her. Three times, Candace had been struck or threatened. She alone had been ignored.

MIKE AND ELLIS moved quickly through hotel staff. Most claimed to have been busy doing something else. The description of the vehicle ranged the gamut from a black sedan, a van of some sort, to pink elephants. Mike's head throbbed, and his focus fluctuated between double and triple vision. Fresh blood dribbled into his ear. They finally convinced a valet to talk – for a generous tip – when Ellis froze.

"Jesus Christ!" He stepped back into Mike. "She was right."

Mike squinted, looked around him and felt his stomach sink. He didn't need all his faculties to recognize the man closing the distance from the street to the hotel's rear entrance. It was the mystery man from the market. Same filthy hair and scraggly beard, clothes layered in dust. Gone was the hunched shuffling gate of an old man. This was the Colonel.

Lucius' long legs closed the gap in moments, his face etched with fury. His thoughts circled in an unending loop. *They had to leave. Now.*

"I lost her," Mike said when Lucius was a few feet away.

Lucius halted, looking from one man to the other. "*Where? When?*"

"Just now." Mike swiped at his cheek, smearing bright red into his hairline. "They were breaking into the room when we got back. One of them took a wild shot, got lucky. Me too ..." The headache had turned into a full-blown set by the US Marine Drum and Bugle Corps. "Anyway, by the time Griffin got here, they'd taken the women."

Inside, Lucius raged. His assassination plan was now a rescue. "A mistake they will soon regret." He stalked into the hotel, Mike and Ellis following. "I know where they were taken. Get that cleaned up." He pointed at Mike's head. "Fifteen minutes." To Ellis he said, "I need a change and a razor."

"Colonel?" Ellis stopped walking, a myriad of questions blazed on his features.

"I don't have time for *your* explanations as to what the *fuck* you are doing here, nor the inclination to offer any." Lucius strode to the elevator. His cache of emotional control and patience strained to the limit anticipating what was to come.

Within the allotted time, Mike had staunched the flow of blood with Celox clotting powder, sealed the edges of the wound with good old-fashioned SuperGlue and traded his jeans and t-shirt for head-to-toe black tactical wear. Ellis and Lucius were similarly dressed when they rapped on his door. They carried the bug-out bags prepped before their arrival in Istanbul.

"How's the vision?" Lucius asked.

"Just singles." Mike hedged the truth. Singles if he didn't turn too fast or look down, or up, or to either side, but he was sure that would correct itself as the time for the infiltration and rescue got closer.

Lucius stepped in close. His eyes darted from one pupil to the other assessing their size and nodded, satisfied. "Fair enough." Stepping back, he continued, "Laz's compound is less than a hundred yards up from the shore of the Bosporus. It's steep, but the footpath is easy. We can't have twisted ankles on the way down." He opened a worn, hand-drawn map of the compound and surrounding property.

Mike tapped the map exactly where Lucius had imagined their landing. "Henneby AJAX inflatable. Aluminum hull, ten-passenger, silent prop." He nodded toward Ellis. "Good thing we put that on the list."

"It's with the plane. We'll get it on the way, not a problem," Ellis said.

The preparations for rescue became a precision dance of securing land and sea vehicles and weapons, and selecting weak points of entry or attack on the compound. Most difficult was waiting until dark to put the plan into motion.

After sunset, the small, inflatable military watercraft drifted to the sliver of beach below the Lazarashvili compound.

"I'm still not a hundred percent on how you're getting in?" Mike said as the three of them slipped onto the rocky shingle.

Lucius looked toward the front gates. "Where he least expects me." He pointed to the wooded trails around the outer walls. He'd given them detailed instructions about points of entry learned over weeks of reconnaissance. "He'll have called in extra sentries. We'll make a sweep outside the walls. Not a sound." Both Chapman and Griffin nodded at the kill-in-silence command.

"Find your perch," Lucius said to Griffin. "Whatever they do to me when I go in, don't take anyone out until I'm inside. I don't want someone getting itchy fingers and killing me too soon." He fixed a suppressor to the barrel of his Russian MP-433 Grach. He would have preferred his SIG Sauer, but since he would be discarding his weapon before entering the compound, the Grach would do and be less evidence of a Western presence if found when this operation was over. "Go in in thirty no matter what."

The sounds of boat traffic on the Bosporus and the city surrounding the property echoed off the water and provided cover for their deadly sweep of the brush outside the compound walls. If anyone inside heard the muffled grunts, lethal knife attacks or the soft pops of suppressed muzzle fire, they didn't rush to the aid of the perimeter guard.

Exactly where Lucius had directed him, Ellis found a utility shed housing the compound's back-up generator. He didn't think the original builders intended for the property ever to be under siege. The remote spot was perfect. Thirty yards uphill from the main house, he could lie flat and see all but the very front of the property. As he looked through the scope on his rifle, he located an office, five bedrooms, and a dozen more rooms with the windows barred.

"Ten armed in the main courtyard. At least that many shadows in the house," he spoke above a whisper into the comm device.

Mike balanced on a boulder across from the main gate. If he squinted, he could make out the hull of their escape boat through the ornate bars.

"In place, Colonel," he said. They heard the faint hum when Lucius disconnected his device, then silence.

Moments later, Ellis and Mike watched from their respective locations as Lucius scaled a wall, went through a hedge, then scuttled around trees until he was close to the main drive. He stepped out behind the guards and walked toward the front entry.

Ellis held his breath and forcibly kept his finger off the trigger as angry blows from humiliated guards rained down on his Colonel.

"Fuck. He's inside," Mike said, and they began their wait.

CHAPTER SIXTY-FIVE

L ucius knelt, bound and bleeding, on the marble floor in an office on the third floor of the villa. He quelled the urge to spit the blood pooling in his mouth across the Persian carpet, swallowing it instead. Kenna would admire the rug, and a spray of fresh blood would distress her when Lazarashvilli brought her in.

And he would bring her, Lucius knew with certainty. Laz would not be able to resist the opportunity to taunt him, to destroy him slowly, body and soul, using Kenna as the instrument of torture.

And so, he waited.

KENNA PACED, then sat, then paced. She'd stopped counting the steps, that was the first phase of full-blown insanity. She was alone now. Frankie had been taken soon after Candace. She folded her hands in her lap and closed her eyes.

"God, I don't know what I'm supposed to do," she sighed. "I'd have an answer if I hadn't waited until it was a last resort to ask, but I did, so now what do I do? Did I imagine everything? Was I just wishing he was alive? Is all of this for nothing?"

The lock on the door clicked. Kenna raised her eyes to see a surprisingly handsome man stroll through the door. His slight limp accentuated his aristocratic bearing.

"Please continue with your prayers, Miss Campbell," he said politely.

There was something too overtly solicitous about him, and it sent a chill through her blood. Kenna stood slowly. "I'm finished."

"Are you sure?"

She nodded.

He held out his hand. "David Lawrence." She'd recognized his voice; the introduction wasn't necessary. When she didn't return the gesture and shake his hand, he opened his arms wide and said, "Welcome to my home." Kenna didn't respond and he scowled. "I hope the absence of original art pieces in the guest lounge ..." he began to say and smiled at her raised eyebrows, "... hasn't offended your tastes. But you never know who might try to steal something."

Kenna crossed her arms, her balled fists hidden.

"You should thank me for not having you taken to my distribution warehouse. I assure you, Miss Campbell, you would *not* have been handled with such delicacy." He waved his hand to encompass the sealed room and chuckled. "My associates find naked, drugged, and well-sampled merchandise much easier to manage."

Kenna thought she might vomit, but hid her revulsion. "Lazarashvilli," she said with resigned recognition. "Where are Candace and Frankie?"

He acted as though her knowledge of his true identity didn't faze him, but he admired her bravado and moved closer. "Your concern is touching. They are, as yet, unharmed."

"You obviously haven't seen Candace," Kenna glared at him.

"Unfortunate, that, but necessary I'm afraid. You three are an impressive force together, and Vlad is new to his position," Lazarashvilli said with false contrition. Kenna assumed this was the name of the thug who'd taken them and struck Candace. "He doesn't appreciate the persuasive effect of a velvet touch. Hans would have used less visible motivation."

"Hans? Vlad?" Kenna laughed. "I'm going to die in a cartoon with moose and squirrel." Visibly tired of this game, she asked, "Why are we here?"

"Yes, yes! My surprise. Please follow me." He was ebullient, almost giddy. When Kenna hesitated, he added, "I promise, no tricks. You will love this."

The two beefy hired guns who, along with the brutish Vlad, had taken them from the hotel were in the corridor and fell in behind Kenna. Lazarashvilli led her up a grand, central stair-case, passing the second-floor landing and up another flight to the third floor. "My residence," he said with a slight bow gesturing her towards another massive, carved set of doors guarded by two more drones.

Abandoning his polite façade, Lazarashvilli stepped into the room ahead of Kenna and turned to watch her enter the room.

Lucius looked up and met Kenna's eyes.

"Luc," she breathed, and, for a fleeting second, a smile broke over her face like a brief appearance of the sun on a clouded day. "I knew it."

"Yes, you did, love," he croaked and managed a partial smile for her. Inside, he warred with elation at seeing her and his horror at meeting her in this evil place. He could not afford to be hobbled by emotions.

She didn't move or seem aware that he had been savagely beaten and was tied hand and foot. She was overwhelmed to find him alive. Kenna's heart hammered in her chest. She'd almost convinced herself that her conviction that he was alive was all in her head.

"I must say, Miss Campbell, your reaction to my gift is somewhat unfulfilling," Lazarashvilli said.

At those words, Lucius' condition pierced her consciousness like a hot needle. She whipped her head around. "What? You want a cookie?"

"*There* she is, Chaerea!" Lazarashvilli crowed as he clapped. "No milquetoast for *you*." He gestured to Kenna. "Please have a seat." When she didn't move, his tone harshened. "I insist." One of his goons made a move toward Kenna, ready to force her into a chair.

She crossed the still pristine Persian carpet and knelt by Lucius. She placed a hand tenderly on his bruised cheek, then laid it on his thigh.

Lazarashvilli scowled. "I've been a polite host, and yet I'm disappointed that you refuse my hospitality."

"I'm sure you are," Kenna said.

He tsked her. "There is no need for sarcasm, Miss Campbell."

"I don't need etiquette lessons from you."

"No, of course not." He flipped open a folder that had been sitting on his desk. "Orphans raised by degenerate criminals seldom do."

Kenna stiffened. The realization that this loathsome person knew details about her, including, it seemed, the death of her parents, unsettled her.

Praying Ellis was in place and determined to stop this twisted circus before Lazarashvilli pulled anymore on that volatile thread, Lucius spoke up. "That's enough," he said so low Lazarashvilli barely heard him. "Let's get on with this."

"Very well. Remember later that you did insist we move on,"

Lazarashvilli said, putting the coming unpleasantness at Lucius'
feet.

"I admit I was surprised to discover the existence of the lovely
Miss Campbell." He leafed through the dossier. "I expected another
raven-haired beauty. Not that you aren't breathtaking in your own
right, my dear. I'll bet he didn't tell you I knew his first wife, did he?
Or that *all* of this," Lazarashvilli said, circling his arms through the
air, "is about avenging her ... unfortunate end." He pouted at Kenna.
"It's never been about you, Precious. But," he clapped his hands
together once, "our Lucius always had a *penchant* for damsels in
distress. I'll bet he could smell it on you, couldn't he?" Lazarashvilli
tipped his head back, his lip curling as he inhaled.

Lucius' jaw cracked watching Lazarashvilli raise his nose in
the air, like a stag in rut catching Kenna's – his prey's – scent.

"Tell me, dear, do you still have nightmares?" He said in a
conversational aside, "They often restrained her in the hospital
to stop the thrashing. Did you know that, Lucius?"

Lucius did know. He'd held her through a few sweat-
drenched episodes in the last months.

Kenna's body jerked as if Lazarashvilli had kicked her.

"Enough," Lucius growled.

Lazarashvilli ignored them. "My goodness! You healed
remarkably well!" He examined a Polaroid as if it was the first
time he'd viewed it. "I would not have recognized you, save the
hair, of course. Have you seen these, Lucius?" He directed his
comments to Kenna, but waved the small stack of photos in
Lucius' direction. "I'm certain he has. Our Lucius is quite deft at
ferreting out information. Did you snoop on your lover, Lucius?"
Every time Lazarashvilli spoke his name, it held a predatory,
even possessive, note, as if the jackal had named his rabbit.

"Defensive wounds. Hmm. Are those the scars on your hand
that you so lovingly – one might say, obsessively – stroke?" he

nodded at the motion occurring in Kenna's lap. She clenched her fists to stop. "It's not to my taste," he lied, "this approach to discipline, but these photos and the evident after-effects are an excellent testimonial. You'd be surprised." He chuckled. "Well, perhaps you wouldn't be, at how many of my customers prefer the combat."

His forehead furrowed in false dismay as he pretended to read, "No visible evidence of sexual assault? Shame that. One might say amateurish." He clucked his tongue in disappointment and then bent to look in Kenna's eyes. "A condition we shall soon remedy, no?" The fear reflected in Kenna's transparent face gave him a perverse thrill.

However, Lucius' stillness irked him. *Could the man not be provoked?* Lazarashvilli struck him hard across his bent back with his cane. The snarling, wolf-snout handle caught Lucius on a shoulder blade.

Lucius inhaled on a hiss and groaned, but remained upright and focused completely on Kenna. Willing away his usual emotionless façade, he poured all his faith and love for her into his expression. When she finally looked at him, surprise infused her features.

Lucius pulled his wounded lip into a grin. He spoke as if they were alone in the room. "Why do you always look so surprised?"

Lazarashvilli laughed merrily. "You actually love this urchin. Oh, my dear Lucius. *I* thought you were merely *fucking* her. This gets better and better. And you know, I *was* almost convinced you were dead. You would have had me, Lucius." He waggled a finger. "If she had not come to your rescue." He returned his focus to Kenna. "That scene in the market this afternoon was priceless. Thank you, my dear. And your lovely friends, of course. Let's not forget *them*."

His glee brought bile up in Kenna's throat. Everything she'd done had tipped the next domino to this end.

He frowned when his phone made a soft tone indicating an incoming call. Perched on the corner of his desk, watching every look Kenna and Lucius exchanged, every muscle twitch between them, he answered.

"Vincent! How is the climate in the UK? I always dreaded London in the autumn." He paused to listen and chuckled. "Your timing could not be more fortuitous. Just today, I have acquired three new treasures your associates will absolutely salivate over." He sent a pleased smile to Kenna. "Yes, *quite* spirited. I'm in the crosshairs of deep, green daggers as we speak. Of course, of course." He pulled out his cell phone and aimed it at Kenna. "Look at me, or I will call Vlad. He's been pining to rip the hair from your skull," he snarled at Kenna, the false solicitous manner was gone for the moment. *"Say cheese!"* Kenna turned and stared blankly at him. He couldn't read the movement of her lips but was certain there was a "fuck you" under her breath.

Hate rolled off Lucius like the shimmers of a desert mirage. Lazarashvilli only grinned, pressing the landline receiver to his chest to muffle the conversation from this Vincent person's ears. "He's about to do something foolish, Kenna."

Kenna rose and glared at Lazarashvilli. Standing between him and Lucius, she too had had enough. Having her own pain exposed was bad enough. Using it to whip Lucius was more than she could tolerate. And the fact was, one of his eyes was swollen shut, and his hands were bound so tight his fingers were purple. He probably couldn't manage a fist, if he were free.

"Go fuck yourself," she said in a low whisper this time. "Oh, but ..." She pasted on her best Scarlett smirk. She'd had her fill of his false hospitality and smiles, her eyes lingered on his groin when she said, "You can't really do that. Can you?" She'd over-heard more than she'd let on of Mike's story on the plane.

Lucius' jaw clenched and a warning hiss came from between his lacerated lips. Kenna and Lazarashvilli both looked down at him.

Kenna jumped as a voice came from the forgotten receiver. "David? David!"

Lazarashvilli turned his back to Kenna and Lucius. "I'm sending you a sample photo of the first one now. The others will take me a few minutes." He made a mental note of the necessity to capture Candace's image from the undamaged side of her face. "I'll need an answer today, Vincent."

Hanging up, he turned and spoke to Lucius. "Consider this my parting gift." He then advised Kenna. "If you cut him free, you will watch him die a slow and painful death." He saw the defiance in her glare. "Test me, Kenna. *Please*, test me," he said as he strode out the doors.

CHAPTER SIXTY-SIX

The second the half-hour was up, Mike was over the wall. Sticking to the shadows, he made it to the corner of the villa closest to the kitchen without detection. Around him he could hear the subtle *whoosh-thap, whoosh-thap* of Griffin's rifle shots finding their targets. One felt uncomfortably close as the hum buzzed past his left ear. Mike looked back in time to see a guard rounding the side of the house fall.

"I took out two in a bunk room on the first floor, but I can't see more than shadows. The outside is clear," Griffin said into his headset. Mike signaled that he'd heard him and made his way to the kitchen door. He saw two thugs in the kitchen, and they were so jumpy one almost shot a third guard coming through the door that led from the interior of the house.

"The redhead needs more ice," he said.

"She should have ducked," said the one closest to Mike.

All three chuckled at the joke as Mr. Ice reached for the freezer door. *Pop. Pop. Pop.* The two who were seated barely moved as they slumped in their chairs. The wall behind them now sprayed with blood. Mr. Ice dropped to his knees, then tipped over like an empty beer bottle.

Mike shoved all their handguns into the pockets and waist-band of his pants, then rifled through Mr. Ice's pockets where he found a magnetic card key he hoped would give him access to the room Griffin had indicated probably held prisoners.

As he hastened down a carpeted hallway, Mike noted that each door had a card reader and a one-way peephole that worked only from the corridor. He checked the first aperture and confirmed that no one was inside that particular room. He swiftly checked the other rooms as he made his way down the hall.

When he came to the door of the second room from the northwest corner, he put his eye to the peephole and said, "The hell?" He rapped lightly on the door and spoke sharply. "Stand back from the door." He swiped the card he'd lifted from the guard through the reader and heard a gratifying click as the lock disengaged. He slipped inside and Frankie dropped the chair she'd been wielding and threw herself into his arms.

"Oh, my God! We *knew* you'd come!"

His heart lifted and then fell when he saw that other than Frankie and a few sticks of furniture, the room was empty.

"Where are Candace and Kenna?"

"*They separated us!* First Candace, then they moved me here. I don't know where they are! We've got to find them – they hurt Candace!" She sobbed and banged on his chest with tight fists.

"How long ago?"

She put her emotional storm on pause, thought for a moment, looked at her watch and answered, "Candace about an hour ago. Me, less – maybe thirty minutes? One of the goons came in and took my picture about five minutes ago."

Mike bent down and removed a compact SIG Sauer from an ankle holster and handed it to Frankie.

"Stay close behind me and shoot anyone who comes up behind us. Don't shoot *me* ..."

"Oh, please!"

"... or Chaerea ..."

"He's *here*?! That's where they've taken Kenna, then. Wherever Luc is, that's where they'll have Kenna."

He mentally acknowledged the truth of her statement. Checking to make sure she had control of her weapon, he gave her another caution to stay close and turned to check the other rooms on the second floor.

It was several minutes later and one more neutralized guard before they found the room where Candace was being held.

Candace stood defiantly facing the door, ready to meet whatever threat came through it, as Mike and Frankie slipped inside. Mike's stomach clenched when he saw the damage to her face, but stowed his reaction for later. Frankie ran to Candace and hugged her carefully, conscious of the loaded gun in her right hand.

"Are you okay?"

"Yes! Are you?"

"Where's Kenna?" Candace looked around.

"Luc's here!" Frankie said. "I bet they've taken her to wherever he is."

"We've got to get to them!"

Mike closed the door and approached, arms wide like they were wearing suicide vests about to blow. "Slow down, slow down. No one is leaving this room before you tell me what you know and we have a plan. Start with telling me about what happened at the hotel ..."

"You got shot," Candace pointed out.

"Yeah, after that. Give me a rundown on the men who've been holding you – have you seen or talked to their boss?"

"The goon that shot you, slugged Candace."

"Then all three goons stuffed us back into the elevator ..."

"... then into a van."

"I cannot believe no one, not even some Western tourist, batted an eye," Candace complained.

Mike snapped his fingers in front of their faces. "Focus, please!"

"You know what happened next. They brought us here and then separated us. They didn't tell us anything. We never saw anyone else, and we never saw your buddy, Laz."

"Stay put, I mean it." With warnings to shoot anyone who came through the door – other than him, Griffin, Chaerea or Kenna – he left to identify where Kenna, and most likely Chaerea, were being held.

As he moved through the building, he wondered where the guards were, the ones that he hadn't taken out. He still moved with caution to clear each room and passage before slipping quietly up the stairs to the third floor. He ducked into an alcove as two beefy guards, the first he'd seen on this reconnaissance, raced toward the stairs. His swift steps were soundless on the carpet. When he caught them, his silenced shots obliterated their brain stems. Chapman dragged each body into the alcove, then waited a full minute to see if any more followed. When none appeared, he trotted in the direction from which they'd come, clearing empty rooms, until he got to a large suite at the end of the hall. Double doors, twelve feet tall, stood ajar.

CHAPTER SIXTY-SEVEN

"We don't have much time," Lucius said with much more strength and command than she'd realized he had left. Although wounded, his internal clock told him the designated half hour had passed and the planned breach of the compound was being carried out.

"What do you mean?"

"If he's going to get photos of Candace and Frankie, he may be disappointed. I don't know how long Chapman and Griffin needed. Go to the window. Be still and wait for a red dot on your chest."

Kenna moved to the window. Her legs felt like Jello. "Why did you leave me?" she asked, her back to him.

"What?" Lucius said in a tone suggesting this was not the time.

"We might not survive this, and I need to know. Why did you leave me when I loved you so much?"

Lucius shifted to look at her, safely tucking away her declaration, though his heart banged in his chest. "He would have come for you. He *was* coming for you."

"So?"

"I had to kill him, Kenna."

"You're not answering the question." Her voice trembled, as the pain of being left washed over her again. "Why did you let me, let us, believe ... were you coming back?"

"No," he said softly. "It was for the best. If you believed – if the world believed – Laz would too, and I would have," he paused before saying, "exterminated the vermin."

"And never come back to me."

"I have to keep you safe. Doing what I do, there will always be someone like him. Evil does not exist in a vacuum. You would heal, and find someone to give you a life –"

"*Do I look healed?*" she shouted, cutting him off. "You kind of screwed the pooch on that one, Colonel. When you are wrong, it's epic! And what's with leaving me money? I guess it's better than leaving me a tip on the nightstand. Seriously, what about me says *this* was a good plan?" She waved her hands over herself, gearing up for more, as the red laser light bounced across her chest.

"Kenna!" Lucius barked. "Listen to me, now. You have to get Laz to the window."

Kenna looked down at the place where the dot had been, then out into the darkness. "How?"

"He will come to you. He won't be able to stay away. Lie to him. Seduce him."

"Seduce him? He has no dick!"

"He's a man. He hates me. And you are ..." he started to say, "an irresistible temptation," then shook his head. "A sharp blade in his hands."

"A knife would be better than this." She popped her hip and cupped her breasts. "I left my *psychopath seduction kit* in my other cleavage."

"Goddamnit, Kenna!"

"Don't you curse at me!" The massive doors creaked, and she

barely paused. *Don't start thinking too much, but think fast, Kenna.* "You're on your own, asshole."

Lazarashvilli walked into the room, his temper visibly chained. "Lover's tiff. How poignant."

Kenna crossed her arms and blew out a snort, keeping her back to them. "Not hardly." Kenna turned. "I, we, may be more valuable to you, Mr. Lazarashvilli, than you anticipated."

"Kenna," Lucius groaned his part in the farce.

She stepped away from the window, focusing solely on Lazarashvilli. "Frankie's father would pay any ransom you asked. Candace has friends with serious money, not to mention contacts in the US government. No questions asked, if they get their princesses back." She combed a hand through her hair and draped it over one shoulder. "Undamaged."

Lazarashvilli stepped closer. "And what about you? Will no one pay your price?"

Kenna took a small step away, then stood still. "You are surrounded by brutes. Even for an urchin, I am no brute. You could keep me." She glanced down at Lucius. "And it would destroy him."

Lazarashvilli closed the distance and grabbed the mass of her hair, tugging so hard she yelped. The gesture arched her back, thrusting her breasts toward him. "How stupid do you think I am?"

"I don't. I didn't mean to," Kenna gripped his wrist. The threat of having her hair torn out was very real.

"Of course, you did. You aren't the first to try and distract me as valiant rescuers attempted to breach my security."

"Attempted?" Kenna groaned, the only one in this room oblivious to his game.

"Coy does not become you, Kenna. My clients will be sorely disappointed, but accidents happen. The photos will have some commercial value. Depraved fetishists, you know."

Kenna choked on a grief-filled moan as fat tears spilled down her cheeks. How could she ever tell their families? She wouldn't. She would be lost in this monster's world. Lucius would not survive this time. Will, Mr. Henneby, Candace's parents whose photographs had radiated safety and love, the Senator, all would carry the burden of never knowing.

Lazarashvilli jerked Kenna's head harder, ripping her out of the spiral of despair. "Open my trousers. Feel what you are offering to service." His spittle dripped on her cheek. "Now!"

Kenna squeezed her eyes shut and tried to shake her head. He dragged her to his desk and pulled a gun from the top drawer. She flinched at the press of cold metal against her head.

"Take off my pants," he said in her ear.

"Please, don't," she pleaded, keeping her eyes closed tight.

"You can save him, Kenna," Lazarashvilli wheedled, and she felt the absence of the steel muzzle against her temple. She knew where he now aimed.

Kenna swallowed hard and, with her right hand, fumbled with his belt buckle and zipper.

"Reach in. You want to seduce me. How willing are you to touch the horror he left me with?"

Nothing of him was familiar. Where smooth flesh should have been, she felt only hard, deformed puckers and rivulets of skin that reminded her of old avocados or rubbery rotting fruit. Twin rubber tubing taped to his groin led to separate collection bags strapped to his thigh and calf. Her groping disturbed the apparatus and made the scent of waste and decay rise like a noxious cloud between them. Kenna gagged.

Lucius watched, willing her to inch Lazarashvilli closer to the window and Griffin's line of sight. When her hand disappeared, and she appeared to be touching the man so intimately, he wretched.

"Why, Lucius, surely you appreciate the poetry of this

moment. You mutilated me. I returned the favor with Sofia. And now, your last love is desperately trying to find something to wrap those lovely lips around."

Lucius spit blood and bile on the rug and then began to laugh. "It wasn't me."

Kenna and Lazarashvilli stilled.

Lucius choked and spit again. "It wasn't me. My young, vengeful Captain fired the shot. I would not have bothered with shooting your cock and balls off. Blowing out your brains would have satisfied."

Lazarashvilli, his grip loosened on Kenna, shifted to gape down at Lucius. "It was your order."

Rising to his knees, Lucius nodded and said, "He won't make that mistake again."

In that instant, everything Mike, Ellis and Rainsborough had drilled into her crystalized in Kenna's mind. Without thinking, her fingers wrapped around the medical tubing and ripped it away as she slammed her knee into his ruined groin. Lazarashvilli screamed and fell to the floor, releasing both Kenna and the gun to curl into a fetal ball. Pain paralyzed him.

Lucius tucked and rolled out of the line of fire in case Lazarashvilli managed to get a shot off in his direction. He struggled to his knees and found Kenna standing over their enemy, the gun pointed at Lazarashvilli's writhing body. A pinpoint of red danced around the room unable to find the kill shot.

"Shit!" Griffin said, as he realized Kenna was standing between him and Laz's head.

"What?" Mike's voice barked in his ear.

"Kenna's blocking my shot. Where are you?"

"Heading to the third floor."

"Fuck!"

———

"KENNA," Lucius said gently. "Come to me."

She didn't take her eyes off her target. "You can't hold a gun."

"Just come to me, honey. Untie me. It's okay."

The croaking laughter startled them as Lazarashvilli rolled to his back, arms spread in a crucifixion pose. "Shoot me."

"Kenna, don't do it. Come to me, baby." Her eyes flickered toward him at the uncharacteristic endearment.

Lazarashvilli choked out another laugh. "He's afraid if you kill me, murder will taint your soul."

Kenna stepped closer, she couldn't miss at this distance. Lazarashvilli's face contorted in a grimace and then vanished as the explosion from her hand echoed in the room.

Kenna threw herself back. Lazarashvilli lay lifeless. She expected to see a shocked open mouth and bright red, dime-sized hole between his eyes, like in the movies. The remnants of his skull spread over the floor. She was oblivious to the blood, bone and flesh that had spattered over her like confetti.

"He was going to kill you."

"It's okay, baby. It'll be okay." Lucius fought to keep his voice gentle and steady. He wasn't certain he could stand. Whether Chapman had succeeded or failed in his mission, they had to get moving. "Kenna."

"Huh?" She looked at him uncomprehending. "He was ..."

"I know. You need to cut me free. We need to get out of here, to the water."

Kenna blinked, then began tearing open desk drawers. She spotted the letter opener on the blotter and raised it to show Lucius. He weakly attempted to raise his hands. She sawed through the thick tape binding his wrists, and Lucius winced as blood vessels and nerve endings roared back to life.

When his feet were free, he gestured to a chair he intended to use to stand up. "Bring me that."

"Oh, fercryinoutloud!" Kenna squatted under his arm. "Just don't fall down the stairs."

He almost smiled and kissed the top of her head. Lucius leaned heavily on her, willing sensation other than thousands of bee stings to return to his lower extremities. He struggled to stay upright and tried to shove Kenna behind him as Mike burst through the doors.

Mike skidded to a halt. "Lookin' good, Colonel."

"Candace? Frankie?" Kenna asked, hope and fear in her voice.

"We'll pick them up on our way down," he moved to offer Lucius his support opposite Kenna.

"I got him," she said, and Mike nodded.

The exodus from the compound bordered on anti-climactic. They met no resistance thanks to Mike's and Ellis' housekeeping. The silence of the massive villa was ghostly.

"Where are the no-neck goons?" Frankie whispered, lest she speak the devils' names and summon them into being.

"Cockroaches," Mike said. She didn't need to know that he and Griffin had eliminated them all. "Once they figured out we were in and Laz was dead, they vanished into the woodwork."

CHAPTER SIXTY-EIGHT

E verything happened so fast, their escape so efficient, so precise. There were no screaming villagers or exploding fortresses. Lazarashvilli's henchmen hadn't chased them to the water's edge, peppering the ground and shallow bank with bullets. The five of them had walked out a small garden gate, down some steps and climbed into the water-craft. The only sign of hurry came from Ellis who, bringing up the rear, hit the water's edge, ready to shove the craft off the sandy gravel and vault into the boat.

"Wait!" Kenna skidded to a stop. "There are others. In a warehouse. He said we were lucky we weren't taken there." She looked to Lucius first, then to Mike and Ellis. "We can't leave them."

Behind her, Ellis shook his head. It was safe to assume the victims of Laz's human trafficking had been the first collateral damage of this mission.

"Kenna," Lucius raised a throbbing hand and clasped her arm. "Get in the boat. We can do this at the hotel."

"What if they are locked in a cage or ... or ... or one of those shipping crates. It happens all the time. We can't let them die in there."

Mike, Frankie and Candace all turned to look over their shoulders when lights and sirens sprang to life, heading in the direction of the compound.

"Colonel!" Mike hissed.

Lucius looked at Ellis and raised his chin. The Captain hauled Kenna up in his arms and dumped her into the boat before pushing them off. She had no choice but to be still and quiet, or they might be caught.

Mike took point, Ellis sat in the back.

The trek from where they'd hidden the boat to the hotel was more arduous and spectator-worthy than when they'd returned from the market. Between Candace's face, Lucius' halting progress and the grim expressions on Mike and Ellis, people stared and whispered. Or, as when the women had been taken, turned away in convenient ignorance.

In the lobby, Ellis stopped, reached inside his hip pocket and said "Luc" – the first time he'd ever used the man's name – and passed him a room key. He refused to look his mentor and brother-in-arms in the eye. "Five thirty-six. End of the hall." He then peeled away from the group and was gone.

"Where's he going?" Kenna asked, watching Ellis disappear into the pre-dawn gloom beyond the hotel's *porte cochere*.

"'To finish his job," Lucius offered no further explanation or a window to ask for more.

When they reached their floor, Mike gestured the direction to their rooms, saving Lucius the trouble of reading room signs.

As Mike, Frankie and Candace approached the women's suite, Mike clasped Candace by the upper arm and steered her further down the hall toward his room, saying, "Excuse us. We've got some things to talk about, and I want to see to her face."

He pulled Candace into his room. As he was closing the door, she wrenched her arm from his grasp.

"Stop manhandling me!"

He reached for her hand and caught her wrist instead. "Hold still. I want to get a close look at your face."

"It's fine."

"It is not fine." He pulled her into the bathroom and turned on the bright overhead lights. "Let me see." He cupped her cheek in his free hand like it was a fragile egg.

Candace rolled her good eye, but after seeing her battered face reflected in the big plate mirror, she let him examine her swollen mouth and cheek. When he pressed gently on the bony orbit around her blackened eye, she yelped and flinched away from his touch.

"I hope the bastard who did this is one of the assholes I left staring sightless at the kitchen ceiling or in the halls at Laz's hellhole. Wish I could kill him all over again," he muttered. He led her back into the bedroom and gently pushed her into an easy chair, saying, "Stay." He snatched up the ice bucket and left the room.

In minutes, he'd filled a hand towel with ice and held it lightly against her bruises. In turn, she stared at the grim expression on his face.

"It's not that bad, is it? I've sthopped – *stopped* – lisping." She pressed the tip of her tongue against a bicuspid and found it only a little bit loose.

"Do you mean, will you ever be beautiful again, or will you be forever deformed? I think I can assure you the damage isn't permanent."

"I am not that vain! I just don't like people staring at me like they did when we came through the lobby."

He snorted. "That might have been because we all looked like we'd been through a pitched battle. And we have been. The attention wasn't all about you, although that shiner does glow like a wingtip strobe light."

Offended, she struggled to get up from the deep-cushioned chair. "Thank you. I'm feeling so much better, I believe I'll head back to my room now."

Chapman gently, but inexorably, pressed her back into the chair. "Not yet, Ms. Fisher. We have that other little thing to talk about – you rushing to my rescue when you three should have been taking that elevator to the lobby and getting hotel security to put you in a safe place. What were you thinking?"

"I guess I was thinking I could save your miserable life or something equally insane." Her poor face hardened into an obstinate expression. "No man left behind. Isn't that your motto?"

"Wrong branch of the service, but I get it. Did you forget the evade-and-escape portion of our training program? You nearly got yourselves killed, not to mention the rest of us."

"Untrue!" Candace was indignant. "If we hadn't been taken to Laz's villa, we'd all still be looking for Luc, and God knows when we would have found him or if he'd have been alive when we did."

"You're wrong." When she opened her mouth to argue, he held up a hand. "Luc came straight here from the marketplace, but by then you'd all been kidnapped. If you'd left me and protected yourselves, we'd probably all be here more or less in one piece and you wouldn't have a broken face."

She calmed herself with effort. "I'll admit it all happened too fast for development of a real plan ..."

He laughed derisively.

"... but Luc, Griffin and *you* were finally able to put an end to Laz's reign of terror."

Mike interrupted, "It was really Kenna ..."

"Even better! My *point* is that recriminations over whether or not we followed our training serves no purpose now, and *it's just pissing me off*!" She managed to stand this time and made it as far as the door to his room before he whirled her around and pushed her against the wall.

"Oh, no. You do not leave in the middle of this discussion on your high horse without hearing me out."

"Completely unnecessary," she sniffed. "I know exactly what you're going to say, and it changes nothing. Save your breath."

He kept her fenced in with arms braced on either side of her head while he studied her with a warring mix of exasperation and humor. At the moment, exasperation was winning. Unable to think what to say or do next, he held her gaze and lowered his mouth carefully to hers. A spark like a static charge arced between their lips, and they broke apart, stunned and staring.

The line of tension between them broke on the instant, and Chapman buried his face in her neck, using lips and teeth to tease the taut muscle leading to her shoulder. Candace futilely pushed against his chest with both hands, her fingers curling of their own apparent volition until she gripped his shirt in fists that pounded weakly against the wall of rigid muscles.

"We can't," she moaned.

"Oh, yeah," he whispered. "We can."

"But I don't like you!"

"I don't like you either, but somehow that's not getting through to my body." He chuckled as he felt her hands trail down to the waistband of his pants and fumble with the fastenings. He leaned his hips away from her to give her more space and cupped the back of her head with one hand to kiss her again, reminding himself to be gentle with her bruised mouth, while he hiked up her shirt and engulfed a plump breast in the other. Its perfection filled his palm with lush warmth and felt like fine silk, the nipple tightened like a ripe berry.

In unspoken accord, they bared only the essentials as they

reeled toward the bed. In one move, he lowered her and plunged inside to the gratifying sound of her gasp. Her sharp inhale was echoed in his deeper tone when she wrapped her legs around his lower back and closed the last millimeters between them.

In mere minutes, they collapsed, breathing hard and vibrating from the shared implosion, their legs entangled and their clothing pushed into bizarre configurations.

Mike lay back with a contented smile on his face.

"This didn't happen."

He turned his head to stare at her incredulously. "It definitely happened. Are you delusional?"

"Maybe it's more accurate to say it can't happen *again*."

"Why the hell not?"

Candace graced him with her most condescending look. "Again. I do not like you, Chapman."

"What's that got to do with it?" Mike rolled up to sit on the side of the bed, and reached for his phone. He called the Henneby pilots to let them know to file the flight plan and be prepared to take off when the original group, plus two, arrived.

As MIKE DRAGGED Candace down the hallway, Frankie stared after them for a quick breath and then with a world-weary sigh let herself into the empty suite. After checking in the closet, the bathroom, behind the shower curtain and finally under the beds, she flopped backward onto one of them and let her eyes drift shut. After a few minutes of this behavior, her jangled nerves and the silence overlaid by the rush of air from the air conditioner got to her, and she rose to drag herself zombie-like to the minibar.

With the contents of three little bottles of whisky safely in a glass, she fished around in a bag for her cellphone and placed an international call to Will. He hadn't wanted either her or Kenna to make this trip, and he'd made her promise she would keep him posted.

He picked up on the first ring. "Frankie?"

Maybe it was adrenaline, maybe it was scotch, but she wouldn't let herself think it could be anything else when her stomach fluttered at the sound of his voice. "Yeah. Just calling, you know, to let you know I'm – we're okay."

"Good. That's good." He was glad she couldn't see him silently look to the heavens and cross himself in thanks, something he hadn't done since he was a kid.

"She was right. He's alive."

"*No shit.*" Fighting to keep his tone light he added, "She'll probably never let any of us forget it."

Frankie laughed, "I think that's a given." *I wish you were here right now.*

"When will you be back?" *I really need to see you.*

"We should be back early tomorrow, I think." Frankie cleared her throat softly. "Will you ... will you be around?" *Please?*

"I should be." *Count on it.*

After a few minutes of listening to each other breathe, they said goodbye.

She dropped the phone beside her on the bed and sat there trying to decide whether she had enough left in the tank for a shower. A sniff at an armpit and the shower won. With a groan, Frankie hauled herself up and trudged, trailing clothes, to the bathroom. She wondered where Candace was. Looking forward to sleeping the entire trip back to New York, she smiled, "At least we won't have to drug Kenna this time."

No longer needing Kenna as a crutch, Lucius cupped her elbow and walked down what seemed to be the longest corridor in creation to room five thirty-six. Every step jarred his bones. His head pounded. The blow across his back from Laz's cane ached and burned; he knew there would be an ugly bruise. He rolled his shoulders, *what was one more blight among the many?*

He went straight to the phone and called for a bottle of bourbon, then opened the minibar and downed two of the miniature bottles of scotch.

"Is that wise?" Kenna winced at the unintentional judgment in the question.

Lucius glared with his open eye. "Yes. Call it a celebration of your life. Cheers." He downed a third without looking to see what it was and grimaced as the inexpensive rum burned his throat.

"I need to know," she picked up her unanswered questions from before.

"Christ, Kenna! Can we save the post-mortem?" He no longer had the physical or emotional strength he'd always called on for his Job-like patience with her.

Scared, wounded and completely unprepared for the fallout of life and death situations, Kenna could only see her own pain and fear and doubts. He'd left her.

"Why did you have to fake your death? Why weren't you coming back?" She sagged on the bed. "Why, Luc?"

A knock on the door brought his bourbon and bought him a moment to gather his reserves. He leaned his head against the closed door. "I believed it was only my heart I risked, and I would break it a thousand times to keep you alive."

"But, I loved you."

He spoke low, between clenched teeth. "How precisely was I to know this ... gem of intelligence? I tend to doubt utterances made in the throes of passion." He smirked at her.

Kenna sprang to her feet. "I'm here, aren't I? Would a woman who didn't love you make up some fucking fantasy in her head that you're alive, when everyone said you were dead, and travel halfway around the world to save your ungrateful ass? What more do you want?"

Lucius grabbed the bottle by the neck and stalked from the room. Self-recrimination gnawed his insides. "A shower."

Kenna sank back to the edge of the mattress and stared at the closed door. It seemed like a long time before the water came on. She assumed he was draining the bottle in the meantime or struggling to get undressed. His hands were stiff, and she had no idea how severely his body had been beaten before she saw him.

How was he to know? Too afraid of a broken heart, so certain of his eventual exit from her life, Kenna owned her role in the self-fulfilling prophecy. The protective barriers – or façade of them – the perpetual testing of his commitment, devotion, *love* had been the very thing that allowed Lucius to believe she could survive without him.

Slowly, she rose and walked to the bathroom door. The sound of running water covered her entrance. Lucius' arms were braced on the shower wall as scalding water beat down on his bowed head and shoulders. The untouched bottle sat beside the sink.

Kenna covered her cry of shock and despair with both hands. She could see bruises along his ribcage and the angry welt where Lazarashvilli struck him with the cane, but these were not the source of her anguish. Bisecting Lucius' lean muscular back, from his left shoulder to right hip was a new, gnarled scar that oddly reminded her of a topographical map of the Colorado River's course through the Grand Canyon, complete with silvery tributary scars branching out where the wound had healed without benefit of surgical sutures.

Desperate to comfort, soothe and atone, she climbed fully clothed into the glass enclosure and wrapped her arms around him. She pressed her cheek to his back and kissed the center of the scar.

Lucius controlled his immediate instinct to fight off whatever had him in its grasp and closed his hands over hers.

"How did you survive this?" she wept.

He turned in her arms, and lowered his mouth to hers, "You."

Every cell in her body burst to life. The tenderness toward his wounds and his own fatigue dissipated on the fog of the hot water. Lucius' hands were everywhere, tugging her blouse over her head, but the wet fabric stuck to her skin.

"Let me," she said when his swollen fingers fumbled with the button of her cargo pants.

He kicked them to the corner of the stall and backed her against the cold tiles. They'd known hunger, passion and desire for each other before. Now there was only raw need. Not for mere sexual gratification, but to possess and be possessed, an undeniable affirmation of their existence.

Placing her hands around his neck, Lucius gripped her thighs, lifting her to wrap her legs around him.

Kenna leaned in to kiss him, sweeping her tongue over his as he pressed himself fully into her silky warmth. They stayed there for several long minutes, breathing together, the water cocooning them. Neither moved to hasten this union. They had, at times, lost all hope of ever finding it again. Kenna raised her head.

"Don't move," he groaned against her neck. "I haven't the strength to ..." She tipped her hips toward him. "Love," he warned.

She had the temerity to giggle and nip his neck, then smile

triumphantly as his body gave in, with violent jerks that seized his muscles and emptied all thought from his mind.

His legs trembled with the effort to be gentle as he set her feet on the shower floor. He touched his forehead to hers, his chest still heaving. He wanted to say something. Promise her more. Promise her happiness.

Kenna stood on tiptoes to kiss him. "Be still and let's get you to bed."

He raked his eyes over her. Wet hair was matted to her head. Another man's blood and body still clung to her. "No." He upended the entire bottle of shampoo on her head. "I'll not take you to bed with him all over you."

Until that moment, Kenna hadn't noticed the remains that had knotted in her hair and stuck to her face, neck and arms. Meticulously, Lucius picked pieces from her hair, inspecting every inch of her as he lathered her from head to toe.

"Wait." She pulled away a suds-covered foot. "I'm supposed to be taking care of you. This was about you." He stood and smiled weakly, then traced the shell of her ear with his tongue, a soapy palm cupping a full breast. "I'm a selfish bastard, Kenna. This *is* all about me."

"Oh," she moaned, arching into his touch. "Well, then."

CHAPTER SIXTY-NINE

E ver vigilant as they boarded the plane for home, there was an unmistakable air of celebration that came with the mid-day sun. Mike and Ellis boarded the plane last, their mission accomplished only when the doors were secured. Ellis, a lone island without any apparent joy in their escape, retreated to the farthest seat in the rear of the cabin. He paused only long enough to say one word to Lucius. "Fifteen."

"What did he mean?" Kenna asked Lucius while she fussed to make sure he was comfortable.

"He found fifteen of Lazarashvilli's victims. They will have medical attention and a place to stay," he said matter-of-factly and reached for his seat belt.

No surprise, Mike took the same seat he'd occupied on the trip into Istanbul and stretched out as before, relaxed and at ease with headphones in place and a directive to the flight crew to wake him only for lunch before landing.

He annoyed Candace no end. She took a seat next to Frankie and pulled out her stupid book, but watching Kenna was far more entertaining.

Lucius was alive, and for the moment, Kenna was attached

to him like a limpet. She hadn't left his side or removed her hand from his as they'd climbed the stairs from the tarmac to the plane. Frankie and Candace nudged one another as they watched her hover and fret over his every move and need. Frankie used her phone to covertly take a picture to send to Will.

When Lucius gently told Kenna he could buckle his own lap belt, they erupted into a fit of giggles.

"What?" Kenna said.

"Nothing," Frankie said, winking. "But if you try and help him to the lavatory ..." She motioned with her thumb between herself and Candace, who was holding her cheek, the throbbing exacerbated by the laughter. "*We'll* know you're getting your membership card in the mile-high club."

Somewhere around forty thousand feet, with their seats reclined, Kenna laid her head on Lucius' chest, counting the heartbeats. She was so grateful to have him alive and back with her. "I love you," she whispered. He would never again doubt her heart.

A chill, autumn tailwind pushed a fully recovered Candace through the door of Marco's. She spotted her two friends perched on stools at the miles-long polished nickel bar and wove her way through a group of squealing office workers in tiaras to reach them.

"I should have known corporate work would take as many hours," Candace said, unfurling her scarf and claiming her seat. "But I'm on the Henneby account, and there is no Palmer Ross. Life is good."

"We should drink to that." Kenna winked. "Or to those!" She pointed to Candace's electric blue peep-toes.

"What? These old things?" Candace laughed as she crossed and re-crossed her legs.

In moments, The Bartender stood across from them, his long arms braced wide on the bar.

"What will it be tonight, ladies?" His Welsh accent was always a source of feminine thrills.

"Uhm ... something warm, yet bracing?"

"Nothing too sweet."

"I'm in the mood for Calvados ..." Kenna wore the dreamy

look on her face that had come to mean she was thinking about Lucius.

A smile quirked chiseled lips, as The Bartender studied each young woman in turn with startling blue eyes.

"Give me a few. I have an idea."

As he turned to walk away, Candace hiked herself up onto the rung of her barstool and leaned on the bar to admire his retreating butt.

"Careful," Frankie snorted. "You fall on your ass and those shoes are *mine*."

For the next few minutes, they resumed the longstanding debate on whether The Bartender was an aspiring actor or merely a model.

"What are you looking at him for anyway, missy?" Kenna nudged Candace with an elbow.

"Because."

"We thought, you know ... you and Mike ..." Frankie waggled her brows and fanned her face with the drinks menu they wouldn't be needing.

"I'm sure I don't know what you're implying," Candace said in a haughty tone.

"She's implying that you two hit the sheets hard and heavy in Istanbul and, normally ..." Candace snorted. "... *normally*, that means a man and a woman have started a little sumpin' sumpin'." Kenna smirked at her.

"Well, you two can just disabuse yourselves of *that* assumption." At their skeptical expressions, she said, "No, really. That was a ... I don't know what exactly. It was touch-and-go-but-we're-still-alive' sex?"

"If you say so." Frankie didn't look convinced. Neither did Kenna. "Calvados?" Frankie said turning to Kenna. "You could have that every night, if you moved in, you know."

"Has he recruited you too? I moved out of the old gallery loft." Kenna reminded them. "Baby steps."

"My mom always says, 'This love business isn't for sissies,'" Candace said.

The Bartender appeared at that *apropos* moment to place before them three snifters of an amber liquid, garnished with cinnamon sticks and wafting a warm, spicy apple fragrance. Kenna, Frankie and Candace stared in awe at the drink, then up into sparkling eyes.

They sipped contemplatively for a few minutes, sighing over the aromatic drink that tasted like warm apple pie in a glass.

"What is it?" Kenna breathed.

He tilted his tousled head and gave each woman a smile that seemed meant for her alone. "I think I'll call it 'Eden's Fall.'"

That night they toasted Candace's mom, The Bartender and love.

THE END

AUTHORS' NOTE

The Bartender, lovingly featured throughout *Eden's Fall* (and who will reappear in *Winter's Thaw* and *Venus Rising*) has a creative mind when it comes to cocktail mixology. In the Epilogue, he invented the "Eden's Fall."

We greatly enjoyed the process of inventing this drink, which is deliciously appropriate for a chilly fall day or evening. Here is the recipe, if you'd like to try it for yourself!

Best wishes – K R Brorman, C C Cedras, S A Young

EDEN'S FALL

Makes 3

Steep three cinnamon sticks in eight ounces of hot water
Combine in each Brandy snifter:
1 ounce hot, steeped cinnamon water
2 ounces Calvados
1 teaspoon wildflower honey
1/2 ounce or a generous splash of Ginger Beer
1 grind of fresh nutmeg
Garnish with cinnamon stick

Salute!

DEDICATIONS

For my husband, Gregg, and our children, Joe Scott and Kate, thank you for making room in our life for Mom to have dreams too.

For Keith Cedras, our first fan, first technical advisor and intrepid taste tester, forever in our hearts and on every page to come.

For our parents, brothers and sisters, and chosen family around the world who never stopped asking "Is it done yet?" It's done! Your belief kept us writing.

HUMAN TRAFFICKING

The exploitation of one human being by another is the basest crime. And yet trafficking in persons remains all too common, with all too few consequences for the perpetrators. ~

YURY FEDOTOV, EXECUTIVE DIRECTOR
UNITED NATIONS OFFICE ON DRUGS AND
CRIME - GLOBAL REPORT ON TRAFFICKING
IN PERSONS 2014

To report suspected human trafficking:
1-866-347-2423

To get help from the National Human Trafficking Hotline:
1-888-373-7888
or text **HELP** or **INFO** to
BeFree (233733)

ACKNOWLEDGMENTS

Cover by Fiona Jade, of Fiona Jade Media
www.fionajademedia.com

Copy edits by Adele Brinkley, of With Pen in Hand
www.withpeninhand.net

Our deepest gratitude to those who offered honest, unvarnished advice, critiques and suggestions, and volunteer editing through numerous drafts.

    Melinda Wilkins - Alpha reader
    Marc Howard - Alpha reader
    Kris Meyer - Beta reader
    Sandra Hagman - Beta reader
    Holly Ghere - proofreader

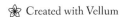 Created with Vellum

CPSIA information can be obtained
at www.ICGtesting.com
Printed in the USA
BVOW08s0825171217
503006BV00001B/109/P